Battle Mage

Book Two of the Vellhor Saga

BY
Mark Stanley

Foreword

Battle Mage
First published by Dragontale Publishing Limited 2024
Copyright © 2024 by Mark Stanley

All rights reserved. No part of this publication may be reproduced, stored or transmitted in any form or by any means, electronic, mechanical, photocopying, recording, scanning, or otherwise without written permission from the publisher. It is illegal to copy this book, post it to a website, or distribute it by any other means without permission.

This novel is entirely a work of fiction. The names, characters and incidents portrayed in it are the work of the author's imagination.

Any resemblance to actual persons, living or dead, events or localities is entirely coincidental.

Mark Stanley asserts the moral right to be identified as the author of this work.

Second edition

Paperback ISBN: 979-8333578488

Hardcover ISBN: 979-8333939319

Cover art by David Leahy

Dedication

*To my amazing wife,
I love you to the moon and back*

The Story So Far

Here's a quick summary of the key elements from *Elven Blood*.

Races of Vellhor

Dwarves - The Dwarves of Vellhor are a warrior race governed by a complex structure of chiefs to the different clans and their elective councils. Political rivalries between and within clans can make co-operation difficult and hereditary accession to the role of clan chief uncertain.

Elves – The Elves are skilled if diminutive (similar in height to Dwarves) masters of magic. Their society is organized around different cities within and around the Great Elven Forest. A particular feature of their society is that elf children are almost always born as twins. A single birth is so rare as to be considered a very bad omen with the child being ostracized and likely to be blamed for any ill events. Elven and Dwarven societies and bloodlines were once close but have drifted apart over the centuries.

Humans – The humans of Vellhor can practice magic but are not as adept as the Elves. Their society is organized around various minor kingdoms and dukedoms with the trading caravans the cities depend on often needing protection from bandits.

Drogo - The Drogo Mulik are a fierce and brutal race of lizard-like people, standing over seven feet tall. Drogo society is organized in warlike clans that will take Drogo of other clans as slaves as well as other races. The Drogo have occupied old dwarven fortresses as their realm has expanded. They worship the dragon god Nergai and their great chief Junak is seeking to reincarnate Nergai in physical form in Vellhor.

ᛁᚾᛏᛏ GLOSSARY

Main Characters

Gunnar - Dwarf – Is the heir to the chief of Clan Draegoor. He discovered treachery in another clan while serving in the border stronghold of Fort Bjerg. He escaped with the aid of his fellow soldier Karl and an avatar of one of the dwarven gods Draeg. Gunnar has discovered a surprising ability to use magic, albeit one he cannot control well yet. Draeg explained this is because Gunnar has a small trace of elven blood in him and that this confirms he is the individual identified in a prophecy that links the dwarven and elven race.

Anwyn - Elf – Anwyn was born as a single child and consequently cast out from Elven city of Stromyr to live in the Great Elven Forest. She has been expertly trained by her parents in magic and combat. Her grandfather Alden returned from his travels to reveal he had identified Anywn as the prophesied Elven Seishinmori – a leader who would unite the elven tribes, The same prophecy said she would marry a dwarven leader who Alden has discovered is called Gunnar.

Kemp - Human – Kemp is a mage of who has a rare ability to work with – have an affinity with – several elements. He is interested in researching the history of dragons and journeyed into Sandarah to find evidence for his theories. While there he discovered the tomb of Nergai and – by having had a human spy named Harald travel with him – inadvertently led Junak and the Drogo Mulik to the lost tomb.

Ruiha - Human – Is a feared and capable assassin who has fled her old employer Faisal, leader of The Sand Dragons gang. She accompanied Kemp in his quest and killed the traitor Harald but was herself captured and put into slavery as a gladiator in the Drogo Mulik dungeons. Ruiha was able to avoid Harald's magic charm and the evil aura of Negai's tomb – which nearly turned Kemp – because she is not affected by any magic.

Supporting Characters

Dakarai - Drogo - Dakarai is a miner from one of the clans Junak conquered. His wife and son were brutally killed by Junak's soldiers but Junak was impressed by the way Dakarai fought back, so he was enslaved rather than killed. In the slave pens he has met and allied with Ruiha.

Lorelei – Fae – Lorelei is a small telepathic creature from the forest who has become Anwyn's companion and guide. Lorelei not only has magical abilities of her own but is able to bolster Anwyn's own powers.

Havoc – Stonesprite – Havoc is a small divine creature gifted by Draeg to Gunnar to aid him in his struggles. Havoc has only just managed to form a bond with Gunnar and is still young, learning and chaotically unpredictable. However, his control over earth and stone is a useful attribute.

Karl – Dwarf - Karl is Gunnar's fellow soldier, loyal companion and last survivor of the patrol that was undone by Dwarven treachery – when Dwarven crossbows were sold to an ambush party of Drogo. Despite their hardships, Karl remains good humored and is quick to poke fun at Gunnar.

Thalirion – Elf – Thalirion is an ancient Elf, who was the previous seishinmori and who has travelled many different worlds and universes. He has returned to Vellhor to support and guide Anwyn as she strives to unify Elves and Dwarves.

Key Events from *Elven Blood*

Anywn defeated several attempts by elves to kill her or her family as they blamed her for a blight affecting crops. Under instruction from Alden she set off in search of her prophesied companion Gunnar and the site of the Elven Sacred Tree. With the help of Thalirion she and Lorelie were brought to meet Gunnar, Karl, and Havoc. Thalirion explained that Gunnar and Karl needed further training in the shadowy realm of Nexus – also known as the Echo realm – before they would be able to take up the prophesied role of uniting and leading their respective nations in the coming war. The portal to get to Nexus would be found at the sacred tree.

Junak with Kemp's inadvertent help located the Tomb of Nergai but has so far been unsuccessful in resurrecting the dragon god. While Ruiha was captured, Kemp somehow slipped into the realm of Nexus where he is being haunted by the spirits of people he had somehow wronged, betrayed or let down in life.

Junak, with the aid of his shaman Shon'anga managed to find and get to the sacred tree just as the party of Thalirion, Gunnar, Karl, Havoc, Anywn and Lorelie arrived. In the battle that ensued, although many Drogo were slain, Shon'anga managed to set the sacred tree on fire destroying it before he himself lost an arm and his staff. The last flicker of life from the Sacred Tree was just sufficient to open the portal and allow Anwyn and her companions to escape to Nexus.

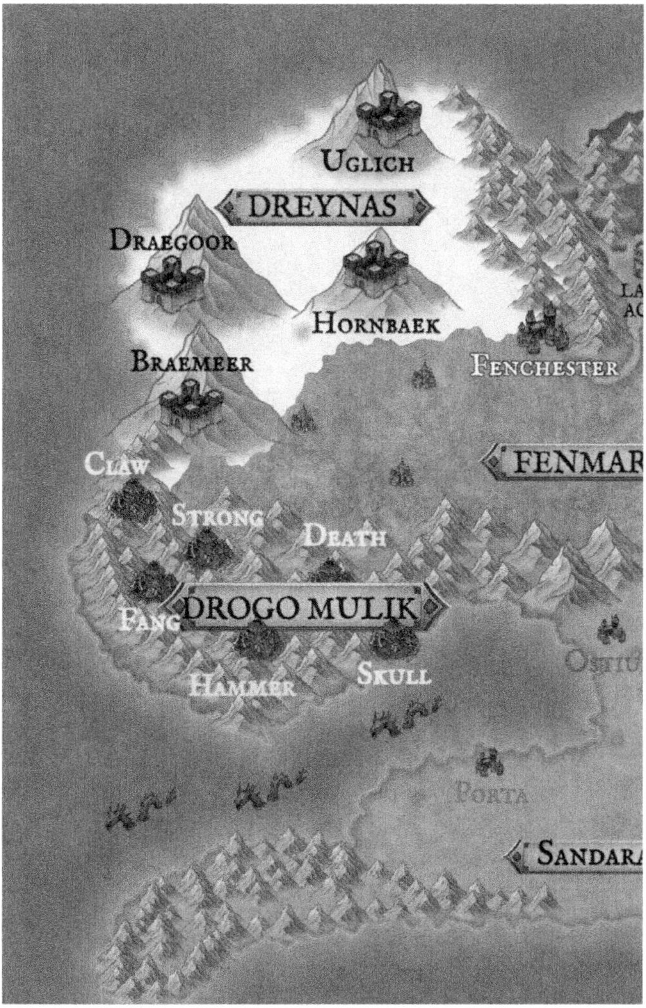
Uglich
DREYNAS
Draegoor
Hornbaek
Braemeer
Fenchester
FENMAR
Claw
Strong
Death
DROGO MULIK
Fang
Hammer
Skull
Porta
Sandara

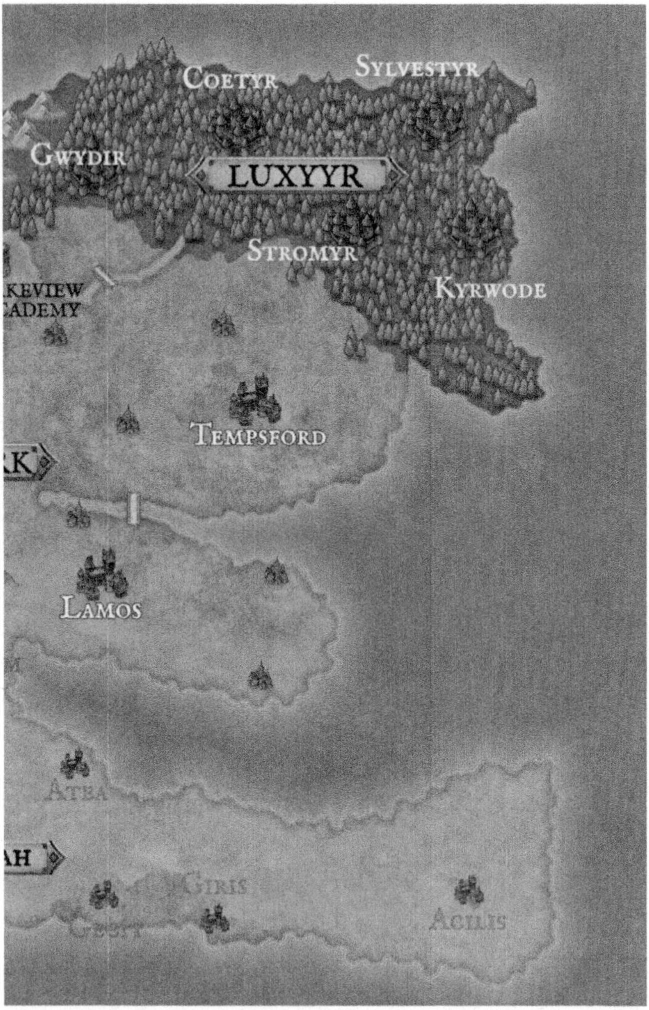

Coetyr
Sylvestyr
Gwydir
LUXYYR
Stromyr
Kyrwode
Tempsford
Lamos
Giris

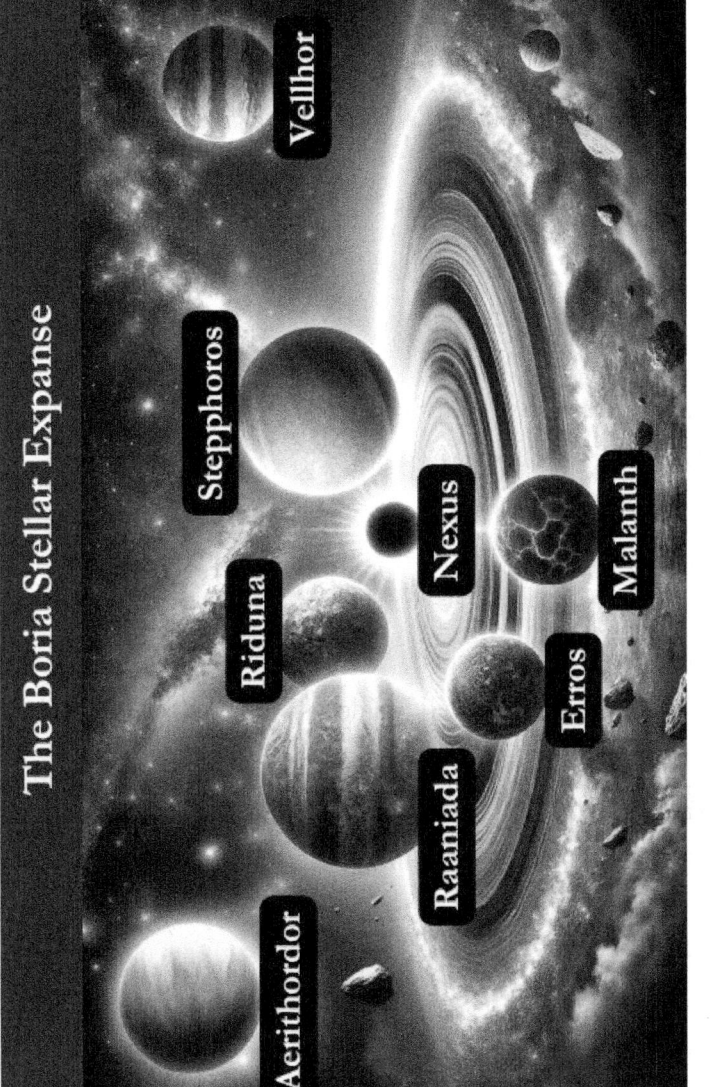

Contents

Prologue	16
1. Shadows and Echoes	22
2. The Pit	39
3. The Path to Mastery	49
4. Pursuit of Shadows	61
5. Echoes of the Dark Forest	77
6. Building Alliances	93
7. The Herald's Fury	110
8. The Tower	121
9. Sacrifices	142
10. The Daemonseeker	157
11. Forging Bonds and Shadows	168
12. Beneath the Arena's Shadow	189
13. Forged in Absence	201
14. The Weight of Destinies	216
15. Forging Paths and Perils	227
16. When Fate Whispers	239
17. Advancing	255
18. The Sovereign's Dilemma	269
19. The Enigmatic Ally	283
20. Gunnar's Gift	295
21. The Labyrinth	309

22. In Exile	324
23. The Crown	335
24. The Fight for Draegoor	350
25. The Descent into Darkness	360
26. Fellron's Stand	379
27. Uninvited Guest	387
28. Battle of the Second Tower	400
29. Reunited	412
Afterword	426
About the Author	430

Prologue

Redemption

"In the heart of redemption, every scar becomes a story of healing and renewal."

Shon'anga

Shon'anga struggled to suppress the whimper that threatened to escape his lips as the physician painstakingly cleaned and re-wrapped the stump of his severed arm. The pain was unbearable and, despite his best efforts, a soft cry slipped out, betraying his agony. It felt as if every touch of the cloth was a dagger piercing his flesh.

As punishment for his failures, Junak had decreed that he was to receive no pain relief during the procedure. Shon'anga clenched his teeth, gritting against the torment as Junak's words echoed in his mind: "You live or die by the hand of Nergai. He will test the strength of your faith."

The weight of those words bore down on him like a mountain, testing not just his body, but his spirit. Shon'anga closed his eyes, his thoughts a whirlwind of pain and doubt, his faith wavering in the face of such relentless suffering.

Shon'anga's mind grappled with the grim reality of his situation. He knew that his chances of survival were slim at best. Among the Drogo, physicians lacked the advanced medical knowledge and surgical expertise of other races. The absence of anesthetic compounded the direness of his condition. Yet Shon'anga had somehow survived the harrowing procedure and was in the slow process of recovery.

During the operation itself, Shon'anga had drifted in and out of consciousness, each awakening accompanied by waves of excruciating pain. But with each return to consciousness, he found himself clinging to a glimmer of hope. The fact that he was now on the path to recovery, rather than descending into the darkness of the underworld, sparked a flicker of optimism within him. Could it be that his faith had been tested by Nergai and found to be steadfast?

As he reflected on his experiences, Shon'anga delved into the inner workings of shamanism. He pondered the stark contrast between those who wielded magic for personal gain and those who dedicated themselves to serving their god, Nergai. Until recently, he had dismissed the latter group as mere zealots, their devotion blinding them to reason. However, when Junak, the ruler of the Claw clan and now all the Drogo Mulik, had approached him, emphasizing the importance of piety and devotion to Nergai, Shon'anga had found himself reluctantly playing along. After all, he knew that Junak would have sought another shaman had he not complied with the facade.

Now, gazing down at his missing limb, doubts still gnawed at Shon'anga's mind like hungry beasts. Had he made the right choice in aligning himself with Junak and embracing this newfound faith? Despite his reservations, he reminded himself that he was alive, and in Junak's eyes, his survival would be seen as a testament to his unwavering devotion.

Shon'anga's thoughts drifted to the precious crystals he had obtained from Chronos, that enigmatic figure who had unlocked secrets of magic previously beyond his reach. Among them was the coveted 'fate crystal,' a rare artifact capable of tracing the strands of destiny. With each use, it required replenishment of aura, a skill he had also learned under Chronos's tutelage.

Despite being a Drogo shaman, notorious for their struggles with meditation and aura manipulation, Shon'anga had mastered these techniques under Chronos's guidance. Yet, he hesitated to share this knowledge with his fellow shamans, preferring to keep this advantage to himself, a secret reservoir of power in uncertain times.

The portal crystals shimmered with aura, their potential untapped yet palpable. Shon'anga couldn't help but marvel at their beauty and power. Once activated, they would fulfil their purpose, transporting warriors across vast distances with unmatched speed. The sheer magnitude of this magic defied everything he had ever known or learned about the arcane arts. Keeping both a fate crystal and a portal crystal on a leather necklace, Shon'anga found himself subconsciously clutching and rolling them in his fingers, especially since losing his hand.

The smooth surface provided a comforting distraction amidst his turmoil.

Along with his hand, Shon'anga had lost his staff in the attack on the Elven tree. It was a devastating blow, and he mourned its loss as much as his severed limb. While his hand was undeniably useful, his staff held immeasurable power.

It had amplified his magic, elevating him above his peers. Without it, he feared his abilities would diminish, rendering him vulnerable in a harsh world fraught with danger.

With a heavy heart, Shon'anga sighed as he rolled onto his side, seeking solace in the embrace of sleep, if only to momentarily escape the weight of his losses and uncertainties.

Shon'anga awoke to a deep, gravelly voice calling his name. "Shon'anga... Shon'anga..." the voice called in its deep baritone. Shon'anga shifted his gaze in a darkness so absolute, it shocked him. Despite living underground his entire life, he was certain he had never before witnessed such total absence of light. There was always a shaft somewhere in the underground world letting sunlight or moonlight in. If not, torches and lanterns were scattered everywhere across the Scorched Mountains, ensuring enough light for the Drogo to see. He searched for something, anything, that might break up the absolute darkness, maybe a patch which was slightly lighter or darker than its surroundings, but he couldn't distinguish anything in the black.

"Shon'anga..." the voice called again.

"Who's there?" Shon'anga replied, his voice raspy from disuse.

Suddenly, fire erupted in the distance, a fierce burst of flame that illuminated Shon'anga's surroundings in a blazing inferno. For several heart-stopping seconds, the intensity of the light nearly blinded him, leaving him disoriented and bewildered. As the flames subsided, shock coursed through him as he realized he was back in the tomb of Nergai once again.

Briefly, a surge of panic gripped him as he wondered if he had inadvertently activated one of the portal crystals in his sleep. Hastily, he reached for his necklace, fingers fumbling in the darkness, only to find both crystals securely in place.

As the fire faded, torches lining the cavern walls flickered to life, casting eerie shadows and providing a dim illumination that allowed Shon'anga to see. But the sudden appearance of light paled in comparison to the awe and terror that seized him as a massive, black-scaled dragon emerged from behind the gigantic coffin.

The dragon moved with a deliberate, almost regal grace, each careful step resonating with unimaginable power. Shon'anga's heart raced, his breath catching in his throat as he scrambled to his feet and instinctively prostrated himself on the cold stone floor. Every fiber of his being trembled in the presence of the colossal creature, feeling the reverberations echo through the chamber with each heavy footfall of the dragon's clawed feet.

"Master," Shon'anga said fearfully. "How may I be of service to the great Nergai?"

"Shon'anga." Nergai responded, with puffs of smoke coming from his nostrils as he spoke. Shon'anga tried to suppress a shiver of fear. "Your failure has cast a shadow on our cause, but you will soon have the opportunity to redeem yourself. Make no mistake, however, I will be watching you closely, Shon'anga. Displease me and I will shatter the very foundations of your existence."

"What the master wills, his most humble servant will provide." Shon'anga said, still prostrated against the hard floor.

"Excellent, Shon'anga," Nergai said with what the shaman took to be a smile. "Now, I believe it is time for you to earn a new staff..."

1.

SHADOWS AND ECHOES

"In the heart of darkness, where shadows dance and echoing fears linger, true strength is forged in the bonds of unity and the mastery of one's inner light."

Gunnar

As Gunnar stepped into the magical gateway set within the ancient roots of the Sacred Tree, the air crackled with arcane energy and he felt a momentary disorientation that was both exhilarating and unsettling. It was as if reality itself were shifting around him, the fabric of the world bending and morphing.

Inside the portal, Gunnar found himself engulfed in a kaleidoscope of swirling colors, a mesmerizing dance of vibrant hues defying nature's laws. He had anticipated a passage akin to the fiery tunnel of the Endless Bridge, but instead of heatless flames, arcane symbols flashed in the darkness, tracing ephemeral patterns in the air. Their luminescence served as a guide through the corridor between realms. With unsteady steps, Gunnar and his companions followed Thalirion into the unknown.

As they advanced, Gunnar sensed the Sacred Tree's magic fading and with it the portal's essence rupturing. Its once-sturdy form flickered like a dying flame, its brilliance diminished its fibers strained.

A glance toward Anwyn revealed tears streaming down her cheeks, mirroring the devastation felt by the group. In that moment, witnessing the depths of her despair, Gunnar felt a sudden resolve to shield her from such grief in the future.

Emerging into the Echo realm of Nexus, made a stark contrast with the vibrant spectacle of the portal. Gunnar found himself shrouded in darkness. Twisted black and grey trees dotted an obsidian landscape, with shadows clinging like a dense cloak to every outcrop. The air hung heavy with an otherworldly stillness, occasionally broken by distant echoes whispering through the branches, while the ground seemed to writhe in shadows.

What unsettled Gunnar most, however, was the thick mist enveloping everything. Glancing back, he watched as the portal dissipated with an eerie silence, vanishing like smoke, leaving only a lingering chill. The once-potent magic of the Sacred Tree reduced to a faint memory.

"What is this place?" Karl asked apprehensively, his gaze darting around in the darkness.

"Welcome to the Echo Realm, Karl," Thalirion stated somberly. "The darkness and the mist is unfortunately something you will have to acclimatize to. There is no sun here. Darkness reigns in this realm."

As Dwarves, Gunnar and Karl were accustomed to the absence of sunlight, but the mist that enveloped them chilled them to the bone with its eerie touch. Gunnar saw Anwyn shudder in evident discomfort at the prospect of perpetual darkness.

"Thalirion, how do we return to Vellhor with the Sacred Tree gone?" Anwyn's voice trembled.

"You are correct, Anwyn," Thalirion began. "The Sacred Tree is destroyed. There are, however, alternate routes back to Vellhor. If you recall, I mentioned a rumor of another gateway in the Scorched Mountains. We will need to find it in order to return."

"And our training?" Gunnar asked.

"That started the minute you stepped out of the gateway, Gunnar," Thalirion responded cryptically.

Gunnar glanced at his companions, about to voice more questions, but Thalirion interjected. "This realm thrives on fear, Gunnar." His voice carried weight, echoing in the darkness around them. "Recall my earlier words about the fate of magical beings in Vellhor: when they meet their demise, their essence transfers to Nexus, giving rise to a Spectral Echo. However, in this spectral ascent, a transformation takes place – the Spectral Echo becomes increasingly erratic, feeding on the fears of the living."

As Thalirion spoke, Gunnar felt a knot form in his stomach, apprehension rising within him. "Prepare yourself," Thalirion continued, his words cutting through the misty air, "for the initial phases of your training will revolve around the exploration and understanding of your deepest fears. In this realm, we shall work tirelessly to unearth the shadows that linger in the recesses of your mind, confronting them head-on."

Gunnar swallowed hard, his mind racing with the implications of Thalirion's words.

"The essence of your training will be the mastery of fear," Thalirion's gaze bore into Gunnar's. "Transcending its grip and transforming it into strength."

Karl looked up, his voice hesitant as he addressed the venerable elf. "Thalirion," he began, "I have not been named in this prophecy. What is my destiny? What is my purpose in all of this?"

"Ah, Karl, I'm glad you brought this up. From a magical perspective, we each have our strengths and our weaknesses. For example, Karl, like most male Dwarves, you have no arcane ability for anything other than craft magic, correct?"

"Aye..." Karl replied hesitantly. "Although, I've not worked in a mine or forge before, so I've never practiced it. Never had the need to in my current line of work. Truth be told, Thalirion, I'm not even sure that I can use craft magic..."

"You have the ability to practice craft magic, Karl. If you did not, then you would not have been permitted to enter the gateway at the Sacred Tree." Thalirion's response was measured and kindly, but lacked the elf's usual enthusiasm. Gunnar guessed that the pain of losing the sacred tree still weighed on him.

"So I am to be a Stone master, or a Forge master then?" Karl asked.

"If that is what you wish to do, Karl. Only you can make that decision. I will not force you to do anything you do not want to do."

Karl stood in silence, and Gunnar saw how the significance of Thalirion's words settled around him like the mist in the Echo Realm. Gunnar's thoughts drifted back to their conversation in the cell at Fort Bjerg, with Karl's talking of his desire to leave the army, a wish forged out of discontent and the longing for a different life. As he watched Karl, Gunnar wondered whether anything had changed in the fateful days since then.

"Where do we go now, Thalirion?" Anwyn broke the silence.

"We must head to the Tower of Absence. The last time I was here, it took me six days to get there from where the gateway opened. However, in this realm, the landscape shifts constantly. It may be farther or closer than that now."

"How is it that the landscape can move?" Gunnar's brow furrowed in perplexity at the notion of his surroundings being able to shift.

"As well as time operating at a different pace compared to Vellhor, the surrounding shadows are constantly shifting. This means that the landscape is in a constant state of movement. It is impossible to map out the Echo Realm. By the time someone had completed their map, the topography would have completely changed, rendering it useless."

The companions glanced down at the ground, the uncertainty swirling within them mirroring the writhing shadows beneath their feet. A whisper of unease creeping into Gunnar's thoughts.

"Is it solid? The ground, I mean," Karl enquired.

"Yes, it is indeed solid, as solid as the ground in Vellhor," Thalirion assured him.

"Except it moves…" Karl muttered beneath his breath.

Anwyn took Lorelei from her shoulder, holding the tiny Fae in her hand before asking, "Will the Spectral Echoes of those we have killed remember us, Thalirion?"

Thalirion's brows furrowed as he studied her expression. "Your question comes not out of fear," he observed, his tone more statement than enquiry.

Hanging her head, she glumly replied, "Not fear, no. Shame, guilt, remorse, disgust. All of those emotions yes to some extent, but not fear."

"Hmmm, interesting, something we will have to delve into further once we reach the Tower of Absence," Thalirion responded firmly.

Lorelei must have communicated something with Anwyn then, for Gunnar caught a fleeting smile gracing Anwyn's face and Anwyn mouthed "thank you" toward the little Fae creature.

At that point Thalirion raised his staff and slammed the shaft into the floor. A luminous beam of green light pierced upwards into the sky, illuminating their surroundings.

Anwyn

Stepping out of the gateway, Anwyn was immediately enveloped in a dense magical aura that hung heavily in the air, pressing against her skin, thick and suffocating. It slowed her movements as if her magic swam through molasses.

She glanced back at the magical gateway that had transported them, a stray tear tracing down her cheek in silent lament for the loss of the Sacred Tree.

As her gaze swung onto the dark trees looming in the distance, Anwyn felt a creeping sense of unease. Despite their apparent vitality, there was something unsettling about them—their shades of grey and black, the aura they exuded. This environment made a stark and unsettling contrast to the vibrant, life-filled forests she knew so well. An involuntary shudder rippled through.

Her sharp elven eyesight caught glimpses of movement in the distance. Shadowy figures, ghostly apparitions, darting between the tar-black trees. Anwyn's heart quickened as she recognized them as the Spectral Echoes Thalirion had described back in Vellhor. A chill ran down her spine at the feeling of being watched by unseen eyes.

The realization that some of these Echoes might remember her as the Elf who had ended their lives sent a sharp pang of regret through Anwyn. She had never taken a life before, yet circumstances had forced her hand repeatedly in recent weeks. Each memory weighed heavy on her heart, a burden of remorse she couldn't shake.

But in her turmoil, the gentle presence of Lorelei came, offering solace and perspective. The tiny Fae reminded Anwyn that she wasn't solely responsible for these deaths; her attackers had made their own choices. Anwyn leant gratefully into the reassurance, finding a glimmer of peace amid the storm of her emotions.

With a resounding thud, Thalirion drove his staff into the ground, sending a surge of anticipation coursing through Anwyn. She held her breath, eyes fixed on the staff as a dazzling emerald light burst forth from its tip. The vibrant glow cut through the darkness, illuminating the landscape in a brilliant hue.

In the newfound radiance, the shadowy figures Anwyn had glimpsed emerged into full view taking on ghastly shapes before her eyes. Anwyn shivered at the sudden clarity about their sinister presence and braced herself for the looming confrontation.

As their surroundings lit up with the brilliant green light, Thalirion surveyed the group of travelers, his gaze piercing and unwavering. "Now we make our way to the Tower of Absence," he declared. "Once the Keeper of the Gate sees my light, he will respond in turn."

Anwyn followed Thalirion's gaze and spotted a distant pin- prick of green light emerging on the horizon.

"Ah, and there we go!" Thalirion remarked with satisfaction, but his tone became stern as he cautioned, "This realm is unforgiving. You can see the Echoes around us, yes?"

Anwyn glanced around, noting the spectral forms lingering in the shadows, and nodded solemnly along with the others.

"Good," Thalirion acknowledged with a serious expression. "They should ignore us for now, but the longer we take to get to the tower, the more accustomed they will become to our presence. They may begin to test our strength. Be wary of attacks and keep control of your fear."

A shiver of apprehension ran through Anwyn at the thought of facing these spectral beings.

"The second they sense your fear," Thalirion continued, his voice dropping to a grave whisper, "they will be drawn in like ants to sugar. Their lust for it makes them little more than rabid wolves around raw meat."

Anwyn swallowed hard, resolving to steel herself against the encroaching darkness and the creatures it harbored.

"How do we defend ourselves should they attack?" Gunnar asked.

"Frosteel or fire are the only two things we know of that can kill a Spectral Echo," Thalirion replied.

His words set Anwyn's mind racing.. "I can create fire," she said before glancing at the dwarves with a pang of concern, "but, as far as I am aware, neither Gunnar nor Karl can."

"Correct, Anwyn," Thalirion affirmed "And they do not have any Frosteel. The crude iron weapons they took from the Drogo will offer little protection." Anwyn's heart sank at the confirmation of their dire vulnerability in this unforgiving realm.

A sudden glimmer of hope dawned on Thalirion's face, and he turned urgently to Anwyn. "Anwyn, can you sense the aura here?"

Anwyn furrowed her brow, reaching out with her senses to grasp the essence of the realm around them.

She nodded warily, her mind grappling with the strange heaviness of the magical aura surrounding them. "Yes," she murmured, "it feels slow, almost sluggish."

Thalirion nodded. "Try and conjure a ball of fire in your palm, please Anwyn," he said with an air of urgency.

Anwyn hesitated for a moment, her thoughts racing but then she focused her will, attempting to summon the flames that danced within her, concentrating on tapping into her magic's familiar rhythms. Summoning something as simple as fire hadn't taxed her since she was a young Elfling. But now, in this horrid place, she struggled. Her first attempt produced nothing more than a puff of smoke and a sweaty brow. Her second attempt was only marginally better, yielding a faint spark. Frustration knotted her stomach as she grappled with the realization that her powers faltered in this unfamiliar environment. She turned to Thalirion, hands spread helplessly, hoping for solace and guidance from his counsel.

"It's the aura here," he responded gravely. "It is far thicker than in Vellhor. In Vellhor, the aura is weak and thin. Eventually, the thickness of the aura here will make you much stronger, but initially, it can be quite tricky to summon the strength to practice even simple spells. We must start by meditating and learning how to draw this aura into our spirit."

Anwyn nodded, though Thalirion's explanation only increased her unease. Mastering the nuances of this new magic would require patience and resilience, qualities her father had desperately attempted to instill in her. As memories of her father's teachings surfaced, Anwyn couldn't help but wonder how successful he had been in preparing her for challenges such as these. Anwyn settled into a sitting position, legs crossed, readying herself for meditation.

Thalirion cast a glance at Gunnar and Karl, who lingered standing. "Well, come on then, you two." He gestured for them to join. "This is your first lesson!"

Karl glanced at Gunnar and chuckled. "I think I'll leave this to you, boss!" He made a move to turn away but was stopped short by a stern glare from Thalirion.

"I don't think so, Karl. Get back here and sit down!" Thalirion insisted. "Despite what you stubborn Dwarves think, you do have the ability to practice magic, and therefore, you can draw aura into your spirit!" His scolding tone left no room for argument.

With a huff and a grunt, Karl reluctantly settled down next to Gunnar, who had Havoc resting on his knee. Anwyn couldn't miss the amusement flickering in Gunnar's eyes as he tried to suppress a laugh at Karl's rebuke. The sight of their camaraderie momentarily eased her worries, and she couldn't resist a chuckle at Karl's expense.

Havoc, however, made no attempt to contain his amusement. His laughter echoed through the clearing, boisterous and contagious, as if he had struck a vein of Frosteel.

"Right," Thalirion's voice commanded their attention. "Now that we are all in position, we will focus on our breathing. Get the breathing right, and the rest will be much easier. Anwyn, what breathing technique do you use?"

The question caught Anwyn momentarily off guard.

"I am not sure what the technique is called, Thalirion," she admitted. "My parents simply taught me to breathe in for five seconds and then breathe out for five seconds." She couldn't shake the feeling that perhaps she should know more about the intricacies of her own practice.

"Hmmm, I see." Thalirion stroked his chin thoughtfully. "Indeed, it's a good method, and in all honesty, more than adequate for the weak aura on Vellhor. However, here in Nexus, a far superior meditation approach is required. This technique is known as the 'Abyssal Radiance Technique'. Begin by drawing in a long breath. Count to five as you breathe in; Anwyn's approach is good here. However, before you exhale, you will need to draw in a short, sharp breath." Thalirion watched closely as each member of the group followed his instructions.

"Now," he continued, once they had all followed his instruction, "I want you to roll that breath around your core, where your spirit is, like a mortar and pestle grinding herbs. Roll it around three times and slowly exhale."

Anwyn closed her eyes and focused, rolling the breath around her core, feeling its presence resonate within her spirit. With each rotation, she sensed her core expanding slightly, the energy pulsating through her being. As she exhaled, a sense of strain lingered in her spirit, evidence of the intensity of the technique. Despite the challenge, she couldn't help but feel a surge of anticipation, eager to open her awareness to the surrounding aura and draw its power into her spirit.

Opening her eyes, Anwyn glanced round at her companions. Gunnar's face had flushed red, beads of sweat glistening on his brow as he struggled to maintain the technique. Karl lay sprawled on the ground, coughing and spluttering, clearly overwhelmed by the exercise. Anwyn felt her heart quicken at the sight of their discomfort and hoped they could quickly find their footing in this unfamiliar practice.

"How... in... all... that... is... holy... are we expected... to... do that?" Karl's words were punctuated by labored breaths as he struggled to regain his composure.

Thalirion stood hands on hips, frowning, but a subtle smile played on his lips. "It seems, Karl, that we may need to leave off the broadleaf for a while!" he remarked. Karl just grunted in response, still catching his breath.

"Gunnar, how did you find the method?" Anwyn asked.

Gunnar rubbed the back of his neck, considering his response. "It was difficult, sure enough," he admitted. "But I feel with more practice, I'll be able to master it."

Anwyn nodded appreciatively at Gunnar's determination to improve despite the initial challenge.

"Excellent!" Thalirion exclaimed, his voice brimming with enthusiasm. "We'll stay here for the night and make a start first thing when we wake tomorrow. Gunnar and Karl, you two spend the rest of the evening working on the Abyssal Radiance Technique. Anwyn, we will move onto introducing aura to the technique now."

Anwyn felt a surge of excitement at the prospect of delving deeper into their magical training and embracing the mysteries of the aura.

The three companions nodded their agreement, each eager to progress in their magical training. Gunnar and Karl settled down next to each other, with Havoc now asleep, and began practicing the Abyssal Radiance Technique.

Anwyn shuffled closer to Thalirion. Closing her eyes, she focused on her breathing, following Thalirion's instructions with precision. Inhaling deeply, she sucked in a short breath before rolling it around her spirit. With each rotation, she felt a connection to the aura surrounding her, a tingling sensation coursing through her being. As she exhaled, she released the energy back into the world, a sense of empowerment coursing through her veins.

"Brilliant, Anwyn. Your technique is flawless already!" Thalirion's praise filled Anwyn with pride, a smile spreading across her face. She had concentrated hard to master the technique, and Thalirion's validation was an acknowledgement of her efforts.

"Now we will introduce aura to the technique. First, as you are aware, you need to open your awareness to the aura surrounding us. Can you feel it?" Thalirion's question prompted Anwyn to focus on the energy permeating the air. With a d she confirmed she could sense the subtle currents of aura enveloping them.

"Now, I want you to connect to the aura before you begin the technique," Thalirion's voice was steady and reassuring.

Anwyn took a deep breath to compose herself as she prepared to integrate the aura into her practice. She felt a twinge of doubt ripple through her at Thalirion's instruction to connect to the aura before beginning the technique. Usually she would connect to the aura in the midst of her breathing technique. The idea of connecting beforehand seemed foreign and unfamiliar.

Taking a moment to gather her resolve, Anwyn reminded her- self of her determination to master this new skill. With a deep breath, she focused her awareness on the aura surrounding her, allowing its energy to flow through her being. It took several attempts, each one bringing her closer to understanding the subtle nuances of connecting to the aura before commencing the technique.

Eventually, through perseverance and practice, Anwyn found her rhythm. The sensation of connection became more natural with each repetition, until she finally mastered the art of connecting to the aura before beginning the technique. A sense of satisfaction washed over her at overcoming yet another hurdle in her magical training.

"Now, with the aura connected to your spirit, when you take the short sharp breath, I want you to imagine opening a tap, and letting the aura fill up your spirit for the duration of the short breath," Thalirion instructed.

Anwyn hesitated, apprehensive at the prospect of flooding her spirit with aura. It was a stark departure from her usual method of slowly dripping aura into her spirit. Yet, she trusted Thalirion's expertise. Steeling herself, she took a short sharp breath and imagined opening the tap. Immediately a surge of energy flooded into her spirit, thick and potent. The sensation was overwhelming, the sheer intensity of the aura leaving her feeling suffocated. Panic gripped her as she struggled to breathe.

In her moment of distress, Thalirion came and stood behind her with a calming presence. The gentle pressure of his hand on the small of her back eased the sensation of drowning in the overwhelming aura. Anwyn felt relieved as the intensity began to subside with Thalirion's steady support amidst the tumult of energy.

"Okay, that was good." Thalirion reassured her. "Now, instead of opening the tap fully, I want you to open it slowly. Let's try again."

The two Dwarves and Anwyn dedicated themselves to practicing the Abyssal Radiance Technique for what felt like an eternity, pushing themselves to the brink of exhaustion. Anwyn felt a surge of pride as she gradually mastered the technique, her spirit filling with aura without the looming threat of fainting.

Thalirion's encouraging words and unwavering belief in her abilities bolstered her confidece, Anwyn knew that with time and perseverance, she would emerge from this trial stronger and more resilient than ever.

As she observed Gunnar and Karl's progress, Anwyn had to admire their determined commitment. Despite the unfamiliar challenge of wrestling with magic, they refused to succumb to defeat, battling on through endless repetitions of the technique.

Gunnar's ability to hold his breath and execute the breathing technique without passing out was impressive evidence of his tenacity. Karl's sporadic coughs and splutters served as a reminder of the hurdles they still faced, but even he had occasional success in carrying out the technique which augured well for the future.

When Thalirion finally called a halt to their practice session, Anwyn felt a sense of accomplishment wash over her. Although mastering the Abyssal Radiance Technique was just the first step in their journey, each step forward made them stronger and more united in their quest for mastery and enlightenment.

As Thalirion instructed them on the logistics of setting up their camp for the night, responsibility for lighting the main fire settled on Anwyn's shoulders. She was determined to prove her proficiency in the arcane arts and, ignoring any offers of help, focused all her concentration on conjuring a spark.

Despite her best efforts, the flicker of flame remained elusive. Anwyn gritted her teeth in frustration. She was sure success lay very close, and she was determined to seize it.

Meanwhile, Gunnar and Karl set about gathering more wood to feed the fire. Anwyn couldn't help but admire the strength in their sturdy frames as they labored industriously on the simple task.

As Thalirion etched runes into the ground, Anwyn marveled at his expertise and mastery of the arcane arts. The barrier of protection he created would shield the camp from encroaching shadows and she was filled with awe at his skillful craftsmanship.

However, Karl's talent for runes took Anwyn by surprise, his keen eye for detail proving invaluable in replicating Thalirion's designs and each stroke of his hand bringing the ancient symbols to life.

As the protective runes began to glow with ethereal light, Anwyn finally managed to bring the fire to blazing life . She felt a sense of peace settle over their makeshift camp as the dancing flames cast a warm glow upon her weary face to soothe her troubled mind.

As the group gathered around the fire, exhaustion weighing heavy on their weary limbs, Anwyn felt a sense of camaraderie fill the air as they took solace in each other's company.

Anwyn, Lorelei, and Thalirion shared a quiet moment of mourning for the Sacred Tree. They shed tears for memory of their fallen sanctuary one of many sacrifices to be made in the name of their quest.

Meanwhile, Gunnar and Karl appeared lost in their own contemplations, frowning presumably at the perils facing Dreynas and the treachery of Gunnar's uncle Wilfrid.

Despite the somber atmosphere, Havoc's playful antics brought smiles to their weary faces as the tiny Stonesprite wrestled with Karl's meaty hand.

As the fire crackled softly and the stars twinkled overhead, the four companions, bound by fate and forged in adversity, slowly succumbed to the embrace of sleep.

2.
THE PIT

"Amidst the growls and chaos, she stood tall, defying the odds with every strike."

Ruiha

As Ruiha stood amidst the tense atmosphere of the pit, adrenaline surged through her veins. Each growl and snap from the bonebacks reverberated through her, a
chilling reminder of the peril she faced. She couldn't help but notice the hunger in their eyes, a primal instinct driving them to view her as nothing more than a meal. Her muscles tensed, ready for the inevitable clash ahead. The eerie shadows cast across the arena by the dim torchlight added to the sense of foreboding. But Ruiha's gaze remained steady her body poised for action. Despite the feeling of being trapped, like a cornered animal fighting for survival she refused to let fear consume her.

With every moment, the crowd's anticipation grew, building like a storm on the horizon. She knew that the coming battle would push her to the limit of her abilities. But she also knew that she wouldn't go down without a fight.

Surveying the daunting pack of bonebacks, Ruiha's thoughts hummed with strategic calculations. The ferocity of these creatures wasn't the only threat; their sheer numbers could easily overwhelm her. She scanned the pack looking for an alpha amongst them, a leader whose demise could disrupt the pack's cohesion.

Drawing on her experience of wild dog packs roaming the grim alleys of Gecit, she sought signs of dominance among the bonebacks. Her eyes narrowed as she identified several larger specimens exhibiting traits of potential alpha status. One in particular with a ghostly pale hue, exuded a sense of intelligence and authority unmatched by the others.

Ruiha honed in on this boneback, with its regal bearing and keen gaze, as the pack's alpha. She grimly set this creature as her primary target, a key to dismantling the pack's unity.

Ruiha stretched her body and then swung her sword in few swift fluid motions, flexing her muscles with practiced ease, steeling herself for the imminent challenge.

Glancing across the arena, she locked her gaze with the alpha, a silent declaration of her readiness to fight to be the top predator to make the bonebacks recognize her as the alpha in this pit. They were entering *her* domain, a world of blood, gore, and death, and she would impose her authority on them all.

As a gong struck, its rich, deep sound reverberating through- out the arena, the crowd erupted into a frenzy of screams and shouts, consumed by bloodlust. With the release of the chains, the bonebacks charged forward eagerly, driven by instinct and hunger. Yet, amidst the chaos, the alpha waited, its calculating gaze fixed upon Ruiha before it slowly stalked towards her, a silent challenge in its eyes.

Ruiha tightened her grip on the hilt of her sword, squaring her shoulders as she braced herself for the onslaught. The bonebacks drove forward, their scales glinting ominously in the dim torchlight as hunger fueled their relentless ferocity. The horde surged towards her, a chaotic mass of snapping jaws and razor-sharp claws, a dense cloud of dust rising in their wake.

Ruiha spun into action, fluidly evading the first boneback's lunging attack and countering with a precise slash through its forelimb, sending scales and bone fragments scattering.

The arena reverberated with the clash of steel against scales, punctuated by the guttural roars of the bonebacks. Maneuvering seamlessly through the chaos of the pack, Ruiha spun with the agility of a dancer delivering calculated strikes that speared flesh and severed necks or limbs.

As the alpha circled cautiously, Ruiha could feel the weight of its gaze upon her, its intelligence observation of her movements, contrasting with the primal instinctive attacks of the lesser bonebacks. Despite her focus on dispatching the smaller threats, Ruiha could feel the pack leader's scrutiny.

With each strike, Ruiha inched closer to her target, her movements flowing with the deadly grace of a trained assassin. Amidst the frenzy of the arena, her skill captivated the bloodthirsty audience, each maneuver showcasing her lethal artistry.

However, the weight of boneback numbers began to tell driving her back against the unforgiving arena wall. The danger heightened Ruiha's senses, sending her sword whirling in a desperate defense, as she felt the alpha's presence looming closer. Sensing her vulnerability, the pack leader seized the opportunity, lunging with a thunderous growl. Ruiha dodged its attack with a nimble side-roll, but found herself forced into a defensive stance on her knees.

Glancing around, Ruiha spotted a discarded spear, partially obscured by dust on the arena floor. She wasn't sure if it had been left intentionally or by oversight, but the weapon's extended reach offered a crucial advantage. The words of her hated mentor, Faisal, echoed in her mind: "Luck favors the brave and laughs at the coward." She disengaged from the alpha, deftly avoiding its snapping jaws as she claimed the spear.

The crowd erupted in cheers as Ruiha wielded the newfound weapon, holding the bonebacks at bay. With the alpha fully committed to the attack, she faced it head-on in a primal contest of strength and skill.

As the crowd's cheers reached a fever pitch, Ruiha scored a deep gouge in the alpha's side. The spectators erupted in a collective roar.

As the alpha staggered, Ruiha seized her moment of opportunity. With a surge of adrenaline, she stepped in and drove her sword deep into the creature's chest. The once-cunning alpha crumpled lifeless to the arena floor.

The remaining bonebacks, rendered suddenly leaderless by the alpha's defeat, hesitated before bowing to accept Ruiha's dominance.

With the alpha vanquished and the horde subdued, the crowd's initial frenzy gave way to an eerie silence. Ruiha stood amidst the aftermath of battle, a solitary figure in the center of the arena. But then the spectators began a rhythmic stomping on the stone ground that grew and filled the air, a steady drumbeat of respect and awe for the undefeated champion before them. With each thunderous stamp, the chant of "Shadow Hawk, Shadow Hawk, Shadow Hawk" echoed around the arena.

Turning away from the adulation, Ruiha silently walked back to her own cage, stoically refusing to partake in the spectacle of celebration. She wouldn't let her captors reduce her to a mere source of entertainment for their bloodthirsty desires.

As Ruiha slumped into the corner of their dim, cold cell, exhaustion washed over her. Blood seeped from her wounds, a painful reminder of the brutality of the pit. With no medics to tend to the fighters' injuries after the matches, many slaves were left to suffer and die alone in their cells—a grim fact of life under Junak's rule, she thought bitterly.

"You live then, Shadow Hawk!" Dakarai's called across the cell.

She met his gaze wearily and rasped, in a voice strained with fatigue, "Barely. Bonebacks, a whole bloody pack of them, I reckon."

Dakarai's eyes widened in surprise, but he remained silent. Instead, he reached for a rag among their scant belongings and wet it on the walls of their cell. He had told Ruiha that the cell's dampness was due to groundwater seeping through the underground rock. Somewhere deeper below lay a pool of water known as an aquifer, a vital source of fresh, clean water for the Drogo. The knowledge offered Ruiha a small glimpse into the intricate workings of their captors' infrastructure, and the complexities hidden beneath the surface of their brutal existence, but for now she was just grateful that it gave her cellmate a means to tend to her wounds.

Despite Dakarai's meticulous ministrations, Ruiha couldn't suppress a wince at the pain coursing through her battered body. His pale, scaled hands were a stark contrast to her own dark-bronze skin, yet they moved with surprising delicacy, gently navigating the jagged claw and bite marks that marred her flesh. It was a skill born of necessity, he had once confided, the result of raising a boisterous Drogo son. Though his words had been light, a shadow of sorrow and loss had lingered in his eyes.

In a quiet moment when he was re-wetting the cloth, Ruiha posed the question that had been weighing heavily on her mind. "How did the recruitment go?"

A smile tugged at the corners of Dakarai's lips. "Not too bad!" he replied cheerfully. "Six new candidates, all young and strong. Corgan plans to speak with them further in the days to come."

Despite the pain pulsing through her body, Ruiha felt a glimmer of hope stir within her. "And any word yet on the Dwarves?" she asked, her thoughts drifting to the two dozen stout warriors who had been brought in days prior and then abruptly vanished from sight, leaving an air of mystery in their wake.

"They're set to fight this afternoon," Dakarai replied. "But as for who they'll face, well that's still unknown though I'm sure Corgan will have the details soon."

Ruiha nodded, though a sense of unease settled in the pit of her stomach. The arena's unpredictability was a constant source of dread, its whims dictating the fate of its unwilling participants. She knew all too well the dangers that lurked within the confines of the pit.

She posed her next question carefully, masking concern beneath an air of casual curiosity. "And when is your next bout, Dak?" Her heart sank at the thought of him facing the same brutal fate that befell so many in the arena. Although he was a formidable warrior, even his strength could only carry him so far in a fight designed purely to entertain others.

"In a few days, I believe," Dakarai replied with a hint of relief. "It'll give me extra time to bolster our ranks. But Ruiha, I think it might be time for the Shadow Hawk to lend a hand with recruitment."

Ruiha tensed at the nickname she despised. "I'll consider it," she muttered through gritted teeth. Though she loathed the name 'Shadow Hawk', she knew the importance of their cause outweighed her personal feelings.

As Corgan approached, Ruiha couldn't help but notice the stark contrast between him and Dakarai. Where Dakarai exuded strength and ferocity, Corgan appeared more reserved, his stature smaller and his frame less muscular. It was said that he had once served as a clerk for his clan's shaman, a role that had shaped his scholarly appearance and introspective demeanor. Despite being a Drogo, known for their fierce and barbaric nature, Corgan stood out for his calm and contemplative disposition—a quality that had thus far spared him from the brutality of the pit.

"The Dwarves fought yesterday," Corgan began, his voice tinged with excitement. "No casualties, by all accounts. They paired them off in twos, pitting them against a variety of monsters."

Ruiha nodded, her mind already analyzing the implications of their latest development. "They were likely testing their strength," she mused. "Now they have some idea of their capabilities, the coming battles will be more challenging."

"We must devise a way to approach and recruit them," Dakarai said.

"Indeed, their strength would be invaluable to our cause," Corgan agreed.

"We can't delay any longer, Corgan." Ruiha couldn't keep the urgency from her voice. "I fear opportunities—and potential allies—will dwindle if we don't act swiftly."

"You make a valid point." Corgan frowned thoughtfully. "I heard about your match yesterday, Ruiha. It must have been a trying ordeal."

Ruiha grunted an acknowledgment. There was little use dwelling on the vicissitudes of their predicament—their focus needed to remain on survival.

"I've heard reports of other matches lately, ones with unfair advantages," Corgan went on, his voice tinged with concern.

"Are they trying to thin our numbers?" Dakarai's question hung in the air, a sobering reminder of the ruthlessness of their captors.

"It seems that way, Dak. Which is why we can't afford to waste any time," Ruiha interjected, her tone grave.

"And there's something else you should know." Corgan confessed, with a tremor of anxiety perturbing his usual composed demeanor. "I've been called to fight this afternoon."

A ripple of concern passed between Ruiha and Dakarai at this revelation, but Dakarai spoke first, his voice infused with genuine warmth, "Good luck, my friend." He went on to add, "You'll prevail, I'm certain of it. Let your cunning and intellect guide you through the fray. Remember, strength isn't always the key to victory." His words of earnest encouragement conveyed a faith in Corgan's intelligence and resourcefulness whatever the circumstance.

Corgan's smile wavered, a tear glistening in the corner of his eye. "In the arena, I'll face an adversary I cannot defeat," he confessed, his voice tinged with a bittersweet acceptance of his fate. "I've been chosen as mere fodder for the crowd's insatiable bloodlust. But even in my final moments, I choose to embrace my fate, knowing that the Shadow Hawk will endure as a symbol of hope for our enslaved brethren." He turned to Ruiha, with a pleading gaze. "Just promise me, Ruiha, that you'll lead our fellow slaves to safety, away from this endless horror."

Ruiha shifted uncomfortably, gaze fixed on the ground between them. "Corgan, you can't speak like that," she said. "Dak's right. You'll find a way through this."

"I've known for some time that I'm not cut out for battle," Corgan confessed in a resigned voice. "I'm a scholar, a scribe—not a warrior. Today, I'll face my end, and I need you to promise me that you'll lead our people to safety. Please, Ruiha, you are our only hope."

Ruiha initially baulked at the enormity of Corgan's request. But then she saw the flicker of desperate hope in his eyes and the sincerity of his belief in her ability to lead.

Stiffening her resolve, Ruiha met Corgan's gaze, her voice steady as she made her pledge. "I promise I will, Corgan," she whispered.

As Corgan walked away, Ruiha and Dakarai were left in somber silence. "I fear for him too," Dakarai confessed, his voice tinged with concern. "But we must hold onto hope. Stranger things have happened."

Ruiha nodded and, with a firm voice, declared her acceptance of the role Corgan had demanded of her. "Now it's time for the Shadow Hawk to lead," she said. "I'll continue seeking recruits. Together, we'll find a way out of this hellhole."

As Dakarai walked away, engaging his fellow Drogo in conversation, Ruiha could already see the change in him. Gone was the weary slump of forlorn indifference, replaced by a stiff-backed determination to reclaim what was lost. She watched him with an admiration tempered by wariness; their path to freedom would require every ounce of their newfound resolve.

3.
THE PATH TO MASTERY

"Mastery is found in the persistence to see through the haze."

Gunnar

Gunnar had devoted himself to mastering the intricate Abyssal Radiance Technique under Thalirion's watchful eye. However, the thick aura enveloping the air presented a formidable challenge, its sluggish essence hampering his efforts with a dense, almost tangible haze. Gunnar was growing increasingly frustrated, as he realized that understanding and mastering this vital but elusive technique might require more from him than he had anticipated.

As they journeyed through the ever-shifting landscape, Gunnar delved deep into his consciousness. With each breath, he surrendered to the pulsating energy of Nexus, feeling its discordant rhythms reverberate through his being. Amidst the swirling chaos threatening to overwhelm his senses, he clung to a fragile thread of control, a glimmer of understanding hinting at boundless potential.

Gunnar remained acutely aware that mastering the breathing aspect was merely the first step on a path fraught with difficulties, but it took four days of traversing the unsettling landscape of Nexus before he achieved even a partial mastery of the Abyssal Radiance Technique. That morning—although the absence of sun, moon, or stars cast doubt on the time—Thalirion, seemingly pleased with that progress, told Gunnar he would now teach him how to connect with the surrounding aura.

"What exactly is aura, Thalirion?" Gunnar's inquiry left Thailirion dumbfounded.

"Are you telling me the Dwarves of Dreynas have forgotten this much of the arcane arts?" he asked in astonishment.

"It seems so, Thalirion," Gunnar's said sorrowfully. "We seem to have forfeited much knowledge over time."

Thalirion lifted his hand to his face, his fingers thoughtfully stroking his smooth chin. "Tell me, Gunnar," he began with a curious tone, "what do you understand about the arcane arts?"

Gunnar reflected for a moment, his brow creasing as he gathered his thoughts. "Firstly, I'd never even heard the term 'arcane arts' before our paths crossed," he admitted before going on hesitantly, as he trawled through his limited knowledge. "From what I've learned, mages can manipulate elements—water, fire, earth, wind, and aura." He shifted uncomfortably, a flush of embarrassment coloring his cheeks, as he confessed, "But honestly, my training didn't delve deeply into the realm of magic."

"Hmmm," Thalirion mused. "Indeed, it is true that mages can control aura, however, the concept that it is somehow similar to the elements is completely wrong. Aura is an invisible presence, undetectable by mundane senses, but perceivable by magical beings. Aura is like a reservoir of magical energy, acting as the lifeblood of the magical realm. It is the subtle echo left behind by spells cast, by magical creatures, and by enchantments that have touched the fabric of reality. This energy is all around us, threading its way through the air, soil, and all living things. Magical beings draw upon this aura to replenish their spirit, similar to sipping on water to slake one's thirst."

Gunnar spent the remainder of the morning in a fruitless effort to expand his awareness to the surrounding aura. Thalirion had assured him that he would definitely recognize the moment it happened. Learning that Anwyn had also initially struggled brought him some comfort, until he discovered she had been only six years old during her first attempts, a revelation that shifted his gratitude into embarrassment and stoked his determination to conquer the technique.

To make matters worse, Karl, having overheard their conversation, burst into laughter and mocked, "If she managed it when she was no bigger than a pebble, this should be easy for you, Gunnar!"

Frustration bubbling inside him, Gunnar could only scowl at the red-headed Dwarf, feeling both the sting of the jest and the weight of his own expectations.

As the weary group of travelers settled for the evening, Gunnar resumed his practice of the Abyssal Radiance Technique. The campsite was carefully arranged around a large central fire, with four fires at the corners of a square, each connected by a line of protective runes.

Gunnar observed how Karl had mastered the rune-work exceptionally well; this was the first day Thalirion hadn't found any errors. Karl accepted Thalirion's nods and compliments with evident pride, visibly thriving under the positive attention.

Meanwhile, Gunnar was focusing on regulating his breathing when Havoc leaped from the pocket where he had snoozed most of the day. Gunnar looked on amazed at Havoc's noticeable growth. It dawned on him that in a few more weeks, Havoc might outgrow his pocket home completely. Gunnar wondered whether the unique aura of Nexus was accelerating Havoc's growth, or if he would have grown just as rapidly back in Vellhor. It accentuated his sense of wonder, tempered with unease, about the mysterious influences at play in this new environment.

In the midst of his efforts to master the meditation technique, Gunnar suddenly realized that he had unintentionally sidelined the nurturing of his bond with Havoc. So he decided to spend some time connecting with Havoc before resuming his meditation practice. He chose a pitch-black log, hauled over by Karl earlier, as his seat, and gently cradled Havoc in his hands.

As he settled in, Gunnar closed his eyes and conjured an image of Havoc in his mind's eye. Without even realizing it, he had engaged the new breathing technique; he felt the stretch of his diaphragm as he smoothly circulated the breath through his core. Mentally reaching out, he whispered in his thoughts, "Havoc, can you hear me?" He could feel a palpable sense of anticipation mixed with anxiety as he attempted this intimate mental communion.

Gunnar's focus intensified, driven by a deep desire to reconnect and strengthen the bond that he feared had weakened due to his recent preoccupations.

Still, nothing happened.

Eyes still closed, he took another long breath before sucking in a quick short breath and rolling it around his core.

"Havoc" he called out. This time he felt a small shift inside him, just a little flutter as he rolled the breath around inside him. It was a faint sign, yet it suggested a potential breakthrough, and Gunnar felt a spark of hope kindle within him.

Attempting the technique once more, Gunnar felt the flutter again, and this time, he actually heard Havoc's response. "Gunnar, you big oaf… how can you not hear me?" came the telepathic chiding. Despite the barb, a wide smile spread across Gunnar's face—it was their first actual conversation.

"Havoc, I would like for us to strengthen our bond. Let us work together," Gunnar proposed earnestly.

Havoc's laughter echoed through Gunnar's mind like the playful dance of leaves in the wind. "Strengthen our bond? Gunnar, you've basically kidnapped me and brought me to this place of misery, and now you want to strengthen our bond?" the Sprite teased mischievously.

Despite the scolding, Gunnar couldn't help but chuckle at the laughter and lightness of Havoc's tone which made him realize the depth of the connection they might already share.

Gunnar concentrated on the swirling energies that linked them, endeavoring to calm the chaotic essence within Havoc. The Stonesprite, however, seemed to have other ideas. A sudden explosion of sparkles encircled Gunnar, enveloping him in a cascade of shimmering lights that tickled his senses and captured the attention of the others. "Havoc, what are you doing?" Gunnar asked in astonishment.

"This place is so gloomy, I'm just adding some light, Gunnar," Havoc replied nonchalantly, as though scattering sparkles was the most natural act in the world.

"Alright, Havoc, but let's try to focus for a minute, okay?" Gunnar implored, hoping to regain some semblance of control.

Havoc gave his bonded companion a skeptical look. "Focus? That sounds boring, Gunnar. I don't want to focus!"

Gunnar tried to explain. "Focusing on our bond and strengthening it will bring us both happiness, Havoc," he said with an encouraging smile.

Havoc didn't respond verbally, but he ceased his exuberant antics, allowing Gunnar to delve deeper into their shared consciousness. As he probed further, Gunnar began to discern the true emotions hiding beneath Havoc's chaotic facade. He realized that the Stonesprite's behavior was more playful than disruptive, an expression of his nature rather than an intent to distract. With this realization came a growing sense of closeness and alignment; their connection strengthened with each passing moment.

After some time, Gunnar felt a shift as Havoc's energy settled into a calm focs. Sensing the right moment, he posed a question born from curiosity and a little hope. "Can you sense the aura around us, Havoc?"

"Magic permeates everything here, Gunnar," Havoc responded. "But in this dark place, the magic is dense—too dense for you to grasp easily."

"But you can feel it, can't you?" Gunnar pressed, his curiosity deepening.

"Yes, I can feel it." Havoc's tone betrayed a subtle pride in his natural affinity for magic.

"Could you guide me in sensing it too? I've been practicing the Abyssal Radiance Technique for days, but I haven't yet managed to integrate the aura into it."

Havoc broke into a laugh. "That's what the old Elf has been calling it?" Havoc chuckled. "What a ridiculous name!"

Despite himself, Gunnar's lips curved into a smile, sharing the humor of Havoc's assessment. The name was indeed cumbersome; even Karl had resorted to simply calling it 'the technique.'

"That is the name he's given it, yes. But can you help me with it?" Gunnar's voice quivered with hope and an edge of urgency. He felt sure that Havoc could prove crucial in bridging the gap in his understanding.

"I can try," Havoc said, in a voice tinged with cautious optimism. "You might be able to sense it through me. If I connect to it, then I can trickle a little into your spirit, help carve the path before you stone the road, as they say…"

Gunnar glanced down at Havoc, one eyebrow raised in mild amusement.

"What? Why that look, you big oaf?" Havoc demanded defensively.

"Who says that?" Gunnar said with a chuckle.

"Everyone says that! Well, everyone who builds paths and roads says it. And if they don't, they should. It's a good saying!" Havoc retorted. Gunnar couldn't help but laugh at Havoc's earnestness and his unique way of viewing the world.

They got to work, with Gunnar concentrating on their growing bond while Havoc carefully began channeling aura into his spirit. Gunnar felt a surge of euphoria; his fingers and toes tingled with an unfamiliar but exhilarating sensation, and a light-headedness swept over him. But just as he was beginning to savor this new feeling, it stopped abruptly. A wave of disappointment flooded through him, leaving him longing for more.

He opened his eyes and saw Havoc visibly exhausted, panting as he lay down in Gunnar's lap. The Sprite's eyes slowly closed with fatigue. "Are you alright, Havoc?" Gunnar asked in concern.

"Tired... but okay..." Havoc's telepathic response was slurred, with evident weariness. "I have one favor to ask before I sleep..." His request, spoken in such a vulnerable state, tugged at Gunnar's heart.

"What is it, Havoc?" Gunnar asked, ready to assist however he could.

"The green Fairy... put in a good word for me..." Havoc murmured, and then his presence in Gunnar's mind faded as he drifted into sleep.

Gunnar couldn't help but burst into laughter at Havoc's unexpected plea, his boisterous chuckles once again capturing the attention of the rest of the group.

Anywn

Anwyn watched from a distance as Gunnar and his Stonesprite, Havoc, shared a private telepathic exchange. She felt relieved to see Gunnar smile and laugh at jokes she couldn't hear, remembering his earlier concerns about failing to connect with Havoc. The sight of the Sprite lighting up the camp with magical sparkles and the joy on Gunnar's face warmed her heart.

She noticed Gunnar's breathing patterns aligning with the Abyssal Radiance Technique—a method she now knew well— and it pleased her to see his progress. Once he fully sensed the surrounding aura, she was confident he would master it. As her appreciation of the rugged and intriguing Dwarf's determination deepened, she felt a flutter stirring in her stomach.

Their interactions often felt awkward, yet he seemed fond of her. His bravery in the defense of the sacred tree and the sympathetic look in his eyes at her distress, had not gone unnoticed.

Their connection was palpable, as deep as the prophecy had foretold, yet their acquaintance was so brief it left Anwyn grappling with the oddness of their situation. She cringed inwardly at the awkward silences when left alone by Thalirion and Karl. A life of outcast isolation had left her ill-prepared for romantic interactions, despite Lorelei's attempts to bolster her confidence by listing her virtues.

Now, settling beside the central fire, Anwyn watched Gunnar cradling Havoc gently before setting him down, and then walking quickly over to her.

"Evening, Anwyn, may I sit please?" Gunnar asked gently.

"Of course." Anwyn sat up with a mix of anticipation and nervousness. "Are you okay?"

Gunnar smiled, evidently still pleased from the success of his work with Havoc. "Aye, I'm fine, thank you. And yourself?"

"I'm well. I think I've mastered the technique now. In the morning I could spend some time with you helping you sense the aura... if you would like," she offered quickly.

"That would be great, thank you," Gunnar replied enthusiastically. "Although, I hope to find it easier tomorrow. I have finally managed to commune with Havoc!"

"I thought you might have!" Anwyn smiled back, then blushed as she added hastily, "I noticed a flash of magic earlier and could hear you both laughing! Not that I was eavesdropping or anything."

"Please don't worry about that!" Gunnar reassured her with a warm laugh. "I do have a message to relay though. Havoc was in a haze of pure exhaustion, so I'm unsure if he really wanted me to say it." He shrugged and then continued, "But he wanted me to put in a good word for him with Lorelei..."

Before he could elaborate, Lorelei appeared, her expression stern. Gunnar's gaze shifted uneasily between the Fae and Anwyn. "Is she upset with me?" he asked quietly.

Anwyn chuckled. "No, no... she's not upset. She's just wondering why the chaotic child—her words—wishes for you to 'put in a good word' for him."

Gunnar hesitated at Lorelei's intense stare. "I assume, Lorelei, that he likes you, and perhaps has asked me to vouch for his character."

Lorelei spun around with a tinkle and darted towards Havoc. Gunnar watched her go and winced, and it was obvious to Anwyn that he was hoping the exhausted

Stonesprite would behave. She was suppressing a laugh as Gunnar turned back to her.

"What?" he asked, puzzled.

"Havoc may be in for a scolding, Gunnar," Anwyn chuckled. As she laughed, she noticed a look of admiration flicker across Gunnar's face. He seemed about to say something, perhaps something more personal, a compliment even, but whatever it had been died unspoken on his lips. Anwyn felt a pang of disappointment wash over her at his reticence. She wished he would articulate those thoughts, craving th deeper connection that his words might spark.

The next morning brought a haunting beauty to their camp- site. Anwyn watched Gunnar, already up and practicing, struggling to connect with the magic that seemed so dense and elusive. She joined him, placing a comforting hand on his shoulder, guiding him through the intricate breathing patterns.

As they practiced, the aura began to envelop them, Gunnar's face showing brief triumph before confusion set in. "I felt it," he said, amazed yet frustrated. "Only for a moment, mind. But it felt... exhilarating."

"I'm so glad you did it, Gunnar. It's easier on Vellhor, and had we been there, I believe you would have already mastered the technique in its entirety!" Anwyn reassured him.

"Thank you for your help, Anwyn, I fear I would have never grasped it without you!" Suddenly, Gunnar leaned forward and embraced her. Shock and embarrassment surged through Anwyn, but those feelings quickly subsided and she felt a warmth she'd never known, safe in his embrace. As they separated, Gunnar coughed awkwardly, his face reddening. "Apologies, Anwyn," he stammered. "I forgot myself for a moment."

Anwyn squeezed his hand, wordlessly, her smile conveying all the reassurance he needed. As they rejoined the group to pack up, Anwyn felt a new connection forming, a bond that promised something deeper amidst the shadows of their journey.

4.
Pursuit of Shadows

"When the path is lost and the shadows close in, keep running toward the light within."

Kemp

Kemp had been sprinting across the desolate landscape for hours, his muscles screaming and his lungs gasping for air. Sweat drenched his weary body, yet he pressed onward, driven by a relentless pursuit. Chilling, ethereal spirits had hounded him continuously from the moment he had awoken in this eerie, nightmarish realm. The beacon of green light he had glimpsed on the horizon had long since faded, leaving him directionless, yet he could not stop his desperate flight.

He knew he would have to halt eventually—to seek shelter and sustenance—but the specters that haunted his steps seemed inescapable. As he ran, Kemp's thoughts wandered, puzzling over how he had come to find himself in this strange, forsaken place.

His memory offered few clues, only a vague recollection of battling a swarm of reptilian warriors. Had he perished in that clash? Was this shadowy world the underworld itself? He thought of Ruiha, stirring a deep longing, as he wondered if she was safe, untouched by the chaos that had torn him from her.

He suddenly remembered the spell Harald had cast, which had suppressed his deepest emotions until it shattered under the strain of battle. The flood of long-stifled feelings had overwhelmed him, like the tumultuous release of water when a dam bursts. It had been a bewildering sensation—feeling truly and profoundly for the first time in ages.

Kemp gradually pushed the terror of the specters to the recesses of his mind as he reflected on his time with Ruiha, on Harald's deep-seated betrayal, and on the mysterious role of the Drogo. When he dared to glance over his shoulder he found, to his surprise, that the spectral pursuers had vanished into the fading mists behind him.

He halted abruptly, hands resting on his knees as he drew deep, labored breaths. Sweeping the sweat from his brow, he gazed across the eerie landscape around him. The trees loomed, black as pitch, their leaves a somber shade of dark grey. Intrigued, he made his way toward a small clearing. Sliding his pack from his shoulders, he dropped it beside him and settled onto a large, dark log.

He sat in silence, allowing himself time to recover, his chest still heaving with the exertion of his flight. The adrenaline slowly receded, replaced by a growing curiosity about his surroundings. As his strength returned, Kemp stood and began to explore the clearing. Out of the corner of his eye, he caught fleeting glimpses of specters darting between the trees. Though, surprisingly, they seemed indifferent to his presence now, as if he had slipped from their ghostly awareness. A sigh of relief escaped him as he continued his survey.

It soon became apparent that others had been here before him. The remnants of a large fire pit dominated the center of the clearing, surrounded by signs of a temporary encampment. The setup was cleverly fortified by four smaller fires, now extinguished, connected by a series of faint runes etched into the earth. Kemp pondered the age of the campsite, feeling the timeless, stagnant air of the place—no wind stirred, no natural sounds pierced the silence.

Turning his attention back to the runes, Kemp circled the clearing, noting that the symbols followed a consistent pattern: eight runes, each repeated twice, connecting the outer fires in an unbroken line. The script was Elvish, elegant and arcane. While he recognized the general form of Elvish runes, these were unfamiliar, save for one, which bore a striking resemblance to the rune for protection. It seemed logical; such runes would fortify a camp against unseen dangers. Deciding it best not to disturb these protective marks, Kemp chose to respect the boundaries set by the unknown travelers.

He settled back onto the log, delving into his pack in search of something to ignite a fire. He chuckled at the futility of the search. As an elemental mage, conjuring flames should have been a trivial matter, needing a mere flicker of thought. Yet, in this peculiar land, his powers seemed to have deserted him entirely.

One by one, he laid out his sparse possessions in front of him. His gaze lingered on a needle and thread, a gift from Ruiha. He smiled softly, touched by the memory of her kindness and unerring practicality. If Ruiha were here, she'd have had a fire crackling already, always ready for any contingency.

While his search for a fire-making tool proved fruitless, his attention was captured by the crown he had retrieved from the ancient tomb. Lifting the intricate headdress, he noticed a faint crack in the gemstone that had once been its centerpiece. The gem, previously alive with magical luminescence, now lay dull and lifeless, its enchantment seemingly snuffed out by the fracture. Despite this, the craftsmanship in its elaborate design was breathtaking. With a sigh of regret, he set it aside and resumed rummaging for his rations.

After consuming some dried fruits, a piece of jerky, and a heavily spiced chunk of flatbread from Lamos, Kemp repacked his belongings, ensuring the crown was securely fastened to his pack. Then, he resolved to attempt a magical ignition once more. Settling into a meditative pose, he closed his eyes and focused intently, trying to summon a flame. A strange sensation fluttered through him, a faint echo of his former power. It was different, unfamiliar, and unsettling.

Curiosity piqued, Kemp delved deeper into this unusual feeling, exploring its nuances. With a deep breath, he probed the mysterious remnants of his magic, seeking understanding and perhaps a way to restore his abilities. As Kemp focused his efforts on conjuring a flame, he expanded his awareness, attuning himself more deeply to the enigmatic sensations that pervaded this strange realm. Concentrating, he realized that the unfamiliarity of his magical struggles was not as alien as he had first assumed. It was like the difference between a stroll on solid, dry ground and a laborious trek uphill through dense, clinging mud. Both were forms of walking, yet one demanded substantially greater effort.

Resolved to intensify his efforts, Kemp channeled more of his dwindling energy into the task of igniting a flame. Fatigue gnawed at him, a remnant of his relentless flight from spectral pursuers, but he pressed on. His training at the academy, though he had not been the most formidable amongst his peers, had equipped him with a refined control over his powers. This skill was proving indispensable now.

Energy surged within him, coursing through his veins towards his fingertips, the intended birthplace of the flame. Sweat beaded on his brow, and he nearly lost his focus as he exerted himself to the limits of his endurance. Then, a tingling sensation sparked at his fingertips, a telltale sign of the gathering magic. Invisible currents flowed from his core, along his arms, and converged in his hands. With one final, determined effort, Kemp ignited a small but steady flame in the palm of his hand. Once the flame flickered to life, maintaining it required minimal effort.

The initial conjuration, demanding and power-intensive, was always the most challenging aspect of elemental magic, be it summoning fire or calling forth a gust of wind. Now kneeling beside the fire pit, Kemp gently coaxed the nascent flame onto the dry, blackened branches left by previous travelers. The wood, already parched and eager for warmth, caught quickly, casting a warm, flickering orange glow that pierced the enveloping darkness of the campsite.

The light, dancing with life, reflected in Kemp's eyes as he watched the fire grow, a small victory in this unyielding, mysterious landscape. This moment of success, however fleeting, bolstered his spirits and strengthened his resolve to reclaim the full breadth of his magical abilities.

However, feeling drained by his magical exertions, Kemp knew he didn't have the energy to summon additional flames directly. Opting for a more practical approach, he picked up a dried branch, still glowing with the ember from his conjured fire, and began the task of lighting the other fires set around the perimeter.

As Kemp brought the glowing branch into contact with the tinder of the final fire, the runes etched around the camp burst into a vibrant green light, shining brightly for a moment before quickly fading back into obscurity. This ephemeral glow confirmed that the magical wards were still a potent safeguard against the lurking perils of this shadowy realm, but also sparked a flicker of hope within Kemp as the brief surge of green light reminded him of the distant beacon he had seen earlier, suggesting that it, too, might provide sanctuary in this forbidding landscape.

With the four fires now flickering steadily, pushing back the chilling darkness and the eerie quiet of the surrounding woods. Kemp felt a much-needed sense of security. He arranged his makeshift camp with weary efficiency, using his pack as a pillow, and settled down next to the central fire.

In the warmth of the flames and the relative safety of the rune- protected clearing Kemp's tension ebbed away. His thoughts of missing friends and the mysterious loss of his powers soon became muddled as exhaustion overtook him. Within moments, his eyes closed, and the rhythmic crackling of the fire lulled him into a deep, recuperative slumber, at peace at last under the starlit sky.

Ruiha

Ruiha was imprisoned in a cage at the center of the pit, surrounded by the other captive Drogo. A line of guards stood watch, their eyes fixed coldly on the prisoners. Between the captives and the guards paced the formidable figure of Captain Drakoth, a giant among the Drogo. In one hand he gripped a massive axe, and with the other, he dragged a battered but still conscious Corgan beside him.

"For all of you who think that you have a chance of escape... think again." Drakoth bellowed. "Corgan here once dreamt of escape. But that dream was a lie, nothing more than a poison-coated dagger, thrust into the heart of your hopes, its venom coursing through your spirit, leaving behind nothing but despair!" His voice boomed across the pit. "Let those who took heart in Corgan's words beware. Behold the fate of liars and dreamers in this pit!" With a sinister chuckle, he hauled Corgan to his feet.

Grinning cruelly, Captain Drakoth announced, "Today, Corgan, you will entertain a different audience." He then turned to the line of guards and roared, "Bring forth his challengers!"

Turning as one, the guards pivoted and made their way toward the archway leading to the prisoners' quarters. Ruiha and Dakarai exchanged worried glances, as they anticipated the emergence of Corgan's adversaries.

Tension mounted as the minutes passed, each one feeling longer and more agonizing than the last. Finally, four armored Dwarves appeared from the shadows. As they stepped into the open, Ruiha noticed their wary eyes scanning the surroundings, likely puzzled by the absence of a cheering crowd. Each Dwarf wore the hard, battle-worn expression of a veteran fighter, clearly outmatching Corgan in every way.

Positioning themselves in the center of the arena, the Dwarves seemed to realize the true nature of the contest as they eyed Corgan, who stood battered and bruised before them. A flicker of confusion and then indignation crossed their rugged faces.

After a brief, muttered consultation, one of the Dwarves stepped forward, his voice gruff and tinged with a heavy accent. "What is this?" he challenged loudly. "I thought you wanted a fight. This will be nothing but an execution!"

"You will fight. And he is your opponent," Captain Drakoth's command left no room for rebuttal. With deliberate slowness, he stepped away from Corgan, leaving the battered Drogo vulnerably positioned in the center of the arena while the captain disappeared through a locked passageway to the side. A moment later he reappeared in the stands and, after a tense pause, he signaled for the match to commence.

One of the Dwarves looked up in disbelief at Captain Drakoth. "He hasn't even got a weapon!" the stout Dwarf protested, his voice echoing across the silent arena.

"I said BEGIN!" Captain Drakoth replied in a ferocious growl. Almost instantly, several arrows thudded into the ground just a few feet in front of the Dwarves—a stark and deadly reminder that their compliance was not optional and the grotesque spectacle would proceed regardless of considerations of fairness or honor.

The Dwarves exchanged resigned glances and then after a brief, intense discussion among themselves, one of them slowly approached Corgan with his hands raised above his head in a clear gesture of non-aggression. Stopping a few meters away, he dropped an axe on the ground in front of Corgan, and without a word, turned to rejoin his group.

As he walked back, three of the Dwarves instinctively stepped aside, clearing a path for him to face Corgan alone. His grip on the axe was firm, his stance resolute, but his eyes betrayed a conflicted spirit, torn between the demands of the situation and his own moral compass.

From her vantage point, Ruiha's attention was drawn to Captain Drakoth in the stands. The fury on his face was palpable, lines of anger etched into his leathered reptilian features at the unfolding scene. His impatience reached its limit, erupting in a bellow of unchecked rage. "Fight!" he screamed, his voice thundering throughout the arena. "I said fight!" he repeated with obvious frustration.

Ruiha could see how the unexpected display of honor among the Dwarves had disrupted the cruel spectacle Captain Drakoth had planned. Their defiance not only challenged his authority but also undermined the atmosphere of fear he strove to cultivate, a breach in his expected order that visibly fueled a deeper anger within him

The Dwarf looked up at Captain Drakoth, his gaze burning with contempt, then shifted his gaze back to Corgan. He nodded toward the axe at the Drogo's feet and said, "Pick it up, I do not want to fight an unarmed opponent."

Watching from her cage, Ruiha felt a deep respect for this Dwarf's insistence on fairness, despite the dire circumstances and Drakoth's looming presence. His actions spoke to a code of honor that resonated with her own values.

Corgan bent to pick up the axe, and Ruiha could see fear marking his every movement. In his large hands, the weapon seemed pitifully small, designed for the shorter stature of the Dwarves. He gripped it awkwardly, unaccustomed to wielding a weapon, his body shaking as if in the midst of a fierce storm. The Dwarf shook his head sorrowfully. Despite his effort to ensure fairness, the fight was still hopelessly skewed.

Ruiha's heart pounded as she watched, her eyes wide with a blend of dread and concern. She longed to look away, to avoid witnessing the impending horror, but she forced herself to watch—for Corgan's sake, and as a poignant reminder of why she must never give up her hope to escape.

When the Dwarf charged, a single tear trailed down Ruiha's dirt-streaked cheek. There was no battle cry, no dramatic flourish—only a swift, decisive swing of the axe that ended Corgan's life. In that grim moment, Ruiha felt a painful gratitude for the swift, merciful end.

The Dwarf turned to face Captain Drakoth, his eyes filled with anger and contempt, but the Captain, unfazed, gave a cold echoing laugh before turning and disappearing through a tunnel.

Magnus

Magnus huddled in the corner of his damp cell, brooding silently. He had been forced to execute a Drogo who was clearly no warrior—a cruel spectacle orchestrated by that sadistic Captain Drakoth, no doubt to prove some twisted point. The memory of the unarmed Drogo haunted him; Draeg's mercy, the lizard hadn't stood a chance.

A sigh escaped him as he lamented the absence of Gunnar more than ever. Since his brother's mysterious disappearance from Fort Bjerg, Magnus had assumed leadership of the Snow Wolves, but under his command, they had been captured and enslaved by the Drogo, reduced to mere pawns in their gruesome games. A heavy burden of guilt weighed on him; he couldn't shake the feeling that he had failed his family, his clan, and his unit.

"Those fuckers are savages," Torain blurted out, trying to snap Magnus out of his dark reverie. Magnus only grunted in response, his gaze fixed vacantly on the floor.

Torain slumped down beside him. "Boss, it wasn't your fault. What happened back there… we did what we could. We gave him the best chance possible."

Magnus looked up, his eyes burning with a mix of anger and self-reproach. "Wasn't my fault? Do you think Gunnar would've done that? In fact, do you think Gunnar would have even let us get captured in the first place?" His voice rose, each word bitter with self-recrimination.

"Listen, Magnus," Torain responded his tone soothing, against the rising storm within his leader. "Gunnar disappeared. I don't know what that bastard Wilfrid did to him, but no one has seen or heard from him since we were released from Fort Bjerg. None of this—none of it—is your fault." The intended absolution in his words did little to ease Magnus's brooding silence, as the dwarf just fixed his gaze on a new spot on the slick wall.

Brenn, Torain's twin, came over and knelt beside them. "Boss," he declared firmly, "never minding how we got here, we need a way out of here."

"Not now, Brenn!" Torain interjected sharply.

"No, he's right, Torain," Magnus countered, a spark of determination flaring in his eyes. "And it's unlikely we'll find Gunnar here."

He saw Torain and Brenn exchange uneasy glances, their silence speaking volumes. Magnus was painfully aware that many in his unit believed Gunnar to be dead, yet he himself couldn't accept that possibility. Gunnar was too capable, too clever, and too damn stubborn to have fallen to someone like Wilfrid.

"He's still out there, lads. He has to be," Magnus said. "And I'll be damned if I'm the one leading the Snow Wolves now."

"That's the spirit, boss!" Brenn cheered enthusiastically "Now, how in Draeg's stone balls do we get out of this damn place?"

"There's fifty or so guards, and only two dozen of us," Torain brought a note of realism to the discussion. "That's not good odds, no matter how you look at it."

"Even more so considering we only have access to weapons in the pit," Magnus felt obliged to point out the limitations of their resources.

"Aye, I wouldn't say we can rush them out there, even with weapons," Brenn chimed in before pragmatically pointing out the immediate obstacle, "And first off, we need to get out of this cell!"

"We will find a way," Magnus asserted as he mulled over their grim situation and limited options.

"We're the bloody Snow Wolves, boss. Of course we'll find a way!" Brenn responded with fervor, his enthusiasm infecting the rest of the group and bolstering Magnus's resolve.

Ruiha

"Bastard Dwarves!" Dakarai erupted, his frustration boiling over as he paced the cramped cell. "They killed Corgan!"

Ruiha watched him, waiting for the wave of his anger to crest and recede a little. She understood the volatile mood among the Drogo; Corgan had been a pillar in their small community—respected and genuinely liked. His brutal death had not just ignited rage, but also stoked fear among them, a fear that they might be next.

Ruiha knew she needed to channel the Drogo's raw emotions away from the Dwarves and towards a collective resolve against their actual enemy—their captors. But finding the right words to unite them was a puzzle she hadn't yet solved. For now, their collective anger and fear filled the air like a dense fog.

Dakarai suddenly spun round at her. "Why are you not angry, Ruiha?" he demanded in a voice accusingly sharp.

Ruiha understood she wasn't the real target of his harsh words; it was the anger speaking, lashing out in pain. She let the bitter reproach pass without challenge. She needed to soothe yet inspire, to redirect their hurt into a focused, fighting spirit.

"Dakarai," she kept her voice level and calm despite the turmoil inside her. "Of course I'm angry. But my anger isn't directed at the Dwarves. It's aimed at Captain Drakoth."

"But they killed him, Ruiha! They executed him!" Dakarai's voice rose almost to a shout, raw with emotions.

"Yes, they did," Ruiha acknowledged, her tone soothing in the face of his agitation. "But who forced their hand? Captain Drakoth did. Remember how they offered him a weapon? That Dwarf—he did not relish his task, Dakarai. Couldn't you see the reluctance, the regret in his eyes?"

"All I saw was him killing my friend, Ruiha," Dakarai's voice dropped to a whisper as the anger surrendered to grief. He sank down next to her, the fight draining from him. "They killed him, Ruiha."

Ruiha felt the weight of his despair, and she placed a hand on his shoulder in silent solidarity. They needed to look beyond their immediate grief and focus their anger where it truly belonged. It was not just about avenging Corgan, but about saving themselves from further destruction under Drakoth's ruthless command.

"And what if it had been me they forced to do it, Dakarai? Or you, even?" Ruiha said softly. "How would you feel then? Corgan's fate was sealed today, whether by a Dwarf's hand or another's. He had come to terms with that reality, and now we must do the same."

Dakarai absorbed her words while a heavy silence filled the space between them. After several moments, he gave a long, weary sigh. "This will set us back, Ruiha. All the work Corgan did for our cause…"

"I know, Dakarai." Ruiha nodded, her mind racing through their remaining options. "But before we can begin thinking about escaping again, we need to deal with the immediate threat among us. We have to find the traitor who betrayed Corgan. If they've done it once, they'll do it again, and next time it might be you or me facing death in the arena."

Dakarai's eyes flickered around the dimly lit cell, his expression clouding with suspicion. "How do we find out who it was?" he whispered, his voice barely audible over the distant sounds of the prison.

"We'll need to be observant, watch for any unusual behavior or slip-ups," Ruiha responded quietly, her mind already formulating the crude beginnings of a plan. "Trust has become as valuable as our lives here. We watch, we listen, and we wait for the right moment to uncover the traitor."

She stroked her chin absently, brow furrowed in thought. "We need to figure out who was aware of Corgan's plans Then we keep a close eye on all of them. The traitor must have received something in return for the information." A question struck her and she turned to the Drogo for his insight. "Dak, what is it that most of us here desire the most?"

"Release," Dakarai answered without hesitation.

Ruiha nodded. "True, but it's unlikely the guards would let anyone go just for that. If the traitor hasn't been released, then what else could they have asked for?"

"If it isn't release, then maybe a reprieve from fighting," Dakarai suggested. "Every breath we take in that pit could be our last. If I couldn't get out, I'd at least ask to stay out of the arena."

"That's exactly my thoughts," Ruiha agreed. "We'll start by identifying those who knew about the escape plans and monitor their movements closely. Everyone is supposed to fight at least once a week; some of us more often. By next week, we should see who's unusually absent from the pit."

As Ruiha laid out the plan, she hoped that during the week of vigilance, the immediate fervor and anger among the imprisoned Drogo might diminish. She needed enough of them to remain motivated and alive by the end of the week for her to enact her strategy. With Corgan gone, she could feel the weight of leadership pressed on her shoulders—and she was determined to honor his memory.

5.
Echoes of the Dark Forest

"In the dense woods, every step forward is a battle against fear and darkness."

Gunnar

Wandering through a dense forest of dark, gnarled trees, Gunnar felt as if shadows and mists coiled around his feet like black and grey serpents. He glanced at Karl, noticing his wince with each deliberately placed step. Even Thalirion, usually sure-footed, had slowed his pace, carefully navigating the eerie woodland.

Perched on Gunnar's shoulder, Havoc, no longer the tiny sprite he once was, had grown significantly to nearly the size of Gunnar's forearm. The sprite, older and evidently more resilient, seemed to thrive, staying awake for longer stretches. Gunnar experienced a familiar tingle in his mind, a sensation he had learned to recognize as Havoc's way of initiating mind- to-mind communication. Once awake, he'd found that Havoc rarely ceased his mental chatter, filling Gunnar's thoughts with a continuous stream of observations and ideas.

"Gunnar," Havoc's voice echoed the unease in Gunnar's mind. "This place is horrible. Stop dawdling and get us out of here!"

"I'm going as fast as I can." Gunnar tried to keep his tone even, hoping his frustration didn't seep into his mental message. He wasn't entirely convinced he had masked it well.

"With those long legs, you should be going faster than you are. That's all I'm saying. I feel like you're being slow on purpose just to irritate me!" Havoc complained, his tone half-serious.

Gunnar glanced at the Sprite, feeling a surge of disbelief and irritation. His face must have betrayed his emotions, because Havoc suddenly burst into laughter. "You look like you're eating a rock!" he mocked.

Despite the irritation, Gunnar couldn't help but be amused by Havoc's barb. A small smile broke through the frustration as he realized that even in dark moments, Havoc could still bring a touch of lightness.

Gunnar seized the opportunity to inquire about Havoc's conversation with Lorelei from the previous evening. Havoc met his question with those unyielding amethyst eyes, then, without a word, hopped back into Gunnar's pocket. Having grown so much, he now barely fitted, his head left poking out as he settled down. "I'm going to sleep. Wake me once we're through this misery…" he murmured before drifting off.

Gunnar chuckled to himself at the faint sounds of Havoc's snores, before his attention shifted to the rest of their group. Anwyn, usually the nimblest amongst them, appeared to be grappling awkwardly with the rough terrain, her movements uncharacteristically labored. Gunnar pushed himself forward, to catch up with her, his muscles protesting against the uneven ground.

It took a strenuous effort to finally draw level, although as he reached her side, Gunnar harbored a suspicion that Anwyn had subtly moderated her speed, perhaps sensing his struggle and allowing him to catch up without making it obvious. He appreciated the gesture, yet chose to keep the suspicion to himself, not wanting to puncture the quiet solidarity developing between them.

"How are you, Anwyn?" Gunnar managed to avoid betraying his breathlessness.

"Good, thank you, Gunnar," she replied, her eyes scanning the dense, dark woods around them. "Though I'd prefer we leave this place sooner rather than later!"

"Aye, that's true enough," he agreed, his gaze following hers through the misty forest.

"And you, Gunnar? How do you fare?"

"I'm okay. But this place doesn't help," he admitted as they maneuvered around a large fallen tree. Pushing past the vine- like black roots, Gunnar found the moment to broach another topic. "I've been meaning to ask you something." He glanced at Anwyn, catching her nod of encouragement. "I can feel the aura around me now, but I just can't seem to connect to it. I haven't managed it since you first helped me." His tone was full of the frustration of his struggle with the mystical forces.

"When we stop again, Gunnar, I'll try to help you. Maybe you just need more practice?" Anwyn suggested gently.

"Aye, you're probably right." Gunnar still felt despondent. He knew mastering such skills was no small feat, yet each failure weighed heavily on him.

"Perhaps Thalirion might be able to assist us as well. If we work together—" Anwyn's words were abruptly cut off by an ear-piercing shriek from above. Both of them instinctively clamped their hands over their ears, wincing as the shrill sound pierced the quiet of the forest. Looking up, they spotted a large bat-like creature descending toward them, its body composed of swirling dark grey smoke and its ethereal wings flapping violently.

"What in all that is holy is that?" Karl exclaimed, pointing up through the dark canopy at the nightmarish figure.

The bat-like creature soared overhead, its screech so deafening Gunnar feared his ears might bleed. With wings that seemed woven from strands of dark smoke and mist, the creature's body was diminutive compared to its expansive wingspan. Amidst the swirling smoky shroud, Gunnar could make out the ominous glow of crimson eyes peering down at them.

Amidst the cacophony, Gunnar saw Thalirion raise his staff, his expression set and focused. A bolt of ice-blue energy surged from the tip, striking the creature squarely in its torso. The impact blasted a hole through the center, and the shrieking abruptly ceased.

With panic etched across his face, Karl turned from Gunnar to Thalirion, his voice tinged with alarm, "Again, Thalirion… what was that thing?"

"A Spectral Echo known as a Shadowwing," Thalirion replied gravely. "We need to hurry. Its nest will be close, and we're vulnerable out here." With that, he quickened his pace, then abruptly stopped and spun around, his finger pressed to his lips signaling for silence. His eyes swept the canopy above as he whispered, "They are in the trees above us. Keep quiet and try to conquer your fear. Remember, fear is like a feast to these Echoes." Without another word, he turned and marched toward the Tower of Absence.

Gunnar noticed Karl swallow hard, and Anwyn shudder beside him; the tension was palpable. Gunnar urged them to quicken their pace to catch up with the seasoned Elf, their hearts pounding with the fear they were trying to suppress.

After about an hour of tense walking, they faced another onslaught. This time, several monkey-like creatures formed from the same dark smoke as the bat descended upon them, shrieking. Thalirion, poised and ready, swept his staff in a wide arc. A powerful gust of wind erupted from it, repelling the shrieking creatures and hurling them backward into the darkness. The swift and capable defense launched by Thalirion momentarily eased the group's fear.

Another echo took flight and Anwyn released shot arrow that passed harmlessly through the spectral creature. Gunnar's frustration mounted as he remembered Thalirion's words about the limitations of their conventional weapons against such foes. He felt helpless, unable to access the surrounding aura or wield any magic, questioning what he could possibly contribute.

Thalirion, as though sensing his plight, called out over the screeching of fresh enemies, "Anwyn, your arrows won't work on these echoes! Use your magic. We must protect Gunnar and Karl." His voice cut through the chaos, redirecting Anwyn's efforts to the critical role of magical defense.

Gunnar saw Anwyn's expression tighten with concentration, the effort of summoning magic in this fraught environment evident in tiny beads of sweat appearing on her forehead. After a moment, she successfully conjured several pebble-sized balls of flame that orbited lazily between her hands. Thalirion, acknowledging her effort with a nod, conjured his own magical attack—a fireball as large as his head that hovered above his left palm while his right hand clamped around his staff, his knuckles turning white from the grip.

With a determined thrust, Thalirion sent his fireball soaring into the canopy. As it blazed a trail through the darkness, Gunnar caught sight of dozens of eerie smoke-like creatures glaring down at them, momentarily exposed by the light. The fireball tore through many of them, scattering them before his eyes could follow its path any further.

Seizing the brief illumination, Anwyn directed her smaller flames with precision, each one targeting a different spectral echo. The creatures emitted anguished howls as they were hit, their forms dissolving into wisps of energy that scattered on the wind.

Then, capitalizing on the moment of chaos among their attackers, they ran. Gunnar felt a surge of adrenaline as they darted through the dark forest, the sounds of the creatures' cries fading behind them. However, as they ran, Gunnar could see the monkey-like echoes chasing after them. The creatures were fast, and Gunnar knew it wouldn't be long before they caught up. They swung from branch to branch effortlessly, whilst the four companions struggled to maneuver around the dense, dark undergrowth. Both Gunnar and Karl tripped and fell more than once, although Thalirion and Anwyn seemed able to keep their footing as they crossed the lethal landscape.

As the spectral monkeys drew nearer, Anwyn unleashed several more tiny balls of fire. Her assault was less accurate this time; only a few struck their intended targets while the rest fizzled out, arcing ineffectively back to the ground.

Thalirion, wielding his staff to conjure another ice-blue ball of energy, similar to the one that had taken down the bat. With precise control, he dispatched the remaining monkeys. Despite the apparent victory, Gunnar could hear more creatures stirring in the canopy above, a reminder that their threat had not fully abated.

The forest began to open up as they continued their flight. The dense, black trees became sparser, and the tangled roots underfoot became less cumbersome, allowing them to quicken their pace. Thalirion periodically launched blasts of energy skyward, and Anwyn sent fireballs hurling into the dark, each determined to ward off any followers.

Feeling somewhat redundant amidst the flurry of magical defense, Gunnar focused on maintaining pace with the group. He and Karl, both veterans of the Snow Wolves, relied on their robust fitness to keep up. Though they lacked the Elves' graceful agility, their sturdy builds powered them through the forest with the unstoppable force of charging boars, ensuring they were no burden to their faster companions.

Relief washed over Gunnar as the Tower of Absence finally came into view, a beacon of safety in the oppressive darkness of the forest. As they drew nearer, Thalirion planted his staff forcefully into the earth, causing it to glow an eerie green against the dark night. Mirroring this signal, the beacon atop the Tower ignited, casting a radiant light that pierced the darkness, illuminating the landscape for miles around. The group, following Thalirion's lead, came to a halt and allowed themselves a much-needed rest. They bent over, hands on knees, each drawing in deep, labored breaths, their bodies heaving with exhaustion.

"We're safe here," Thalirion panted, his voice a mix of relief and fatigue. "We are within the Tower's defences. No spectral echoes can attack us here."

Karl, regaining some of his strength, turned to look back the way they had come, his expression lined with weariness and concern. "How are we supposed to protect ourselves from those things?" he asked, his voice heavy.

"Magic," Thalirion responded simply, regaining his compo- sure. "Magic is the only weapon that can destroy an echo. They are remnants of pure magic, and no mundane weapon or attack can harm them whatsoever."

At Thalirion's words, the reality of their situation settled in on Gunnar; they were not just fighting physical creatures, but against manifestations of raw magical energy. He felt a mix of awe and helplessness, aware now more than ever of the importance of mastering the magical skills he struggled with.

Gunnar exchanged a despondent look with Karl before voicing his frustration, "How, then, can we ever be expected to defeat even a weak echo?"

Thalirion looked at Gunnar, a hint of confusion crossing his features. "Gunnar," he began in an earnest tone, "you can practise magic. That is why we are here. You will master the arcane arts to a degree that is unheard of back in Vellhor."

Gunnar fixed his gaze on the old elf. "Thalirion, please explain to me how I will be able to control magic if I cannot even connect to the aura, let alone conjure a flame!" His voice broke with the desperation of his need for answers and yearning to grasp the powers that Thalirion and Anwyn wielded so effortlessly. He felt as if he was on the brink of a breakthrough that hung frustratingly just beyond reach.

Thalirion pursed his lips in a moment of deep thought and Gunnar wasn't sure he would even respond. But abruptly, Thalirion's gaze sharpened and he fixed Gunnar with an intensity that might have intimidated a lesser Dwarf. "Gunnar," he said firmly, "in the right circumstances, even a loose pebble can bring down a mountain. Here in Nexus, we find those circumstances, and you, Gunnar, are that pebble. Your training will be arduous, I won't sugarcoat it. Prepare for what could be the most challenging twelve months of your life. But remember, you are young, and our true battle with Nergai lies far in the future."

Gunnar stood straighter. "I'm ready to prove myself, Thalirion. I'm not afraid of hard ork." He paused as a thought struck him and he looked up sharply at his Elven mentor. "Wait, did you say twelve months?"

"Yes, Gunnar," Thalirion confirmed, "But remember, time in Nexus operates differently from Vellhor. Here, a month equates to merely a day back home. When we return, only twelve days will have passed in Vellhor!"

Karl paled visibly at Thalirion's revelation. With a hesitant voice, he asked, "Thalirion, what about me? Am I to undergo the same training as Gunnar?"

Thalirion smiled gently at the dwarf's concern. "Karl, you aren't required to undergo the same rigorous training as Gunnar. However, I strongly advise you not to squander this chance. The Tower of Absence is home to many Sages who can teach you skills beyond your imagination. It would truly be a missed opportunity if you left without exploring what they have to offer."

Anwyn's sharp intake of breath caught everyone's attention, and they turned to her with questioning looks. "Anwyn, is everything okay?" Thalirion asked.

Anwyn shook her head in disbelief. "Did you say Sages?"

"Yes, dear. Several of them, in fact!" Thalirion's voice positively swelled with pride.

"How?" Anwyn's skepticism was clear. "Sages are a myth! They're tales from an age when dragons soared through the skies of Vellhor!"

Thalirion's announcement had clearly challenged Anwyn's understanding of their world's history and the very boundaries of what she believed possible. Gunnar could see the gears turning in her mind as she tried to reconcile Thalirion's claims with the stories she had grown up hearing.

"Dragons, Anwyn," Thalirion's smile blended amusement and seriousness, "are very real! In fact, we are currently facing a formidable threat from one. But to address your initial shock—yes, in Vellhor, Sages are considered mythical. The aura there simply cannot sustain a Sage, or anyone of higher magical standing than an Overlord, for an extended period. That's why we choose to reside in places like this."

Gunnar listened intently, realizing the title of Sage or an Overlord denoted great power, and he wondered whether Thalirion himself might be one of these esteemed ranks. Just as he was about to voice that speculation, Karl chimed in with his own query, "What exactly is a Sage? We don't have such tales in Dreynas."

"A Sage is essentially a rank," Thalirion explained. "It's determined by a combination of experience and the strength and amount of one's magical power. A Sage is the first of the advanced rank in the arcane arts, followed by a Sovereign, which is higher still."

"And what is your rank?" Karl promptly asked.

Thalirion bowed with a playful flourish. "I am but a Sage," he declared, his tone light yet proud.

"And how does Anwyn compare to a Sage? What rank is she?" Karl went on.

Thalirion subjected Anwyn to a searching look, and Gunnar noticed her tense up. She took a quick, sharp breath before demanding, "What did you just do to my spirit?"

"I simply conducted a quick scan of your spirit," Thalirion replied nonchalantly, as though such an intrusion were a mere commonplace.

Anwyn wrapped her arms around herself with a huff, arching her eyebrow with displeasure as she turned away. Above her head, Lorelei mirrored Anwyn's offended stance.

Either Thalirion didn't notice Anwyn's reaction or he chose to overlook it as he continued addressing Karl's question. "Anwyn has recently advanced to the rank of Master, which is an intermediate level, two ranks below the advanced level of a Sage. A Master is the highest rank attainable in Vellhor, and achieving it at her age is exceptional progress!" The praise seemed to soften Anwyn's irritation, and her expression became more contemplative rather than upset.

Karl frowned. "Two ranks doesn't sound like much. Surely Anwyn's training won't be as intense as Gunnar's?"

"Ahh, Karl," Thalirion said, "I wish it were that straightforward. But the leap from Master to Sage is vast—like trying to cross a wide river. Many try, and despite having access to far greater resources than we have here in Nexus, only a few succeed."

Their exchange left the group silent for a moment, each pondering the challenges ahead. How much could they each achieve in this mysterious and magical place? Gunnar felt a surge of determination to at least match Anwyn's current level of arcane mastery.

Once the group had recovered from the grueling ordeal in the forest, Thalirion led them on in the journey toward the Tower and the beacon of green light that promised not just respite but a semblance of safety.

Kemp

Each time Kemp glimpsed the bright green light piercing the distant sky, a surge of hope fluttered in his chest. He wasn't sure what the light signified or what awaited him there, but it had become a beacon guiding his weary steps, the only goal that could anchor his wandering spirit. The luminous light was a welcome distraction from the eerie, ghostly creatures that flickered at the edges of his vision in the gloomy expanse. Fortunately, since his arrival in this strange, unsettling land, these spectral figures had kept their distance, neither attacking nor pursuing him.

Since waking Kemp had noticed the light remained steadfast—unlike before, when it had blinked out after brief moments—and he felt reassured by the persistence of its green glow.

He'd spent the night in another abandoned campsite, enclosed by a rune barrier. Once he'd kindled a fire, he'd spent several hours studying the protective runes and copying their intricate fascinating patterns onto a piece of parchment. He thought his future safety might depend on his ability to replicate these protective wards.

Having broken camp and walked for several hours Kemp found himself facing a vast and forbidding forest that stretched without visible end to left and right. It seemed to form an insurmountable barrier between him and the light.

Kemp took a determined breath. The forest might be daunting, but the light beckoned him irresistibly. He stepped forward into the shadows of the trees. As the trees closed in around him, the flicker of hope that the green light represented sustained him.

Gnarled, blackened roots sprawled across the ground, making the terrain treacherous to navigate. The dense canopy obscured the distant light, firing a fear that he might lose his path amid the tangle of thick trees. Yet he pressed on, compelled to chase down. the beacon's light, the only sign of hope he had found in this desolate place.

As he scrambled through the forest, Kemp's mind was a tumult of tangled thoughts. He worried about what had become of Ruiha, haunted by the possibility that the Drogo might have harmed her, though a part of him clung to a belief in her resilience.

He struggled to comprehend the mysterious nature of this place. How had he ended up here? It certainly wasn't Fenmark or anywhere in Vellhor. The more he thought, the more he suspected his arrival here was linked to the ancient tomb he had stumbled upon. He recalled the ominous aura of death magic that had permeated the tomb and his surge of rage as he touched the tomb of Nergai, only for Ruiha to soothe his fury, dispersing it as effortlessly as wind scatters dust.

A horrific screech sliced through the darkness, abruptly shattering Kemp' thoughts. Panic seized him, his hands flying to his ears in a futile attempt to block out the piercing sound. He bolted through the thick undergrowth, pushing his body to its limits.

Running had never been Kemp's preferred mode of action, yet this strange place had forced him into relentless sprints for survival. As he darted through the forest, he caught sight of the pursuing creature—a rat-like being the size of a small dog, composed of dark, smoky wisps. It too appeared to struggle with the rugged terrain, but Kemp knew it was only a matter of time before it would close in on him. He needed to prepare for a confrontation.

He tried conjuring a fireball as he ran, but the effort was nearly impossible while also navigating the perilously uneven ground. The sounds of the creature grew louder, its screeching turning into ferocious growls and howls.

Spotting a fallen tree ahead, Kemp made a split-second decision, leaping over it and crouching behind its cover. No longer in motion, he focused intensely, channeling all his energy into the creation of a small flame in his palms. The stillness helped, though summoning magic in this cursed place was still an arduous task.

Under the intense pressure of imminent danger, Kemp finally managed to summon a modest fireball, just as the creature vaulted the log to land menacingly before him. He hurled the fireball directly into its chest. The creature dissolved into motes of energy, vanishing before his eyes. Relived and exhausted, Kemp took a grateful moment to catch his breath behind the shelter of the log.

As the immediate threat seemed to recede, the pounding in his ears subsided, only to be replaced by distant screeches that reignited his fear. His heart pounding anew, he scrambled to his feet and plunged back into the run.

As he darted through the forest, glimpses of bright green light filtering through the dense canopy buoyed his spirits. He clung to the hope that reaching the light would mean safety and perhaps a way back home—to Ruiha. The trees gradually began to thin, fueling his optimism that he must be nearing his destination.

Finally breaking through the tree line into a small clearing, Kemp saw the source of the light in all its majesty: a towering structure piercing the sky. His legs, rejuvenated by a mix of fear, hope, and desperate anticipation, carried him swiftly towards the base of the tower, each step fueled by the thought of safety and the chance to find his way back to everything he held dear.

Just as he thought he had reached safety, a huge bat-like creature, shrouded in smoke, swooped down upon him. Its sharp talons pierced the skin on Kemp's back and shoulders as it lifted him off the ground. Fortunately, the creature's grip was tenuous, and Kemp, thrashing wildly, managed to break free, tumbling back down. He landed awkwardly and a searing pain shooting through his left calf made him scream out.

Rolling onto his back, Kemp fought through the waves of pain, desperately trying to focus his energy to summon another fireball. The creature hovered closer, full of menace. In a frenzy, Kemp gathered all his remaining strength as a swipe of the creaturs talons sliced through the flesh and bone of his left hand. Miraculously, just as the creature made contact, Kemp's other hand unleashed a small fireball. The impact blew the creature back, disintegrating it into countless motes of dust-like energy.

Staring down in shock, Kemp saw his hand, gruesomely hanging by a thread of skin and muscle, blood soaking his clothes. Oddly, in that horrific moment, his thoughts flickered to Harald—memories of the man's betrayals and death mingling with his own acute physical pain. The mix of shock, loss, and betrayal overwhelmed him completely, and he vomited before the world went dark as the pain drove him into unconsciousness.

6.
BUILDING ALLIANCES

"The foundation of any great victory is laid in the alliances formed along the way."

Ruiha

The five days since Corgan's execution had passed uneventfully. Though, as Ruiha had anticipated, the seething anger once directed at the Dwarves had started to wane.

In the pit, where the shadow of death was a constant presence, grief and rage were luxuries few could afford. A small, secret smile of triumph curled Ruiha's lips at Dakarai's success in redirecting the collective ire from friend to foe—their guards.

Dakarai had survived a ferocious fight the previous day—ribs cracked, a stark gash across his back, and fingers twisted at cruel angles. Yet, despite the vivid bruises and bloodied bandages, victory clung to him like a hard-won cloak.

The injuries, severe as they were, inadvertently served their broader strategy. As Dakarai recovered, avoiding the rigors of training, Ruiha seized the chance to observe and influence the other gladiators in the training sands. This was a critical time to strengthen alliances and mold the raw, simmering energy of the gladiators into a focused force against their true enemies.

Approaching her usual corner where Dakarai waited, she raised her hand in a weary salute before collapsing beside him and taking the roughly hewn cup he offered. The cold and bracing water refreshed her parched throat, offering a brief moment of solace in their relentless struggle

"Tough session today," Ruiha complained, her voice heavy with fatigue. "I dunno if it's the lack of decent food, or if it's the constant training and fighting, but I'm struggling, Dak. I'm due back in the pit tomorrow afternoon. I don't know if my body can take it!" The words just spilled out. Her body ached in places she hadn't known could feel pain, each muscle and bone crying out for rest that was nowhere in sight.

Dakarai looked at her with the deep understanding born from sharing the same trials. "We don't have much time, Ruiha," his voice was low and his tone urgent. His eyes, usually full of fight, had dimmed with the grim realities of their predicament.

"There are only twenty or thirty of us remaining," he said before adding with a note of bitterness, "Plus the Dwarves." He sighed "They're trying to wear us down, so we die quicker out in the pit."

Ruiha felt a chill run through her despite the stifling atmosphere of their surroundings. Dakarai's words simply echoed her own fears— each day could be their last, and every fight in the pit was potentially fatal. She drew a deep, steadying breath. She had to believe in Dakarai, in herself, and in the slim chance that they could turn their fate around.

Ruiha finished the cool water in her cup with one long gulp and wiped her mouth dry with her sleeve. She leaned closer, her voice low. "The Dwarves were training today.

Well, most of them were. The thinner our ranks get, the more we'll find ourselves training alongside them." Her eyes darted from side to side, vigilant for any unwelcome ears that might overhear their clandestine conversation, before whispering, "I want to speak to their leader. I need to know if they're willing to join us in our plans to escape."

Dakarai laughed, a harsh, stark sound in the muted atmosphere. "What plans, Ruiha? We have ideas, but no concrete way to execute them. We can't even speak openly about them yet!"

"That's exactly why I need to speak to the Dwarves, Dak!" Ruiha's whisper grew fierce, urgent. "Haven't you seen them? I'd gladly trade my sword arm if they aren't warriors or soldiers of some kind! They must be planning an escape, just as we are. We can help each other."

Dakarai gestured toward the slaves sharing their cell. "Do you think they're ready? To work alongside the Dwarves, I mean?"

Ruiha paused. "For most of them Corgan is already forgotten history. We've lost so many, another fallen Drogo, no matter his esteem, barely registers." She threaded her fingers through her long dark hair with a sigh of frustration. "If they can't grasp that we need to escape soon, we'll all be mere carrion for the crows."

Dakarai's brow furrowed in confusion before he shook his head. "I suppose that's another one of your surface dweller sayings?" A faint smile split his somber expression, before he went on, "But you're right. Death has become a trivial constant among us; we've been steeped in it for too long."

"We need to flush out this rat, once and for all, Dak. Until we know who it is, we can't approach anyone about our plans, for fear of being exposed like Corgan was," Ruiha said.

Dakarai's reptilian gaze swept over their cell, his eyes narrowing as he considered their fellow inmates. "I have my suspicions. There are three Drogo who have not yet fought. One of them has missed at least one training session, too."

"Hmm, interesting," Ruiha mused, before asking, "Have any of them been scheduled to fight?"

"One of them has," Dakarai replied, his voice dropping to match hers. "His fight is tomorrow afternoon. The other two, no scheduled fights have been planned."

"And these two remaining Drogo?" Ruiha's gaze flickered around the cell, drawing on everything she had learned in the back alleys of Gecit as she searched the faces and postures of their cellmates for any hint of duplicity. "Who are they?"

"One is older," Dakarai said in a cautious tone. "Perhaps in his fortieth year."

Ruiha knew from her many discussions with Dakarai, that Drogo rarely lived past fifty, a consequence of their harsh, unforgiving lifestyle combined with a dire absence of medical knowledge. To be forty was to teeter on the edge of ancient in their brutal society, making every day a gift or a curse, depending on one's perspective.

"And the other?" she pressed him.

"The other is my main concern," Dakarai replied, his voice lowering even further. "He is young, younger than me. And he was due to fight on the same afternoon as Corgan, you know, before his… death."

Ruiha could see the strength of Dakarai's suspicion in her friend's steady gaze and deep frown. The timing of the young Drogo's scheduled fight could not be mere coincidece. She took a moment to consider their next move, before looking up at Dakaai. "We should lay a trap. See if we can get him to make a mistake…"

"How do we do that?"

Ruiha leaned in closer. "I want to spread a rumor, Dak," she whispered, her voice steady despite the flicker of excitement that danced through her. "Something that will get his attention. And hopefully make him slip up."

―――――◆―――――

Magnus

Magnus grunted, muscles straining as he parried a hefty swing of an axe. The blow was forceful enough to have reduced his wooden shield to splinters had the axe been crafted from iron rather than wood. And if the axe had been made of frosteel? Magnus didn't like to think about it, but the grim reality was that his head might have been severed, lying several feet away from his torso.

"Wipe that stupid grin from your face, Brenn!" Magnus admonished irritably as he readjusted his shield for the next assault. "This isn't a bloody game!"

Brenn grinned with all the exuberance of youth. "No disrespect, boss. But isn't a game exactly what we're doing?" He gestured at the wooden weapons clutched in the hands of the seasoned Dwarven warriors around them.

Magnus's jaw tightened as he scanned the training ground—a makeshift arena echoing with the clatter of wood on wood and the occasional hearty laugh. This was no game to him. Each swing, each block, each moment spent in the training ring was a preparation for the brutal reality of the pit, where mistakes were measured in blood rather than bruises.

Yet, he found his irritation ebbing slightly as he considered the value of Brenn's ability to find joy in training. Perhaps, Magnus reflected, there was room for levity even here, in the heart of preparation. Maybe Brenn's high spirits could serve as a lesson in resilience, a reminder to find strength in the face of grim prospects

Magnus conceded the point with a sigh. "Aye, I suppose you're right." He said in his deep, rough voice. "But we do need to take this training seriously, Brenn. Each time we take a step into that arena could be our last."

Brenn's grin faded as he nodded in understanding.

"Now," Magnus bellowed, "attack again. And this time, I expect more than a mere tickle!"

Grinning, Brenn dropped into a fighting stance, his lead foot slightly forward, body angled for optimal balance—ready to deliver a more serious challenge.

After their training session, the Dwarves were escorted back to their cell by eight armored guards—the same ones who had brought them out. Throughout the two hours of training, Magnus had been watching them intently, looking for any lapse in their vigilance. He had noticed how the guards' alertness had waned as the session progressed; they'd leaned against the walls, absorbed in the spectacle of the training pairs. Some even placed small bets on the outcomes of the sparring matches, their focus drifting further from their weapons.

Once back in the cell, Magnus approached Uleg, an elder Dwarf whose experience and perception he had come to value. He had tasked Uleg with documenting any potential vulnerabilities or weaknesses in their captors.

"Boss," Uleg greeted him with a tone as casual as if they were sat in a tavern rather than imprisoned in a cell. "Everything okay?"

"Aye, all well," Magnus replied, scanning quickly through the bars to ensure privacy from any nearby guards, before leaning in to murmur, "Eight guards this time. They escorted twelve of us out this afternoon and again, their attention slips during training. Also, on the way back, some seemed more preoccupied with the money they had won or lost on their bets."

Uleg stroked his beard thoughtfully as he absorbed the information. "Hmm," he mused, his frown deepening a network of wrinkles. "Very similar to the report from this morning."

"We need more observations. Any pattern or habit could be our key out of here," Magnus said.

Uleg nodded in agreement. "It's a shame they only let us train with wooden weapons."

"Probably why they're more relaxed. There's no need to be at peak awareness when we don't have the tools to truly hurt them," Magnus replied bitterly. "Even though we outnumber them and they show lapses in vigilance during training, I don't think that's the right time to make our move. The timing has to be perfect."

"You're right, boss. If we rush in without the right leverage or preparation it could spell disaster for all of us." Uleg's voice was heavy with resignation. "Only half our number being allowed to train at a time, and with nothing more than toothpicks..." He sighed deeply. "In a real fight, we'd just be kindling for the fire."

Magnus's eyes sparkled as he considered Uleg's words. "Aye, but surely we have got other options?" he queried. "What of the other reports? There must be more weaknesses we can exploit?"

"Well, we know we can get out of these cells whenever we want. They weren't designed to hold Dwarves. There are no runes, scripts, or protections on the metal bars. Even I could manipulate the metal, and I've never worked with the stuff!" Uleg's voice rose slightly with excitement at that prospect.

Magnus was acutely aware of their potential to escape their cells; it was one of the first things he had tested upon their arrival. Technically, they could break out at any moment. Yet, he harbored reservations. "I still want to keep that card close to my chest. For now, at least," he confessed. "If we were to escape, we'd be running around the godsforsaken mountains lost until we were either recaptured or killed!"

The mountains were unforgiving, a labyrinth of dangers that extened far beyond their captors' reach. Escape without a plan was tantamount to a death sentence, and Magnus was not about to lead his people into a trap of their own making.

"Aye," Uleg agreed solemnly. "We also don't have our weapons, so we'd essentially be running around with our hands tied behind our backs."

Magnus knew it wasn't just about escaping; it was about surviving long enough to make that freedom meaningful. Not only surviving the trials of the pit but also surviving once they were free.

"Any news on the scouting mission from last night?" Magnus asked. They had sent their best scout into the heart of danger. The stakes were high, and Andrin's skills were their best shot at understanding the enemy's layout. As he pictured Andrin manipulating the metal bars to slip through last night—warping them with a deftness that bordered on artistry, then meticulously straightening them to erase any trace of intrusion— Magnus felt a mix of pride and concern.

"Not as much as we hoped," Uleg replied with a frown. "However, he found where they're keeping the Drogo slaves, which could prove useful. He's going out again tonight. Hopefully, he'll be able to get some more information."

Magnus mulled over the potential of the new information—and what it might cost them. After a moment, he said. "Tomorrow evening, I want to make contact with the Drogo slaves. I think forming an alliance with them will be our best chance. We can aid their escape, and in turn, they can lead the way out of here." With a firm, decisive nod to Uleg, Magnus turned and walked away.

"Boss," Uleg called after him. Magnus turned, his expression curious. "I know it must be hard with Gunnar... disappearing like that. But I think he'd be proud of how you're handling things."

"He's not dead, Uleg. Have faith. Our handsome leader will be back with us soon enough," Magnus replied.

"Aye, boss, I doubt he's dead. That fella's too stubborn to die!" Uleg chuckled.

Magnus smiled back. Deep down, he was certain: Gunnar was still out there.

Ruiha

The rumor had started slowly, Dakarai mentioning it casually to two slaves, who passed it on to others. Before Ruiha realized it had caught and spread like wildfire through the cells. "Rainok is fighting this afternoon." The whisper reached Ruiha from a shadowed corner of the cell as she approached Dakarai, who leaned against the cold metal bars, gazing at the exit that seemed tantalizingly close yet agonizingly unattainable.

"So," Ruiha said, pulling Dakarai back from his distant thoughts. "What are you brooding over? Our plan is beginning to move."

Dakarai released a long sigh. "If things go well, we could all be free soon. But then what? Where do we go? They destroyed my home, and everyone I knew and loved is gone."

Ruiha shared his sentiment more than she cared to admit. Her own past seemed like a distant dream; she could never return to Gecit, the sandy city of her childhood. Despite its rife undercurrents of crime, she would miss the city's enigmatic beauty.

She had never known her family, and the only significant figure in her life had been Kemp, the mage whose kindness and strange innocence had offered her a rare sense of warmth. She clung to the hope that he was still alive, though the likelihood of their paths crossing again dwindled by the day.

However, as she watched Dakarai's forlorn figure, she saw the more immediate need to jolt her Drogo friend from his despair. "I know it's daunting, Dak," she began, "but what's the alternative? Let those who stripped everything away finish us off? Come, escape with me and we can truly live! We can seek our revenge, start anew. We'll find a place beyond Junak's reach."

Dakarai's response was a soft chuckle as he shook his head. "Where could we possibly go that Junak couldn't find us?"

"You could come to Fenmark with me." Her voice trailing off as she realized the absurdity of her own words. Dakarai, a Drogo, would likely be hunted in Fenmark, seen as a monster not a refugee. By the look he gave her, either he knew the truth of it, too, or he loathed at the thought of being a surface dweller.

"Or we could go to Dreynas," Ruiha seized at another thread of an idea. "If we help the Dwarves escape, they might feel indebted to us, right?"

Dakarai shook his head sadly. "You obviously don't understand the history between our two races, Ruiha. If a Drogo is seen in Dreynas, execution is immediate. The same fate awaits any Dwarf caught in Drogo Mulik."

"Dak," Ruiha sighed with frustration. "We have to believe there's a place for us beyond these walls. Anything is better than staying here, right? Come on, snap out of this gloom. Let's strategize, not despair!"

Dakarai gave a curt nod before stretching his limbs as if trying to force out his doubts. "I'm sorry, Ruiha," he apologized. "I don't know what came over me, I guess I'm just weary, weary of all this."

"Well, don't let it happen again!" Ruiha smiled as she delivered a playful punch to Dakarai's arm, before asking if Dakarai had been keeping tabs on Rainok's movements.

"Yes, I have," Dakarai responded. "And I've also got two trusted Drogos monitoring his every move."

"And? Has he done anything yet?" Ruiha pressed. Rainok's actions—or inactions—could be vital in dictating their next move.

"Apart from panic," Dakarai chuckled. "No, not yet. I believe he has only just found out."

"Okay, we need to keep a close watch on him. As soon as he does anything suspicious, I need to know!" Ruiha said before turning to walk away.

"Of course," Dakarai called after her, his voice echoing slightly across the cell. "As the Shadow Hawk wills it!"

It was only a few hours later that Dakarai approached Ruiha with a new development.

"Rainok spoke to a guard earlier. Unfortunately, we couldn't catch the conversation. But he's told at least four people that there is no fight happening."

Ruiha mulled over this for a moment before responding. "Dak," she asked, "if you found out you were supposed to fight, would you go ask a guard to confirm it?"

"Of course not!" Dakarai scoffed. "They'd beat me half to death just for bothering them!"

"Exactly!" Ruiha exclaimed. The implications of this young Drogo's actions went beyond the betrayal of Corgan;

by derailing their plans he had cost them precious time—time during which more prisoners had perished.

"We need to kill him!" Dakarai's temper flared as he too realized the enormity of Rainok's betrayal.

To Dakarai's obvious astonishment, Ruiha shook her head. "No..." she said. "No, we wait. This information could still be valuable. In the meantime, we'll accelerate our efforts with those we trust."

The shock was evident on Dakarai's face, his features tightening in incredulity. "No, Ruiha... Rainok must pay for his betrayal." His words were choked with anger. "It is the Drogo way... I cannot stand..."

Ruiha interrupted him, placing her palm gently against his chest, forcing him to focus on her instead of his anger locking gazes to ensure he truly listened. "Dakarai, Rainok will die. I promise you, I will kill him myself. But not before we've found a use for him. If we act now, the guards will get suspicious, and their increased vigilance will make our escape even more difficult."

Dakarai's expression remained tense but he slowly nodded in agreement. "I asked you to lead us," he admitted, his voice softening as he bowed his head. "I will trust your judgment."

Magnus

Being so far underground, the absence of any natural light made it impossible to distinguish night from day; the only clue lay in whether the torches and lanterns outside the cells were lit. Having spent his entire life in subterranean darkness, Magnus was unfazed by navigating the pitch-black tunnels. He had assigned Andrin the task of locating their weapons, while he and Brenn decided to visit the Drogo prisoners.

As he neared their cells, Magnus hesitated for a moment, a flicker of doubt crossing his mind—what if they alerted the guards? He wrestled with the thought but then dismissed it. The Drogo were surely desperate to escape this hellish confinement. They must share the same dreams for freedom as he did.

Although Dwarves were not renowned for their grace or subtlety, Gunnar and Brenn managed to approach the cells with uncharacteristic silence, startling the large Drogo stationed on the other side of the bars. Was he acting as a sentinel? Magnus speculated. The Drogo seemed frozen by surprise, prompting Magnus to initiate the conversation.

"Good evening," he began, his tone deliberately cordial. There was no need to be rude, he reminded himself. A little politeness never hurt anyone. "Have you got a leader? Someone who is in charge?" He kept his voice low.

The Drogo simply stared, his eyes darting between Magnus and Brenn, his expression one of pure disbelief.

Magnus persisted with a firm but gentle request, "We would like to speak with someone who represents you. Can you call them here, please?"

Before the lack of response could get too uncomfortable, a larger Drogo approached. "Thokkar, you are relieved. Please get Ruiha and DO NOT tell anybody of this," he commanded in a tone that brooked no argument. The smaller

Battle Mage

Drogo, clearly intimidated, hurried off, presumably to fetch Ruiha.

"Thank you," Magnus acknowledged the switch with a nod before venturing another question to try and gauge the hierarchy within the Drogo cell. "Are you in charge here?"

The larger Drogo sized Magnus up with a sweeping glance, eyes narrowing in a disdain the dwarf could almost physically feel. "No, I am not the leader," the Drogo replied with a curtness that bordered on outright hostility. "Thokkar has gone to get her. I am Dakarai. And you are the one that killed my friend."

As the tension between them mounted, with the persistence of Dakarai's glare, Magnus again questioned his wisdom in seeking an alliance with the Drogo. Yet, there he stood, committed to seeing it through.

Choosing diplomacy over aggression, he spread his hands in a gesture of apology. "I am sorry that I killed your friend, Dakarai. The act of executing someone innocent and defenseless has haunted me. I did my best to allow him a chance to defend himself, but when it became clear he could not, or would not… I tried to make it as painless and quick as possible." Magnus lowered his gaze, acutely aware that no words could restore the life lost or erase the big Drogo's grief.

To Magnus's surprise, Dakarai's expression mellowed. Moments earlier, anger radiated from him like heat from a furnace, but now, he looked down at the Dwarf with an unexpected softness—sympathy, perhaps? "She was right about you," Dakarai said simply before stepping aside to allow someone through.

To Magnus's complete shock it was a human woman who appeared before him. He could only stare speechless as his previous assumptions unraveled before this new, unexpected figure.

The woman, her dark skin contrasting with even darker hair, looked down at him, a small, knowing smile playing across her youthful face. "Welcome to the pit," she said. "I am Ruiha. I would invite you in, but..." She tapped gently on the wrought iron bars that separated them, her eyes twinkling with amusement.

Before Magnus could react, Brenn stepped forward, his hand reaching out to touch the bars. With a grunt of effort, he bent and warped the metal out of shape, his face lighting up with pride at the stunned expressions on Dakarai's and Ruiha's faces. "No need to apologize, we can let ourselves in!" he announced cheerfully, gripping the next bar and bending it too, clearing a path for him and Magnus to enter.

"Erm, come on in then," Ruiha said, her brow furrowing with confusion. "Please, tell us why you are here?"

"I am Magnus, the Acting Commander of the Snow Wolves of Draegoor," Magnus declared, puffing out his chest proudly.

"We want to escape, and we're wondering if you would like to come with us," Brenn blurted out before Magnus could urge him to restrain himself.

"Aye," Magnus interjected, shooting a stern glance at Brenn. "He's right. We're planning on escaping, and we thought that strength in numbers would increase our chances of success."

The human and the Drogo exchanged a knowing glance before Dakarai cut straight to the heart of the matter. "Tell us of your plans," he said. "We are formulating our own arrangements, and we will not be used as fodder to help you escape!"

Magnus felt a pang of unease at Dakarai's sharp tone, but he strove to maintain a calm demeanor. "Nor do we ask you to." He raised his hands in a gesture of peace. "We merely wanted to begin negotiations. In truth, our plans are somewhat... lacking."

"Well, that makes two of us, Magnus," Ruiha admitted with a wry smile, her gaze shifting between Magnus and Dakarai. "We have recently had a rat infestation, which has set us back somewhat. But today, we have resolved that issue," she said, her eyes flicking toward Dakarai.

Magnus responded, "As you saw, we can manipulate the metal bars of the cells. But we lack an opportunity for escape, and we also lack knowledge of the terrain. We believe that you can offer us the knowledge of the terrain?" He directed his gaze at Dakarai and was relieved by the Drogo's, firm nod of affirmation. "So we just need to contrive an opportunity for escape," he concluded.

Again, Ruiha and Dakarai exchanged a glance before Ruiha responded. "I believe that we may have a plan to create such an opportunity," she said, before adding, "But it will risk many lives, and if unsuccessful, I doubt we will ever have another chance."

"We're all ears!" Brenn exclaimed with all the bright eagerness of youth and inexperience.

Magnus sighed inwardly, wishing he had brought the more levelheaded Torain or Uleg instead of the excitable Brenn.

7.

THE HERALD'S FURY

"Every setback in the quest for power is a lesson, every victory a step toward ultimate control."

Junak

Junak hurled a wooden chair against the stone wall of his chambers. It shattered into splinters, joining the remains of the three previous chairs.

"Lies!" he fumed, pacing around the room. "Prove to me that he has spoken to you, Shon'anga! I am his herald in this realm."

"Master," Shon'anga said, his voice trembling. "He spoke to me in my dreams, immediately after my operation. I would not lie to you."

The urge to pick up the pathetic shaman and throw him into the wall, along with the chairs, boiled inside Junak, but he held himself back, just growling in anger.

"He tasked me with replacing my staff." Shon'anga continued to grovel, nervously rubbing the stump where his hand once was.

"You must be confused, Shon'anga," Junak replied sharply. "In your pain-induced state, you simply had a dream. That is all." Even as he said the words, Junak knew them to be false. Shon'anga would not risk his ire unless he was certain that Nergai had indeed spoken to him. The sniveling Drogo was too fearful and weak to lie about this. Doubt gnawed at Junak. Could it be true? He hated the idea that Nergai would bypass him, yet the fear in Shon'anga's eyes suggested sincerity. The shaman's trembling wasn't just from pain; it was genuine terror.

"Master," Shon'anga pleaded. "I do not wish to displease you. However, my vision was real. The great Nergai came to me and tasked me with finding a new staff." He gulped nervously. "He made it clear to me that you were his Herald and that I am a mere servant."

Junak saw through the lie, an obvious attempt to placate him, but still felt somewhat appeased by the shaman's words as he settled into the one remaining chair in his chamber. "We failed him, Shon'anga," he admitted with a deep sigh. "We failed to kill either the Dwarf or the Elf, and now I fear for what is to come."

Junak had never admitted his fears to anyone before. Fear was a sign of weakness, and he never let anyone see his weaknesses. However, Shon'anga's pitiful trembling presence was sufficient reminder of Junak's own power to allay that reservation. Junak knew he could destroy the shaman without raising his heart rate, let alone breaking a sweat.

Nonetheless admitting his fear felt strange, almost foreign but unexpectedly liberating and he found himself savoring the moment of vulnerability, confident that Shon'anga would never dare use it against him.

"Master, the divine will of Nergai has been set into motion. He did not fear for the future. He has a plan, I am certain of it. I have my part to play. And your part, Master, is to lead us." Shon'anga bowed respectfully.

Junak accepted the shaman's submission with a swipe of his hand that was much about dismissing his own weakness as commanding his one-armed servant "Shon'anga, clear up this mess and then meet me at the arena. We must discuss these plans you mentioned." He stood up, turning to leave with renewed purpose. "But first, I need some entertainment to take my mind off the pressures of leadership."

As Junak watched the pair of scaled beasts circling the large Drogo, a vague memory surfaced. He recalled encountering this Drogo during one of his raids, back when he seized control of the Drogo Mulik lands. The warrior's survival meant he had impressed Junak in combat; otherwise, he would have been executed.

THE HERALD'S FURY

The Drogo gladiator gripped a longsword in one hand and a spear in the other, facing the creatures with cool determination. Junak noted the absence of fear in his eyes.

The scalemaws, eight-foot-long pale green lizards with elongated snouts full of razor-sharp teeth and six short, stubby legs, could move with lightning speed. Their deadly reputation came not just from their speed but from their teeth, which could rip through flesh, muscle, and bone effortlessly. More lethal than their bite was the venom they secreted. Harmless on the skin, however it caused immediate cardiac arrest once it entered the bloodstream. The two motionless Drogo on either side of the scalemaws were grim evidence of this fact.

Junak could only admire the remaining Drogo's unwavering stance and, despite himself, felt a flicker of hope the warrior would prove victorious. His strength and bravery might yet serve Junak's interests in future conflicts.

As the beasts slowly approached their prey, snapping their powerful jaws the Drogo remained deathly still, apparently waiting for the beasts to get closer within range. Scalemaws usually hunted in packs, and these two seemed perfectly in sync, approaching the Drogo from different angles to divide his attention.

BATTLE MAGE (THE VELLHOR SAGA VOLUME 1)

Junak felt a surge of anticipation course through him, fists clenching with the thrill of the fight. He reveled in these moments, savoring the rush of adrenaline when lives hung in the balance. Watching the Drogo stand his ground, Junak marveled at how different creatures reacted when their lives were at stake. Would they attempt to flee? Stand and fight? Do something unexpected?

He relished forcing his subjects into a corner, knowing that pressure birthed diamonds within mountains. Without it, the diamond would remain mere dirt. His rise to the top was evidence of that, and he wanted his army of diamonds to rise with him. This Drogo's display of courage and skill could be invaluable, a potential diamond among his ranks.

While other races had grown complacent, the Drogo remained strong and formidable, dismissed as barbaric by those who failed to understand their power. Junak, however, saw beyond the misconceptions. With Nergai's guidance, he knew that the Drogo would ascend to dominance across the realm of Vellhor. His own personal triumphs were proof of that; guided by the hand of his god, Junak had single-handedly allied the weaker clans of the Drogo Mulik, creating a unified force for the first time in Drogo history. Junak's confidence swelled as he watched the Drogo warrior, hoping to see the spark of greatness that could elevate their people even further.

THE HERALD'S FURY

The scalemaw facing the Drogo made a sudden lunge but the warrior was ready for it, dropping and rolling aside before rising in a new position with both scalemaws directly in front of him. Clever, Junak thought, appreciating the tactic of turning two opponents into one.

Dust swirled as the scalemaw landed, its partner snapping its jaws in frustration. Junak couldn't tell if the Drogo had planned it this way but, as the beasts distracted each other, he seized the moment to spear one through the eye in a single, fluid motion. Then, wheeling round, he decapitated the other with his sword. Junak's jaw dropped, stunned by the Drogo's effortless dispatching of both creatures.

As the large Drogo hacked at the speared beast to ensure it was dead, Shon'anga approached. "Master," the shaman whined. "Are you ready to discuss our plans?"

Junak struggled to focus on Shon'anga's words, his gaze still drawn to the warrior towering triumphantly over the lifeless scalemaws. The victorious Drogo, bloody sword raised high, awaited the guards who would soon escort him back to his cell. Junak felt a complex array of emotions—admiration, unease, and even a twinge of jealousy at the Drogo's prowess.

As Junak looked down on the bloody tableau, a thought flitted through his mind, almost too quick to catch, a sense that he was missing something, or that something was missin. But before he could interrogate the thought further, Shon'anga's voice pulled him back to more pressing concerns.

"Master, we must discuss our plans. Nergai will not wait for us," Shon'anga urged desperately.

Despite his annoyance at the interruption, Junak reluctantly had to agree with the persistent Drogo. With a loud sigh, he picked up his cup and downed the contents in one draught, The drink–duskfire–was brewed only in Drogo Mulik and, much like his subjects, was strong and bitter.

BATTLE MAGE (THE VELLHOR SAGA VOLUME 1)

"Fine." He belched and wiped his mouth on his arm before adding with a mix of resignation and irritation, "I assume your plans involve this staff?"

"Correct, Master!" Shon'anga nodded eagerly. "Nergai showed me an image of the staff. It was the most powerful weapon I have ever seen! Made from shadows and forged in the mystical realm of Nexus. The staff will be invaluable for our cause."

Junak noticed a tear forming in Shon'anga's eye as the shaman described the wonderous staff. He found himself weighing the risk of trusting Shon'anga with such power, against the potential of having so great a weapon wielded on his behalf. However, if the staff was as powerful as claimed, it could change everything.

"Hmm, I agree. If the staff is as potent as you say, it would certainly help us with our plans. And Nergai wills this?"

"Yes, Master," Shon'anga affirmed immediately, the small Drogo's excitement bordering on passi. "Our divine lord has also shown me exactly where the staff is, and how I can retrieve it!"

Shon'anga grasped his necklace, fingering the two large crystals given to him by Chronos. Junak had considered taking the stones from the shaman but, as he himself lacked the comprehension to harness their power, seizing them would have been pointless.

THE HERALD'S FURY

Watching Shon'anga, Junak couldn't help but feel uneasy. If the staff truly existed and held the power Shon'anga claimed, it could shift the balance of their struggle. Yet, there lingered a fear—an insidious doubt—that this path might lead them into unforeseen peril. Nonetheless it was not his place to question what Nergai had commanded. It would be done. It must be done.

"Very well, Shon'anga. You will gather a small team of your best shaman and a handful of warriors and set forth as soon as you can," Junak ordered. Obeying Nergai's wishes was non-negotiable, but as the leader of the Drogo, he needed to ensure his subordinates weren't deceiving im. He would have a spy among the warriors accompanying Shon'anga. Caution was paramount.

After they had discussed the logistics of this mission, Junak's attention swung back to his greater plans. "Are we any closer with our attempts to resurrect Nergai?" he asked searching Shon'anga's expression for any flicker of deceit.

A shadow of frustration crossing the Shaman's features. "We are making progress, Master, but it is slow. The rituals are complex, and the necessary components are difficult to acquire."

BATTLE MAGE (THE VELLHOR SAGA VOLUME 1)

Junak nodded at the expected, yet still disappointing, respnse. "You are, of course, aware that the resurrection of Nergai remains our main objective, Shon'anga?" he said. "We cannot let trinkets blind us to our true purpose."

"Of course, Master. And I am certain that the staff will assist in resurrecting Nergai." Shon'anga gave a deep bow, evidently eager to end the conversation, but Junak more questions for the smaller Drogo.

Junak knew he had too much at stake to afford any missteps. The resurrection of Nergai was the goal that overshadowed all others and every action had to be aligned with this purpose. The defeat at the sacred tree had shaken him, forcing him to scrutinize every detail and potential flaw in their planning. He couldn't escape the feeling that pursuing the staff, no matter how powerful it might be, could divert them from their true mission of resurrecting Nergai.

"And the humans?" Junak asked. "Have they been in contact yet?" The humans had been the ones who found the tomb and it wouldn't be long before their Duke requested the army he'd been promised in return. Junak's reaching out to the humans, dwarves, and elves had been a calculated risk, navigating the intricate webs of their politics and hierarchies to find those most willing to betray their kin for more influence, power or hard cash. But for every gain there would be a time when the price had to be paid.

"They have," Shon'anga began, "and they know we've found the tomb of Nergai. But they have not yet requested our troops."

"Inform me as soon as they do so, Shon'anga."

"Yes, my Lord," the shaman responded.

"And what of the Dwarves? Have you any update on that situation?"

Shon'anga paused, likely sifting through the latest intelligence. "My Lord, the Dwarven general we had originally tasked with finding the tomb of Nergai has unwittingly paved the way for us to mount an attack as soon as we are ready. Following the fruitless outcome to his search, the further negotiations that you instructed, my Lord, have enabled us to create dissent and discord among their leadership. Soon, we will have a puppet leader in power of one of their most fearsome clans."

Junak's lips curled in a satisfied smile. The Dwarves, once staunch and unified, were now fracturing as the seeds of discord he had planted bore fruit. This was his strength— exploiting the weaknesses of others. Each manipulated alliance, each sowed betrayal, brought him closer to resurrecting Nergai and securing his dominance.

The success of his intricate web of intrigue and subversion in Dreynas was especially pleasing. The Dwarves, so proud of their military superiority and vaunted code of honor, were about to be deeply disillusioned. It had just taken one jealous and power-hungry relative of a clan chief to initiate and manipulate installed a power struggle that would ripple through the clans, weakening thm all. As Shon'anga continued his report, Junak's grin widened in delight at more evidence of the Dwarves' internal discord. The satisfaction of seeing his plans unfold so seamlessly was intoxicating.

"The general requested that we remove certain obstacles from his path to becoming clan chief. Some of those obstacles should come out to fight in the arena shortly." Shon'anga gestured towards the fighting pit with his stump. "Our troops managed to capture their most feared unit, the Snow Wolves." As the shaman spoke six armored Dwarves marched into the pit.

The sight of the captive Snow Wolves, forced to be arena combatants for his amusement, filled Junak with a sense of triumph. This was more than just a victory; it was the fulfilment of a vision, a testament to his determination to dominate and reshape the world according to Nergai's plan.

As the Dwarves entered the pit, Junak felt a surge of anticipation. The forthcoming spectacle was a mere prelude to the larger conflict brewing. "Excellent, Shon'anga," he said. "This progress will go some way towards making up for your failures in the Elven Forest." The bitter memory of those failures reminded Junak of something. "And the Elves, Shon'anga… do you have a report on the success of our machinations in Luxyyr?"

Shon'anga eagerly accepted the chance to move on from his past missteps. "Indeed, Master. While we have struggled to identify anyone in Luxyyr willing to negotiate with us, we have managed to sow discord among their cities. The spells we cast ravaged the groves surrounding Gwydyr. As superstitious as the Elves are, they have blamed each other. Eventually, the Elven Council will have to come out from hiding and deal with the issue. We have also begun attacking other groves, though I am yet to receive a report regarding that situation."

The progress of Junak's plans in Luxyyr had been slower than he had hoped. With the Elves being even more wary of outsiders than the Dwarves he had been forced to use human intermediaries to approach the Elves. However, each attempt to probe their hierarchy for vulnerabilities had failed miserably. While he had come to understand that the Elven Council ruled supreme in Luxyyr the group were as impenetrable as a locked chest, and infiltrating their ranks had proven impossible.

Still, they had met with some success against the Elves. The poisoned groves, the discord among their people, and the recent destruction of their Sacred Tree were all small victories that helped ease the sting of their failure to kill the Dwarf and Elf as Nergai had commanded. With his mind somewhat at ease, Junak could bide his time. He would focus on his other projects until an opening arose in Luxyyr.

8.
The Tower

"Reaching the destination, the journey's trials fade into the triumph of arrival."

Gunnar

Gunnar craned his neck, gaze climbing the impossibly high peak of the tower. It seemed to rise forever, white brick stark against the dark, dreary surroundings. The height made him feel small, a sensation he wasn't accustomed to and didn't particularly enjoy.

The group faced a pair of massive wooden doors, easily twenty feet high and ten feet wide. Gunnar couldn't help but wonder at their size—what were they expecting to come through here, giants? The sheer impracticality of it amused him.

Thalirion stood a few paces ahead, staff raised. With a dramatic flourish, he slammed it into the ground. The doors rumbled, slowly creaking open. The theatrics were impressive, though Gunnar suspected Thalirion relished the showmanship a bit too much.

"What would you do without that staff of yours?" Karl teased.

Thalirion shot the red-headed dwarf a sideways look, eyebrows arching in mock annoyance, before striding through the enormous entrance.

Gunnar followed him into an antechamber of marvelous grandeur. Crafted from pristine white marble, the gleaming walls reflected the golden light from a majestic chandelier. Between the intricately carved columns, decorative sconces with dancing flames lined the walls. The awesome magnificence of the place momentarily overshadowed the grim reality outside.

Venturing further into the vast space, Gunnar ran his finger-tips across the engravings on one of the massive columns. The cool marble was smooth beneath his touch, and as he inspected the patterns more closely, he noticed they portrayed warriors in various dynamic poses. Most held magical weapons, depicted with bolts of lightning, fireballs, or streams of energy emanating from them. The artistry was stunning, each detail meticulously rendered, and Gunnar couldn't help but feel a pang of envy at the prowess and power these figures represented.

Anwyn was also examining the carvings and the soft, golden light highlighted her focused expression.

"They're wonderful, aren't they?" she whispered, her voice filled with the same awe he felt.

"Absolutely," he replied. "The detail is incredible. Makes you wonder about the stories behind each one."

He turned back to the columns, his thoughts swirling with admiration and curiosity. Each warrior, each weapon, seemed to tell a tale of epic battles and legendary feats that had Gunnar's mind wandering to the challenges of their own journey.

Lorelei fluttered up and down on Anwyn's shoulder, making a tinkling sound like a tiny bell. The delicate noise briefly broke the heavy silence of the chamber and Anwyn turned to Gunnar. "Lorelei can sense a familiarity with the power of this place."

"She should be able to feel it, Anwyn," Thalirion interjected, walking toward them with a hint of pride. "I imbued this very room with my own magic."

"You?" Anwyn queried in surprise. "You helped build this place?"

Thalirion shook his head with a soft chuckle. "Build? No, no, no. This place is millennia older even than I am. I merely assisted with a redecoration of the magical protections for this particular room."

"You did?" Gunnar asked, his gaze wandering around the vast chamber. "What did you do to it?"

Thalirion's features softened as he recalled a memory. "In order to advance here, every novice must complete a series of tests or trials after each training period. When I was a student, a long, long time ago, one of my early tests was to remove all the magical protections from this room and then re-install different protections based on what I had learned. After my test, a Sage would attempt to break in. Once they could no longer manage to enter without triggering an alarm, I was deemed to have passed the test."

Gunnar's mind buzzed at the daunting thought of altering such an ancient and powerful place. His admiration for Thalirion's skill only grew as he realized the depth of knowledge and mastery it took to succeed in such a trial.

As Anwyn's gaze scanned the room, she asked, "How long did it take for you to pass?"

Thalirion stroked his jaw in contemplation. "I believe this particular trial took me around three months."

"Three months?" Gunnar echoed. "That doesn't seem so long."

"You're right, Gunnar," Thalirion agreed. "Casting magical protections and enchantments is one of my stronger suits. Some novices took three years or longer to pass this trial."

Anwyn's eyes widened, and Gunnar noticed a flicker of envy in her expression, as if she wished she possessed such natural talent. The realization that they were surrounded by centuries of accumulated knowledge and effort made the room feel even more imposing.

Gunnar gulped, his face paling slightly. "We don't have three years, Thalirion. We have one." The task ahead felt more unobtainable than ever.

Thalirion nodded, as if anticipating Gunnar's worries. "I believe we intend on fast-tracking your training somewhat..." As they reached the end of the large antechamber, Thalirion gestured to some plush leather seats in the corner. Each sofa had a table in front of it with various books scattered across them. "Please, take a seat. Someone will be along shortly to see to us. In the meantime, feel free to help yourselves to some food and refreshments."

Gunnar glanced over and noticed a table laden with food and drink just beyond the seating area. His stomach let out a low rumble of hunger. Karl was immediately running full-speed towards the table and, with a chuckle, Gunnar followed, his spirits lifted by the prospect of food.

Anwyn

As Anwyn waited on the comfortable sofa, she couldn't help but wonder how much food the average Dwarf could consume. Were Gunnar and Karl particularly hungry, or was it a Dwarven trait to eat so much in one sitting? She was fairly sure that between them, they had consumed two whole loaves of bread, a wheel of cheese, three whole chickens, an entire roasted pig, and a dozen large frothy ales. Even Havoc had eaten his fill and now lounged on the chair across from her, looking as though he may fall asleep again. Anwyn glanced back at the Dwarves, still eating with gusto.

Gunnar eventually wandered back over and sat down next to her, a look of contentment on his face that made her smile. "Are you not hungry, Anwyn?" he asked with a note of concern.

Was he worried about her? She had eaten a few slices of bread, some cheese, a slice of chicken, and some wonderfully roasted vegetables. She looked back at him, perplexed but amused. "I ate more than enough, thank you. I feel quite full, actually!" She gently patted her stomach. "What astounds me is how you and Karl could possibly eat so much food!"

Gunnar chuckled, leaning back comfortably. "Dwarves have hearty appetites, especially after a long journey. Food is more than sustenance for us; it's a way to bond and celebrate."

Anwyn nodded at this small insight into their culture. Seeing Gunnar and Karl enjoy the simple things brought a sense of normalcy and camaraderie to lighten the daunting prospect of their mission.

THE TOWER

Gunnar laughed and patted his own stomach. "And, it seems as though Karl is still going!" He glanced over at the red-haired dwarf, who looked ecstatic upon discovering a selection of honey cakes and sweet treats further up the table.

"Indeed, he is!" Anwyn chuckled. "I fear he may pop, however!"

"Karl has always been known for his penchant for food," Gunnar admitted with a soft chuckle. "Thank Dreyna there's no broadleaf here! We'd never be able to get him to leave!"

As Anwyn and Gunnar sat in a moment of shared amusement at Karl's prodigious appetite, a large door at the end of the antechamber began to creak open. Anwyn glanced at Gunnar, whose eyes were already fixed on the door. Thalirion, who had been sitting on another sofa engrossed in a book, stood up and walked towards the slowly opening door.

When the door had fully opened, a figure strode out that left Anwyn momentarily speechless. It was clearly male, with the heavily muscled torso of a human, but the head of a fierce bull. Two large pale horns protruded from the creature's head, curving upwards and ending in sharp points.

The creature let out a soft grunt upon seeing Thalirion, which sounded welcoming to Anwyn's ear. Thalirion returned the gesture with a warm smile before the two embraced, patting each other on the back. The height difference between the two was stark with the newcomer towering over Thalirion, making the elf seem diminutive. Yet, their embrace was one of equals, filled with mutual respect.

BATTLE MAGE (THE VELLHOR SAGA VOLUME 1)

"Thraxos!" Thalirion exclaimed. "It's been too long! Too long by far! How are you? I see you're a Sage at the Tower now!"

"Thalirion. Indeed, it has been too long. As you know, Sovereign Tarsha looks after us well. I cannot complain," Thraxos replied, his tone refined and surprisingly gentle.

Anwyn's mind wrestled with the paradox of the creature before her His fierce, almost terrifying appearance was at odds with the learned and elegant tone of his voice. She found it difficult to reconcile the contrasting impressions but reminded herself that the world was full of unexpected wonders, and allies could come in the most surprising forms. Swallowing away her initial instinctive reservations, she realized she still had much to learn and understand about this complex new world around her.

Thalirion patted Thraxos on the back one last time before turning to Anwyn and Gunnar with a small flourish. "Please, may I introduce you to my companions, Gunnar and Anwyn."

Gunnar, who had been quietly observing, stood and nodded in acknowledgment. Anwyn followed suit, offering a polite smile while her mind buzzed with questions about the rich tapestry of Thalirion's connections.

THE TOWER

Thraxos nodded a courteous greeting before turning back to Thalirion with a serious expression. "Thalirion, is there not another member of your party?"

"Only Karl, over there, Thraxos. Why?"

Thraxos's gaze settled on the large wooden doors the group had entered through. "Our boundary alerts went off shortly after your party requested entrance. We allowed them to pass through our protections, assuming they were part of your group."

"They're not with us, Thraxos. We haven't seen anybody on our travels through Nexus." Sadness colored Thalirion's features as he continued, "We weren't followed either. The passage to Vellhor, via the Sacred Tree, was obliterated once we crossed through. We will have to find a new route back."

Anwyn felt a pang of empathy with the grief in Thalirion's words. The destruction of the Sacred Tree was more than just a tactical setback; it was a profound loss, one that must touch him especially deeply. The tree had been a vital link to his homeland and a symbol of something greater.

"We witnessed the disappearance of its power here." Thraxos placed a hand on Thalirion's shoulder. "It must have been difficult, Thalirion, to see something so cherished destroyed."

Thalirion let out a long sigh. "Yes, indeed it was. The Sacred Tree meant so much to us Elves. It was a symbol of Her power on Vellhor, and now…" He shook his head sadly, a tear creeping down his cheek. "Now, it's gone. Destroyed."

Anwyn's own heart ached for the loss. She would have offered words of comfort but felt that silent solidarity better fitted this moment of mourning. The destruction of the tree was a wound that would take a long time to heal.

BATTLE MAGE (THE VELLHOR SAGA VOLUME 1)

"Her song may have ended, Thalirion, but her sweet melody continues in the heart of every Elf in Vellhor. You..." Thraxos's gaze scanned the group of travelers before he continued, "and your companions bear the responsibility for rekindling Her song and defeating the evil which destroyed your Sacred Tree!"

Thalirion smiled at Thraxos's words. "And so, the novice becomes the master... or Sage as it was."

Thraxos let out a low, rumbling chuckle. "Indeed, Thalirion. I am merely telling you what you would have told me once. But, alas. I must see to this intruder. I doubt it is something we cannot handle, however it worries me that someone has managed to get this far into Nexus without us detecting them." With that, the huge, muscled half-human half-bull creature turned and left, leaving Anwyn with so many questions.

"Thalirion," she said hesitantly once Thraxos was far enough away not to hear them. "Who, and what, was Thraxos?"

Thalirion chuckled. "Thraxos is a Minotaur, Anwyn. They do not exist in Vellhor. He is from a realm known as Stepphoros. Minotaurs and Centaurs inhabit their lands. Their realm is a boundless grassland of scattered nomadic clans." Thalirion paused and shook his head sadly.

"Unfortunately, the two races have been locked in a brutal war for hundreds of years and the once beautiful landscape has been ravaged by their potent and destructive magic."

THE TOWER

"So they're warriors hen?" Karl called over through a mouthful of cake.

"They weren't always, Karl. Although Minotaurs may be built like warriors, they used to be a society of academics and scholars. Artists and sculptors. Now the constant fighting has taught them to use their arcane arts for war, and if I am honest, it is something they have excelled at, unfortunately."

"And the Centaurs?" Gunnar asked.

"The Centaurs are bands of travelling warriors. Their heads and torsos resemble that of a human. However, their lower bodies are that of a large horse. They are a notably aggressive race."

Karl's eyes widened. "Horses, you say… amazing."

"Anwyn, you have more questions?" Thalirion asked.

"Yes, Thalirion… many questions…" Anwyn replied.

With a mock flourish and a smile, Thalirion responded, "Then please, ask away!"

"Firstly, who is 'She'?" Anwyn asked. "I thought Thraxos might be referring to The Spirit of the Forest, but you spoke of her as if she were a tangible being."

"She has no name, Anwyn. She is the Mother of the Forest. The Goddess of the Elves, although we do not call her that. She is the unifying Spirit who guides every Elf in

Vellhor. And you are her Seishinmori, Anwyn. Selected by Her to represent Her will."

Anwyn felt a shiver run down her spine as her role as Seishinmori suddenly felt heavier, more profound although the idea that she was chosen by a deity to represent Her will filled her with both pride and trepidation.

BATTLE MAGE (THE VELLHOR SAGA VOLUME 1)

Thalirion's eyes softened. "Yours is a great responsibility, Anwyn. But remember, She chose you for a reason. Trust in Her guidance and in yourself."

Gunnar placed a reassuring hand on her shoulder. "We're with you, Anwyn. Whatever comes next, we face it together."

She took a deep breath, feeling the support of her companions and the silent strength of the Mother of the Forest withn her. With a steady voice, she asked, "How many realms are there, Thalirion? I've only ever known Vellhor, but now we're in Nexus and you say there's Stepphoros too. Are there more?" It felt surreal, as if all the rules and limitations she had ever known had shattered like a vase falling to the floor. The vastness of the multiverse was daunting but also exhilarating.

Thalirion paused, his eyes thoughtful. "There are seven inhabited worlds, Anwyn. There is, of course, Vellhor, and you now know of Stepphoros. The others are Raaniada, Malanth, Erros, Riduna, and Aerithordor. The seven worlds make up the Boria Stellar Expanse."

Gunnar and Karl exchanged a look which Thalirion noticed, saying, with a nod, "Yes, yes. Aerithordor, the godly Dwarven realm of our dear friend Draeg, whom I met at this very institution! The realm is a part of the Boria Stellar Expanse."

Gunnar nodded in understanding but still seemed confused. "Apologies, Thalirion, but aren't there eight realms, including Nexus?"

"Well noticed, Gunnar," Thalirion said. "You are correct. However, Nexus is not a world as such. It is a form of a pocket world, magically powered by the seven realms. Each world sends its most promising and talented inhabitants here for training and education. Thus far, no Drogo or human from Vellhor has been permitted to train here."

Before they could continue, the doors burst open, and Thraxos entered with an unconscious human draped over his shoulder.

Kemp

Kemp awoke groggily, his vision blurred, and saw a sea of bright white so intense that he had to close his eyes again immediately. Disoriented, he tried to recall what had happened and how he had ended up in this place of pure, brilliant, painful white. As the memories flooded back— the battle with the bat-like creature—his eyes shot open. He winced at the pain but forced himself to persevere. He raised his arm and gasped in horror; where his hand had been there was just a bandaged stump.

A pained sob escaped him. What was he going to do without his hand? The realization hit hard—he was a cripple now. Would he still be able to cast magic as he once did? He tried to calm himself, knowing his hands weren't necessary for harnessing the arcane arts, but the loss felt overwhelming and rational thoughts were elusive.

Staring at the stump, he experienced a strange sensation, as though his missing fingers were twitching. The phantom feeling made him nauseous. Suddenly, a low, gravelly voice emanated from the corner of the room. Kemp's heart raced as he turned and saw a massive, muscled man with the head of a bull approaching. Panic surged through him, and he scrambled to escape, only to find himself restrained.

"What do you want? Who are you?" Kemp pleaded, trying to summon his magic, but panic and fear overwhelmed him.

"Calm, human," the bull-man said, his voice surprisingly soft and gentle. "You are in The Tower of Absence, and before I answer any of your questions, I have some of my own."

Kemp eased back slightly. He was still afraid and confused, but the initial shock had subsided somewhat. As his senses returned, he realized that someone, presumably this creature, must have tended to his wounds when it would have been easy to kill him. That fact at least should earn the creature a measure of trust.

"Please," Kemp implored. "You need to help me get home. I don't know where I am."

The bull-man eyed him suspiciously. "We have elixirs here that can force you to speak the truth. I will not hesitate to use one if I believe you are lying or misleading me."

Kemp nodded vigorously, his dirty chestnut locks bouncing. "I have no clue where we are or how I got here. I woke up in this place a few days ago and followed the light of a green beacon until I arrived at a forest. And now I'm here."

The bull-man nodded as if this were an everyday occurrence. "How did you make it past the spectral echoes? They would have ripped you to shreds."

Kemp raised his stump in answer. The bull-man nodded, conceding the point. "I am still surprised you managed to get here in one piece." He winced and apologized. "I'm sorry. That was insensitive. What I mean is, I'm surprised you managed to make it through at all."

Kemp conceded the point with a nod. He knew he probably wouldn't have made it without finding the little campsites that offered him protection along the way and said as muc to the bull-man, who continued nodding as if he already knew the answers.

As Kemp spoke, he felt a mix of relief and unease. The bull- man's gentle demeanor contrasted sharply with his imposing appearance, creating an unsettling incongruity. However, the creature's concern for his wounds and genuine curiosity about his journey formed the beginnings of a thin thread of trust.

The bull-man concentrated his focus on Kemp's chest for a moment. A cold shiver ran through Kemp, making him feel as if the creature had penetrated his very core, his essence. "You practice the arcane arts?" the creature asked. Kemp nodded. "Yet you are weak. Where do you come from?"

Kemp wondered at the bull-man's words. He had never been called weak before. Lazy or useless, maybe, but never weak. His magic had always been his strength. How could this creature sense his power by merely looking at him? It seemed impossible. Deciding the bull-man must be referring to his physical state or his current injured condition, Kemp replied, "I am from Fenmark."

The bull-man grunted. "Vellhor," he mumbled. "Did you come through the Sacred Tree?"

Kemp looked at him blankly, unsure of what he meant. "I was in the Scorched Mountains. There were few trees there. I found a tomb, and then the Drogo Mulik attacked. I was knocked unconscious, and when I woke, I was here." He glanced around the pristine white room, remembering the gloom outside. "Well, not here... I woke up outside in the darkness."

He thought he saw a flicker of surprise in the bull-man's eyes, but he couldn't be sure. Reading the expressions of a creature with the head of a bull was challenging. Despite his confusion, Kemp felt a strange sense of connection with the creature, a glimmer of understanding that he hoped might lead to some answers.

"What is your name?" the creature asked.

"I am Kemp. Who are you, if you don't mind me asking?" Kemp responded, trying to sound polite despite his anxiety.

"Welcome to the Tower of Absence, Kemp. I am Thraxos, one of the Sages here. Once you feel able, you are welcome to make use of our facilities while we decide what to do with you."

"Decide what to do with me? What do you mean? I want you to send me home, Thraxos!" Kemp exclaimed, panic rising in his voice.

"Ordinarily, Kemp, that is what we would have done. However, there has been a complication with the portal leading to Vellhor. It may take a while for us to resolve."

The bull-man stood up to leave, saying, "Until that time, please feel free to make use of the Tower's many benefits."

Kemp's mind raced. He had been thrust into an unfamiliar world, faced with deadly peril, and now told he couldn't return home immediately. Thraxos's calm yet authoritative demeanor made it clear that arguing wouldn't change anything, but frustration and helplessness swirled within him bordering on a panic that he knew would do no good.

Taking a deep breath, Kemp tried to steady himself. "Thank you, Thraxos. I'll try to make the best of it." Despite his attempt at composure, he couldn't help but wonder what lay ahead in this mysterious tower and whether he'd ever find his way back to Fenmark.

"Wait, Thraxos." Kemp called after Thraxos, but the bull-man had already left the room. Alone and with no answers forthcoming, exhaustion settled over Kemp. With nothing else to do, he surrendered to the wearinss and fell into a fitful sleep, his dreams haunted by visions of home and the strangeness of his new reality.

When he awoke a few hours later, Kemp felt a mix of disorientation and determination. Thraxos had said he was free to make use of the Tower's benefits, so he decided to explore and find out exactly what those benefits included. Maybe, just maybe, he'd find a way back home or at least understand his new surroundings better.

The place was a maze of immaculate white marble. Kemp marveled at how they kept it so clean and pristine, his thoughts wandering to the kind of magic or labor required to maintain such a state. He walked for almost an hour without encountering another living being. The silence and emptiness amplified his sense of isolation. Anxiety started to creep in as he realized he had long ago lost track of where he was and the way back to his room. Still, he kept walking, trying to take in every detail.

All the rooms he passed seemed to be dormitories, making him assume this was the accommodation quarter of the Tower. The monotony of identical rooms heightened his desperation to find something different, something that would give him more insight into this mysterious place. His mind buzzed with questions about the purpose of the Tower and its inhabitants.

Eventually, he came across a large stairway leading both up and down. Unsure which direction would prove more informative, Kemp hesitated for a moment before deciding to go up. He climbed several flights of stairs until his legs ached, each step echoing in the silence, before finally coming across a landing with a door. With a sigh of relief, he pushed open the door.

It opened onto a corridor stretched straight for about a hundred feet, glass doors lining each side at even intervals. As Kemp approached the first door, he finally saw signs that he wasn't alone in the giant Tower. Peering through the door, he observed several people, a mix of different races. There were a few Elves, Dwarves, and more creatures like Thraxos. He even spotted someone who appeared human until the person turned, revealing an extra set of arms.

The group was gathered around one of the shadow-spirits, a Spectral Echo, as Thraxos had called them. This particular Spectral Echo resembled a giant butterfly and remained un- moving while the group examined it. Kemp's curiosity was piqued. What were they studying? The room hummed with a quiet intensity, the kind of focused energy he associated with scholars and researchers deeply absorbed in their work.

Moving on to the next room, Kemp found only three occupants, all Dwarves. Various tools—hammers, scalpels, knives, tongs, and chisels—lay scattered on a large table to the side. In the centre of the room was another table, this one covered with shadowy limbs, presumably from the Spectral Echoes. The Dwarves seemed to be conducting experiments, dissecting and analyzing the limbs with meticulous care.

Each door Kemp checked revealed more of the same: groups of individuals, sometimes diverse, sometimes not, all engaged in some form of study or experimentation. It became clear that this floor of the Tower was a hub of scientific inquiry. Some rooms featured a figure who seemed to be a lecturer, guiding the others—students, Kemp assumed—through complex tasks. Kemp felt a mix of intrigue and apprehension.

This place was dedicated to understanding the mysteries of the Spectral Echoes, among other things. He wondered what kind of knowledge and power were contained within these walls. The presence of so many different beings working together also gave him a sense of hope. If they could coexist here, perhaps there was a way for him to find his place in this wrld. Maybe the Tower held the answers he sought, not just for returning home, but for understanding the broader mysteries of his existence.

Intrigued, Kemp decided to explore further. He returned to the staircase and headed up one more floor. Climbing several flights left him even more out of breath, but curiosity pushed him onward. When he reached another landing, he pushed open the door, expecting a layout similar to the floor below but was shocked to find he was wrong.

He had entered a large gymnasium. Dozens of creatures were engaged in various exercises or locked in combat training. As he ventured further into the room, a stray bolt of lightning flew over his head, and he ducked instinctively. Surprisingly, nobody gave him a second glance.

Kemp walked over to a particularly vicious-looking training match. He saw a human with a scorpion's tail protruding from his back facing off against another bull-man. The bull-man charged, the impressive speed and power of his strides suggesting some kind of magical reinforcement. The scorpion-man waited, almost patiently, for his opponent to get closer.

In an instant, the bull-man was upon him. Kemp thought he was about to witness the scorpion-man become impaled by the sharp horns protruding from the bull-man's head. But at the last second, the scorpion-man jumped high into the air, focusing his hands below him and releasing a stream of energy that pinned the bull-man to the floor. The bull-man quickly recovered as the scorpion-man landed. Fire blazed in the bull-man's eyes and hands as he spun around, launching two large fireballs before charging again. The scorpion-man slipped to the side, deftly avoiding both the fireballs and the charge.

Kemp watched, captivated by the intense training session. The display of power and agility was mesmerizing, and he couldn't help but feel both awed and intimidated. The creatures here were formidable, each possessing unique abilities honed through rigorous training. The gymnasium buzzed with energy and purpose, a stark contrast to the quiet, clinical atmosphere of the previous floor.

He realized that this Tower was not just a place of learning but also of strength and combat prowess.

A newcomer walked up to the bull-man and his adversary and waved the match to an abrupt halt. The bull-man continued to blaze with fury, shouting in objection, only to be met with a violent shock of magic from the newcomer. The bull-man's eyes widened in fear before he dropped to the floor, trembling.

Kemp realized the new arrival was likely a combat instructor, a supposition that was confirmed as he shouted to the gathered group, "A warrior's strength is not defined by the power of one technique alone, but by his repertoire of techniques. By lacking adaptability, versatility, and strategic finesse, you make yourselves weak." He turned to the trembling bull-man. "Urlok, you rely on your charge far too often. It has become predictable. What was once your strongest asset has now become a weakness. You need to work on at least two additional techniques or you will no longer have a place here." With that, he turned and walked off toward another group of students.

Kemp absorbed the instructor's words with a mix of admiration and anxiety. The emphasis on versatility and strategic finesse resonated with him. It was a stark reminder that he needed to develop his own skills if he hoped to survive and find a way home.

As he left the training hall, his stump throbbed painfully, and he noticed it had started bleeding again. The bandages would need replacing soon. Exhausted and in pain, Kemp decided it was time to find his way back to his quarters.

Descending the two flights of stairs, his vision began to blur. He stumbled a few steps before white dots appeared in his periphery, and he fell to one knee. In a haze state, he saw Thraxos escorting a group consisting of two Dwarves and two Elves. As Thraxos noticed Kemp sprawled on the floor, blood seeping from his wound and across the white marble, he sighed and picked up his pace. Kemp's last thought before blacking out was a mix of frustration and helplessness. He had so much to learn and adapt to, and yet his own body was betraying him at every turn. The darkness closed in, swallowing his awareness before Thraxos reached him.

9.
Sacrifices

"The measure of one's dedication is reflected in the sacrifices they are willing to make."

Magnus

Magnus stood side by side with Torain, grim determination etched across both of their faces. In his hands, he held a crudely made Drogo axe. The Drogo would wield this weapon single-handedly. However, Magnus's smaller stature obliged him to use both hands. Torain had just a simple sword and a small, round shield. Their opponent, a large cavern spider, towered over them menacingly. Magnus suppressed a shudder at its sleek, ebony carapace, glistening with a sickly sheen under the glow of the arena torches.

As the Drogo guards released the spider from its chains, its eight angular legs, each as thick as tree trunks, skittered across the dusty arena floor, propelling the creature forward with unsettling speed and agility. Razor-sharp claws protruded from the ends of its limbs, glinting ominously in the faint light, ready to tear flesh apart.

Adrenaline surged through Magnus's veins, the rough texture of the axe handle pressing into his palms. The weapon was more than a tool; it was his lifeline. He stole a glance at Torain, whose face mirrored his own resolve. There was no room for hesitation.

The cavern spider lunged, its fangs dripping with venom. Time seemed to slow as Magnus calculated his move. Every muscle in his body coiled with tension, he surged forward with a thunderous roar. The axe, an extension of his will, cut through the air and met the spider's armored carapace with a resounding impact, sending a jarring shock up his arms. The creature recoiled, a horrific screech of pain echoing through the arena.

Magnus's breath came in ragged gasps, the taste of iron on his tongue. The spider's venomous fangs hovered perilously close, but he held his ground, tightening his grip on the axe, his mind focused solely on the deadly dance between predator and prey.

Meanwhile, Torain darted in from the side, his sword flashing like lightning as he engaged the spider in a whirlwind of metal on flesh. Each strike looked like a gamble with death. The spider's claws lashed out, but Torain's small, round shield deflected its venomous attacks with practiced ease.

The battle raged on in a cacophony of clashing metal and monstrous roars. The cavern spider onslaught was relentless, its fury palpable, but Magnus and Torain fought back with unwavering determination. Their weapons struck with deadly precision, a symphony of violence pushing the monstrous arachnid to its limits.

Magnus felt every moment stretch into eternity, the weight of his axe an extension of his will. Torain's movements were a blur of speed and precision. Neither of them had room for error or time for doubt.

As the battle reached a crescendo, the cavern spider lunged forward at Torain who, ever vigilant, parried the creature's attack with his sword and shield, deflecting the deadly strike just in time. But in the chaos, he left himself momentarily exposed to another razor-sharp claw that sliced through the air with lethal accuracy. Torain staggered back, a guttural cry of pain escaping his lips as the sharp claw tore into him, leaving a deep, jagged gash across his torso.

Magnus's heart clenched as he saw the blood seeping from Torain's wound, staining the dusty floor a deep crimson. He could see the agony in his friend's eyes, the fierce determination that refused to yield despite the pain coursing through his body. Roaring with fury, Magnus redoubled his efforts to subdue the monster. Each swing of his axe became a torrent of righteous fury, driving the cavern spider back with relentless force.

The creature's carapace cracked under his assault, but even as he fought to protect his injured comrade, a cold dread gnawed at Magnus. Torain's wounds were severe, and Magnus fought with everything he had, not just for his own survival, but for the life of his friend.

In a final, desperate attack, Torain summoned the last ounces of his strength, his muscles straining against the weight of exhaustion as he launched himself into the fray. With a primal roar, he clashed with the monstrous creature, his blade flashing in the dim light.

Despite Torain's undeniable courage Magnus could see the toll that the battle was taking on him. With each passing moment, Torain's movements grew more sluggish, his breaths coming in ragged gasps as fatigue threatened to overwhelm him.

With a mighty roar, Magnus maneuvered into position under the carapace of the monster. With savage precision, he struck at an earlier crack his axe had made in the monster's armored hide. The devastating blow split the cavern spider's carapace in half and the creature finally crashed to the ground, defeated.

As the dust settled, Torain lay gravely wounded, his body battered and bloody from the ferocious battle. With victory secured, Magnus sighed a breath of relief and, with a swift, calculated motion, he lost his axe beneath the sandy arena floor before hoisting his injured comrade onto his shoulders to carry him to safety.

Together, they disappeared into the darkness of the exit tunnel, leaving behind the fallen cavern spider along with the cheers and bloodlust of the savage spectators.

Ruiha

"Are you sure, Ruiha?" Dakarai asked for what felt like the one- hundredth time that day. Ruiha could see the anxiety gnawing away at him, making his voice tight. "I'm not happy with this plan. It is too risky," he continued, his footsteps quickening to keep up with her determined pace.

Ruiha stopped abruptly and turned towards Dakarai. "Dak," she began in an exasperated tone, "this has been the plan for the past few days."

Frustration boiled over in Dakarai's expression. "I know!" he burst out, "And my objections have remained the same. It is too risky!"

Ruiha resumed her walk forcing Dakarai to trail behind her through the dim cell. "I agree. It's risky. But how else can we get all the prisoners and all the guards into the pit together? With no spectators! As far as I can see, it is our only option."

Dakarai sighed but said nothing. Ruiha knew he had no alternative plan. She had confirmed with the Dwarves that all the Drogo and guards could be in the pit at the same time. Dakarai hadn't been happy when she'd explained how she planned to do that, but there was no other choice. This was their opportunity for escape, and she had to seize it.

Reaching her destination, she turned to Dakarai and whispered, "It's now or never, Dak. Are you with me?" Reluctantly, he nodded his agreement.

Ruiha's mind was buzzing. She knew the risks of their plan but she couldn't let fear paralyze her.

This was their only shot, and she was determined to make it count.

"Okay, good. Now move away from me. I don't want Rainok to associate you with this. We will need you to coordinate things in my absence."

Dakarai let out a long sigh as he shifted away from her, blending into a group of nearby slaves. Ruiha steeled herself. Every moment counted, and any hesitation could mean the failure of their escape. Her heart was pounding. She had to be convincing, had to make Rainok believe in the urgency and possibility of their plan.

"Rainok!" she called over, her voice steady despite the butterflies in her stomach.

The Drogo shifted uncomfortably, his eyes darting from left to right, as if harboring some secret guilt.

"Rainok, come over here," she called again, injecting a touch of impatience into her tone. "I have a proposition for you!"

The young Drogo still hesitated, his wary eyes betraying his reluctance, before he finally approached her. "Shadow Hawk," he acknowledged her, lowering his reptilian gaze in deference, and Ruiha had to suppress a look of irritation at the nickname. "How can I help?" Rainok continued, in a tone that mingled suspicion with curiosity.

Ruiha's eyes flickered around, pretending to ensure no one was watching, and she lowered her voice to a tense whisper. "Rainok, we're escaping. Are you in?" Her pulse quickened as she watched his face closely, seeing the conflict between fear and the longing for freedom.

The Drogo eyed her silently for a moment. "Dangerous words after what happened to Corgan," he remarked. "Before I commit to anything, I need to understand the plan in full. I do not wish to throw my life away on a false hope."

Ruiha's irritation flared. "False hope?" she snapped. "Rainok, if we do not escape, we are all going to die in here. How can you not see that?"

Rainok raised his hands placatingly. "Listen, Ruiha. I appreciate that. However, unless you have a solid plan, we'd be throwing our lives away pointlessly."

Suppressing her frustration, Ruiha took a deep breath and began explaining their fictional escape plan. As she laid out the details, Rainok listened intently, nodding along eagerly. Despite her earlier irritation, she could see the spark of hope igniting in his eyes.

After their conversation, Ruiha watched him leave, her mind racing with the possible outcomes.

"Do you think it'll work?" Dakarai asked, once Rainok was out of earshot.

"It has to." She stared after the disappearing Drogo for a long moment before adding, "I doubt he'll be able to keep that information to himself for long. I wouldn't be surprised in the slightest if the guards come to collect me for questioning before the end of the day!"

It took just three hours.

The guards stormed into the cell, fully armed, beating any Drogo unlucky enough to be in their way. They carved out a path straight to where Ruiha and Dakarai were sitting and surrounded the pair, weapons glinting in the faint torchlight.

Ruiha and Dakarai immediately raised their hands in surrender. This moment was part of their plan, and Ruiha had made it clear to Dakarai not to intervene. She desperately hoped they would leave him behind and focus solely on her.

To her gratification, Captain Drakoth snarled, "Stand up, human. You are coming with us!"

Rising to her feet, Ruiha stared into the guard captain's reptilian eyes. "What is this about?" she demanded. Her only answer was an armored punch to the face.

As Ruiha gradually regained consciousness, the reality of her surroundings settled in—a cramped, desolate cell devoid of any comforts. She sat up slowly, gingerly touching her swollen jaw, wincing at the lingering pain from Drakoth's punch. The dull ache served as a harsh reminder of the precariousness of her situation.

Time seemed to stretch on endlessly. The oppressive silence of the cell was broken only by the distant, echoing footsteps of guards. When one finally passed by and noticed her awake, he ran back the way he came. Ruiha's heart pounded, the sound of hurried footsteps, and the dim corridor amplifying her dread. Left alone once more, doubts began to creep into her mind. What if they executed her here, in this cell? Her plan would die with her, and there would be no chance of escape. She tried to shake off her concerns. The guards would surely want to make an example of her, as they had done with Corgan. Slowly, like the gradual creep of dawn over the horizon, her confidence began to return.

The guard soon reappeared, and with him came the imposing figure of Captain Drakoth. His presence sent a chill down her spine, his steely gaze fixed upon her like a predator assessing its prey.

"Shadow Hawk... have you been plotting against us?" Drakoth's words dripped with sarcasm, but beneath the mockery, Ruiha sensed a simmering anger.

She stared back defiantly, refusing to be intimidated. "Plotting?" she retorted, bitterness threading through her voice. "I have no idea what you're talking about, Captain."

"We know of your plans, human! Stop the pretense!" Drakoth's voice thundered through the chamber, his anger boiling over as he advanced on Ruiha. "You think you can outwit us, but your schemes have not gone unnoticed."

Ruiha squared her shoulders, unwavering in the face of Drakoth's wrath. "I shall not dignify your questions with my words," she insisted in a steady voice.

Drakoth's jaw tightened at her defiant tone, his eyes narrowing with unrestrained hostility. "Your audacity knows no bounds, human!" he growled. "But mark my words, your treachery will be punished."

"I fear neither your threats nor your false sense of power, Captain," Ruiha retorted in a firm even voice, despite the storm brewing within her. Each word was a gamble, a calculated risk meant to fuel the flames of rebellion. "For every action you take against me, the flames of rebellion will only burn brighter."

Her words hung in the air, a bold challenge to Drakoth's authority. She knew she was treading a dangerous path, deliberately provoking him in hopes of forcing a public punishment, a message to the other slaves that resistance was futile. Should she push him too far, however? Well, that wasn't worth thinking about right now, she decided.

Drakoth's lips curled into a cruel, reptilian snarl. His eyes gleamed with malice as he seized Ruiha's arm in a vice-like grip. "You dare defy me?" he hissed. "Very well, Shadow Hawk. Your fate is sealed."

With his free hand, he delivered a brutal backhanded blow to Ruiha's face. Pain exploded through her skull as she staggered and fell to the floor. Although stars danced in her vision she refused to give him the satisfaction of letting out a cry.

With a swift motion, Drakoth signaled to the guards, who moved forward to restrain Ruiha, their faces masked in cold indifference. As they dragged her away, her heart pounded with trepidation. Her plan was now in motion, and the fear of things going wrong still loomed heavily over her, but her resolve only grew stronger. Fueled by a burning desire for justice and freedom, she would be a beacon of defiance in the face of her captors. Even in chains she would not be silenced.

Magnus

"Quick... he's bleeding out!" Magnus cried as he rushed back into the cell. He tenderly lowered Torain to the floor and began removing the clothing around the large slash wound across his abdomen. "Uleg! Come here. Bring something to stem the blood!" The urgency in his voice echoed through the cramped cell.

Uleg dashed over with a bundle of rags and knelt beside Magnus, his face creased with concern at the sight of his injured comrade.

"Hold on, Torain," Magnus muttered, his hands working swiftly to staunch the flow of blood. Memories of past battles flooded his mind, but none had felt as dire as this moment. He grimly applied pressure to the wound, his steady actions born of years of experience and training with the Snow Wolves.

Uleg wasted no time, tearing the rags into makeshift bandages and pressing them firmly against Torain's torn flesh. His trembling hands betrayed his fear. "Stay with us, Torain," he urged, his voice thick with emotion. "We'll get you through this."

Brenn ran over, despair etched on his face. "Torain!"

He knelt beside his brother, eyes wide with desperation. "What happened, Magnus?" he pleaded.

Magnus, his teeth clenched, quickly recounted the fight, vivid memories of the battle flashing through his mind— every strike, every moment that led to Torain's injury. He noticed the tears streaming down Brenn's bearded cheeks but couldn't afford a second to console the young Dwarf.

Uleg, seeing the anguish on Brenn's face, gripped him by the shoulders in a fatherly gesture. "Listen, lad. Why don't you give us some space? We'll get him patched up alright." Brenn nodded absently, the numbness of shock settling in as he rejoined his comrades who attempted to console him.

The minutes stretched on, an oppressive atmosphere of fear weighing heavily on everyone present in the cell. Amidst it all Magnus and Uleg worked tirelessly, determined to save their friend's life. Magnus drew on every technique he had learned, every scrap of knowledge that might make a difference, while Uleg's steady hands mirrored his resolve to fight off death's encroaching shadow.

After what felt like an eternity, the bleeding finally began to slow, and Torain's shallow breaths grew steadier. Magnus let out a heavy sigh, his shoulders sagging with exhaustion, but the relief washing over him was a momentary balm to ease the tension that had knotted his muscles. "He's stabilized," he announced, his voice hoarse with emotion.

But their respite was short-lived. The sound of approaching footsteps echoed outside their cell, a grim reminder of their imprisonment. Fear clawed at Magnus's heart as he and Uleg covered over their makeshift medical efforts, with swift practiced movements, bracing themselves for whatever fate awaited next.

"Ready yourselves, Dwarves!" one guard bellowed as he peered into the cell. "You'll all be back in the pit this evening." The proclamation was delivered with cold finality before the guards turned on their heels and departed.

Magnus and Uleg exchanged grim glances. This was the opportunity they had been waiting for, the chance to set their plan in motion. Yet the bleak reality was that Torain's survival still hung by a thread, and time was not on their side.

With a decisive nod, Magnus turned to Uleg. "This is it then," he declared. "We have to make our move now."

Uleg nodded grimly, his hands shaking as he helped Magnus lift Torain from the ground. Together, they carefully maneuvered their injured comrade towards the back of the cell.

"Boss," Uleg's urgent whisper made Magnus glance up from his burden. "Boss, he ain't going to make it. If we had a few days on our side... But a few hours?" Uleg's voice trailed off as he noticed Brenn rushing over.

"He made it, then!" Brenn exclaimed, his expression full of desperate hope.

"Aye, lad," Uleg said gently, "we stopped the bleeding. Now he needs time to recover." His gaze shifted to Magnus, the unspoken truth hanging between them.

"What do you mean? Time? We've got to be back out there this evening!" Brenn demanded, panic rising in his voice.

"Listen, Brenn." Magnus interrupted solemnly. "Your brother has suffered a horrific wound. He could take days, if not weeks, to recover fully. The fact that we do not have that time means we need to decide what to do. As you know, we've been called back into the pit. That can only mean one thing..."

As Brenn digested the devastating news, Magnus's heart ached. He hated being in this predicament, but he couldn't imagine how Brenn must be feeling. The young Dwarf's eyes darted between his wounded brother and Magnus, struggling to reconcile hope with reality. Brenn had been present for the negotiations with Ruiha and Dakarai and knew, better than any of them, that this was their only opportunity to escape. They were all in with this final hand, and the stakes had never been higher.

Magnus grappled with the impossible choice before them. The urgency of their plan clashed violently with the brutal reality of Torain's condition. His own resolve wavered as he looked at Brenn, the anguish and determination in the young Dwarf's eyes a mirror of his own internal turmoil.

"What do we do, Boss?" Brenn asked, his voice unsteady and weak.

"We take a vote on the matter." Uleg interrupted. "It wouldn't be fair to lay this decision on one head alone."

"Aye," Magnus replied, glad the decision had been taken away from him. "I'll gather the lads."

His expression was grave as he gathered the other Dwarves into a circle in the dim confines of the cell, looking from one worried face to another. "We all know what's at stake here," Magnus began, his voice low but resolute. "Torain's life hangs in the balance, and with it, our only chance at freedom. We must decide whether to end his suffering now and attempt our escape, or to wait for his recovery and hope for another opportunity."

The Dwarves exchanged anxious glances. They understood the gravity of the situation, but each Dwarf had known Torain for years. They had served together, laughed together, and bled together. It wasn't an easy decision to make.

"I say we end it now," one Dwarf spoke up eventually, his voice tinged with resignation. "We don't know how long he'll take to recover, if infection doesn't get him and we can't afford to wait. Our own lives depend on it."

Some murmured their agreement, but Magnus heard a chorus of dissenting whispers protesting against the notion of sacrificing one of their own.

"We can't just give up on him," another Dwarf argued defiantly. "Torain is one of us. We owe it to him to give him a fighting chance."

The debate raged on, each Dwarf voicing their own fears and convictions as they grappled with the impossible decision before them. But as the arguments grew heated and tensions reached a boiling point, all eyes turned to Brenn, the youngest among them, whose final vote would tip the scales one way or the other.

Brenn drew a hesitant breath. They all knew that whatever choice he made would haunt him for the rest of his days. But before he could speak, Torain stirred, his eyes fluttering open as he looked up at Brenn with a mixture of pain and determination.

"I can't have you making that decision, brother," Torain croaked, his voice barely above a whisper. "I can't have this burden looming over you."

Before anyone could react, Torain reached into his pocket and produced a small broken blade, its glinting edge catching the dim light of the cell. With a swift motion, he drew the blade across his own throat, a grim determination in his eyes as he embraced the finality of his fate.

Brenn let out a cry and ran over to his brother as the rest of them watched in stunned silence as Torain's lifeblood spilled onto the cold stone floor, his self-sacrifice a testament to the unwavering bond of brotherhood that bound the Snow Wolves together. In that moment, as the echoes of Torain's final words reverberated through the cell, Magnus surveyed his companion's grim expressions and could see that, whatever awaited them in the pit, they were resolved to be worthy of Torain's sacrifice.

10.

THE DAEMONSEEKER

"Beware the Daemonseeker, for he is of the Shadowforged. With dark magic as his ally, he tames the shadows, his power a force of nature and night."

Fellron

As the mist clung to the dark lake, only the reflection of the wolf moon shimmered in Fellron's unsettling, jet-black irises. Taking steady, measured breaths, he waited patiently. Hours passed, the moon dipping and the first rays of daylight emerging from the distant mountain peaks.

It was when the sun touched the frosted tree branches, slowly melting the ice and adding an irregular drip, drip, dripping noise, and the mist began to dissipate, that he saw it. An almost imperceptible ripple in the center of the lake, then a larger one off to the left. His fist tightened on his crossbow, already drawn for hours. He took a steadying breath. It wouldn't be long now.

A sinuous, mottled green and brown tentacle emerged from the water's surface. Slowly, almost apprehensively, it ex- tended its reach until it felt the shore. Fellron could see the rows of tiny, barbed suckers covering the tip, perfect appendages for grasping prey and navigating the lake's treacherous underwater terrain.

The tentacles stretched out in eerie silence, seeking, searching, hunting. So slow were its movements that, had Fellron not been lying in wait, he doubted he could detect its approach in the low light of dawn.

As the tentacle approached, it froze almost a meter away from him. With unnatural speed, the Kraken emerged. Its bloated body, covered in slimy, mottled scales of dark greens, dirty browns and deep purples, blended seamlessly with the lake's murky waters. Its monstrous head, adorned with multiple eyes emitting a sickly glow, boasted jagged, needle-like teeth capable of tearing through flesh and bone with ease.

The creature emitted a bone-chilling screech as it approached Fellron with such speed that it took all of training to remain still and track the monster. Picking the opportune moment, when the creature's maw was at its widest, Fellron squeezed the crossbow's trigger. Thousands of faint runes all over his body emanated a soft glow before disappearing. The magically enhanced bolt pierced the soft palate within the Lake Kraken's open jaws, piercing its brain and killing it instantly.

Standing at his full height of four and a half feet, Fellron wiped beads of sweat from his brow, the cool mountain air doing little to alleviate the heat of battle. Pushing his weariness aside, he silently made his way to the creature's corpse, his heart pounding with a mixture of adrenaline and grim satisfaction. Unsheathing his axe, he dismembered the monster with practiced efficiency. Its head, still dripping thick, black blood, was a grotesque trophy that he wrapped in cloth and stuffed unceremoniously into a sack.

With a sharp whistle, he summoned Ghost. Fellron's only companion was a creature of pure elegance and strength. The sight of the majestic wolf sprinting towards him brought a rare smile to Fellron's face. Ghost's thick fur, pristine as freshly fallen snow, shimmered in the early morning sun. His eyes, a piercing shade of icy blue, radiated intelligence and wisdom. Although exceptionally large for a wolf, Ghost moved with wraith-like grace, navigating through the snow-covered terrain of the Frost Mountains without a sound. His massive paws, adorned with silver-tipped claws, left a trail of imprints in the snow, marking his passage with an almost mystical aura.

The contrast between Ghost's silent, graceful approach and Fellron's own heavy, weary steps was not lost on him. As the wolf reached him, Fellron knelt, burying his hand in the thick fur, drawing comfort from the warmth and the steady presence. "Good boy," he murmured, his voice a rough whisper against the backdrop of the silent mountains.

The wolf puffed out a breath of misty air, no doubt expressing his disdain for the unpleasant smell lingering from the dead Lake Kraken. He eyed the blood-drenched sack, shuffling slightly to the side with a look that could only be described as wolfish indignation.

"Bloody Dreyna!" Fellron sighed, shaking his head. "Come on, ya' fastidious pretty boy! I'll clean ya' up when we get to Uglich for Dreyna's sake!" He gave Ghost a playful pat on the rump. "Now get on with ya'. I'm freezing my bits off in this hellhole!"

Fellron chuckled at his own grumbling, as he secured the sack to the wolf's harness. Ghost, ever the dignified creature, gave a resigned huff but stood patiently while Fellron meticulously checked his weapons, ensuring everything was in place before he hopped onto Ghost's back. As they set off, the absurdity of their situation struck him. Here he was, a Daemonseeker of the Shadowforged, riding a giant, overly dignified wolf, carrying a stinking sack of monster parts through the icy wilderness. "Just another day in paradise, eh, Ghost?" he muttered with a wry grin.

Fellron knew the two hooded dwarves in the corner of the dingy tavern were watching him. Their pale skin and slightly larger builds suggested they were from Draegoor, a long way from home which made Fellron even more cautious. It wasn't unusual for dwarves to stare at him—he struck an odd, if not fearful, sight. His irises were completely devoid of any color or variation, a deep, solid black that seemed to drink in the light. The lack of facial hair, a stark contrast to the bushy beards of his kin, along with the faint rune scars etched across his skin, marked him as an unsettling and disturbing figure in Dwarven society.

These traits identified him as a Daemonseeker of the Shadowforged. Besides the burdens of constant vigilance and isolation that his duty entailed, the fear he instilled in his own kind left Fellron more alone than he cared to admit, always an object of unwelcome attention and suspicion. Aware that his mere presence could provoke hostile reactions, he kept a wary eye on the two Dwarves from Draegoor.

The bartender, an old Dwarf with coppery skin characteristic of Uglich, a lengthy grey beard, and a substantial barrel-like stomach, approached Fellron. The Dwarf's eyes were wary and the hands holding the pitcher trembled. "Another ale?" he asked, his voice quavering as if anticipating Fellron might strike him down with dark magic.

Fellron nodded, offering a tight smile that did little to ease the tension. "Aye, top it up, and bring out a plate of meat and potatoes too, will ya'," he replied gruffly.

As he took the freshly poured ale, his fingers brushed against the cool metal, the faint runes etched into his skin tingling slightly, a reminder of the power and responsibility he carried. He glanced across at the two hooded figures, their intentions still unclear, before taking a gulp of ale. The bitter taste grounded him in the present. No matter the stares, the suspicion, or the isolation, he was a Daemonseeker, and he would fulfil his duty.

Fellron could feel the weight of the Dwarves' attention as they continued to watch him, faces hidden beneath their hoods. He stared back at them. If they wanted a confrontation, they would find him more than ready.

"More ale, when you get a chance!" Fellron called to the old Dwarf. "And while you're about it, hurry up with that food." Then he took a deep breath and turned to his onlookers. "And if yous' two have something to say, then get your asses over here and say it!" Better to face whatever was coming head-on and still enjoy his evening if he could.

The two exchanged a brief glance before standing and making their way over. The one with bright copper hair and a matching beard flecked with grey nodded as he approached. Fellron mused, perhaps they didn't fancy a fight after all. Yet, he remained vigilant—nobody ever died from being too careful. The other Dwarf, slightly taller and thinner, with dirty blonde hair, didn't acknowledge him, his expression unreadable.

"Evening, lads." Fellron greeted them with a nod. "I can't help but notice, but yous' two have been staring at me for the past hour."

The red-haired Dwarf settled beside him, while his companion stood. "Daemonseeker," he greeted. "We've been sent to find you. Our clan chief needs your skills."

So, Fellron thought, customers, not enemies, then. The bartender brought Fellron's ale and plonked it down. The dark liquid had a dirty-colored froth on top. Fellron took a deep drink, savoring the bitter, tangy taste, then wiped the froth from his upper lip with his sleeve. The ale here was good. He noticed the blonde Dwarf staring at the faint rune scars on his hand.

"Which clan?" Fellron asked gruffly, although he already knew the answer.

"Erik the Blood, Draegoor clan chief," the blonde Dwarf replied instantly.

Fellron eyed the Dwarf. "Former clan chief, from what I hear…" The Dwarf twitched with anger. "And sit down, for Dreyna's sake! You're making me as wary as a mouse in a room full of cats, lad."

After a moment, the red-haired Dwarf beckoned his companion to sit. "Come, sit down, Rorik. We're here as friends." Rorik sat hesitantly, moving the stool further away as he did.

"Lad," Fellron began, "I don't bite. You came here looking for me, remember? Now, why don't we get down to business?"

"Aye, you're right," the red-haired Dwarf said. "I'm Arvi, and this is my companion, Rorik."

"Fellron," the Daemonseeker tapped his own chest.

Arvi continued with a glance at Rorik. "You'll have to excuse him. He's not as... open-minded as our clan chief and I."

More like he's scared shitless of the Shadowforged and our dark practices, Fellron thought, but he said, "Aye, that's understandable. The Shadowforged have an unfavorable reputation among the clans, unfortunately."

The blonde Dwarf snorted. "You're a secretive cult of daemon worshippers who use forbidden dark magic." He glared at Fellron.

Maybe there will be a fight after all, Fellron thought. "What's got his knickers in a twist?" he muttered to Arvi.

Arvi laughed. "Oh, never mind him. Anyway, back to business. Our clan chief needs your assistance with a sensitive issue."

"So I've heard. But I'm not in the business of fighting battles for deposed clan chiefs. Neither are my brothers and sisters," Fellron said. "You'd be better off raising an army and reclaiming your territory by force."

"Aye, that's the plan. But we need you for something more... specialized," Arvi stated.

Fellron raised an eyebrow. "You've got my attention, Arvi. Better keep it. My interest won't last long."

"Erik the Blood needs you to find Gunnar and his unit of Snow Wolves," Arvi said, getting straight to the point.

Fellron had heard the rumors: Gunnar, the heir to Draegoor had turned traitor, along with his elite unit. At least that was the tale being spun in taverns all the way from Braemeer to Uglich, anyway. However, Fellron knew that things were never that simple, especially when it came to clan politics.

"I'd heard that Gunnar is dead, and the rest of the Snow Wolves have defected to the Drogo Mulik," Fellron replied.

"That's bullshit." Rorik said angrily, glaring at Fellron with his thick arms crossed over his chest. "If you believe that, then this conversation is pointless."

"I didn't say I believed it, ya' fool. I said, that's what I'd heard!" Although Fellron had never met Gunnar, the Dwarf's reputation for integrity and honor, along with that of his unit, was well-established. Fellron had gathered this knowledge over the years from several reliable sources and had no reason to doubt it.

Arvi raised his hands in a placating manner before the discussion could get any more heated. Fellron was beginning to like this Dwarf. He seemed to have his head screwed on straight, and Fellron could respect that.

"Listen, lads, nobody knows what's happened to them. Personally, I don't believe the rumors that they're traitors, and neither does Erik. That's why we're here."

Fellron gestured for him to continue.

"Erik has mounted a small army of loyal Dwarves, mainly his personal guard and soldiers who defected from the usurper Wilfrid's leadership. Before he reclaims what is rightfully his, Erik wants his sons and the Snow Wolves by his side."

Fellron considered the strategy Arvi had laid ot. This mission was starting to sound intriguing, and perhaps even worthwhile. Erik's approach was sound. By bringing Gunnar and the Snow Wolves back into the fold, he'd simultaneously clear their names and take back his throne. Proving Gunnar's innocence now would, when the time eventually came, ensure Gunnar's own succession was clear of objections from the other clan chiefs. Besides that the Snow Wolves were the best unit under Erik's command...

"What of the other clans? Surely the clan chiefs are happy to step in and help Erik?" Fellron questioned.

"Not likely. The Drogo crisis has taken priority. The council has opted to stay out of Draegoorian affairs with the threat from the Drogo Mulik looming. Apparently, they can't afford to waste warriors on infighting. All they care about is Draegoor sending troops. They don't care whether they are under the command of Wilfrid or Erik." Arvi spat the final words, his frustration and irritation at the situation shattering his self- restraint.

Fellron nodded. He understood how the council operated. In their defence, they had more than the affairs of an individual clan to worry about. However, in the same breath, Fellron could see the cowardice and betrayal in their actions. Erik had been their stalwart ally for decades. They owed him a certain level of loyalty. Fellron wondered how the situation with the council would play out should Erik manage to reclaim his throne.

"I'll admit, Arvi. I have some sympathy for Erik, truly I do. I met him once, and he seemed a good Dwarf. However, I'm not sure what he thinks I'll be able to do."

"You're a Daemonseeker of the Shadowforged, Fellron. Renowned as the best trackers and hunters in Vellhor! You go toe-to-toe with monsters of the deep. You have mastered the forbidden arts. Rumor has it you can even communicate with magical beings! Are you telling me, Fellron, that there is nothing you can do? That there is no aid you can provide?" Arvi pleaded.

"Ahh, Dreyna strike me and my compassionate heart down, will ya'!" Fellron grumbled. "Aye, I can find 'em… if they're still alive." In truth, he could also find them even if they weren't alive, but he thought he'd keep that to himself. "What d'ya expect me to do once I've found 'em, though?" He really did curse his compassionate heart. The damn thing had got him into more trouble than he'd care to remember.

"Thanks, Fellron," Arvi said with a respectful bow. Even Rorik had a grateful look. "They're alive, I'm certain of it. All I ask is that if you find them, bring them back to Erik. If, for whatever reason, you can't, report back to Erik with news of their whereabouts."

"There'll be a fee, lads. I'm not about doing my job for nought but goodwill."

"Aye, of course." Arvi pulled a large cloth bag from his cloak and unceremoniously dropped it on the thick oak bar. The bag landed with a muffled thud, its contents hinting at the weight of the metal within. "Five thousand hammers now. Five thousand if you return without them. Ten thousand should you return with them."

Fellron opened the bag and retrieved one of the frosteel coins, known as hammers. He rubbed the coin between his fingers and closed his eyes, feeling the precious metal sing in his mind. This was a generous offer, Fellron knew. The city had only paid him a thousand hammers for the lake kraken he'd brought in earlier, and that monster had been terrorizing the populace for almost six months.

"Aye, lads. A generous offer, indeed." Fellron sighed, wondering what in Dreyna's name he was about to commit to. "I'll accept your offer. Give me three weeks and either way, you'll know where they are."

The two Dwarves looked at each other skeptically before Arvi asked, "Are you sure that'll be long enough? It'll take you almost three weeks to get to Fort Bjerg. That's the last reported sighting of them."

"Aye, it's plenty of time," Fellron replied. He knew that with Ghost carrying him, they'd be at Fort Bjerg within the week, and once there, it wouldn't take long to figure out what had happened to them. The thing that worried Fellron the most was how easy the job sounded. From his experience, the easier a job sounded, the more complications he normally came across.

The bartender finally returned with the food and drink, and the two Dwarves left Fellron to his meal and his thoughts. As he dug in, he couldn't help but wonder what was in store for him this time. With a final sigh, he downed his ale and stuffed a roast potato into his mouth, silently cursing Erik and his problems.

11.

Forging Bonds and Shadows

"When shadows loom and challenges rise, it is unity and resilience that light our path."

Gunnar

After Thraxos had tended to the unconscious, bleeding human they found in the corridors, the Minotaur led them to their quarters. Gunnar and Karl shared a
room while Anwyn and Lorelei were shown to a private room next door.

The room Gunnar shared with Karl was surprisingly spacious. Like the rest of the Tower, it was made from pristine white marble. Two large beds flanked the room, each with its own bedside table and small writing desk while two large oak cupboards stood opposite the beds. Gunnar chuckled at the lack of belongings they had managed to bring.

The walls were lined with intricately carved wooden frames, each containing hand-painted scenes of battles depicting mythical creatures and unfamiliar races. A solid wooden door led to an adjoining washroom, which delighted both Dwarves with its large metal bath. The water came from a small pipe protruding from the marble wall, surrounded by a mixture of strange runes.

"Hot, cold," Karl pointed at two runes on either side of the pipe.

"What does the rest mean?" Gunnar queried as he studied the three remaining runes.

With a shrug, Karl touched one. Nothing happened. "'Aint got a clue, boss," he said. "But I'm up for filling the tub and getting in!"

"Aye, that's a good shout!" Gunnar agreed eagerly. Karl didn't hesitate to press the hot rune and they watched in awe as steaming water poured from the pipe.

While the water filled the tub, Karl examined the remaining runes. He pressed one at the bottom of the pipe. The tub started draining. Quickly, he pressed it again, and the water ceased draining and began filling once more.

"Okay, so that empties it," he mused aloud. "Wonder what this one does…" He pressed the rune above the pipe, and the water began bubbling gently. "You've got to be kidding me!" Karl marveled. "This place is amazing, Gunnar!"

Gunnar laughed and pressed the final rune. Nothing seemed to happen at first, but soon the unmistakable scent of lavender and pine sap filled the air, and the water turned a milky colour.

"Scented soap!" Karl exclaimed with pure glee as he began undressing. Gunnar chuckled and left the room, leaving Karl to enjoy his bath.

Once Karl had finished he emptied and cleaned the bath, ready for Gunnar. As Gunnar waited for the tub to fill, Havoc wandered in and hopped onto the sink. He pressed his small stone hand on the hot rune, and steaming water began filling the sink. With a smile, he stared at Gunnar and tentatively dipped his toe into the water. Gunnar stared in stunned silence.

"What?" the Stonesprite questioned, raising an eyebrow. "Are you expecting me not to have a bath?"

Gunnar turned and pressed a rune, and the room slowly filled with the scent of lavender and pine. He undressed and lowered himself gingerly into the hot, soapy water. The heat and steam seeped into his tired, aching muscles, and he let out a long sigh, closing his eyes.

"I didn't realize that Stonesprites needed to bathe, is all," Gunnar said out loud rather than mind-to-mind, enjoying the simple act of speaking in the quiet room. He paused, savoring the warmth. "Are you looking to freshen up for anyone in particular, Havoc?" he teased.

Havoc let out a low chuckle. "Aye, Gunnar." The Stonesprite sighed with pleasure as he immersed himself in the sink of hot water. "I'll be honest with you, I reckon that Lorelei may have a thing for me!"

Gunnar laughed. The Stonesprite's serious expression made the situation even more amusing. "Lorelei, you say? Well, if that's the case, you'd better make sure you're squeaky clean. Can't have you showing up to woo her looking like you've been rolling in dirt."

Havoc grinned. "I'll take your advice, Gunnar. Never thought I'd be getting tips on romance from someone so handsome!"

Gunnar blinked in surprise, then laughed. Only his closest friends called him "handsome," and he never expected to hear it from Havoc. He wondered if Karl had been teasing him within earshot of the Stonesprite.

"Handsome, eh? Did Karl put you up to this?" Gunnar chuckled, shaking his head. The nickname always felt like a jest among his comrades, but hearing it now, in this unexpected moment, warmed his heart a bit and he relaxed further into the tub.

Cracking an eye open, he peered over at Havoc. "Anyway, what makes you think Lorelei is interested in you?"

"Well, Gunnar, when a female gets angry at you, it's like a cat pretending to be a mountain lion—all hiss and no roar. In fact, I've decided to take it as a compliment; she's merely showing me her ferocious affection."

Gunnar couldn't help it. He burst out laughing, even wiping a tear from his eye at the Stonesprite's reasoning. The idea of Lorelei's cross tinkles and chimes as affection was too much.

"So you're telling me," Gunnar managed between bouts of laughter, "that if she's mad at you, then you're probably doing something right?"

"Aye," responded Havoc. "Either that, or you're doing some- thing terribly, terribly wrong!"

Both the Dwarf and the Stonesprite laughed until they cried, the sound echoing off the marble walls, the moment of shared amusement unwittingly strengthening their bond beyond anything they had achieved since Gunnar had named Havoc and initiated their connection. Gunnar sank deeper into the water, feeling the last of his tension melt away. He glanced over at Havoc, who was now splashing water playfully, and felt a surge of gratitude for the unexpected ally and friend that the perilous journey had given him.

After their baths and a short nap, both Dwarves became restless. Eager to explore the Tower and commence their training, they agreed to ask Anwyn to join them. Havoc opted to stay in their room while Gunnar and Karl went to knock for Anwyn.

A few moments after Gunnar gently tapped on the door, the handle rattled. Anwyn peeked her head around the crack in the door, her golden hair still wet. Gunnar's heart skipped a beat. "Apologies, Anwyn," he stuttered. "Sorry for disturbing you. We were wondering if you'd like to come explore the Tower with us?"

He thought he saw her cheeks flush slightly before she nodded. "Of course. Just give me a moment to get ready."

As the two Dwarves waited outside her door, Gunnar couldn't help but think about how Anwyn's presence ruffled his usually confident demeanor, leaving him fumbling awkwardly for words.

Meanwhile, Karl wandered over to the door on the other side of their room—where Thraxos had taken the injured human. He placed his ear against the door, curiosity clearly getting the better of him.

Gunnar raised an eyebrow. "What are you doing?" he asked in a hushed voice.

"Just checking," Karl whispered back. "I'm curious about what's happening in there. Thraxos seemed pretty worried about that human. Also, I mean, if he's going to be our neighbor, it might be worth getting to know him."

"And?" Gunnar asked curiously. "Is he in there?"

"Dunno, boss. Can't hear anything with you talking to me!" Karl joked.

Gunnar shook his head in resignation and let the Karl press his ear back to the door to resume his eavesdropping. "Sounds like he's in there with someone, boss. There's definitely a conversation taking place. Either that, or he's talking to himself!" The red-haired Dwarf laughed as he wandered back toward Gunnar. "By Dreyna, this Elf is taking her time!" he muttered.

Gunnar felt a mix of amusement and impatience. Anwyn's meticulousness was something he appreciated, but Karl's restlessness was contagious. As he waited, he couldn't help but think about how their dynamics were evolving—Karl's curiosity, Anwyn's grace, and his own sense of responsibility towards the group.

Anwyn finally emerged from the door, a mischievous twinkle in her eye. "Sorry for the delay, Karl," she quipped having clearly overheard Karl's muttering. "You know us Elves. We like to make sure every leaf is perfectly in place before we grace you mere Dwarves with our presence!"

Karl smiled sheepishly, and Gunnar let out a low laugh.

"My apologies, Anwyn," Karl began, surprising Gunnar with a low sincere bow. "I've been told I'm not the most patient Dwarf in Dreynas. Sorry if I offended you."

Gunnar was slightly shocked at Karl's unexpected humility, a change from his habitual recourse to a sharp retort, which made Gunnar reflect on how their experiences were reshaping them.

"No offense taken, Karl," Anwyn replied with a warm smile. "Now… where shall we go first?"

"Let's start with the training grounds," Gunnar suggested. "We need to get a feel for the place if we're going to be spending a lot of time here."

As they walked through the Tower, Gunnar glanced between his companions appreciating how Anwyn's easy going nature balanced Karl's rough edges. Despite the looming challenges, moments like these made the journey ahead seem a bit more bearable.

Kemp

"So, Kemp," Thraxos, the big Minotaur, began in a matter-of-fact tone, "you lost your hand to a Shadowwing. Unfortunately, our assessment reveals that your magical strength falls short for self-healing. In Vellhor, you might have managed, but here in Nexus, where the aura is stronger, you're having a tough time tapping into it." Thraxos droned on, as if reciting the most mundane of reports.

"There is some good news, however," he stated flatly, as though there was, in fact, no good news. "We can replace the hand fairly easily. However, we would have to craft a prosthetic from the soulshards of several spectral echoes in order to achieve this. Your hand would look… odd… in Vellhor."

Kemp stared blankly at the stump, the deep red stain seeping through each replacement bandage, frustrated rather than comforted by the Minotaur's clinical tone. "Can you define odd, please?" he asked, masking his unease with a studied politeness.

Thraxos continued impassively, "The prosthetic will have a faint, ethereal glow and might be slightly translucent. In Vellhor, where people are not accustomed to such things, it might draw unwanted attention."

Kemp nodded slowly. The idea of an ethereal, glowing hand was surreal, but the practical necessity of having a functional hand outweighed concerns about its appearance. Still, he couldn't shake the feeling of being marked as different, forever changed by his encounter with the Shadowwing.

"How soon can it be done?" Kemp focused on the practical aspects, trying to suppress the rising tide of anxiety.

"With the right materials, we can start immediately," Thraxos replied in the same level tone. "The process is straightforward, though the results may take some getting used to."

Kemp took a deep breath, steadying himself. The prospect of adjusting to a spectral hand was daunting, but he had to face it head-on.

"How long will it take to learn how to use it?" Kemp asked.

"It will take time to relearn how to grab or hold things," Thraxos explained. "But it will also give you the ability to use shadow magic."

Kemp thought about Harald, the Shadowmage who had betrayed them, and shook his head. "What does that mean?"

"It means you'll be able to control and conjure shadow magic," Thraxos replied, his tone almost condescending. "I can't give you a full lecture on shadow magic here, but in time, you'll learn to harness it."

Kemp considered his options. "What if I opt not to replace the hand?" He already knew he needed a hand Living without one forever was unimaginable, but he had to ask.

Thraxos looked at him curiously. "Then the corrupted magic from the Shadowwing would slowly creep up your arm. In about three weeks, it would reach your heart, and you would die."

"Okay then, how quickly can we replace the hand?" Kemp said immediately.

Thraxos smiled. "We have several students already stitching together a prosthetic prototype for you."

Kemp nodded, feeling a mixture of relief and trepidation. The thought of a spectral hand was unsettling, but with death as the only alternative, he would have to adapt to this new reality. Determination surged within him. He would learn to use the new hand, master the shadow magic, and continue his journey. There was no other option.

Gunnar

Gunnar, Karl, and Anwyn made their way up to the next level. As they emerged from the doorway, a large Dwarf greeted them. "Good afternoon, and welcome to the Spiritsmithing department," he proclaimed proudly. "I am Sage Thadwick from Aerithordor. I am responsible for this entire department. During your spiritual scan, we will discover if you have a natural magical talent for Spiritsmithing. If so, then no doubt you will be in one of my classes." He clapped his hands loudly and spun around. "Now please follow me so we can get the scans underway!"

Gunnar exchanged an apprehensive glance with Karl. Spiritsmithing was a prestigious craft, but he had always relied on his physical strength and combat skills. The notion of possessing a magical talent felt alien and intimidating.

"Excuse me, Sage Thadwick," Anwyn asked. "Could you explain to us what a spiritual scan is, please?"

Gunnar thought back to how Thalirion had assessed Anwyn's strength and wondered if this would be a similar process. The memory of Thalirion's probing made him uneasy, particularly how uncomfortable Anwyn had looked during that scan. The idea of another invasive scan didn't sit well with him, but he knew they had to go through with it.

Thadwick turned back to Anwyn, his expression softening slightly. "A spiritual scan is a way to assess your innate magical abilities. It's a harmless process that allows us to understand your potential in Spiritsmithing. You will feel a gentle energy flow through you, revealing your magical strengths."

Gunnar took a deep breath to steady his nerves. He glanced at Anwyn, who seemed calm but curious. Her presence reassured him, reminding him that they were in this together. As they followed Sage Thadwick, Gunnar couldn't shake the mixture of excitement and dread. While the scan could open new possibilities, it would also mean confronting a part of himself he had never known.

The first scan revealed that Karl, as Gunnar had suspected, had a latent talent for craft magic and Spiritsmithing. Gunnar could see the excitement in his friend's eyes as he bombarded Sage Thadwick with a barrage of eager questions. Gunnar's mouth bent into a proud smile, knowing and seeing how much his red-headed friend relished this opportunity.

Gunnar's own results were less clear to him. Apparently he had an aptitude as a battle mage. The term was intriguing but vague, leaving him unsure of what to expect. Battle magic sounded useful, but he wondered what it specifically entailed. He would find out soon enough, as his instructor was apparently on their way to meet him.

Anwyn's result, however, seemed to baffle Sage Thadwick. Gunnar watched with growing concern as Thadwick conducted the scan again. Anwyn's worried look mirrored his own unease. He had always known Anwyn to be exceptional, but the Sage's reaction hinted at something extraordinary, perhaps even troubling.

"Is there a problem?" Anwyn asked, her voice tinged with apprehension.

Thadwick shook his head, though his expression remained one of astonishment. "No, no... everything is fine. It's just that you have shown an aptitude for all the major skills."

"And... that's bad?" Anwyn asked with a worried frown.

Gunnar saw the alarm in her eyes, so he focused on the positives. "Anwyn, that's incredible," he reassured her warmly. "It means you have limitless potential."

Thadwick nodded, his initial surprise giving way to a more composed demeanor. "No... it's not bad, Anwyn. It's fantastically good, in fact. Yet I'll admit, somewhat surprising. I have only ever witnessed this from one other Elf..." His voice trailed off as Anwyn, Karl, and Gunnar shared a look of confusion.

But then Thalirion swept in greeting the Sage like an old friend. They embraced and exchanged pleasantries, before Sage Thadwick asked with a glance at Anwyn, "I'm assuming you have conducted your own scan on Anwyn?" Thalirion's smile widened. "Indeed, Thadwick! You seem confused?" Thadwick nodded, and Thalirion gestured for Anwyn to come over. "Anwyn has been chosen as the Seishinmori."

Gunnar noticed clarity dawning in Sage Thadwick's eyes. "Which means…" Thadwick's gaze shifted to Thalirion, and Gunnar saw a wave of sadness sweep over him.

Letting out a long, contented sigh, Thalirion responded, "Yes, I am giving up my mantle as Seishinmori."

Gunnar's mind struggled to grasp the weight of what was happening. Although the term Seishinmori was new to him, the significance was clear. Thalirion, a figure of great power and wisdom, was passing his title to Anwyn. Gunnar looked at Anwyn, who stood determined despite her evident surprise and nervousness. His heart swelled with pride and a fierce desire to protect her, knowing how life-changing this revelation would be.

Thadwick, however, looked downcast at the news, and Gunnar wondered why. The sadness in Thadwick's eyes suggested a deeper significance than a mere title, a burden that came with the mantle of Seishinmori. Gunnar's curiosity was piqued, but before he could ponder further, a large figure barged into the room.

At first, Gunnar assumed it was a man, given the figure's height and size. However, sharp talons at the ends of the intruder's hands revealed otherwise. This wasn't entirely human.

The newcomer grunted a greeting to Thadwick and Thalirion before turning towards the Dwarves. "Which one of you is Gunnar?" he asked, his voice devoid of emotion.

"Ahh, Commander Aelric!" Thalirion greeted. "How are you?" The commander cut a striking figure. Tall and broad-shouldered, he wore a pristine surcoat adorned with the insignia of his rank, each metallic emblem polished to a gleaming sheen. Gunnar couldn't help but notice the absence of the commander's left eye and the sprawling burn mark marring the left side of his face. As Commander Aelric turned towards Thalirion, Gunnar's gaze lingered on the sight of wings folded tightly against the commander's armor.

"I am wondering why I am down here collecting this Dwarf..." the commander grumbled, his tone gruff and impatient.

Despite the commander's brusque demeanor, Thalirion responded with a chuckle. He directed Gunnar to stand, gesturing towards the commander. "Gunnar, meet Commander Aelric. He once led the Arovian Air Force in his native realm of Raaniada," Thalirion introduced. Turning to the commander, he continued, "Commander, allow me to present Gunnar, Prince of Dreynas and," he added, "your newest battle mage... trainee."

Gunnar's drew in a sharp breath, startled at the unexpected revelation. "Sorry, did you say Prince?" he exclaimed, hardly noticing arl laughing beside him.

Thalirion ignored Gunnar completely and focused on Commander Aelric. "Now, come on Aelric. You can't still be mad at me? It's been what? Two centuries?"

Commander Aelric gave Thalirion a deadpan look, with a slight twitch in his only eye. Gunnar couldn't help but feel a pang of anxiety. This scarred, formidable man would be his instructor, and Thalirion had angered him so much that he held a two-century grudge.

Gunnar sighed inwardly. The title of "Prince" felt like a burden rather than an honor, and the knowledge that his mentor had a strained history with his new instructor only deepened his unease. He realized bleakly that the path ahead might prove steeper and more treacherous than he had first thought.

As he tried to steady his breathing and calm his racing thoughts, Gunnar felt a mixture of dread and determination. He couldn't afford to show weakness, not now. Thalirion, seemed unfazed by the tension, but Karl's laughter was starting to die down.

"Great," Gunnar muttered under his breath, steeling himself for what was to come. He knew he had to prove himself, not just as a battle mage, but as someone worthy of the title he had been given.

Kemp

Kemp awoke with a start, the strange sensation at the end of his arm an immediate, unsettling reminder. His new hand, securely attached to his wrist, was impossible to ignore.

Thraxos had been right—it looked... bizarre. The hand was woven from what Kemp could only describe as thick, tangible shadow, a dark, opaque substance that seemed to drink in the light around it.

As he flexed his fingers, a cold, eerie sensation coursed from the material through him. It was a chill unlike anything he had ever felt, a disconcerting contrast to the warmth of his living flesh and a tangible sign of the shadow magic that now pulsed within him. Kemp tentatively tested the capabilities of his new appendage and the shadowy material responded with unexpected fluidity. It moved unnaturally, almost as if it had a will of its own. Kemp's brow furrowed in concentration, his mind wrestling with the alien nature of the hand. He tried to make it perform simple tasks, but it resisted, moving only to flex open and closed.

FORGING BONDS AND SHADOWS

Each attempt felt like a battle of wills and, although frustration bubbled up within him, he also felt a strange fascination. There was power here, something dark and potent. The hand was not just an extension of him; it was a conduit to something deeper, something he had yet to fully understand.

Kemp's thoughts raced as he continued to experiment, the cold sensation a persistent presence. The shadow magic was alive, a dark current running through him, altering him in ways he could not yet fathom. He couldn't help but wonder whether he could learn to master his new appendage—or if it would master him.

Kemp looked up as he heard the heavy footsteps approaching, and Thraxos's massive form cast a long, ominous shadow across the room. "How does it feel?" the Minator rumbled, his voice a deep, resonant echo.

Kemp flexed his new hand, feeling the eerie sensation of shadow and magic intertwining with his flesh. He marveled at the seamless integration of the arcane and the biological that felt both alien and intimate. "It's... strange," he admitted, still grappling with the surreal nature of his transformation. "But I think I could get used to it."

"Good," Thraxos nodded with a glimmer of satisfaction dancing in his eyes. "While you were unconscious, we performed another scan of your spirit." Thraxos's eyes narrowed slightly, his tone more inquisitive. "Do you possess an affinity for the elements?" he inquired.

BATTLE MAGE (THE VELLHOR SAGA VOLUME 1)

Kemp nodded. "I received my education at Lakeview Arcane Academy in Fenmark," he replied proud of his association with the Academy.

Thraxos seemed unimpressed, his blank expression explained when he confessed, "I'm unfamiliar with that institution." He drew in a breath before continuing, "However, it's apparent from our examination that you lack experience in meditation. Your spirit appears depleted and unable to tap into the aura, which contributes to its weakened state."

Kemp's brows furrowed, his pride giving way to confusion. Meditation? He had always associated it with relaxation and mental clarity, not with strengthening magical abilities. The concept seemed foreign, almost contradictory to what he had learned. Magic, in his understanding, was about energy manipulation, spells, and incantations, not quiet introspection. His mind also wrestled with the idea of the spirit as a source of magical strength. To Kemp, the spirit had always been an abstract concept, linked to morality and emotions rather than something tangible that could be strengthened or depleted. The notion challenged his foundational beliefs about the nature of magic and his own capabilities.

As these thoughts churned within him, another term caught his attention: aura. Thraxos had mentioned it before, yet Kemp realized he had never encountered the word in his formal studies. What else had he not been taught? What other fundamental aspects of magic had his prestigious education overlooked?

"Thraxos," he began, his curiosity tinged with a hint of frustration, "you mentioned my aura earlier. What exactly is an aura, and how does it relate to my spirit and magical abilities?"

FORGING BONDS AND SHADOWS

Thraxos's expression remained impassive, unimpressed by Kemp's genuine curiosity and thirst for knowledge.

"I find it perplexing that someone who has supposedly studied the arcane arts would know so little," Thraxos remarked, with an air of skepticism. "If your knowledge of magic is as lacking as your understanding of the spirit, meditation, and aura, then it's no wonder your spirit is in such a state."

Kemp's confusion deepened. How could his education at the prestigious Lakeview Arcane Academy have left him so ill- prepared? The notion that he—and perhaps all humans from Fenmark—were viewed as ignorant by those more versed in the arcane arts struck him as both unfair and disheartening.

Yet, Thraxos's disdain kindled a spark of defiance within Kemp. The dismissive tone and harsh critique stung, he wouldn't let Thraxos's words diminish his worth or potential.

"I may not have all the answers," he conceded, his voice steady, "but I am eager to learn." He met Thraxos's gaze head-on with an intense stare. "If you're willing to teach me, I'll do whatever it takes to get stronger."

In that moment, Kemp felt a shift within himself. He wasn't just a student from Lakeview anymore; he was someone who would forge his own path, master the mysteries of the spirit and aura, and prove his worth not only to Thraxos but to himself.

Thraxos frowned. "I see little point in tutoring someone so ignorant in the arcane arts," he grumbled, doubtfully. "What good is teaching elemental magic to one who knows so little and possesses such a weak spirit?"

Kemp's shoulders sagged as Thraxos's stinging words cut deep, gnawing at his confidence, yet something inside him refused to yield.

"I may be inexperienced," he said, straightening his back, "but I want to learn. If you're willing to teach me, I will prove myself worthy of your instruction."

Thraxos regarded Kemp for a long moment, his gaze intense and probing. Kemp's heart was pounding, the silence amplifying his doubts, but he held his ground, returning Thraxos's stare with his own steely determination.

Finally, Thraxos gave a reluctant nod. "Very well," he conceded. "But know this, Kemp: the path ahead will not be easy. If you are to succeed, you must be prepared to push yourself beyond your limits. This training may very well kill you."

Kemp's heart raced at Thraxos's words, a mix of fear and exhilaration coursing through him. The prospect of the challenges ahead was daunting, but the chance to prove himself, to grow stronger, burned like a fire within him.

"What must I do?" he asked, leaning eagerly forward.

"Patience," Thraxos tone brooked no argument. "Control over your shadow hand must come first and it will not prove esy. It is a manifestation of your spirit, and as such, it will require discipline and focus to command. If you can control your hand by the end of the week, you will have proven to me that you have what it takes to at least commence training in the elements."

Kemp had no idea of a week would be enough time, but Thraxos's offer filled him with hope. "Thank you, Thraxos," he said earnestly. "I won't let you down."

Under Thraxos's stern guidance, Kemp plunged into his new training routine. The Minotaur provided him with a set of basic forms to practise with his shadow hand, each movement designed to hone his control and precision. Kemp repeated the forms tirelessly, his muscles and mind aching with exertion. Although the fluidity of shadow hand's movements continued to defy his attempts at control, Kemp kept pushing himself, sweat dripping from his brow as he struggled to master each motion.

Thraxos also introduced him to mind control techniques. Despite being labelled 'basic', Kemp found them anything but. They required intense concentration, a level of mental discipline he had never known. He focused, channeling his thoughts and intentions, trying to direct the energy of his spirit—though he still wasn't clear about what that truly meant—toward his shadow hand.

Every exercise pushed Kemp to his limits. His body ached, and his mind felt stretched thin, yet he persisted. The connection between his mind and the shadow hand grew stronger, the movements becoming slightly more responsive. Each small success fueled his determination, the spark within him growing into a flame. He could feel the power within the shadow hand, a mysterious force that he was slowly beginning to understand.

The most challenging aspect of Kemp's training was the meditation technique. Thraxos had explained that mastering this would be crucial not only to control his shadow hand, but also to advance in the arcane arts. It required intricate breathing techniques that felt completely unnatural to Kemp. The first time he attempted it, he had been left gasping for breath, feeling like he was drowning on dry land.

With Thraxos's guidance, Kemp slowly acclimated to the technique. Each inhale was an effort to draw in the pulsating energy of the aura, envisioning it as tendrils of ethereal light weaving through the air around him. But the connection remained elusive, slipping away like a fleeting dream upon waking.

From his seat, Thraxos observed Kemp's struggle, offering occasional words of guidance and encouragement. "Focus, Kemp," he urged softly, his voice a reassuring presence in the otherwise silent chamber. "You must attune your senses to the subtle currents of energy that surround you. Only then can you begin to harness their power."

Kemp tried to heed his words, but silencing the clamor of his thoughts proved difficult. Doubts and uncertainties gnawed at his consciousness. Could he truly master this arcane art, or was he destined to falter at the first hurdle?

Despite the doubts that threatened to overwhelm him, Kemp pressed on. Each controlled breath brought a faint glimmer of progress, a stirring of something ancient and powerful deep within his soul. It was a small victory, but a victory nonetheless.

As evening fell and Thraxos departed, Kemp persisted in his meditation, determined to unlock the elusive spark of aura. Hours passed, and just when weariness threatened to overtake him, he felt it—a subtle yet undeniable surge of energy coursing through him. Sweat dripped from his brow as euphoria washed over him. He collapsed onto his bed with a contented smile, wondering if he might be the first human to experience such a phenomenon. Triumph filled him, but so did exhaustion and, with a sigh, Kemp surrendered to sleep.

12.

BENEATH THE ARENA'S SHADOW

"Amidst the shadows, the strength of true allies shines brightest."

Ruiha

The torches lining the walls blurred past as Ruiha fought to stay conscious. Dragged through the tunnel, her thoughts flitted chaotically, unable to latch onto anything. Reeling from the blows Captain Drakoth and his guards continued to inflict, a doubt gnawed at her—had all her efforts been for nothing?

An alarming thought of how easily she could die here and now flickered briefly, but she felt a surge of relief when Drakoth signaled a halt. Not for the cessation of pain, though that was welcome, but because she knew they had spared her for the pit. Drakoth wanted her death to be a spectacle, a grim lesson for all.

Each step was a torment as the guards, indifferent to her suffering, dragged her over jagged terrain. The stone ceiling gave way to a vast cavern, the ground turning sandy—this was the pit. The arena she now knew so well. With a jolt, they dropped her, knees hitting the floor with a thud. She lay there, gathering her strength.

On Drakoth's command, two guards hoisted her upright. She swayed, then steadied, scanning the arena. Relief flowered as she saw Drogo imprisoned in cages at the arena's side. Armored guards encircled the periphery, a stark reminder of her peril. About fifty guards, with only fifteen to twenty armed with long-range weapons—less than half. Most wielded swords and axes.

A wry smile touched her lips as she assessed the odds. "That makes things a little easier," she mused quietly. Her eyes darted back toward the imprisoned Drogo slaves, desperately seeking Dakarai. A tense moment stretched until she found him, gripping bars of metal, his expression grave. At first, she thought his demeanor reflected their dire circumstances, but then she saw him shaking his head and gesturing frantically across the arena floor. Panic widened his eyes, and a chill of foreboding crept down her spine, the urgency of his message sinking in.

Scanning the pit, her initial chill turned into icy terror. Dozens of shallow holes dotted the arena floor, a grim testament to the discovery and removal of the cache of weapons they had hidden over the past week. Her heart plummeted. She turned back to Dakarai, mouthing a silent apology. He shook his head defiantly, eyes blazing with determination. "Fight!" his silent plea echoed across the distance. Nodding, she steeled herself for what lay ahead.

"Ah, welcome." A twisted smile stretched across Captain Drakoth's reptilian features. "I see you've all been eagerly anticipating today as your escape day, haven't you? Well, it seems that fate has other plans." A cruel chuckle escaped him. "Instead, you shall have the pleasure of witnessing the Shadow Hawk fight for her very survival!" He paused dramatically, savoring the tension. "And who might her fortunate adversaries be? Why, none other than… YOU!"

Ruiha's heart ached as her gaze fell on the Drogo slaves. The thought of fighting them, knowing their defeat meant their death, weighed heavily on her. Facing Dakarai, should he be brought out, filled her with dread. A tear trailed down her cheek as she grappled with the impossible choices before her.

She scanned the arena, searching for an escape from this nightmare and spotted the Dwarves confined in a cage behind the imprisoned Drogo. She longed to communicate a plan, but knew any attempt would draw the guards' attention.

Her thoughts shattered as Dakarai was dragged out to be her first opponent. Emotion overwhelmed her at the sight of her closest ally, the one who had shared her struggles and offered unwavering support, now destined to be her opponent in a fight to the death.

Tears welled in her eyes. How could she raise a weapon against Dakarai, the one who had shown her kindness amid cruelty? The one who had welcomed her, despite their differences. Yet, the brutal reality left her no choice but to steel herself for the inevitable confrontation.

As the tension in the arena peaked, a guard approached, his footsteps thudding against the sandy floor. Smirking, he tossed two swords to the ground between them, the metallic clang reverberating through the silence.

Ruiha's heart pounded as she and Dakarai reached for the weapons. Their eyes met briefly, a silent acknowledgment passing between them, before focusing on the looming figure of the guard.

The guard's eyes gleamed with sadistic amusement, his reptilian lips curling into a cruel sneer. He gripped his own sword tightly and stepped back, signaling the start of the battle.

Facing each other, Ruiha and Dakarais eyes spoke volumes as they made a silent pact to fight with every ounce of strength and skill they possessed. The outcome would be left to fate and their abilities as warriors.

Ruiha took a deep breath and tightened her grip on her sword, adrenaline heightening her senses. Across from her, Dakarai mirrored her stance, his expression a mix of determination and resignation.

The world around them faded, leaving only the two friends poised for the inevitable clash. Captain Drakoth's primal roar signaled the start of the fight, his voice echoing through the arena like a death knell.

The first strike was exchanged, the sound of steel meeting steel ringing out as Ruiha and Dakarai danced around each other in a deadly ballet of swords.

Despite their unspoken agreement to give it their all, it was clear neither Dakarai nor Ruiha fought with their full strength. Their movements, while swift and precise, lacked the ruthless efficiency of true combat, and Ruiha deliberately missed an opening to strike at Dakarai.

Captain Drakoth's erupted in fury erupted at her hesitation. He raised two scaled fingers in the air in a silent command to the guards. They sprang into action, and with sickening thuds, two bolts pierced the chests of the nearest pair of Drogo slaves. Their bodies crumpled lifelessly against the cold metal bars, executed as punishment for Ruiha's timidity

A sense of dread clouded the airat Drakoth's vicious decree. From the corner of her eye, Ruiha saw the caged Dwarves growing increasingly restless, their angry shouts echoing from their cell. But she couldn't focus on them for long. Above the din of the arena, Drakoth's furious shout pierced the tension. "Fight, human," he screamed. "Fight, for Nergai's sake. Fight!"

She turned to see him aiming a crossbow at Dakarai. Reacting swiftly, she lunged, her blade leaving a shallow gash across Dakarai's ribs. He shouted in pain and stepped back. Anguish pressed in on Ruiha chest as she readied herself to face the impossible choices bearing down on her.

Suddenly, the Dwarves swarmed from their cage through suddenly twisted bars into the pit. It seemed they would rather meet their end in combat than remain at the mercy of their captors. Chaos erupted as Drogo guards scrambled to maintain order, but the element of surprise tipped the scales in favor of the Dwarves.

Magnus and his comrades surged forward with a mighty roar, and descended on the unprepared Drogo guards, clenched fists flying. As the skirmish unfolded, the Dwarves wrested weapons from the fallen guards, gaining a crucial advantage.

Ruiha and Dakarai exchanged a knowing glance, and joined in the fight side by side, their blades flashing in the dim light of the arena. As the battle raged on, their extensive training sessions paid off as they seamlessly synchronized their movements. Fighting back- to-back, they cut through the Drogo guards with precision and determination. Each strike left fallen weapons scattered for the eager Dwarves to seize.

Ruiha's heart pounded, not just from the exertion of battle, but from the sheer will to survive and protect those she cared about. The clash of metal and the shouts of combatants filled the air, but amid the chaos, a fierce clarity emerged. She and Dakarai fought as one formidable force. With every swing of her blade, Ruiha rejoiced that she was no longer a captive fighting for her life; she was a warrior. A leader. A beacon of resistance against their oppressors.

Dakarai's presence beside her, his movements mirroring her own, bolstered her resolve. They carved a path through the enemy ranks, their blades a blur of deadly efficiency. The arena, once a place of dread, transformed into a battleground where hope and defiance clashed against tyranny.

The Dwarves, emboldened by their success and by the sight of Ruiha and Dakarai's prowess, fought with renewed vigor. Magnus, wielding a captured sword, led a charge that further disrupted the Drogo guards' ranks. The once-overwhelming enemy forces faltered, their confidence eroded by the unexpected ferocity of their prisoners.

Ruiha could feel the tide turning. She and Dakarai pressed their advantage, cutting down the remaining guards with relentless determination. The arena floor, littered with fallen Drogo and discarded weapons, stood as a testament to their resistance.

In that moment, amid the chaos and bloodshed, Ruiha realized they were no longer just fighting for survival. They were fighting for freedom, for a chance to break the chains that had bound them for so long. That realization fueled her every move, propelling her toward the total victory they so desperately needed.

Amidst the tumult, a lone Dwarf broke away from the melee, sprinting towards the cages containing the Drogo prisoners. Channeling his mastery of craft magic, he focused his energy on the metal bars, bending and twisting them until they finally yielded to his will, freeing the imprisoned Drogo.

With a triumphant cry, the liberated Drogo surged forth, their eyes alight with newfound hope and fury. Armed with weapons scavenged from fallen guards, they joined the Dwarves, decisively turning the tide of battle.

The arena echoed with the clash of steel and the roar of combat as the combined might of the Dwarves and Drogo overwhelmed their oppressors. The Drogo guards found themselves steadily pushed back, their ranks thinning under the relentless assault.

Ruiha stepped back from the fray, needing a moment to evaluate the situation. With the guards close to being overrun, they needed an escape plan. Her eyes scanned the arena until she found Magnus, deep in the thick of the fighting, wielding an oversized axe to hack at the guards.

Grabbing Dakarai's hand, she navigated through the chaotic battle, swiftly dispatching any enemies in their path. Within moments, they reached the forefront of the battle. Despite her calls for Magnus to turn, he was ensnared by a primal bloodlust. Ruiha recognized the sensation all too well—the pounding in her ears, the singular focus on the clash of blades, the blurring of everything else.

She needed to get closer. Approaching from behind, she made a piercing scream of his name and he finally turned, wild eyes gleaming. She beckoned him and he complied, a sense of calm washed over his features as he disengaged from the fray.

"We need a plan to escape," Ruiha said to Dakarai and Magnus.

"Isn't that what we're doing?" Magnus panted.

"No," she countered firmly. "We're currently fighting to the death with these guards. The escape comes next."

Dakarai nodded, his gaze fixed on the exit leading to their cells—the only point of entry or exit any of the slaves had ever used. "I suggest we take a hostage," he proposed.

Ruiha nodded curtly. "That could be our best shot. We need leverage."

Magnus, regaining some composure, suggested, "We could use Drakoth. He's the key to their command."

"Agreed," Ruiha said. "But we need to act quickly before the guards regroup. Magnus, lead the Dwarves and Drogo. Keep pushing them back. Dakarai and I will get Drakoth."

Magnus nodded, with a steely gaze. "Stay safe," he muttered, gripping his axe tighter.

Ruiha and Dakarai moved with purpose, cutting through the chaos toward Drakoth. Each step was a calculated move, every strike a deliberate action to clear their path. As they neared the Drogo Captain, Ruiha's pulse quickened, knowing the next moments could decide their fate.

Drakoth, sensing their approach, turned, his eyes narrowing. "You think you can challenge me?" he sneered.

Ruiha's grip tightened on her sword. "We're not just challenging you," she said, her voice unwavering. "We're ending this."

The clash was immediate and fierce. Drakoth's strength and speed were formidable, his sword a blur as he met their attacks. Ruiha and Dakarai moved in sync, their strikes coordinated, but Drakoth parried each blow with terrifying ease. The metallic clang of their swords echoed through the arena, a symphony of desperation and defiance.

Drakoth's laughter cut through the noise. "Is this the best you've got?" he taunted.

Ruiha gritted her teeth, frustration mounting. Every move she made felt like a test, each strike a measure of her resolve. She had faced many battles, but this one carried the weight of freedom for her and the others.

Dakarai lunged forward, his blade aimed at Drakoth's side. With a swift motion, Drakoth sidestepped and countered, his sword slashing across Dakarai's arm. He cried out in pain, stumbling back. Ruiha's anger flared, a fierce protectiveness driving her forward. She swung her sword with renewed vigour, forcing Drakoth to focus on her.

"Your defiance is admirable, but futile," Drakoth hissed, his strikes becoming more aggressive.

Ruiha parried a powerful blow, her arms shaking from the force. Sweat dripped down her face, mingling with the dust and blood. She caught Dakarai's eye, saw the determination burning there, and felt a surge of resolve. They had to keep fighting, no matter the odds.

Drakoth swung his sword in a wide arc, forcing Ruiha to leap back. She stumbled, regaining her footing just in time to block another strike. The sheer power behind his attacks was overwhelming. She needed to find an opening, a moment of weakness.

A flash of movement caught her eye as Dakarai circled around, attempting to flank Drakoth. Ruiha seized the opportunity, launching a series of rapid strikes. Drakoth deflected each one, but it diverted his attention. Dakarai lunged again, aiming for Drakoth's unprotected side.

For a brief moment, victory seemed within reach. But Drakoth, with uncanny speed, twisted and drove his elbow into Dakarai's chest, sending him sprawling. Anguish and rage surged through Ruiha. She attacked with everything she had, her blade a blur of steel and desperation.

Drakoth's defences faltered under the relentless assault. Ruiha pressed on, her strikes becoming wild, fueled by raw emotion. She saw a flicker of doubt in Drakoth's eyes, a moment of hesitation. Seizing it, she thrust her sword forward with all her might.

The blade sank into Drakoth's chest, the look of surprise and fury in his eyes freezing as the life drained from him. Ruiha's breath caught in her throat, realization dawning. She had meant to subdue him, to capture him and use him as leverage, but in the heat of the battle, her intentions had turned deadly.

Drakoth collapsed to the ground, his body limp and lifeless. Silence fell over the arena, the battle momentarily forgotten as all eyes turned to the fallen captain. Ruiha stood over him, her chest heaving.

Dakarai struggled to his feet, clutching his wounded arm. "You did what you had to," he said in a strained voice.

Ruiha shook her head. "I didn't mean to kill him," she whispered, the anguish and relief intertwining in a tangle of emotions. "We needed him as a hostage."

"Well he's dead now," Dakarai said. "But we're still alive, and so are the others. We need to finish this and get everyone out."

Ruiha nodded, steeling herself. The battle was not over. With Drakoth dead, the remaining guards were leaderless, their morale shattered. She and Dakarai turned back to the fray, rallying the Dwarves and Drogo. The tide of the battle had well and truly turned as they fought to secure their freedom.

As Ruiha strode through the chaos of the arena towards Magnus, her eyes locked onto a figure she had momentarily for- gotten: Rainok, the treacherous bastard who had orchestrated Corgan's execution and nearly caused her own death. Anger surged within her, a fire burning brightly in her veins as she closed the distance with purposeful strides.

Each beat of her pounding heart echoed the rage that fueled her steps. Wordlessly, she approached Rainok and as he turned to face her, surprise quickly morphed into fear. Before he could speak, she drew her blade with lightning speed, the steel glinting menacingly in the dim light.

She struck him hard with her free hand and he crumpled to the ground, his eyes wide with shock and disbelief. Ruiha stood over him, righteous fury filling her voice as she uttered her parting words.

"Go to your god knowing this, Rainok; your treachery made our success possible. In the end, traitors like you always meet their fate. Consider this justice for Corgan." With deliberate slowness, she slid the tip of her sword into Rainok's heart, watching the fear and pain drain from his eyes as his life slipped away.

The act brought a grim satisfaction, not so much pleasure in the kill as a matter of justice having been served. Turning away, weariness seeped into her bones, drained by the cost of their struggle.

She moved towards Magnus, who was still in the thick of the fighting wielding his oversized axe with brutal efficiency, and caught sight of her. His expression, a mix of exhaustion and resolve, mirrored her own. "Ruiha," he shouted over the din, "we need to keep moving!"

"I know," she replied, her voice steady despite the tumult within. "We're almost there."

Together, they continued to fight, side by side with the remaining Dwarves and Drogo, each swing of their weapons bringing them closer to the elusive goal of freedom. As the last of the Drogo guards fell, the arena echoed with the victorious cries of the liberated. The path to freedom now lay open before them; scattered with the lifeless bodies of both friend and foe, but there, nonetheless.

13.

Forged in Absence

"Through struggle and sacrifice, a leader is forged from the flames of determination."

Gunnar

Throughout their journey from Sage Thadwick's office to Commander Aelric's, silence weighed heavily on Gunnar. The air between them was thick with unspoken judgments.

Aelric halted abruptly by a door which appeared to be their destination. Gunnar presumed it must lead to the battle mage training rooms as Aelric turned to face him. The scar across the Commander's face seemed to pulse with a life of its own, reflecting the anger in his one remaining eye. "You stand within the walls of the Tower of Absence," Aelric began, coldly. "Let me make one thing crystal clear: absence is the key to your survival here. Yes, you will learn the art of war, the craft of combat, and the discipline of death. But above all, you will learn the absence of fear, the absence of hesitation and doubt, the absence of mercy, the absence of weakness, and the absence of ego. These traits will not be tolerated, excuses will not be accepted, and failure will not be an option. You will either emerge from this Tower as a battle mage hardened by absence or you will die here. The second you step foot into this room, there will be no other options available to you."

As Aelric's gaze bore into him, Gunnar felt a steely determination harden within. The stakes were brutally clear, and the Commander's words were a challenge he silently accepted. He would not let fear, hesitation, or doubt rule him. Mercy, weakness, and ego would find no place in his heart. This was not just about survival; it was about transformation.

Although Gunnar had expected the training to be challenging, the first two weeks showed how he had grossly underestimated the magnitude of the ordeal.

Commander Aelric's evident disdain for him was a constant undercurrent that left Gunnar questioning why someone with such palpable contempt would choose to train anyone. Gunnar discovered that despite Aelric's status as a Sage, he preferred the title of Commander, a nod to his military years, distinguishing himself from the more scholarly Sages who oversaw the training departments.

He also quickly realized that Vellhor was among the weakest of the seven realms in the arcane arts. The thin aura and lack of knowledge gave Vellhorians a weakened spirit, many exhibiting poor meditation habits or possessing only a rudimentary understanding of magic. Despite these shortcomings, the Tower of Absence regularly accepted applicants from Vellhor, which explained the presence of Dwarves and Elves from his home realm.

Upon joining the battle mage training department, Gunnar learned about the four distinct types of mages: battle mages, elemental mages, craft mages, and shadow mages. The spiritual scan unveiled latent talents and abilities within individuals, guiding them towards training in disciplines where they were most likely to excel. Battle mages, Gunnar discovered, were a rare breed. They possessed a unique blend of martial prowess and magical aptitude, seamlessly integrating combat skills with arcane knowledge to become formidable warriors on the battlefield. This fusion of talents set them apart but brought with it significant training demands.

As the days of rigorous training passed, Gunnar had to grapple not only with the physical demands of the training but also with the psychological toll of Commander Aelric's relentless scrutiny. Every mistake was met with scorn, every success downplayed. Gunnar's frustration grew, not just from the harsh training, but from the gnawing question of why Aelric singled him out for such intense disapproval.

Yet amid the grueling routines and harsh criticisms, Gunnar began to appreciate the depths of his own resilience. The training was molding him, pushing him to tap into reserves of strength and determination he hadn't known he possessed. He saw glimmers of his potential as a battle mage, moments where the fusion of his martial skills and burgeoning magical abilities felt seamless and powerful. Despite the challenges Gunnar was determined to emerge from this training as a fully-fledged battle mage, ready to face whatever lay ahead.

Every day was a relentless trial of endurance. From the crack of dawn until late at night, Gunnar and Havoc were pushed to their limit in physical and mental challenges under the watchful eyes of three merciless instructors.

Commander Aelric, with his imposing presence and unsympathetic demeanor, led the training with imperious commands and swift punishments. The respect Gunnar had for Aelric's expertise was entwined with a deep-seated fear of failing to deliver and error-free performance.

Sage Zanders and Sage Raveena were equally demanding. Zanders focused on the physical, driving Gunnar through endless combat drills and tests of stamina. Raveena, on the other hand, honed Gunnar's magical abilities, demanding precision and focus that left his mind reeling.

Their teaching methods were brutal, making free use of a variety of punishments. Any mistakes met with immediate consequences. Havoc's presence, rather than being supportive, often added to the strain. His dark humor and chaotic behavior grated on Gunnar's nerves, adding to the challenges of an already intense environment.

The training was excruciating. Gunnar's body ached constantly from the demanding exercises. His muscles screamed for rest, but rest was a luxury he couldn't afford. Mentally, he was pushed to the brink. The intense focus required for spell- casting and combat maneuvers left his mind in a perpetual state of exhaustion.

Yet, despite the pain and fatigue, a spark of stubborn Dwarvish determination kept Gunnar going. While the instructors constantly reminded him how exceptionally fortunate he was to receive personal instruction from three Sages. Each reminder felt like a twisted joke, a cruel taunt.

As he lay on his bunk each night, every muscle in his body screaming, Gunnar would allow himself a moment to reflect. The days were brutal, but he could feel himself changing, growing stronger. He was not the same Dwarf who had walked into that room two weeks ago. He was being forged, bit by bit, into something more formidable. A weapon.

There were some brief moments of solace to be had in the time he shared with Karl each evening. It was usually a mere hour before exhaustion claimed him, but it provided an anchoring connection to normalcy and friendship. Encounters with Anwyn were rare and fleeting, deepening his sense of isolation amidst the relentless training. Yet, Gunnar clung to the hope of emerging from the Tower of Absence as a battle mage of unparalleled strength and skill.

His daily routine was a relentless barrage of physical and mental challenges. The mornings were divided between combat training and spell-casting. Drills and sparring sessions honed his weapon skills, agility, and reflexes, through armed and unarmed combat. Each exercise leaving him bruised but sharper.

After intense combat sessions, he praciced incantations and rituals to control arcane energies with precision. Within a few days, Gunnar had managed to tap into the aura, igniting his latent magical abilities, however the mental focus required for magic was exhausting.

After a brief but welcome respite for lunch the afternoon began with physical conditioning to build his strength and speed, followed by tactical training sessions exercising his strategic thinking and adaptability. Devising moves to outmaneuver imaginary foes and anticipate their actions was as mentally taxing as the stamina training had been physically demanding.

Each day concluded with mental discipline sessions that included meditation, visualization exercises, and mindfulness techniques. These practices were designed to cultivate his mental and spiritual resilience, preparing him for the advancement to Master and eventually Overlord. Despite the exhaustion, Gunnar found these sessions grounding. They offered a moment to center himself, to reflect on his progress, and to steel his mind against the challenges ahead.

Punishments within the Tower of Absence were merciless. Thise that didn't involve excruciating pain, would instead encroach upon Gunnar's scarce time for food and rest. Varying from brutal physical assaults to performing menial tasks under the scrutiny of various Sages, each penalty extracted a toll on his already taxed body and mind. Among the instructors' preferred methods was the dreaded 'pit of absence,' a chamber devoid of light, warmth, comfort, sound, food, or even water. Even Havoc was not permitted to keep him company during these punishments. With no sense of time passing, he would be left to confront his shortcomings in utter isolation.

His instructors had mentioned the Corpselands, as the ultimate trial awaiting him at the culmination of this phase of his training. Despite his inquiries, they remained tight-lipped, and all he gleaned was that although most trainees faced the trial after their first year at the Tower, Gunnar would be facing it in less than three months…

Gunnar had known the training would be challenging, but he hadn't anticipated the ordeal it would become under Commander Aelric's watchful eye. The disdain in Aelric's gaze was a constant reminder of how little he thought of Gunnar. The Commander, despite his status as a Sage, clung to his military title, perhaps to distance himself from the more scholarly Sages who led the training departments.

Every morning, Gunnar found himself alone in the training yard, pushing his limits. The clink of his sword against the practice dummy and the hum of his magic were the only sounds that accompanied his grueling routines. Aelric's sharp voice echoed in his mind. "Vellhorian meditation is as weak as their magic. Focus, Gunnar!" The sting of those words drove him harder, determined to prove his worth as a battle mage.

The memory of his spiritual scan with Sage Thadwick was still fresh. The sage had looked at him with a mixture of curiosity and respect when the scan revealed Gunnar's latent abilities. "A battle mage," Thadwick had announced, confirming Gunnar's unique blend of martial prowess and magical aptitude. It was a rare designation, one that demanded rigorous and demanding training.

One evening, after a particularly exhausting session, Gunnar collapsed onto the ground, staring up at the darkening sky. The thin aura of Vellhor had always made meditation difficult. He remembered overhearing other Sages discuss the realms during his early days at the Tower. "Vellhor's thin aura and poor magical education make it the weakest," one had said, and Gunnar couldn't help but feel the truth in those words.

Despite the challenges, the Tower of Absence regularly accepted applicants from Vellhor. The presence of Dwarves and Elves from his home realm was a testament to that. Gunnar often wondered if the Tower saw something in Vellhorians that others did not.

As he continued his solitary training, Gunnar reflected on the different mages he had learned about upon joining the battle mage training department: elemental mages, craft mages, and shadow mages. Each had their own unique talents and specialties, but none combined martial and magical skills quite like battle mages.

The training was rigorous, demanding a seamless integration of combat skills with arcane knowledge. Gunnar's sessions were a blend of physical and magical exertion, leaving him exhausted but exhilarated. The fusion of combat and magic felt natural, exhilarating even. As he trained, the weight of Aelric's scorn seemed to lift slightly.

Commander Aelric watched from the shadows, his expression unreadable. Gunnar didn't need his approval to know he was improving. The thrill of his newfound abilities and the prospect of what he could become fueled his every move.

One evening after the grueling classes had finally ended, an exhausted Gunnar found himself ambushed by several students led by a towering Minotaur named Urlok. Though Gunnar had never crossed paths with Urlok before, he had heard enough whispers to know of the Minotaur's brutal reputation.

"It's the Dwarf who thinks he's special," Urlok scoffed.

"Wonder why he thinks that?" retorted one of his companions. "Maybe he needs bringing down a peg."

Surrounded by hostile faces, Gunnar surveyed the scene with a calm that surprised even him, unsure whether it was his training at the Tower or his time with the Snow Wolves that granted him mastery over the primal instinct of dread.

"Either piss off or make it count, lads," Gunnar said. He sighed heavily as he heard their chuckles in response. "You've been warned," he grumbled, shaking his head.

With a ferocious snarl, Urlok lunged forward, his massive fists wreathed in crackling orange flames. Gunnar's instincts screamed for him to meet the onslaught head-on, to clash in a whirlwind of steel and fire. But his recent training in the arcane arts gave him options—subtler yet more potent tactics.

Gunnar tapped into the wellspring of power within him, feeling the familiar rush of energy as he reached out to manipulate time itself. Memories of his first encounter with time manipulation, battling the golem, flooded his mind.

As Urlok's fists hurtled towards him with bone-shattering force, Gunnar surrendered to the tranquility of his inner calm, allowing time to slow to a crawl around him. In that suspended moment, he felt a sense of clarity and purpose, his every movement guided by the ebb and flow of temporal currents.

With practiced grace and the luxury of manipulated time, Gunnar effortlessly sidestepped Urlok's thunderous charge, feeling a slight breeze as his opponent moved past him. Without hesitation, he swiftly retaliated with a lightning-quick jab aimed at Urlok's exposed midsection.

Energy crackled as Gunnar's fist found its mark, the impact sending a shockwave rippling through the air. In that fleeting moment, time seemed to stand still completely, allowing Gunnar to savor the satisfaction of his precise strike before the inevitable chaos of battle resumed.

Urlok grunted in pain and launched himself at Gunnar with a roar that seemed to shake the very foundations of the

Tower, his horns gleaming in the dim light. Gunnar braced himself, summoning the arcane energies coursing through his veins to shield himself from the impending onslaught.

As Urlok closed in, Gunnar's senses sharpened with the battle magic coursing through him. The crackle of magic filled the air, intensifying with each passing second. With flames licking at his massive form, Urlok charged, but his movements were sluggish compared to Gunnar's magically augmented sense of time.

Gunnar's movements were a blur of speed leaving the Minotaur with a broken cheekbone and several cracked ribs.

Tapping into the essence of his spirit, Gunnar channeled the swirling energies around him, intricately weaving them together until Urlok staggered under the magical pressure, before Gunnar unleashed a sudden surge of magic that sent Urlok crashing into the wall.

In a final desperate gambit, Urlok charged head down, his horns aimed straight for Gunnar's heart. But Gunnar was ready. With a flicker of his fingers, he summoned a barrier of shimmering energy that deflected the Minotaur's attack, sending him crashing to the ground with a deafening thud.

As time resumed its normal course, Gunnar stood over the fallen Minotaur, his breath ragged from the intensity of the struggle. He knelt beside Urlok. "It is the absence of mercy that forges a warrior's steel," he whispered, his voice carrying the weight of an executioner. With a swift motion, he grasped Urlok's horns with both hands and, with magically enhanced strength, snapped them off.

As the horns of the Minotaur clattered to the ground, Gunnar stood u and turned to confront the onlookers, his gaze meeting that of Commander Aelric. The commander's expression was inscrutable.

In that moment, Gunnar felt a profound shift within himself. He had come to the tower as a warrior. Now he was a battle mage. Yet as he stood amidst the aftermath of his victory, a flicker of doubt tugged at the edges of his consciousness.

Had the Tower changed him for the better, honing his skills and fortifying his spirit? Or had it wrought a darker transformation, hardening his heart and blurring the line between justice and vengeance?

Aelric

Aelric turned from the fight in the hallway, his expression thoughtful. The Dwarf had conducted himself well, but that lumbering ox Urlok was about as useful as wings crafted from lead. Aelric shook his head, certain the Minotaur wouldn't last long in the unforgiving Corpselands. Casualties were common in that realm, and Aelric couldn't alter the final trial even if he wanted to. Either Urlok would surprise him and become a battle mage, or he would die. It was that simple. It was that brutal.

Aelric's disdain for the Dwarf lingered like a bitter aftertaste. Normally, he had the authority to recommend candidates for battle mage selection to the Sovereign. But this Dwarf, ushered in by Thalirion no less, was thrust into his department, and Sovereign Tarsha insisted on Gunnar's training under Aelric's personal tutelage.

Aelric sighed, acknowledging his own stubbornness. His centuries-long feud with Thalirion drove his reluctance, fueled by the Elf's responsiblity for the accident that claimed Aelric's eye and left the searing burn scar across his face. Despite his antipathy, Aelric begrudgingly recognized Gunnar's progress. However, the decision to expedite Gunnar's training ensured Aelric could absolve himself of responsibility whatever happened. The implicit directive was to push the Dwarf to his limits. If Gunnar succeeded, it would be a triumph but if he faltered and perished in the trial, Aelric could remind them he had never endorsed Gunnar's candidacy from the start.

After witnessing Gunnar's performance against Urlok, Aelric accepted, with some reluctance, that it was time for the Dwarf to face a greater challenge. He made his way to the instructors' chamber where Sages Zanders and Raveena, were engaged in a hushed discussion.

Sage Zanders, a warrior hailing from the realm of Malanth, greeted Aelric with a nod. Standing tall like Aelric, Zanders' scars bore witness to the experience of long-fought battles, His piercing blue eyes radiated an aura of authority, while his unique trait—a serpentine scorpion tail from his Malanthian heritage—loomed ominously over his shoulder, ready to strike at a moment's notice.

Sage Raveena was an Elf from the realm of Erros, epitomizing grace and lethal beauty. Aelric caught a glimpse of her smile as she glanced up at him, her tall stature and silver hair distinguishing her from the shorter Elves of Vellhor. While her expression projected unwavering loyalty to Commander Aelric, her every movement—fluid yet calculated—spoke of the danger lurking behind her beautiful facade.

Aelric joined them at the table, the flickering torchlight casting shifting shadows across the room, as they discussed the details of the impending trial for the Dwarf whose stubborn determination had managed to draw their grudging respect.

Sage Zanders leaned forward, his scorpion tail twitching restlessly behind him. "This trial must push him to his limits," he growled, "Gunnar's strength lies in his raw power, but he lacks finesse. We need to test his adaptability in combat."

Sage Raveena, her eyes shimmering with an ethereal glow, nodded in agreement. "Indeed," she murmured, her voice carrying an otherworldly resonance. "But let us not forget the importance of mental fortitude. Gunnar's struggles with doubt could be his undoing. We must select a trial that challenges his resolve as much as his physical skills."

"Agreed," Aelric conceded, as he considered the many trials available to him. Eventually, he looked up, his mind made up. "The Labyrinth seems an adequate trial for Gunnar at this stage."

The two Sages shared a look before Raveena's soft voice broke the silence. "That trial is designed for an Overlord. Gunnar is only in the Foundation Element, not yet a Master, even."

Aelric looked thoughtful for a moment. "Then we will allow him to complete it with companions." The three instructors looked at each other before they nodded their agreement, their decision confirmed.

"What of the final trial, the Corpselands? When will he undertake that?" Zander's tail twitched as he spoke.

"In just under three months' time," Aelric confirmed.

Raveena, her seductive voice grabbing the attention of both Aelric and Zanders, spoke. "We must consider the risks. Gunnar hasn't encountered adversaries of this magnitude before. While Urlok presented a challenge, it doesn't reflect the level of difficulty of the Corpselands. Even the Labyrinth, despite its challenges, won't adequately prepare him for the dangers of this final trial. Are we prepared to accept the consequences if he fails?"

Sage Zanders scoffed dismissively. "Failure is a luxury he cannot afford," he declared, his scorpion tail lashing out emphatically. "Gunnar must prove himself worthy. If he cannot rise to the challenge, then he is not fit to bear the title of battle mage."

Sage Raveena's expression remained inscrutable as she spoke, her words carrying an undercurrent of caution. "Which one of us could have faced the Corpselands before a year?" she whispered. "Gunnar's journey has been accelerated, and he has shown great skill, yet will three months be long enough? Let us not underestimate his potential. Imagine what we could create if we had the full year!" Her eyes gleamed with excitement at the thought.

Aelric nodded thoughtfully. The opportunity to grant Gunnar more time for training would be ideal. But time was a luxury they couldn't afford, not with the looming threat on the horizon. "We must strike a balance," he declared. "Time is not on our side. He has three months before the Corpselands. The Sovereign has made that clear. If successful, he is to begin his training in the Intermediate

Element to become an Overlord immediately upon his return."

The two Sages glanced at each other. Although they hid their surprise well, Aelric could still sense it. He continued, "We will proceed with the final trial as planned and monitor Gunnar's progress closely. If it becomes apparent that he is not ready, we will come up with a contingency."

Personally, Aelric had few doubts Gunnar would be ready. Sovereign Tarsha had already approved the use of every performance-enhancing elixir the Tower could manufacture. He would stuff the Dwarf full of pills and potions until he was on the verge of bursting if he had to.

14.

THE WEIGHT OF DESTINIES

"A heavy heart often carries the seeds of profound change."

Thalirion

Thalirion faced Sovereign Tarsha, head of the Tower of Absence, within the grand council chamber. Typically reserved for gatherings of Sages and the Sovereign to address significant affairs, the chamber now hosted only Thalirion and Tarsha.

Seated at the head of the grand table, Sovereign Tarsha basked in the soft torchlight, commanding attention with her regal presence. Tall and graceful, she epitomized the beauty typical of the Elves of Erros. Opulent waves of black and gold hair framed her face, and cascaded around her shoulders, glistening like spun silk in the dimly lit chamber.

In contrast, Thalirion stood a foot shorter, a testament to his Elven lineage from Vellhor. Though lacking in height compared to the Elves of Erros, his quiet dignity commanded respect. "Your Grace," Thalirion began, "I come seeking counsel regarding the dire situation in Vellhor."

Although Sovereign Tarsha regarded him with sympathy her tone was reserved. "Speak, Thalirion," she said. "I am aware of the issues in Vellhor, but I would appreciate hearing your assessment of the situation."

Thalirion took a deep breath. "As we already knew, the Drogo Mulik are attempting to raise their god, Nergai," he explained, his voice grave. "They have already destroyed the Sacred Tree, the spiritual emblem of The Great Elven Forest, and with it the only viable portal to and from Nexus. Should they succeed in resurrecting Nergai, he will bring untold destruction upon Vellhor and potentially the seven realms."

Sovereign Tarsha's brow furrowed. "I understand the threat posed by the Drogo Mulik and their god, Nergai," she replied, her voice tinged with regret. "But as Sovereign of the Tower of Absence, I am bound by certain restrictions. We cannot interfere in the affairs of realms or engage in political conflicts." She sighed heavily. "As much as I regret the situation, there is unfortunately nothing I can do."

Thalirion's expression hardened. "But surely, Your Grace, the might of the Tower could quash this threat before it escalates further," he pressed, desperation creeping into his voice. "With the power of the Overlords, Sages, and yourself, we could stand against Nergai and protect our lands."

Sovereign Tarsha sighed heavily, her gaze falling to the floor. "Believe me, Thalirion, if it were within my power, I would do everything in my capacity as Sovereign to aid Vellhor," she confessed, her voice tinged with sorrow. "But the laws that bind us are strict, and to violate them would risk destabilizing the delicate balance of power among the realms."

Thalirion clenched his jaw in frustration, but he could not fault Tarsha's reasoning. The laws that governed the Tower were ancient and immutable, designed to maintain order and prevent the escalation of conflicts between realms.

"Then what can be done?" Thalirion demanded. "Surely, you cannot stand idly by as Nergai threatens to engulf us all in fire and ash."

Sovereign Tarsha's expression reflected the anguish of her own powerlessness. "I have agreed to train Gunnar and Anwyn to raise them to the ranks of Overlords and potentially even Sages," she explained, her voice heavy with resignation. "But beyond that, my hands are tied. I can offer no more aid."

Thalirion's heart sank at her words. "Surely, Sovereign, there is something you can do. No matter how small, any aid will be appreciated greatly."

Tarsha looked pensive, her slender finger and thumb gently rubbing her porcelain face. "I can allow you to request aid from any Master, Overlord, or Sage who originally hailed from Vellhor." Thalirion nodded appreciatively, but before he could speak, Tarsha interrupted him. "Remember, Thalirion, I said request. You are not to order anyone. If they wish to provide aid, then so be it."

Thalirion knew there was little else he could do. Even this small concession from the Sovereign would help their cause immensely. He bowed his head deferentially.

"Thank you, Your Grace, for your counsel," he said, his voice tinged with sorrow. "I will return to Anwyn and do what I can to prepare her for the coming storm."

Sovereign Tarsha offered him a sympathetic smile, her expression one of shared burden. "May the spirit of the forest watch over you, Thalirion," she said, softly. "And may you find the strength to weather the trials ahead."

With a final nod of gratitude, Thalirion turned and made his way out of the council chamber, his heart heavy with the knowledge that the fate of Vellhor hung in the balance and that the full aid of the Tower would not be forthcoming.

Outside the council chamber, the bustling activity of the Tower continued, oblivious to the weighty discussions that had taken place within. Novices hurried past, lost in their studies and training, while the hum of magical energy permeated the air, a constant reminder of the Tower's purpose.

Thalirion wandered the halls aimlessly, his thoughts consumed by the looming threat of Nergai and the seemingly insurmountable obstacles they faced. He knew he had to remain strong for Anwyn and the people of Vellhor, but the burden of responsibility weighed heavily upon him.

As Thalirion turned a corner, his eyes widened in surprise at the scene unfolding before him. There, amidst the echoing corridors of the Tower, Gunnar and a Minotaur Thalirion knew to be Urlok were engaged in a fierce fight. Spells crackled through the air, accompanied by the resounding thud of powerful blows.

Thalirion watched in awe as Gunnar, the once magically inept Dwarf from Vellhor, displayed a level of skill and mastery that surpassed his wildest expectations. The transformation was remarkable—from a mere novice two weeks ago to a formidable battle mage, potentially even closing in on the rank of Master. Gunnar had come a long way in a remarkably short time.

Yet amidst his admiration, a pang of concern tugged at Thalirion's heart. He couldn't help but worry that in Gunnar's rapid ascent through the arcane arts, he may have sacrificed a part of his pure spirit. But it was an inevitable consequence, Thalirion supposed. When one needed to progress as swiftly and as far as Gunnar did, sacrifices were bound to be made.

With a heavy sigh, Thalirion tore his gaze away from the spectacle before him. He knew there was little he could do to intervene—Gunnar was already well beyond his tutelage. Instead, he turned on his heel and made his way back the way he came, the clatter of horns falling to the floor echoing in his ears as he left the scene behind.

Anwyn

The air within the training chamber crackled with raw magic as Anwyn stood poised in the center, surrounded by torches casting flickering shadows on the white marble walls. She focused her thoughts, attuning her mind to the elemental forces pulsating around her. With a whispered incantation, she summoned an orb of flame into existence, its fiery glow casting an ethereal light upon her features. With a steady hand, she manipulated the flames, guiding them through intricate patterns and shapes, honing her control over the element of fire.

Stretching the orange orb, she elongated it until it resembled a three-foot stick. Creating two large air pockets at either end, she switched her breathing pattern to conjure a new element—water. Filling the air pockets with conjured water, she twirled the stick, marveling at the combination of two opposing elements. Positioning the stick vertically as though it were a bow, she summoned air and mimicked pulling back its string. As she released, she uttered a soft incantation, and a bolt of lightning shot forth.

Anwyn had learned that creating lightning involved combining fire, water, and air in a precise manner. It began with conjuring fire, infusing the surrounding air with intense heat. Water enhanced conductivity, facilitating the flow of electricity within the charged atmosphere. Finally, air served as the conduit for the electrical charge, guiding it toward the target. Through focused concentration, a brilliant bolt of lightning was formed.

Lorelei, Anwyn's familiar, jumped up and down on her shoulder, her bell-like chatter bringing a smile to Anwyn's face. "I know," Anwyn said softly. "This would never have been possible in Vellhor."

Thalirion coughed, startling Anwyn. She hadn't noticed him enter the chamber. "Ahem... it is possible in Vellhor. The elemental forces are just not understood properly there." Anwyn bowed her head in both greeting and acknowledgment, knowing her mentor was correct.

"Remember, Anwyn," Thalirion's voice echoed through the chamber, "the elements are potent forces. Respect and understand their powers, and they will serve your commands."

Anwyn nodded attentively, her mind racing with the implications of Thalirion's teaching. The elemental forces had always fascinated her, but under Thalirion's guidance, their significance had become clearer. Fire, with its passion and destructive potential, demanded respect and control. Water, flowing and intuitive, held the secrets of emotion. Air, with its boundless freedom and clarity, whispered truths beyond the tangible. And earth, solid and grounded, nurtured growth and stability.

Remembering her parents' teachings and the countless hours spent practicing with them Anwyn now realized how little they truly knew.

Under Thalirion's direction, Anwyn's understanding of the elements had expanded beyond what she had ever imagined. She saw the interconnectedness of all things—the balance between creation and destruction, fluidity and stability, freedom and constraint. Each element held a key to unlocking greater power within her.

However, as she continued her training, Anwyn had appreciated that mastery of the arcane arts required more than just power and knowledge—it demanded reverence for the powers governing both the arcane and the physical. With each passing day, she grew more determined to unlock the secrets of the elements and wield their power with wisdom and humility.

Thalirion's voice cut through her reverie, bringing her back to the present. "Now, Anwyn," he continued, his tone grave yet filled with anticipation, "let us delve into the path of advancement within the arcane arts."

Anwyn listened intently as Thalirion outlined the progression of mastery in the arcane arts. "At the foundational level," he began, "one starts as a Novice, learning the basic principles and techniques of magic. It is a time of discovery and experimentation, laying the groundwork for future growth."

"In Vellhor, under the tutelage of your parents," Thalirion continued, "you reached what we call the Intermediate Element, attaining the rank equivalent to what we know as a Master. Here in Nexus, you have demonstrated a deeper understanding of magic, honing your skills and delving into more complex spells and incantations. I believe you are on the brink of advancing to the next rank: Overlord."

Anwyn's heart swelled with pride at the realization of how far she had come. She had achieved the level of Master during her training in Vellhor, which she thought was her limit. Now, under Thalirion's tutelage, she stood on the verge of advancing to Overlord. A month ago, she didn't even know what an Overlord was.

Thalirion's voice brought her back to the present. "Beyond the realm of Mastery lie the Advanced Elements—Overlord, Sage, and Sovereign. These titles represent the pinnacle of magical attainment, achieved only by those who have proven themselves worthy of wielding great power."

Anwyn's pulse quickened at the mention of these titles. To become an Overlord, a Sage, or even a Sovereign was a dream she had dared not voice aloud since she discovered what they were. Yet now, with Thalirion's guidance, it all felt within reach, as if the stars themselves were aligning to grant her deepest desires.

"And for those who seek true mastery—the truly exceptional," Thalirion's voice took on a solemn tone, "there exists the Expert Element, where only the most gifted and dedicated practitioners dare to tread. Here, one may aspire to become a Supreme Archmage, wielding power beyond imagination and shaping the very fabric of reality."

Anwyn's honey-colored eyes locked onto Thalirion's. "Is there a Supreme Archmage here? At the Tower?" she asked. Thalirion let out a small chuckle and gently shook his head. "Apologies, Anwyn. There have only ever been four Archmages in the history of the Boria Stellar Expanse."

Anwyn was puzzled. "Is the rank of Archmage attainable then?"

"Everything is attainable, Anwyn," Thalirion paused, allowing his words to linger, "but the path to such heights is fraught with challenges and sacrifices. To reach the pinnacle of power, one must possess not only exceptional talent but also unwavering determination, unyielding resolve, and a boundless thirst for knowledge."

Anwyn absorbed his words, her mind racing with questions. "And what of those who have achieved the rank of Archmage? What becomes of them?"

A shadow crossed Thalirion's face. "The fate of Archmages is a mystery. Some say they ascend to a higher plane of existence, transcending mortal limitations. Others believe they withdraw from the Boria Solar Expanse completely, seeking solitude and contemplation of the cosmos. And then there are whispers of darker fates, of power consuming them utterly."

Anwyn's heart quickened at the thought of such fates, both wondrous and terrifying. "I… I understand," she murmured, her gaze fixed on Thalirion, searching for answers in his enigmatic demeanor.

"But fear not, Anwyn," Thalirion said, his voice soft yet reassuring. "The journey you embark upon is yours to shape. The path you tread may be fraught with uncertainty, but it is also filled with boundless potential. Trust in your abilities and let your passion guide you. Only then will you unlock the secrets of the arcane arts and forge your own path."

Anwyn nodded, determination flickering in her eyes. "I will not falter," she declared, her voice steady with resolve. "I will strive to become more than I am."

Thalirion smiled, a glimmer of pride shining in his eyes. "Then you are ready, Anwyn. Ready to take your understanding of the arcane arts to new heihts."

Thalirion paused, allowing Anwyn a moment to absorb the significance of his words. "As you embark on the journey to becoming an Overlord," he went on solemnly, "you must prepare yourself for profound transformations—both in mind and body."

Anwyn's breath caught in her throat, her heart pounding with excitement and trepidation. She had heard snippets of such discussions before, but a full explanation from Thalirion was something she had not anticipated.

"In terms of your mind," Thalirion continued, "you will undergo a profound expansion of consciousness. Your capacity for understanding and manipulating magical energies will increase tenfold, allowing you to grasp the most intricate spells and incantations with ease."

Anwyn's mind raced with the possibilities. To be raised to such heights was both exhilarating and daunting, like staring into the vast expanse of the night sky and realizing just how small one truly was.

"But with this heightened mental acuity comes great responsibility," Thalirion's voice brought her back to the present. "You will be tasked with wielding magic of unprecedented complexity and potency, and the consequences of your actions will ripple through the fabric of reality itself."

Anwyn nodded, determined to bear the burden of her destiny.

"And as for your body," Thalirion's voice took on a gentler tone, "it too will undergo changes as it becomes attuned to the flow of magical energy. You may find yourself experiencing heightened senses, increased stamina, and even physical enhancements such as strength and agility."

Anwyn's eyes widened in astonishment at the thought of such physical transformations. She had always known that magic had the power to reshape reality, but to witness its effects firsthand on her own body was something she had never imagined.

"But be warned," Thalirion cautioned, his expression grave, "the path to becoming an Overlord can be dangerous, and the toll it takes on your body can be great. The rigorous demands of magical training can lead to exhaustion, strain, and even physical deformities if one is not careful."

Anwyn swallowed hard. She knew that the road ahead would be filled with challenges and obstacles that would test her strength and resolve to their very limits. But she also knew that she was ready—ready to embrace her destiny and become the master of her own fate.

15.
Forging Paths and Perils

"Strength is born from the fires of trial and the shadows of challenge."

Karl

Compared to Gunnar's grueling training regimen, Karl knew he had it easy. He could see the haunted look in Gunnar's eyes when he returned in the evenings, always exhausted, his body battered and bleeding from the day's trials. When Gunnar didn't return in the evening, when days passed without a word from his friend, worry gnawed at Karl's insides.

Each time Gunnar went missing, Karl's concern grew, his imagination conjuring up the worst possible scenarios. And when Gunnar finally did return, it was as if he had been through the void and back—a broken shell of his former self.

Karl's training was a leisurely stroll compared to the torture the aspiring battle mage endured. Yet, despite the stark contrast between their experiences at the Tower, Karl couldn't help but admire Gunnar's resilience and determination. Not once had the Dwarf uttered a complaint or a foul word toward his instructors or about his training.

Karl's own training in the arcane art of craft magic had captivated him from the moment he set foot in the Tower igniting a passion within him he hadn't known existed. Though he had only been training for a few weeks, Karl had already made up his mind to stay at the Tower for as long as possible, eager to delve deeper into the mysteries of Spiritsmithing.

What seemed like a lifetime ago, back when they were prisoners in Fort Bjerg , he had told Gunnar of his desire to leave the army. Shortly afterwards they had stupidly hurled themselves off a cliff. Karl chuckled at the absurdity of it all, reminded of Hansen—or Draeg, the god of fate, as he now knew him to be. Shaking his head, Karl marveled at the twists and turns of fate that had led him to this moment. "Talk about being in the wrong place at the wrong time," he mused.

Despite being unwillingly dragged into this storm of chaos, Karl felt this was exactly where he was meant to be. Under the guidance of Sage Thadwick, Karl's journey into craft magic had taken on new depth and complexity. The eccentric old Dwarf, with his bushy beard and twinkling eyes, proved to be a font of wisdom and knowledge, imparting the secrets of Spiritsmithing with a mixture of patience and enthusiasm.

As Karl delved into his studies, he discovered that craft magic was not just about understanding runes or weaving spells and enchantments, but about tapping into the very essence of magical energy that permeated the world. With Sage Thadwick's guidance, he learned to perceive the subtle currents of magic that flowed through the air, guiding his hands as he shaped and molded raw energy into intricate constructs.

One of the most fascinating aspects of his training was the art of crafting constructs on the go, in the heat of battle— a skill most Spiritsmiths lacked. But with Karl's military background, being thrust into danger was something he had been well trained for, and being able to remain calm and collected while crafting a construct suited his skill set perfectly.

Thadwick explained that a construct was not merely a physical object but an abstract concept brought to life through mental synthesis. With practice and focus, Karl found himself able to manifest constructs using raw material from spectral echoes and infuse them with his magic, shaping them to suit his needs, ready for battle or moments of crisis.

It was a revelation to Karl that he could create something out of spectral echoes, imbuing them with his will, summoning forth magical constructs that could be used as weapons, for healing, or for simple everyday things.

Under Thadwick's tutelage, one of the first constructs he crafted was a healing orb using the soul shard from a spectral echo that resembled a large dog. Removing the shard was gruesome work, like a butcher preparing a carcass. He grew accustomed to the grim work, however, developing a detached efficiency in handling the spectral echoes' remnants. Once completed, the construct pulsated with soothing energies and emanated a gentle glow, providing a serene ambiance wherever it hovered.

To activate the healing orb, the user would focus their thoughts on the intended recipient, directing the orb to hover near them. As it drew close, the orb would emit a soft hum, and tendrils of shimmering life energy would extend from its core, enveloping the individual in a comforting embrace.

Unfortunately, the power of his construct was limited. The soul shard he used was not finite. Eventually, its power waned, and the construct faded from existence. While these temporary constructs created on the fly could prove extremely useful they were often of limited use and only suited to use in emergencies or the heat of battle.

Fortunately, there were constructs that lasted longer and were far more powerful. These needed to be crafted in what Sage Thadwick called a spirit foundry. Luckily, Karl had access to the Tower's foundry. There, with Sage Thadwick's assistance, he worked on a special project—something that would put his training to the ultimate test.

Understanding the trials that awaited Gunnar, Karl embarked on the formidable task of crafting a magical axe worthy of the battle mage's prowess. Drawing upon his newfound knowledge of craft magic, Karl delved deep into the arcane arts, channeling his focus and energy into the creation.

Each strike of the hammer resonated with purpose, every rune etched and enchantment woven poured not only Karl's skill but also his spirit into the frosteel. He researched tomes and scrolls to identify the most compatible spectral echoes to imbue into the axe. The process was an intricate blend of research, craftsmanship and magic, each element carefully balanced to ensure the weapon's power and resilience.

As the days turned into weeks, the axe began to take shape under Karl's skilled hands, its blade gleaming with otherworldly energy and its haft pulsing with the power of spectral echoes.

Standing before the unfinished axe, his hands still tingling with the residual magic of his craft, Karl felt a sense of pride swell within him. Though the weapon was not yet complete, Karl knew that once finished, it would be a powerful tool in Gunnar's hands, ready to face the challenges that lay ahead.

Kemp

Kemp stood in his chamber, his gaze fixed on the shadowy form of his hand. It had been a week since the appendage had fused onto his wrist, and mastering its capabilities had proven a daunting challenge. During his early efforts, the shadow hand had seemed to have a mind of its own, moving with an unnerving fluidity that defied his commands.

Refusing to give up, he had concentrated harder, pushing past the doubt and uncertainty clouding his thoughts. Slowly, the shadow hand had begun to respond, its movements jerky and uncoordinated at first, but gradually growing smoother and more controlled.

A sense of triumph had surged through Kemp the first time he compelled the shadow hand to obey his commands, making his thumb meet each fingertip in turn. The small victory had filled him with newfound confidence.

Kemp's reverie was broken by Thraxos's sudden entrance, his massive form filling the doorframe. "Show me what you can do," Thraxos rumbled, his voice echoing in the cavernous chamber.

With a determined nod, Kemp demonstrated his control over the shadow hand, performing a series of intricate movements with increasing skill and finesse.

Thraxos watched in silence, his gaze intense. After a moment, he nodded approvingly. "Impressive," he admitted grudgingly. "You have made considerable progress."

Pride swelled within Kemp at the Minotaur's praise. He had overcome countless obstacles to reach this point and was determined to push himself further.

Thraxos regarded Kemp thoughtfully before speaking again. "I believe you are ready for the next step," he said. "But be warned, the trial ahead will test your strength, your resolve, and your mastery of the arcane arts."

Kemp's heart raced with anticipation. He had come too far to turn back now. "I am ready," he declared firmly.

Thraxos nodded, a hint of respect in his gaze. "Very well. Follow me."

Together, Kemp and Thraxos ventured deep into the heart of the Tower, their footsteps echoing in the silence. Eventually, they arrived at the entrance to the Labyrinth, a twisting maze of corridors and chambers shrouded in darkness.

"The Labyrinth is a place of ancient mysteries and untold dangers," Thraxos explained gravely. "Only those who possess true strength and courage can hope to navigate its depths."

With a steady breath, Kemp stepped forward, his shadow hand pulsing with energy at his side. He knew the trial ahead would be the greatest challenge he had ever faced, but he was determined to succeed.

Thraxos's large hand rested on Kemp's shoulder, preventing him from venturing any further. "You misunderstand me, Kemp," the Minotaur said with a snort.

"You are not to partake in this trial. If you did, you would die. You are not strong enough yet."

Confusion crossed Kemp's face as he stared into the depths of the Labyrinth. "Then why are we here?" he asked.

"You are to use the skills you have gained to run the trial for three candidates on the brink of their advancement."

Kemp's shoulders sagged in disappointment. "How will this test my abilities in the arcane arts?" he asked despondently.

"Come," Thraxos said, gesturing for Kemp to follow. Kemp nodded and followed the Minotaur into a spiraling staircase to the side of the entrance. The staircase opened up into a large room. "Welcome to the Viewing Chamber for the Labyrinth trials," Thraxos proclaimed.

The Viewing Chamber was a large room bathed in the soft glow of magical illumination. As Kemp stepped inside, he was struck by the vastness of the space and the panoramic view it offered of the Labyrinth below. Tall arched windows lined the circular chamber, offering glimpses of the twisting corridors and hidden chambers that comprised the arcane maze.

At the center of the room stood a raised platform with three large crystals mounted on it. Each crystal glimmered with an ethereal light, pulsating with raw arcane energy. Kemp could sense the power emanating from them, a tangible presence humming in harmony with the very essence of magic itself.

Thraxos led Kemp to the control panel positioned in the center of the platform. The panel was adorned with intricate runes and glyphs, its surface shimmering with latent energy. Thraxos gestured toward it with a grave expression.

"This is the control panel," he explained, his voice echoing in the chamber. "With it, you will be able to manipulate the obstacles and challenges within the Labyrinth trials."

Kemp studied the control panel intently, his mind racing with possibilities. He sensed the intricate web of magic woven into its design, a complex network of spells and incantations waiting to be unleashed.

"Thraxos," Kemp began, his voice also echoing softly in the expansive chamber, "what exactly are these trials? And why is mastering them so crucial?"

Thraxos turned to face Kemp, his gaze intense. "The Labyrinth is one of many trials at the Tower. The trials are a test of strength, skill, and cunning," he explained. "Those who seek to advance in the arcane arts must prove themselves worthy by navigating the challenges within."

Kemp's curiosity was piqued. "But what do the trials entail?" he pressed.

Thraxos's expression grew solemn. "The trials are different for each participant," he replied cryptically. "They are designed to push you to the limits of your specialism, to test your resolve and your ability to harness the power of magic." Thraxos paused, allowing his words to sink in. "But be warned," he continued. "To control the Labyrinth, you must draw upon your knowledge of the arcane arts, particularly elemental magic. Each obstacle the participants encounter will also test your mastery of the elements—fire, water, earth, and air."

"But I have not studied the elements here in Nexus," Kemp questioned.

"You have a clear affinity with them. Now that you understand how to fill your spirit with aura, your powers will be considerably stronger. Use the knowledge you learned in Vellhor," Thraxos declared.

Kemp nodded. He had spent years honing his skills as a mage in Vellhor, and he was ready to put his knowledge to the test.

With a deep breath, Kemp reached out toward the control panel, his fingers hovering over the runes etched into its surface. He could feel the magic coursing through him, a powerful current flowing from his very core.

Closing his eyes, Kemp focused his mind, drawing upon the elemental energies that surrounded him. With a whispered incantation, he channeled his will into the control panel, commanding it to activate the trials below.

As the crystals hummed to life, the chamber filled with a kaleidoscope of colors, each representing a different element. Kemp could sense the obstacles shifting and rearranging within the Labyrinth, responding to his commands with fluid grace.

With a sense of satisfaction, Kemp opened his eyes and gazed out over the Labyrinth below. The trials awaited, and he was ready to do his part in testing these competitors, armed with the power of the arcane and the knowledge he had earned through years of study and practice.

"Now, Kemp!" Thraxos interrupted. "Let us go back and work on some more exercises. The trials do not commence for another week. During that time, I have plenty for you to do!" As Kemp released his control over the Labyrinth, the colors in the chamber dimmed, and the obstacles ceased their movements. "Will I get to return here before the trials begin?" Kemp asked hopefully. He was looking forward to learning more about how the controls could manipulate the various challenges within the trial.

"Yes, we will spend a few hours here each day learning and understanding the controls and the various obstacles you can operate." Kemp nodded and began following Thraxos back down the staircase.

Upon returning to his room, Kemp settled onto his bed, causing his pack to tumble to the floor with a metallic clatter. The sound intrigued Thraxos who turned back to face the room.

Leaning forward, Kemp retrieved the broken crown that had made the noise and lifted it up before him. Once again, he found himself entranced by the intricate markings adorning its surface.

Thraxos approached cautiously, his expression wary. "This is no ordinary artifact," he murmured. "It holds great power, but also great danger."

As Kemp studied the crown intently, his mind raced with possibilities. Initially, when he first laid eyes on the crown, he felt no magical energy emanating from it. Yet now, a shift had occurred; he could sense the latent potential within it, vast reservoirs of magic waiting to be harnessed. A surge of anticipation coursed through him, tingling in his veins like dormant power awakening. His shadow hand twitched involuntarily, a reflexive response to the magic's call, and Kemp had to exert mental restraint to prevent it from reaching out toward the crown.

"Where did you get this from, Kemp?" Thraxos asked, his eyes darting to Kemp's shadow hand as he watched him struggle to restrain it.

Kemp recounted how he had found the crown in Nergai's tomb shortly before being knocked unconscious and awakening here in Nexus.

Thraxos nodded. "Kemp, may I take this and study it for a while?" he asked. Kemp reluctantly agreed, his hand still twitching to reach for the crown.

Thraxos

Thraxos cradled the broken crown in his hands, the cold metal sending a shiver up his spine as he navigated the labyrinthine corridors of the Tower. The flickering torchlight cast long shadows on the stone walls, making the journey feel even more ominous. His mind raced with questions. What secrets did this crown hold? Why had its power remained hidden from him for so long?

At last, the heavy wooden door to Thalirion's chambers loomed before him. Thraxos paused to catch his breath before raising his hand to knock.

The door creaked open, revealing Thalirion's scholarly visage. "Thraxos, what brings you here?" the Elf welcomed him warmly, before his brows knitted together, eyes widening in surprise as they landed on the broken crown in Thraxos's hands.

Wordlessly, Thraxos stepped forward, extending the crown towards his friend. "Thalirion, I have found something of great significance," he began. "This crown was discovered by the human within the depths of Nergai's tomb." As he spoke, Thraxos couldn't shake the unease that had settled in his chest.

BATTLE MAGE (THE VELLHOR SAGA VOLUME 1)

Thalirion's eyes gleamed as he examined the artefact, his fingers delicately tracing the intricate markings etched into its surface. "Remark- able," he murmured, his voice barely more than a whisper. "This is no ordinary crown."

Thraxos nodded solemnly. "Kemp could sense its power," he explained. The flicker of pride he felt for Kemp's growing abilities was tempered by the looming threat the crown represented.

"Which means the human's abilities are growing stronger," Thalirion confirmed, his expression thoughtful. Thraxos could almost see the wheels turning in the Sage's mind, calculating the implications.

"Yes, he has made good progress," Thraxos admitted, though a furrow appeared on his brow. "However, this crown… I am concerned that I could not sense its power earlier. I have spent much time in its presence." The confession felt heavy on his tongue.

Thalirion's expression darkened. "Indeed," he agreed, a note of foreboding in his voice. "The broken crown holds secrets we cannot begin to comprehend. We must tread carefully, I feel its power is both great and dangerous." Thraxos noted the rare hint of fear in Thalirion's eyes, a reflection of his own anxieties.

With a nod of understanding, Thraxos handed the broken crown to Thalirion. The weight lifted from his hands brought a sense of relief, but also an acute awareness of the peril they now faced. As he watched Thalirion handle the artefact, he couldn't help but feel that this was only the beginning of their trials.

16.
WHEN FATE WHISPERS

"The past haunts us, but it also guides us to our destined future."

Fellron

Kneeling upon the unforgiving, chilled rock of the canyon floor, Fellron closed his eyes, allowing the sensation of stone between his fingers to sing in his mind. The aftermath of battle lay scattered around him—broken bodies and discarded weapons whispered of conflict. Yet, it was the silent witness of the stone that held the truth he sought. The weight of his responsibility pressed down on him, mingling with the cold seeping through his skin.

With deliberate motions, he ground the stone between his fingers, focusing his mind, coaxing it to reveal its secrets. He felt a surge of anticipation mixed with dread; the truth could be a double-edged sword. Gradually, the world around him dissolved, and he found himself transported to a shadowed chamber.

Seven towering Drogo shamans encircled a young, petrified Drogo girl, chanting in tongues unknown to Fellron. His heart clenched as he sensed her fear, raw and palpable. As their ritual peaked, each of their blades struck out, carving deep into her flesh, releasing dark, viscous blood that sizzled upon the ground. He felt a shudder of horror and helplessness, the scene imprinted on his mind.

Abruptly, he was thrust back into the canyon, but not to the present. Instead, he found himself witnessing an event which had happened only weeks prior. His breath quickened as he realized he was watching something critical unfold.

A Drogo shaman was performing rites over a mound of stones. The shaman vanished like smoke, replaced by armored Dwarves. The stones trembled and coalesced into a towering golem, sparking a fierce clash. Fellron's pulse quickened, sensing the gravity of the moment.

Amidst the chaos, only two Dwarves remained, the rest obliterated by the golem's fury. One Dwarf stood forward, resolve clear in his eyes. Fellron's eyebrows raised as he felt a pulse of strong magic emanate from the Dwarf. The Dwarf himself looked confused, unsure as to what had happened. Fellron watched intently as the Dwarf strode toward the golem, which was frozen in time. Then, in a burst of force, the golem shattered, and the Dwarf slumped to the ground, unconscious.

As his surroundings faded like smoke around him, Fellron returned to the present day. He surveyed the battlefield understanding that these valiant Dwarves had sacrificed their lives bravely. It was becoming clear that Gunnar had not turned traitor, and his unit must have been betrayed. The realization sparked a determination within him to uncover the truth and honor their sacrifice.

He let out a sharp whistle, and Ghost came bounding over, the majestic white wolf nestling at Fellron's side. The familiar presence of Ghost provided momentary comfort. With practiced ease, he mounted Ghost and urged him toward Fort Bjerg, where he resolved he would uncover more of Gunnar's story.

Ruiha

Ruiha, Dakarai, and Magnus stood at the edge of the massive canyon, peering into the depths, which barred their path to the other side, sealing off their escape route. Ruiha's heart sank as she looked into the abyss, the sheer scale of it threatening to swallow her hope.

Despite still being deep within the Scorched Mountains, a multitude of fissures and apertures above them allowed enough light to filter through so that they could see the obstacle clearly. Ruiha squinted, trying to gauge just how far the canyon extended.

"I thought you had a plan for getting us out of here," Magnus pressed impatiently as he scanned their surroundings.

Dakarai grunted in frustration, his fists clenching involuntarily. "How was I supposed to know the damn arena would be on the wrong side of this chasm?"

"You're a Drogo, and this is your territory, right?" Uleg interjected, with more than a hint of skepticism. The imposing Drogo glared at the older Dwarf, but Ruiha noted with surprise that Uleg didn't flinch or retreat under the weight of Dakarai's intense stare.

Ruiha surveyed the canyon, her mind racing. This couldn't be it, could it? There had to be a way around. She glanced to left and right, but the canyon extended for miles in each direction, an impassable barrier mocking their desperation.

"There might be a through further down," Dakarai suggested, squinting into the distance where the canyon seemed to narrow slightly.

Although doubtful, Ruiha still nodded her agreement. Anything was preferable to staying here and waiting to be recaptured. "It's worth a try. Let's move."

As they made their way along the canyon's edge, the terrain became increasingly treacherous. Loose rocks threatened to give way beneath their feet, and the sheer drop on one side made their progress slow and perilous and Ruiha could feel the tension in the group mounting.

After what felt like hours of precarious maneuvering through the dark, the escaped slaves finally discovered a steep, winding natural trail carved into the canyon wall by the ravages of time. It was barely wide enough for one individual to pass at a time. Ruiha's heart pounded in her chest, the danger of the path looming large.

"We'll have to go one by one." Magnus eyed the narrow path apprehensively, his usually steady hands trembling slightly as he grasped his weapon tighter.

With Dakarai leading the way, the Drogo embarked on their harrowing descent; it was decided that the Dwarves would wait until the Drogo reached the canyon floor to silence any patrolling enemy scouts or warriors. Each footfall was calculated, every handhold tested for stability. The sound of dislodged stones plummeting into the abyss below reverberated through the canyon, amplifying the danger that already loomed over them. Ruiha's breath hitched each time a rock fell, a silent prayer on her lips for safe passage.

As they cautiously navigated the treacherous path, the canyon's shadows deepened, weaving an eerie tapestry of darkness around them. Each step was a dance with fate, the jagged edges of the cliff-side threatening to nudge them into the depths below. Ruiha's muscles ached with the strain.

A sudden cry shattered the stillness, a desperate primal plea for salvation as one of their own lost his footing and careened helplessly into the chasm. His anguished cries echoed off the canyon walls until with a sickening thud, he was gone, swallowed by the jagged rocks of the canyon below.

The remaining members of the group froze in shock, grief intertwining with fear. Although each one of them had their own experiences with death forged in the pit, even the bravest among them must have felt a chill creep into their hearts at the sound of the anguished scream.

Ruiha called the group to attention, shouting to reach those furthest away. "Listen to me," she began. "We may mourn our fallen friend, but we cannot afford to linger here. We do best honor to his memory by pressing forward together."

She looked down the long line of former prisoners and slaves. "Yes, the path ahead is treacherous. But we have been through harder challenges than this. We must see this journey through to its end. We cannot afford to falter now." Ruiha's voice wavered slightly, but the fire in her eyes reignited the flicker of hope that had threatened to dim in the wake of their loss.

Gripped by a newfound sense of purpose, they set forth once more, their footsteps echoing resolutely along the precarious path until, eventually, they reached the darkness at the bottom of the canyon.

The canyon's floor was shrouded in impenetrable gloom. Shadows danced eerily along the rocky terrain, obscuring Ruiha's vision and lending an air of foreboding to the desolate landscape, but she pressed on, determined to find refuge.

Tall cliffs loomed on either side, their outlines barely discernible in the dim light coming through shafts above them. Craggy rocks littered the ground, posing unseen hazards to the unwary traveler. A distant murmur of water hinted at a river somewhere nearby.

With her senses on high alert, Ruiha strained her eyes, searching for any sign of movement or danger in the dark. She knew they needed to make camp and wait for the Dwarves to make the descent safely. Gathering the others close, she told them, "We must find a place to rest until the Dwarves arrive." She scanned the blackness of their surroundins. "Somewhere well-hidden and defensible." Despite the turmoil within her she managed to project a reassuring calmness and strength.

They all worked together to scour the canyon floor, feeling their way through the darkness with cautious steps. Dakarai's keen instincts led them to a small alcove nestled against the base of a cliff, its rocky overhang offering some semblance of security.

Ruiha breathed a sigh of relief, grateful for Dakarai's sharp eyes. As the fire crackled to life, casting a warm glow upon their faces, Ruiha surveyed their makeshift camp with a sense of satisfaction. Despite the unforgiving surroundings, they had created a sanctuary of sorts, where they could rest and regroup while they waited for the Dwarves to join them. She allowed herself a moment of peace, feeling the tension slowly ebb away.

With the camp established, Ruiha turned to offer the others words of encouragement and reassurance. "We may be in the heart of darkness," she said, with conviction, "but as long as we stand together, we will weather whatever challenges come our way." Her words were a promise, both to her companions and to herself. They were not just survivors; they were warriors on a path to reclaim their destiny.

Fellron

Standing on the precipice of a cliff, Fellron staggered to his knees, the ground tilting beneath him. His breath came in ragged gasps, heart pounding as if trying to break free from his chest. He stared into the chasm, the roar of the river below muffled by the turmoil in his mind. It wasn't the sight of Gunnar and his companion plunging into the river that had unsteadied him. No, it was the Dwarf who had urged them to jump that left him reeling.

Vivid painful memories flooded back, each one a sharp dagger to his heart. The Dwarf's face awakened images Fellron had tried to bury deep within the recesses of his mind. He had met this Dwarf nearly two thousand years ago, a lifetime for most but a blink for Fellron. The attack on his farming village, the monstrous cave worm decimating everything he loved, the Dwarf helping him bury his family, those moments seared into his memory—the way the Dwarf's hands had trembled slightly as they worked, the murmured words of comfort that a twelve-year-old Fellron had clung to like a lifeline.

Fellron's fists clenched at the memory of Hansen guiding him to the gates of the Shadowforged. Each trial he endured, every rune-scar that marred his body, he attributed to Hansen. The hatred fueled his resolve, a constant companion through the darkest times. He could almost hear Hansen's voice, calm and steady, urging him to be strong, to survive.

But, seeing Hansen at Gunnar's side just a few weeks ago, utterly unchanged, as if time had no claim on him, shook Fellron to his core. Fellron had aged, his journey with the Shadowforged marked by the passing years, each scar bearing witness to his struggles. How could Hansen look exactly as he did all those centuries ago? The impossibility of it all made him feel like he was teetering on the edge of reality.

Eventually, Fellron forced himself to stand. "Bloody Dreyna!" The curse slipped from his lips as he steadied himself, his voice trembling with confusion and frustration. "I knew this job wouldn't be worth it." Shaking his head, he trekked back up the tunnel, burdened with the weight of old memories and new uncertainties. The cell where they had kept Gunnar awaited his inspection, but Fellron's mind remained trapped in the past, haunted by the ghost of a Dwarf who should have aged but hadn't. Each step echoed with the memories of that fateful day, the boy he once was and the Dwarf he had unwillingly become.

Ruiha

Magnus gently shook Ruiha awake. "Ruiha, wake up. It's time to move," he murmured, with quiet urgency.

Her eyes fluttered open, sleep fading as recognition dawned. She rose swiftly to her feet rubbing the last dregs of sleep from her eyes.

As Ruiha joined Magnus in rousing their comrades, the camp stirred quickly to life. The Snow Wolves moved with practiced efficiency, their years of training evident in their precise movements.

Alongside them, the former Drogo slaves worked with a new-found purpose, their hands moving with a fervor born not just of dreams of freedom but the chance to reclaim their lives and dignity.

As the first light of dawn began to filter through the fissures above, Magnus urged his companions to move with haste. Their escape had been successful, albeit disorganized, but there was no time to rest on their laurels. Drogo forces could be upon them at any moment, and the thought of capture sent a shiver down Ruiha's spine.

"We can't afford to linger here any longer than necessary," Magnus said, his voice low but firm. "Every moment we delay brings us closer to danger."

Spurred by his words, the group set off deeper into the mountains, leaving the remnants of their camp abandoned behind them. To Magnus's obvious chagrin, they did not have time to cover their tracks and Ruiha felt the weight of their vulnerability to any pursuers that might be closing in.

Magnus assumed the lead with Dakarai by his side as their guide. The combination of Magnus's military expertise and Dakarai's familiarity with the Drogo Mulik territories proved invaluable as they guided the group through the rugged landscape. Light shafts filtered through the jagged peaks, casting long shadows over the rocky terrain as the escapees ventured deeper into the uninhabited heart of the mountains. Ruiha kept her mind focused on the path ahead and her senses alert to every sound and movement.

Uleg followed closely behind Magnus, his wisdom guiding them through the labyrinthine pathways of the mountains. Beside him, Brenn struggled to keep pace, his grief still fresh in the wake of losing his brother. The weight of his sorrow clearly hung heavy upon his shoulders, and, having heard what had happened, Ruiha watched him with concern. She wished she could ease his pain, but knew that only time could heal such wounds.

As they forged ahead through frequent obstacles. Deep crevasses would yawn abruptly before them, threatening to swallow the unwary traveler with their dark depths, but Magnus navigated the hazardous terrain with a sure hand and keen eyes. Ruiha found herself admiring his resolute leadership. She was relieved to pass on the responsibility to Magnus, for a while at least, trusting him to guide them safely.

As the day drew on, they began to hear the distinctive howls of bonebacks. The Scorched Mountains were the reptilian wolves' habitat, and as the howls drew closer, a chill ran down Ruiha's spine

"They're close," Dakarai whispered, as he scanned the rocky terrain. Ruiha could see the apprehension in his eyes, mirroring her own.

Brenn's eyes narrowed as he listened to the howls. "Do you think they'll try to flank us?" he asked, his voice steady, a seasoned warrior ready for battle.

Ruiha exchanged a glance with Magnus. "I don't think so," she replied grimly. "We're being stalked."

Magnus nodded. "We need to be ready," he said in a determined voice. "They won't give up easily."

The group moved forward tentatively, weapons at the ready, bracing themselves for the imminent confrontation. Ruiha's grip tightened on her weapon, her heart a steady drumbeat of resolve.

Magnus scanned their surroundings, his brow furrowed in thought. "We need to find a spot where we can hold them off," he said.

Ruiha scanned the rocky terrain ahead. "Somewhere narrow where they can't surround us," she suggested.

Dakarai, ever resourceful, pointed towards a rocky outcrop- ping up ahead. "What about there?" He indicated a narrow passageway flanked by towering stone walls. Ruiha's hopes lifted at the sight.

Uleg studied the position with a critical eye. "It's defensible," he conceded with a nod of approval. "We could bottleneck them there."

"What's our fallback plan if they overwhelm us?" Brenn asked.

Magnus placed a hand on the younger dwarf's shoulder, meeting his gaze with unwavering resolve. "We'll fight with everything we've got," he vowed, his voice firm. "And if it comes to it, we'll make a strategic retreat. But we won't go down without a fight."

The group didn't have long to huddle in the narrow passageway, before the bonebacks descended upon them with a savage ferocity. Ruiha's heart raced, her body coiled with readiness.

The first boneback lunged forward, its jaws snapping shut with a sickening crunch as it closed in on a Dwarf named Yorain. With a roar of defiance, Yorain swung his axe with all his might, the blade glinting in the dim light as it met the boneback's scaled hide. But the creature's claws tore through Yorain's defenses with brutal efficiency. With a final defiant roar, he fell to the ground, his lifeblood staining the rocky terrain beneath him. Ruiha's chest tightened with grief, but she couldn't afford to mourn.

Magnus and Ruiha fought side by side, their weapons flashing in the dim light as they held back the onslaught of bonebacks. Magnus wielded his axe with deadly precision, his muscles straining with the effort as he fended off the creatures' attacks of. Beside him, Ruiha moved with a grace born of years of combat, her sword dancing through the air as she struck down one boneback after another.

Despite their efforts the odds seemed insurmountable as more and more bonebacks surged forward, overwhelming the defenders with sheer numbers. Brenn fought with wild abandon, his grief fueling his every strike. But in the chaos of battle, he found himself surrounded, his crazed cries drowned out by the savage growls of the bonebacks. Ruiha's tried to push a way towards the isolated dwarf, but she was too far away.

With a roar, Dakarai leaped to Brenn's defense, his own sword flashing as he fought to protect the Dwarf. The bonebacks closed in, their razor-sharp claws tearing through flesh and bone with savage efficiency. Despite Dakarai's valiant efforts, the bonebacks' onslaught threatened to destroy them both

In a desperate lunge Dakrai pushed Brenn out of harm's way just as a boneback's claws sliced through the air where Brenn had stood moments before. Brenn stumbled, his breath coming in ragged gasps as he struggled to regain his footing amidst the chaos of battle.

Ruiha turned from Dakarai and Brenn's struggle to see two Drogo warriors torn to shreds by the vicious bonebacks. Roaring in frustration, she spun around and swiftly decapitated a boneback that had ventured too close, its scaled, bony head rolling across the ground.

Amidst mounting losses, Magnus and Ruiha fought on, with unyielding determination striking down boneback after boneback, with every swing of their weapons, even as their comrades fell around them.

At last, as the group continued to valiantly hold their ground, the bonebacks seemed to sense the difficulty of their prey and began to retreat. Relief was tempered with sorrow as Magnus and Ruiha surveyed the aftermath of the battle and the many they had lost.

Then, just as they began to catch their breath, the rhythmic pounding of drums echoed through the mountains, interspersed with the metallic clanging of weapons and eventually the steady, synchronized footfalls of boots.

Magnus, Ruiha and Dakarai shared a panicked look knowing that victory over the bonebacks was only the beginning and a new, more substantial threat loomed on the horizon.

Fellron

Fellron had pieced together that Gunnar and his companion had been swept downstream for several miles, only to inexplicably vanish without a trace. Meanwhile, the Snow Wolves, under General Bjorn's orders, had been released only to fall prey to an ambush by a small Drogo army shortly thereafter.

As he watched Gunnar and his companion vanish into the ether, Fellron grappled with a rare sense of unease and uncertainty. The image of them slipping away felt like sand through his fingers, a reminder of how elusive truth could be. Muttering staccato incantations, he wove together exotic spells, each flick of his wrist a desperate attempt to penetrate the mystery. With each spell, he delved deeper, seeking clarity amidst the shadows. Yet, despite his efforts, his magic faltered, grasping only fleeting glimpses of Gunnar amidst the haze. The image of Gunnar gathering deer from his traps lingered briefly before fading into obscurity. Fellron's frustration mounted as he sensed a formidable barrier warding off his magic like an impenetrable fortress. The sensation of this unseen force sent a shiver through him.

Fellron's frustrations grew as his divinations failed to reveal the fate of Hansen, the enigmatic Dwarf who had urged Gunnar and his companion to leap from the cliff's edge. Each attempt to trace Hansen's trail through the intricate web of magic that bound their world ended in frustration. The elusive Dwarf remained maddeningly out of reach, slipping through Fellron's grasp like smoke in the wind. Hansen's disappearance felt like a personal affront, as if the very fabric of the realm conspired to hide him. Each search yielded little more than fragments of tantalizing clues and fleeting shadows.

Sighing heavily, Fellron turned and walked away from the underground fort, oppressed by the weight of unanswered questions. Perhaps tracking the Snow Wolves would yield more tangible results. With a sharp whistle, he called Ghost; the wolf appeared at his side as if summoned from the shadows. Fellron patted the soft white fur and Ghost gave Fellron a sideways glance, his eyes reflecting a mix of curiosity and silent judgment.

"Pah! Don't be looking at me like that. As if you could do a better job of finding 'em!" Fellron muttered in frustration. Ghost merely snorted, a puff of mist clouding the air in front of them. "Aye," Fellron sighed, "it's as if destiny itself spirited them away…"

The words hung in the air, reverberating deep within Fellron's core. A look of shocked comprehension dawned on his weathered features, his eyes widening as the realization washed over him like a crashing wave. "Surely not… it can't be that… can it, Ghost?" His voice wavered as he turned to the wolf.

He remembered the words Hansen had sung what felt like a lifetime ago, as they walked together to the gates of the Shadowforged. The poem, once dismissed as mere tradition, now resonated with newfound clarity and significance.

"Born of sorrow and tempered by strife. Reforged, you are the shadow's knife.

Saved from despair by fate in disguise. In the shadows, where your true power lies.

To the realm where shadows reign. Where secrets whisper and darkness wanes.

You emerge a seeker bound by fate. Embracing the void at shadow's gate.

Through trials dire, you'll save your kin. Bound by fate, and yet to begin.

With courage, bold and spirit pure. Their freedom, you'll ensure."

Each verse echoed in his mind with the weight of a destiny long foretold. The words seemed to weave a tapestry of purpose that felt tied to his very being.

It was as if a veil had been lifted, revealing truths that had lain dormant within him all along. The poem wasn't just a relic of tradition—it was a guiding light, a beacon illuminating the path he was meant to tread. It spoke to him, to his purpose, and to the journey that lay ahead.

With sudden clarity, Fellron knew what he must do. For the first time in his life, he felt truly connected to destiny, bound to a course that would shape fate.

Turning his gaze to the horizon, Fellron took a deep breath, the weight of his responsibility settling upon his shoulders like a heavy cloak.

With a nod, Fellron mounted Ghost, feeling the familiar strength of the wolf beneath him. The path ahead might be fraught with danger but it was also brimming with the promise of destiny. The mission was clear: he had a captured unit of Dwarves to free, and he would stop at nothing to see it through.

17.
Advancing

"True power is not in ascending to the highest rank but in mastering each step along the way."

Gunnar

Gunnar broke through to the level of Master two days after his confrontation with Urlok. It was an extraordinary achievement, yet as he stood amidst the brilliant white spires of the Tower, the air tingling with arcane energy, he couldn't shake a lingering sense of detachment.

Stronger now, not just physically and spiritually but also in the arcane arts, Gunnar could feel the very fabric of reality bending to his will. Yet, within himself, he felt unchanged. The Sages had spoken of this achievement as if it would transform him, but as he walked the polished marble corridors, disappointment gnawed at him.

What had he expected? A surge of power coursing through his veins, a radiant transformation of body and soul? He chuckled softly, realizing the foolishness of such naïve dreams. Perhaps true mastery lay not in grandiose displays but in the quiet acceptance of one's own advancement. The marble under his feet felt the same, the air just as charged, but his heart remained heavy with unmet expectations.

Shaking his head, Gunnar continued his slow journey through the labyrinthine halls of the Tower to Commander Aelric's office. Despite the directive to inform the Commander immediately upon his advancement, the term 'immediately' allowed for some interpretation. Enough leeway for Gunnar to justify his leisurely pace although he doubted Aelric would be interested in such justifications should he be in a foul mood.

At last, Gunnar reached Commander Aelric's office and knocked three times on the towering wooden door adorned with intricate carvings. Each firm rap resonated through the corridor like a distant drumbeat.

The door creaked open, revealing a spacious chamber bathed in the warm glow of flickering torches. Commander Aelric sat behind a massive oak desk buried beneath a mountain of parchment and scrolls. At the sound of Gunnar's entrance, he glanced up, his angry scar glinting in the dim light.

He curtly beckoned Gunnar to a worn leather couch nestled in the corner of the room. Gunnar surveyed the spartan space as he settled onto the cushions. The office was devoid of ornamentation, every item serving a practical purpose. Even the pair of formidable swords mounted on the wall behind him bore the scars of countless battles, notches and scratches testifying to their martial history.

A long sigh escaped Aelric, as he stood, his chair grating against the tiled floor. As he approached Gunnar, the dwarf sensed the faint, almost imperceptible sensation of a spiritual scan—something he wouldn't have noticed earlier that morning.

"So," Aelric began gruffly. "You've ascended into the Intermediate Element. A Master, it appears."

"Yes, Commander," Gunnar affirmed with a nod.

Aelric paced back and forth before him, stroking his chin as he deliberated. Finally, he halted and turned his gaze squarely on Gunnar. "I must admit, Gunnar, you have surpassed our expectations. We had not anticipated your advancement for another two or three weeks."

Gunnar was taken aback by the Commander's praise. Until now, he had received no acknowledgment, let alone commendation, from any of the Sages, including Aelric. Amidst the trials and hardships, Gunnar had assumed he was falling short of their expectations. It seemed the opposite was true.

"What are the next steps then, Commander?" Gunnar asked, striving to keep his voice steady.

"Now that you have advanced, we have the rest of the week to prepare you for your first trial—the Labyrinth," Commander Aelric replied.

Gunnar had heard his instructors mention the Labyrinth in the past. "Commander, might I inquire about the specifics of the trial, please?"

Aelric's grizzled countenance hardened at Gunnar's inquiry, his gaze resembling frosteel, void of warmth or empathy and for a long moment Gunnar wondered if he would receive any answer at all. "Very well, Gunnar," he grumbled at last. "The Labyrinth trial was designed for newly ranked Overlords. In certain cases, advanced Masters would be allowed to attempt the trial. Though not many succeed," Aelric added.

Gunnar's heart sank at Aelric's words, his recent advancement to the rank of Master suddenly feeling inadequate in the face of the trial ahead. He shifted uneasily as his new-found confidence waned.

"Commander," Gunnar began, "I've only recently attained the rank of Master. I'm far from advanced, let alone capable of attempting a trial meant for Overlords."

Aelric's eyes darkened, the contempt he held for Gunnar's perceived inadequacy evident in every line of his scarred face. "Absence of fear, absence of doubt," he retorted, with thinly veiled contempt. "The decision has been made. You will face the Labyrinth whether you feel ready or not."

Gunnar swallowed hard, the reality of his situation sinking in like a heavy stone in the pit of his stomach.

As he prepared to leave, Aelric's voice called him back. "Wait," the Commander said, his tone almost hesitant. "Now that you've reached the level of Master, there is something you should know."

Gunnar turned back to face Aelric, curiosity flickering in his blue eyes.

"With your advancement," Aelric continued, "comes the opportunity to utilize some of the Tower's performance-enhancing elixirs."

Gunnar's eyebrows furrowed in confusion. "Elixirs?" he echoed, his interest piqued.

"Yes," Aelric confirmed, his gaze steady. "These elixirs are designed to strengthen not only your physical strength but also your spirit and your lifeline. They will make you more powerful, Gunnar, paving the way for your future advancement."

With deliberate movements, the Commander delved into the folds of his cloak, retrieving a small vial scarcely larger than Gunnar's thumb. Within it a swirling vivid purple liquid, glimmered faintly in the subdued light. Without warning, he tossed the vial toward Gunnar, who caught it deftly in one hand.

"This elixir," Aelric explained, "is designed to bolster your lifeline, Gunnar. A robust and resilient lifeline facilitates swifter and easier recovery than you're accustomed to. While it also possesses a minor boon in strengthening your spirit, that is not its primary purpose. Go back to your room, take this elixir, and meditate according to the Abyssal Radiance Technique that Thalirion taught you. That way, the elixir can be processed by your spirit. Should you react well to this one, you will be entitled to more."

Gunnar's mind raced with possibilities at the potential benefits of the elixir. Could it truly enhance his healing abilities? He rotated the vial in his palm, watching the purple liquid shimmer in a hypnotic dance.

Anwyn

Anwyn noticed Kemp, the Human mage, peering through the glass door of the training room. Thalirion had already instructed her to erect a protective barrier around the room to prevent their spells and training attacks from spilling outside and causing damage. Luckily, the barrier also provided sound protection, ensuring their conversation remained private from prying ears.

Standing before Thalirion, her mentor, Anwyn felt anticipation coursing through her veins like lightning as he spoke, his demeanor grave and his gaze penetrating.

"Anwyn," he began, "in five days' time, you will face the trial of the Labyrinth, a test reserved for those who have attained the rank of Overlord."

A knot of apprehension formed in the pit of Anwyn's stomach at the mention of the trial. Under Thalirion's guidance, she had honed her skills in the elements and as a warrior. But now, faced with the prospect of a trial designed for Overlords, doubt gnawed at her.

Thalirion's voice cut through her inner turmoil. "As Seishinmori, you possess a unique strength," he continued, his tone measured. "You are not bound by the constraints of other Masters. You must prove yourself in the arcane arts of elemental magic, craft magic, battle magic, or shadow magic. However," Thalirion added, his expression serious, "you must focus your energies on mastering only two of these skills for now. Forget the shadow magic. It is not your path. And craft magic would take too long for you to master."

Anwyn nodded. In Vellhor, she had learned some basic attacks using what she now knew to be shadow magic. When her home had been attacked, she had used destruction magic against her attackers. However, she knew her strengths lay within the elements and combat.

"Although you are on the brink of advancement, we cannot raise you to Overlord in the next five days," Thalirion said gravely. "We have strengthened your spirit and skills through training and elixirs to their capacity, and you will have to complete the trial as a Master."

Anwyn frowned. "But as a Master, will I be ready?" she asked, her voice trembling.

Thalirion's gaze softened. "Anwyn, the path to greatness is not without its challenges," he replied gently. "Although you will not advance to Overlord in the next five days, I will train you to the best of my abilities. You will be strong enough. Trust in yourself and trust in me."

As they embarked on their training session, an eagerness to prove herself surged through Anwyn like a torrential wave. She channeled her frustration into every movement, her muscles straining with exertion, her spirit on the verge of bursting.

She urged Thalirion to push her to her limits, sensing a reluctance in him to fully unleash the depths of her potential.

With a sudden burst, she launched a barrage of arcane projectiles towards Thalirion, each bolt crackling with elemental fury. With lightning-fast reflexes, he deflected the onslaught with his staff, a smile playing on his lips.

Anwyn halted mid-step, her breath catching as she realized Thalirion had been smiling the whole time. He wasn't taking their training seriously at all. A surge of anger consumed her, and she couldn't heed Lorelei's voice in the back of her mind, urging her to calm down.

"Thalirion!" she exclaimed, her voice ringing with frustration. "I need you to take me seriously! I don't have time for this. The fate of Vellhor hangs in the balance, yet you refuse to treat this matter with the gravity it deserves."

Thalirion remained composed, though he cocked his head to the side slightly, a furrow creasing his brow as if puzzled.

"You don't believe I am taking this seriously, Anwyn?" he sid with a hint of confusion.

Anwyn hesitated, before asserting, "No, Thalirion. I don't believe you are taking me seriously." Her voice trembled with emotion. "Why do you refuse to help me advance to Overlord? Do you doubt my strength? Do you doubt me?"

Thalirion's gaze hardened, the playful glint in his eyes replaced by a chilling intensity. "I am pushing you to your current limits," he explained evenly. "To push you further would risk damaging your spirit and hindering your potential advancement."

Then, in a sudden surge of power, Thalirion unveiled the full extent of his might, his spirit radiating with an otherworldly strength that enveloped Anwyn like a tempest. The sheer force of his presence staggered her to her core, leaving her gasping for breath as her senses reeled under the overwhelming pressure. As Thalirion veiled himself once more, Anwyn struggled to regain her composure, her mind racing with a newfound clarity. "Why?" she demanded, her voice trembling with a mixture of awe and disbelief.

Thalirion blinked, the intensity fading from his gaze. "You have indeed made progress, Anwyn. But you are not yet ready for the mantle of Overlord," he stated firmly. "The transformation that accompanies such advancement is profound and rushing it could lead to irreversible harm."

"But you said that advancing would strengthen my mind and body," Anwyn countered, her frustration evident in her tone.

Thalirion nodded solemnly. "Indeed, Anwyn. But the process requires patience. Rushing it could jeopardize everything you've worked for. Trust in the journey, Anwyn. Trust in me, please."

Anwyn realized that her desire to prove herself had blinded her to the wisdom of his guidance. Nodding slowly, she resolved to trust Thalirion's judgment and the path he had set before her.

As they resumed their training, Anwyn's movements were more measured, her mind focused on the lessons Thalirion imparted. She understood now that true strength lay not just in power, but in patience and understanding.

Karl

The dim light of the forge danced around Karl as he stood before the anvil, his eyes reflecting the crackling fire. He had long since learned to ignore the heat and the distraction of the roaring flames, so focused was he on his project.

Each strike of the hammer reverberated throughout the chamber as he meticulously shaped the rare metal. . The hammer, forged from the shard of a rhinoceros-like spectral echo, transferred a tiny amount of strength into the axe with every blow, enhancing its power. Karl's own spirit infused every strike, ensuring that only Gunnar, the intended recipient, could harness its full power. He had crafted a collection of hammers, each designed to imbue a distinct aspect into the weapon being forged.

As he laid the hammer down to inspect his work, a smile crept across his face. It was nearly finished, and he could feel the magic emanating from the weapon. He picked up a smaller hammer and a chisel, beginning to etch intricate runes onto its surface. Each stroke brought the ancient symbols to life, weaving an arcane energy around the axe. These runes were not mere decorations; they held the key to unlocking the axe's true potential.

As he etched, Karl muttered enchantments under his breath, his voice low and steady. Each carefully selected incantation was imbued with centuries of magical knowledge passed down through Sage Thadwick's teachings.

With every word, he guided the flow of magic into the axe like a master craftsman shaping a masterpiece.

With each strike of his hammer, each rune etched, and each incantation spoken, the axe became more than just a weapon; it became a conduit for Karl's will and the embodiment of ancient magic. By the time he finished, the axe pulsed with a faint, otherworldly glow.

He took a moment to step back to admire his handiwork, a sense of satisfaction washing over him, before beginning to buff the magical axe to a deep shine.

The heavy door to the foundry creaked open and the stocky figure of Sage Thadwick entered, robes flowing majestically behind him as he strode towards Karl's workspace.

"Karl," Thadwick's voice echoed in the cavernous room. "Is the axe finished?"

Karl faced his mentor with a hint of anticipation in his eyes. "Almost, Sage Thadwick. Just a few small enchantments and it will be ready."

Thadwick's gaze fell upon the axe, his eyes widening in astonishment. He stepped closer, studying the intricate runes etched into its surface and feeling the hum of magic emanating from it.

"By the stars," Thadwick murmured in awe. "This is remarkable, Karl. I have never seen such craftsmanship."

Karl's chest swelled with pride. "Thank you, Sage Thadwick. I have poured everything you have taught me into this creation."

"Still," the Sage continued, shaking his head slowly in astonishment, "this is a truly powerful weapon."

"Without your guidance and the use of the Tower's foundry, it would never have been possible."

Thadwick nodded, his expression serious. "Indeed, Karl. But there is something more to this axe than mere craftsmanship. Its power... it is unlike anything I have encountered before. This could be among the most powerful weapons ever crafted by a mortal."

Karl's eyes widened in disbelief at Thadwick's words which filled him with a sense of accomplishment unlike any he had ever known.

"Thank you, Sage Thadwick," Karl whispered. "Your wisdom brought me to this moment."

Thadwick laid a hand on Karl's shoulder, his touch firm and reassuring. "You have done well, Karl. Your journey as a Spiritsmith has only just begun. May this axe serve you and Gunnar well in the battles ahead."

With a final nod of approval, Thadwick left Karl alone with his creation. As Karl looked upon the axe, he knew it was more than a weapon—it was a symbol of his dedication, his skill, and his unwavering determination to stand against the darkness. With Thadwick's words echoing in his mind, Karl felt ready to face his upcoming trial in the Labyrinth.

Kemp

Kemp had explored the myriad challenges of the Labyrinth numerous times. Initially, the sheer difficulty of each test had astounded him. Every challenge seemed more daunting than the last, designed to push contenders to their limits and test their skills in ways he had never imagined.

Frustrated by the harshness of the trials, Kemp had once accused Thraxos of teaching children to wrestle by throwing them in a pit with bears. Thraxos, however, had quickly dismissed his accusations, urging him to study the competitors and their abilities before passing judgment.

So Kemp did just that, and what he discovered astounded him even more than he had anticipated. He spent days monitoring the challengers, gauging their strengths and weaknesses, and preparing for his role in controlling the various challenges they would face.

Witnessing the blonde Dwarf Gunnar advance to Master status had been impressive, but even before his advancement, Gunnar had displayed formidable prowess. Kemp couldn't forget how effortlessly Gunnar had annihilated Urlok, a Master who had held his title for several months. The memory of that battle lingered in Kemp's leaving him in awe of the Dwarf's potential in combat.

Then there was the female Elf, Anwyn, whose power sent shivers down Kemp's spine. The way she effortlessly commanded the elements was unlike anything he had ever seen. Kemp had watched her manipulate fire and water as if they were extensions of her own body, her eyes glowing with an inner light as she wove spells with fluid grace.

Yet, impressive as Anwyn's abilities were, they paled in comparison to the unveiling of Thalirion's full power. The sheer magnitude of Thalirion's abilities had left Kemp trembling, his knees weak and breathless under the weight of such spiritual pressure. It was a humbling experience, a stark reminder of the vast depths of the arcane arts that still lay beyond his understanding.

And finally, there was Karl. The red-haired Dwarf possessed the ability to conjure weapons seemingly out of thin air. Kemp vividly remembered observing Karl's training session with Sage Thadwick, where a series of constructions launched various long-range attacks.

Karl's task had been to maneuver through the assault course and destroy them. Kemp marveled at Karl's ingenuity, particularly when he created a cannon out of a shadowy lump—a soul shard—manifesting it into a formidable weapon. The cannon discharged three shots before dissipating. Then Karl created a dark, shadowy crossbow to finish the remaining targets. Each arrow released unleashed a torrent of arcane projectiles, each finding its mark with unerring accuracy. The memory of the weapons materializing from the shadows, the air thick with the scent of magic and the tang of metal, filled Kemp with a sense of wonder and admiration.

As Kemp watched these extraordinary beings, trepidation gnawed at him. The challengers' abilities were beyond anything he had ever encountered. The thought of manipulating the Labyrinth's controls to test such formidable opponents sent a thrill of anxiety through him.

He hoped that his ability to navigate and control the Labyrinth would be enough to prove himself to Thraxos. Witnessing these combatants and their immense power had made Kemp more desperate than ever to continue his training in the arcane arts, unlocking his own potential so he could stand among the ranks of these incredible warriors.

18.

The Sovereign's Dilemma

"In the heart of every warrior is the silent battle of self-doubt."

Sovereign Tarsha

Sovereign Tarsha, revered as one of the most formidable individuals in the Boria Expanse, was often likened to the legendary Supreme Archmages of old. Despite her outward aura of power, she battled inner anxieties akin to a child fearing the lurking shadows. While she longed to intervene personally in the tumult of Vellhor, showing favoritism to one realm risked plunging the entire expanse into chaos and igniting a war between the realms that could span decades, if not centuries.

She knew that this so-called god, Nergai, would not be content with Vellhor. If left unchecked, his power would only grow until he posed a threat even to her. Her thoughts were haunted by images of his rage absorbing all the power of Vellhor and amassing untold armies. She dreaded the devastation he might then unleash upon the remaining worlds of the Boria Expanse. Weighed down by that dire prospect, she sighed and, sweeping her long gold and black hair out of her face, summoned an image on the crystal at the center of the grand table.

Sovereign Tarsha watched as Gunnar downed a thumb-sized vial of shimmering red liquid. Judging by its color, she assumed it was an elixir for strength, but without being in the chamber with him, it was merely an educated guess. Aelric could have easily changed the elixir's color for some reason. She shook her head, contemplating Aelric's unorthodox training methods. If she were to name his style, she would call it extreme duress. Yet, she couldn't deny his success as the most effective battle mage instructor the Tower had ever seen. As she observed Gunnar, she worried about the toll such training would take on him.

She gently urged the image to change, and it dissipated like paint in water, replaced with an image of Anwyn. She watched with a mixture of concern and hope as Anwyn meditated while Thalirion paced around her, reading aloud from a tome. The worry was evident in the lines etched in Thalirion's face, and Sovereign Tarsha silently hoped that Anwyn was skilled enough to achieve what they needed from her. Thalirion's methods hadn't changed over the centuries; he always found ways to push his students to their limits. She smiled to herself, recalling his penchant for multitasking. She was surprised he hadn't thrown in a few impromptu attacks for Anwyn to defend against.

As she observed the scene unfolding before her, Sovereign Tarsha couldn't shake the feeling of impending danger looming over them all.

Sovereign Tarsha dissipated the image in the crystal with a single thought and cloaked the orb in a heavily runed black cloth. Standing up from her seat, she paced around the large table in the center of the grand council chamber, as she contemplated the Vellhorian situation. She would need to call a meeting of the Sages soon to gather their opinions and expertise. Their insights would be crucial in navigating the complexities of the situation and assessing the candidates chosen by Thalirion to defend Vellhor.

Whilst her hands were tied, she would urge the advancement of the candidates and ensure the instructors were pushing them to their limits.

Thalirion

The summons jolted Thalirion from his contemplations just as he was considering whether to introduce magically propelled projectiles into Anwyn's training regimen. Having administered several elixirs from the Tower, including one designed to enhance memory, he knew her mind would be in a heightened state, processing information swiftly and efficiently. Projectile evasion would add an additional layer of challenge to the process of mastering the art of meditation while simultaneously digesting information. It could extend her adaptability, and situational awareness.

However, just as had been mulling over the potential benefits of this new training approach, Sovereign Tarsha's call cut through his thoughts like a blade. "Esteemed Sages of the Seven Realms," the telepathic voice commanded. "Your presence is urgently requested in the grand council chamber. Come swiftly, for the fate of the Boria Expanse hangs in the balance."

Thalirion was among the first Sages to arrive at the grand council chambers. As he waited, he observed a mixture of familiar and unfamiliar faces trickling in. Some of the Sages he had formed close bonds with over the years, and they acknowledged him with grim nods. The news of the dire situation in Vellhor, coupled with the destruction of the Sacred Tree, had spread like wildfire throughout the Tower, casting a sombre mood over the gathering.

As the Sages arrived, they each took their seats Thadwick, his intricate beard adorned with metal beads, settled next to Thalirion, fingers fidgeting restlessly with the ornaments. Across from them sat Aelric, his scarred and weathered countenance seemingly to fixated on Thalirion. Perhaps he was indeed glaring, Thalirion mused. Sage Raveena and Sage Zanders flanked Aelric, their expressions aloof and disinterested as they eyed the other Sages in the room. As battle mages they seemed to think their status placed somehow above their peers.

As the last of the Sages settled into their seats, Sovereign Tarsha rose from her throne at the head of the grand council chambers and a hush fell over the room.

"Greetings, esteemed Sages of the Seven Realms," she began. "I thank you all for heeding the summons and gathering here today."

She scanned their attentive faces before continuing. "As you are all aware, the situation in Vellhor has reached a critical juncture. The machinations of the Drogo and their god Nergai threaten to plunge the realm into chaos."

A ripple of concern spread among the Sages. Those hailing from Vellhor exchanged anxious glances, clearly fearful for their homeland. Aerithordor's representatives shifted uncomfortably in their seats, their expressions mirroring the deep concern for the Dwarves of their neighboring realm.

However the concern was not uniform. The Sages from Stepphoros, embroiled in their own internal conflicts, displayed a marked indifference to the plight of Vellhor, remaining unmoved by Sovereign Tarsha's words.

With Sovereign Tarsha's words still hanging in the air, a deep voice resonated from the back of the chamber. All eyes turned as a towering Minotaur from Stepphoros rose from his seat.

"Sovereign Tarsha," the Sage began, his voice a rumble that echoed off the chamber walls, "with all due respect, it is not the Tower's responsibility to intervene in the internal conflicts of individual realms."

His words drew murmurs of agreement from some of the other Sages, as the Minotaur's gaze bore into Sovereign Tarsha. "Where was this level of concern when the Centaurs began their attacks on the Minotaurs in Stepphoros?" he asked with more than a hint of bitterness in his tone. "We continue to endure our struggles alone, without the aid or intervention of the Tower."

Sovereign Tarsha met the Minotaur's eyes with a steady gaze. "I understand your concerns," she replied evenly. "But the situation in Vellhor threatens the stability of the entire Boria Expanse. We cannot afford to turn a blind eye to such a grave threat."

The Minotaur's expression hardened, but before he could respond, Sovereign Tarsha raised her hand, silencing any further objections.

"I am, however, well aware of our constraints regarding the level of intervention we are able to provide Vellhor,"

Sovereign Tarsha continued, her tone firm but measured. "However, we must put aside our differences and work together to find a solution. The fate of Vellhor—and indeed the fate of all the realms— may well rest in our hands," she declared, emphasizing their collective responsibility.

As Sovereign Tarsha's words echoed through the grand council chambers, a tall, handsome Elf from Erros rose from his seat. His silver hair shimmered like moonlight, cascading elegantly around his shoulders, and his piercing blue eyes held a wisdom beyond his years.

"Forgive the interruption, Sovereign Tarsha," the Elf spoke, his voice smooth yet commanding, "but are we not already committed to training candidates from Vellhor?" His gaze turned to Thalirion as he spoke.

Sovereign Tarsha nodded. "Indeed, we are," she replied. "But the events in Vellhor have escalated beyond mere training. We must reassess our approach and determine how best to support the realm in this time of crisis."

The Elf nodded. "Then I trust that together we will find a way forward." he said as he resumed his seat.

As the discussion unfolded, Thadwick, with his intricate beard adorned with metal beads, rose from his seat. "Sovereign Tarsha, esteemed Sages," he began, his voice tinged with excitement, "I must speak of my candidate, Karl. He has shown remarkable promise and ingenuity in his training. Just recently, he crafted a weapon—an axe of extraordinary craftsmanship—that will surely aid Gunnar in his quest."

A murmur of interest rippled through the assembly as Thad- wick continued, with animated gestures, "This axe is not just any weapon. It is forged with techniques passed down through generations of Dwarven Spiritsmiths, imbued with powerful enchantments that enhance its strength and durability. It is a testament to Karl's skill and dedication."

However, as Thadwick was still speaking, an older Dwarf from Aerithordor interjected with evident skepticism evident. "Bah! The demigods of our home-realm could gift an axe of superior quality to what a mere Dwarf from Vellhor could create."

Thadwick's expression hardened, his pride wounded by the Dwarf's dismissive remark. "Respectfully," he retorted indignantly, "I must disagree. This axe, forged by Karl, is one of the most powerful weapons I have ever seen. Its craftsmanship and enchantments rival even the most legendary artefacts of Aerithordor."

Sovereign Tarsha and Thalirion exchanged a meaningful glance. Thalirion had known Thadwick for centuries, and he was not easily impressed. It was clear that Karl's creation held potential beyond what they had anticipated. Thalirion looked forward to seeing the weapon. Clearly, Sovereign Tarsha agreed with him.

"Sage Thadwick," Sovereign Tarsha addressed the smith with a tone of respect, "we are grateful for your insight and for bringing Karl's accomplishment to our attention. Thalirion and I shall personally inspect this weapon after the meeting."

"Thank you, Sovereign Tarsha, Sage Thalirion," Thadwick replied, eyes sparkling at recognition from the highest authority in the Tower. "I am confident that you will be impressed by Karl's craftsmanship."

As the discussion veered towards potential solutions, a woman with a scorpion tail from the realm of Malanth rose from to address the gathering. Her movements were graceful yet imbued with a sense of strength.

"Sovereign Tarsha, esteemed Sages," she began, "may I suggest diplomacy? The Sages could offer to facilitate negotiations between the conflicting factions within Vellhor, acting as impartial mediators to seek a peaceful solution to these underlying tensions."

The room fell quite for a moment as the other Sages considered her proposal, but before Sovereign Tarsha could respond, Thalirion stood to speak.

"With all due respect," he said, his voice heavy with resignation, "diplomatic mediation is unlikely to be effective in this situation. Nergai and the Drogo are driven by a fanatical desire for destruction. They will not listen to reason or negotiation. Their only goal is the annihilation of Vellhor."

Sovereign Tarsha nodded, her grave expression reflecting the grim reality they faced. "Indeed," she replied, sadly, "diplomatic mediation may not be the answer in this instance. We must explore other avenues to confront the threat posed by Nergai and the Drogo."

The woman from Malanth nodded as she sat down, though not without a flicker of disappointment crossing her face.

Another female Sage, a winged Aerovian from Raaniada, rose from her seat. Her wings shimmering iridescently in the light

"Sovereign Tarsha, esteemed Sages," she said, "may I suggest humanitarian aid? The assembly could organize efforts to provide relief to those affected by the turmoil in

Vellhor, such as displaced civilians or communities impacted by the upcoming conflict."

Her proposal elicited many nods and murmurs of approval. "This assistance would not breach the regulations imposed on the Tower's intervention in other realms," she continued in a confident tone. "Similar aid has been provided in Stepphoros during times of crisis."

Sovereign Tarsha and Thalirion shared a look acknowledging the merit of the suggestion. Humanitarian aid would alleviate the suffering of those caught in the crossfire and demonstrate the Tower's commitment to the well-being of all the realms.

"Indeed," Sovereign Tarsha said firmly. "Humanitarian aid will be crucial in this time of need."

However, despite the obvious benefits, Thalirion couldn't shake the feeling that humanitarian aid alone would not provide the solution they sought. The looming threat posed by Nergai and the Drogo demanded a more decisive course of action to confront the danger head-on.

Another Minotaur rose from to address the assembly with a deep resonant voice.

"Sovereign Tarsha, esteemed Sages," he began, "I propose military aid. We could provide training to the military forces of the humans, Elves, and Dwarves within Vellhor, strengthening their defenses and readiness to face their enemies." Even as his suggestion garnered thoughtful consideration, he went on to add a note of caution.

"However," he said with a frown, "we would have to be careful to ensure no breach of the regulations about direct military intervention. The training must be conducted with careful oversight."

Thalirion sensed this was an opportunity to contribute. "I agree," he began. "But first we must convince the nations of Vellhor of the severity of the threat they face. Anwyn, as Seishinmori, must persuade the Elven Council to rally the Elven army. And Gunnar must unite the Dwarven clans, urging them to let him lead them into battle." He paused, his gaze sweeping across the assembly. "As for the humans of Fenmark," Thalirion continued, "I will need to investigate further to ascertain the status how ready and willing they are to join the fight."

Sovereign Tarsha nodded, acknowledging the wisdom of Thalirion's words. "Very well," she replied. "Let us proceed on that basis with caution and determination."

At this critical juncture in the discussion, a Vellhorian Elf rose from his seat, his expression pained and his voice trembling.

"Sovereign Tarsha, esteemed colleagues," he said sadly, "how do we plan to reach Vellhor now that the portal through the Sacred Tree has been destroyed by Nergai's forces?"

His question cast a shadow over the chamber as the fundamental weakness in any plan was thrown into sharp relief. Without a means of swift transportation to Vellhor, any aid – humanitarian or military – to support the embattled realm would be severely hindered.

In the hush that had fallen over the chamber Thraxos rose to speak. "Sovereign Tarsha, esteemed Sages," he began, "there may be a solution to our dilemma." As eager eyes turned towards him, Thraxos explained, "The human Kemp somehow managed to traverse realms and arrive here without using the Sacred Tree. He brought with him a powerful artefact—a broken crown of ancient origin."

A murmur of intrigue rippled through the assembly at the mention of the artefact and its power.

"I entrusted the crown to Thalirion," Thraxos continued glancing across at the Sage. "This artefact may hold the key to traversing between realms without relying on the Sacred Tree."

Thalirion nodded solemnly. "I will conduct further research on the crown," he assured his fellow Sages. "If it indeed possesses the ability to bridge realms, then it may be our best hope of reaching Vellhor and confronting the threat of Nergai." Sovereign Tarsha and the other Sages nodded recognizing the significance of the broken crown.

As the meeting continued, further suggestions from the sages included offering magical support and guidance to the defenders of Vellhor with spells, enchantments, magical weapons, and strategic advice to enhance their capabilities and effectiveness in repelling Nergai's forces. This prompted a free-flowing discussion on measures ranging from protective wards to enhancing fortifications to illusions to deceive and confuse the enemy.

On the back of this another Sage raised the idea of offering logistical and tactical support to help organize and co-ordinate the defenders, for example by ensuring they have access to essential supplies, reinforcements, and strategic planning expertise.

As the deliberations drew to a close, Sovereign Tarsha rose from her throne, ready to summarize the proceedings.

"Esteemed Sages of the Seven Realms," she began, "it is clear that we face a formidable challenge in aiding Vellhor within the constraints imposed by the Tower's regulations. However, I believe we have identified several avenues through which we can provide assistance."

She paused, her gaze sweeping across the assembled Sages. "We will offer magical support and guidance to the defenders of Vellhor, providing spells, enchantments, and strategic advice to bolster their capabilities. "We will also organize logistical and tactical support, ensuring they have access to essential supplies, reinforcements, and strategic planning expertise."

"Furthermore," Sovereign Tarsha continued, "each department within the Tower will be asked to provide a specific number of candidates to aid in training the Vellhorian armies. We require individuals with expertise in combat training, strategic planning, weaponry, and magical support."

Her summary of the Tower's plans elicited nods of agreement from the other Sages.

Sovereign Tarsha scanned the room, identifying the department heads. "Now let us hear how our trainees areperforming." Her gaze fixed first on Aelric. "Commander Aelric," she began, "I woul tell u how Gunnar is faring in his training?"

"Sovereign Tarsha." Aelric rose to reply in his voice gruff, "Gunnar has shown notable progress in his training. Both his dedication and determination are commendable, and I have every confidence that he will prove himself a formidable ally in the defense of Vellhor, given time.".

"Time," the Sovereign said sadly, "is one asset we do not have the luxury of."

The Commander nodded. "We have filled him up with elixirs and potions in preparation for his trial in the Labyrinth. I am confident that he will succeed."

A scorpion-tailed man rose to interrupt the Commander. Given the gaze he received from both Sage Zanders and Sage Raveena, Thalirion wondered how he kept is composure whilst speaking. "Isn't the Labyrinth trial designed for Overlords? How can you be so sure he will pass?"

Commander Aelric didn't acknowledge the man; instead, his gaze remained on the Sovereign. "Sovereign Tarsha," he began, "we will allow the Dwarf to take part in the trial alongside his companions who are both at Master level. The trial will be challenging for three Masters, but not impossible."

Sovereign Tarsha thanked Aelric for his invaluable insights before shifting her attention to Thalirion to inquire. "Sage Thalirion, how does Anwyn fare?"

Thalirion's expression turned thoughtful as he considered his response. "Anwyn is on the cusp of breaking through to Overlord," he said, "yet she is not ready."

He frowned before continuing. "I have concerns for her pushing herself too far," he admitted. "She is desperate to reach Overlord, but rushing her training will have dire consequences without the right foundations."

"However, as you said earlier, time is a luxury we do not have," he concluded, his voice tinged with a hint of resignation. "So we must tread carefully but swiftly if we are to prepare Anwyn— and ourselves—for the challenges that lie ahead."

Sovereign Tarsha nodded. "Thank you, Sage Thalirion, for your insight," she said. "Your concerns for Anwyn's well-being are duly noted." Turning to address the assembled Sages as a whole, she began. "Esteemed Sages of the Seven Realms, today's meeting has provided us with valuable insights and a clear course of action."

Her gaze swept across the assembly, meeting the eyes of each Sage in turn. "Furthermore, we will continue to explore avenues for assistance, including the investigation of the broken crown and its potential to facilitate travel to Vellhor."

"But in the meantime," she concluded in a firm voice, "let us remain vigilant and united in our resolve to protect the Boria Expanse and all its inhabitants. This meeting is adjourned."

19.
The Enigmatic Ally

"In the battle against darkness, allies come from the most unexpected places."

Fellron

Fellron surveyed the group of Drogo and Dwarven former slaves from his concealed vantage point—a rocky crevice in the canyon wall shadowed from view.

Relief washed over him as he noticed them finishing off the bonebacks. He had left Ghost up on the ridge; controlling the wolf around pack animals during a hunt was always challenging. Before diving headfirst into the mission, he needed to assess the situation carefully. His father's words echoed in his mind, "Like a seed planted in fertile soil, patience will bloom into success." Memories of his family flooded back, a pang of longing gripping him. He hadn't thought about them for years, but since his visions of Hansen, thoughts of his family had resurfaced time and again.

He shook off the memory, a brief furrow creasing his brow as he cleared his mind. His gaze drifted around his surroundings, evaluating the scene before him. That's when he heard it— thedistant pounding of drums and the clash of weapons. It was the very threat he had been destined to confront, as foretold in the ancient poem of the Shadowforged.

Fellron weighed his options carefully. Should he join the fight alongside his kin, facing the Drogo warriors head-on? Or would he remain hidden, utilizing his dark magic to aid them from the shadows? Both paths held their merits, but after a moment's deliberation, he resolved that his assistance would be most effective from concealment.

His spells could shape the battlefield without his direct presence, offering a strategic advantage without risking unnecessary exposure.

Focusing his mind, Fellron channeled his magic. A swirling vortex of shadows coalesced around him. With a whispered incantation, he shaped the shadows into a thick, billowing cloak that enveloped the Dwarves and Drogo slaves huddled nearby. The cloak of illusion was more than just a mere shroud—it was a veil of deception that distorted perception and obscured truth. Beneath its shadowy embrace, the Dwarves and Drogo slaves became invisible to the naked eye, their forms blending seamlessly into the surrounding darkness. Besides being unseen, the cloak ensured that their movements and voices remained unheard, masking them all in utter silence. All but one.

A human female stood at the center of the otherwise hidden assembly of Drogo slaves. Fellron was surprised by this anomaly but didn't have time to dwell on it.

To the outside world, they vanished into thin air, leaving no trace of their presence. But to Fellron, they remained just visible, a shimmer in the fabric of reality that only he could perceive. His gaze returned to the human woman who remained completely visible. He didn't want the attackers to see her, so he summoned a wall of shadow and erected it in front of her. She squinted in confusion but remained still, staring at the approaching Drogo through the wall of shadow.

As their pursuers approached, oblivious to the concealed presence of their quarry, Fellron observed their movements closely. With each passing moment, tension mounted among the Dwarves and Drogo slaves—unaware that they had been shrouded by Fellron—who waited nervously, anticipating the impending clash.

Fellron's lips moved in a steady cadence as he muttered more incantations, weaving the threads of dark magic into a second cloak of shadows. Unlike the first, this cloak was not meant to conceal but rather to confound and disorient.

With a flick of his wrist, the cloak unfurled its inky tendrils, swirling around the Drogo pursuers like a fog. As the shadows enveloped them, their surroundings blurred and shifted, casting doubt upon their senses and obscuring their vision.

Confusion swept through the ranks of the Drogo pursuers as they struggled to make sense of their suddenly distorted reality. Shadows danced and flickered at the corners of their vision, whispering of unseen dangers lurking just beyond their reach. Some of the weaker-willed completely froze in terror, whilst others attempted to run away in fear.

Unable to trust their own perceptions, the Drogo pursuers hesitated, their movements faltering as uncertainty tore through them. With each passing moment, the cloak of shadows tightened its grip, ensnaring them in a web of confusion, fear, and doubt.

From the safety of his concealed vantage point, Fellron watched with grim satisfaction as his dark magic took hold. With the Drogo pursuers ensnared in their own illusions, the advantage now lay firmly with the Dwarves and Drogo slaves.

As the clash of steel and the cries of battle echoed through the canyon, the true test of their mettle began in earnest.

Magnus

Magnus's heart was pounding with anticipation. Leading the Dwarves into battle was a weighty responsibility, yet it was one he would bear with honor.

Uleg and Brenn stood beside him grim-faced but resolute. Uleg, gripping his sturdy axe, radiated the quiet strength of a mountain. Brenn's youthful eyes blazed with fiery determination.

Magnus glanced across at Ruiha, leader of the Drogo slaves whose skill with a blade was unmatched. In her, he saw a kindred spirit, a warrior bound by ties of duty and honor that transcended race or creed.

Dakarai stood flanking her. Despite his past as a miner, Magnus knew he fought with the fervor and dedication of a seasoned warrior.

As Magnus stood in the frontline of the Dwarven warriors, Brenn's voice broke through his thoughts, with a note of confusion. "Why aren't they attacking?"

Magnus tightened his grip on his axe, his brow frowning as he scanned the steadily approaching enemy. "I do not know," he admitted. "But it matters not. Our course of action remains unchanged."

"Aye, we fight on," Uleg affirmed.

Suddenly, the approaching Drogo began shouting and scattering in different directions. At first, Magnus assumed it was part of their tactics, some strange attack plan. However, the more he witnessed the Drogo's behavior, the more he realized they were genuinely confused and scared, running around without purpose. Some halted in their tracks and simply screamed at the top of their voices. Although he didn't understand why this was happening, Magnus knew they couldn't waste this perfect opportunity.

Magnus raised his weapon high to rally the Dwarves and Drog and, with a thunderous roar, they charged forward, their battle cries ringing out across the canyon.

The clash of steel was deafening as the wave of slaves broke on their bewildered adversaries. Magnus fought with a fury born of desperation, every strike fueled by a burning desire to get back to Dreynas.

As the fog of confusion slowly began to fade from the Drogo warriors, the battlefield erupted into chaos. Axes clashed with blades, sending sparks flying into the air as blood stained the earth crimson.

Magnus swung his axe with deadly precision, cleaving through the ranks of their adversaries with each thunderous blow. Beside him, Uleg fought with the ferocity of a much younger Dwarf, his stout frame a whirlwind of destruction as he felled foe after foe.

Meanwhile, Ruiha and Dakarai led the Drogo slaves with a cunning and skill that belied their outnumbered status. Moving with fluidity and grace they cut through the chaos of battle like a hot knife through butter, their blades finding their marks with lethal accuracy.

Amidst the carnage, Brenn stood screaming in rage for his lost brother, slicing out a bloody revenge with every strike of his axe. Each swing carved a path of destruction through the enemy ranks.

But for every victory won, there was a price to pay. The Drogo slaves bore the brunt of the enemy onslaught, their screams of pain and anguish drowned out by the cacophony of battle. Despite their courage and determination, many fell beneath the merciless blades of their foes.

The Dwarves, seasoned soldiers with years of battle-hardened experience, fared far better amidst the chaos. Yet even they were not immune to the horrors of war. Magnus, their steadfast leader, watched with a heavy heart as a few of his comrades succumbed to the deadly Drogo blades.

Fellron

Fellron watched the battle unfold. Though the Dwarves and Drogo slaves seemed to be gaining the upper hand, he was concerned at the weight of their losses

A grim resolve settled over Fellron. He had to intervene despite the toll it would take on him.

As the Drogo pursuers charged forward with fresh energy, Fellron summoned his dark magic once more. The surrounding air grew colder, the shadows deepening and twisting at his command. With a whispered incantation, the shadows coalesced, forming into sharp, jagged spears that erupted from the ground beneath the pursuers' feet.

The shadowy spikes pierced through flesh and armor alike, impaling their victims with ruthless efficiency. Fellron's heart pounded with the exertion, each pulse a reminder of the power he wielded and the cost it demanded. The shadow spears wrought carnage among the attackers, their screams mingling with the battle cries of the Dwarves and Drogo slaves.

With each exertion of his dark powers, Fellron felt a draining sensation, his strength ebbing away like sand through an hourglass. The dark magic was a double-edged sword, granting him immense power at the expense of his vitality. His breath grew ragged, his limbs trembling with exhaustion, but he pushed on, driven by the desperate need to protect his kin.

As the last of the shadow spears faded away, leaving behind a scene of devastation, Fellron staggered back. The dark magic had taken its toll, leaving him in a weakened state that threatened to consume him. His vision blurred, and his body screamed for rest, but he couldn't afford to falter.

As he struggled to regain his composure, Fellron could see that his allies needed him now more than ever. He pushed his fatigue aside and focused on the task at hand.

His gaze swept over the battlefield, taking in the sight of the Dwarves and Drogo slaves fighting with renewed vigor. Their determination mirrored his own, a fierce resolve to see their struggle through to the end. Fellron clenched his fists, feeling the remnants of his strength rallying within him.

With a deep breath, he channeled the last of his energy into one final spell. The shadows around him surged, swirling and coiling like serpents ready to strike. He directed them towards the largest group of Drogo warriors, focusing fiercely despite the pain that wracked his body.

The shadows wrapped around the warriors, constricting them with an iron grip. The Drogo struggled, their movements growing frantic as they fought against the inescapable darkness. Fellron's vision darkened at the edges, his strength nearly spent, but he held on, determined to see the spell through.

Finally, with a gasp, he released the spell, the shadows dissipating as the last of his energy left him. He sank to his knees, the world spinning around him. His breath came in shallow gasps, his body trembling with exhaustion. But even in his weakened state, he felt a sense of triumph.

The battlefield fell silent, the remaining Drogo warriors retreating in disarray. The Dwarves and Drogo slaves stood victorious, their faces etched with relief and surprise.

Fellron's vision began to blur. Yet he fought to stay conscious, his thoughts drifting to his family once more. Their faces, long faded from memory, appeared vivid and clear. He had honored their deaths. With that thought, a sense of peace washed over him. In the midst of the chaos and bloodshed, Fellron had found his purpose. He had embraced his destiny, wielded his dark magic for the good of his kin. He knew that whatever came next, he had fought with honor, darkness against darkness.

Ruiha

As Ruiha surveyed the battlefield, adrenaline surged through her veins. The battle had been fierce, the losses heavy, but victory was within their grasp. The air was thick with the acrid scent of blood and sweat; the ground littered with the fallen.

With a fierce cry, she rallied her Drogo slaves. Together, they pressed forward, blades flashing as they cut through the remaining adversaries with ruthless efficiency.

Beside her, Magnus and his Dwarven warriors fought with equal tenacity. The clash of steel against steel made a symphony of the battle, each strike a testament to their determination to see this fight through to the end.

As the battle raged, Ruiha's gaze swept across the chaos, searching for Dakarai. Alarm gripped her when she spotted him locked in combat against three Drogo warriors, his back against a sheer rock face as he fought for his life.

Dakarai moved with a fluid grace, parrying blow after blow from his adversaries. Despite being outnumbered and cornered, he refused to yield. His eyes, filled with fierce resolve, met hers for a brief moment, and she saw the toll the fight was taking on him—the sweat-soaked lines of his horned brow and the heaving rise and fall of his chest.

Without a moment's hesitation, Ruiha charged into the fray, her blade flashing as she attacked Dakarai's assailants with a ferocity that dwarfed their own.

With a fierce cry, she unleashed a flurry of blows, her blade a blur as she struck out with precision born from years of fighting.

As the last of Dakarai's opponents fell beneath their combined onslaught, Ruiha turned to him. "Last push now," she said, wiping her dark hair from her eyes. "We've nearly defeated them."

Dakarai nodded, a look of fierce determination in his eyes, and together they turned and ran back to the main battle.

When the final attackers fell before them, Ruiha felt a surge of triumph swell within her chest. The battlefield lay strewn with the fallen, a testament to the ferocity of the struggle, but – despite their losses and against all odds – they had emerged victorious. With a weary but triumphant smile, Ruiha turned to Magnus.

"You fought well," he said, through labored breaths, still managing a small smirk as he added, "For a human!"

"Have you not heard of the legends told of the Shadowhawk?" she said playfully.

"Aye," he chuckled, "although until recently I had believed her to be a myth!"

Replaying the battle in her mind she turned suddenly serious, to the Dwarf "Magnus," she asked, "do any of your Snow Wolves practice magic?"

"Bah," he scoffed. "Dwarves can't practice magic! The only thing we're good at is craft magic. You saw how we could manipulate the metal on your bars, yes? Well, that's the limit of our magical abilities!" He laughed, the sound hearty despite the fatigue in his eyes.

"Hmm..." she mused, a thoughtful expression crossing her face. "Someone out there was using magic. And it seemed as though they were on our side. Just before the battle began, a wall of dark shadow concealed me. I could barely see through it. And again towards the end of the battle, shards of earth speared through the enemy."

"Aye," Magnus said, his gaze drifting into the distance as if pondering the intricacies of the universe itself. "It may well explain why they didn't attack us when they were in range. Perhaps someone was hiding us."

"And," she continued, "remember their fear and disorientation minutes before our charge? The assistance we received helped turn the tide of the battle, I believe. Whoever it was, I'd like to extend my thanks!"

As Ruiha finished expressing her gratitude, a voice echoed from the shadows saying, "Thanks is unnecessary but appreciated nonetheless." They spun round to find a hooded figure emerging from the darkness.

As the shadows parted, a Dwarf unlike any she had ever seen before approached with measured steps. His eyes, black as the darkest night and piercing, seemed to hold wisdom yet were devoid of the warmth typically found in the eyes of his kin. What struck her even more was the absence of facial hair, a rarity among Dwarves, lending him an unsettling air of enigma

As he moved closer, Ruiha's gaze traced faint lines etched across his skin like whispers of a forgotten language. Upon closer inspection, she realized they were rune scars intricately carved into his flesh, each marking a story of power and mystery. These runes, remnants of forgotten magic, adorned his body like a tapestry of secrets, hinting at a life steeped in strange dark magic.

"I am Fellron," he announced. "And aye, it was I who lent my aid to your cause."

Magnus and Ruiha exchanged glances, their curiosity piqued by this unexpected revelation. Ruiha heard several whispers of Daemonseeker from behind them, the term carrying an air of both fear and reverence.

"But why?" Ruiha inquired, her eyes narrowing with suspicion. "What stake do you have in our battle?"

Fellron's lips curved into a cryptic smile, and she thought she saw a glimpse of warmth enter his dark eyes. "Aye, lassie, it will become clear in due time," he replied, his eyes gleaming with hidden knowledge. "For now, rest assured that our paths have intertwined for a reason."

As the weight of his words settled over her, Ruiha couldn't shake the feeling that their victory, their very survival, had been orchestrated by forces beyond their understanding and that allies could come from the most unexpected places.

20.
Gunnar's Gift

"The bond between friends is forged in the fires of trust and loyalty, a connection that transcends time and trials."

Shon'anga

In the depths of the Scorched Mountains, where the tunnels wound like veins through the earth, Shon'anga plotted his path to power. His nerves jittered like flickering torchlight as he led his party of shaman and warriors deeper into the labyrinthine passages.

The loss of his hand throbbed with every heartbeat, a constant reminder of the battle that had inadvertently set him on this course. The phantom pain seemed to mock him, a cruel echo of past failures. But now, with the promise of the staff echoing in his mind, Shon'anga's thoughts danced with newfound purpose. As they delved deeper into the winding tunnels, Shon'anga's eyes were set on his destination: the tomb of Nergai. There, he would carry out the will of his god and search for the way to breach the barriers between worlds. Failure was not an option.

As Shon'anga guided his party towards the hidden chamber, he tried to shake off the lingering fear of Nergai's wrath or Junak's contempt. Each echoing footstep was a whisper of destiny, each breath a pledge of commitment.

A sudden roar shattered the silence. Shon'anga faltered, his body nearly betraying him in the face of the thunderous sound. From the darkness a pack of scalemaws erupted, their reptilian forms twisting with lightning speed, their long snouts filled with row upon row of razor-sharp teeth hungry for flesh. They halted mere metres away from the Shon'anga's group, their ravenous gaze fixed upon their prey.

The warriors instinctively formed a defensive barrier, weapons poised to strike as the scalemaws slowly stalked forward. An attacking scalemaw caught one of the shaman off guard with the sheer speed of its lunge. The victim found himself ensnared within the creature's deadly jaws as a vice-like grip crushed bone and jagged teeth tore through scaled flesh. The shaman was dead before the poison reached his heart.

With a rallying cry, the warriors leapt into action, their blades glinting in the dim light as they clashed with the ferocious beasts. Despite their stubby legs, the scalemaws moved with astonishing agility, darting in and out of the shadows to strike with deadly precision.

The battle raged on, the air thick with the scent of blood and sweat as the warriors fought desperately to defend themselves and the unarmed shaman. With each swing of their weapons, they carved through the scalemaws, pushing back the ferocious onslaught.

As chaos unfolded around him, Shon'anga's mind raced desperately. The weight of a portal crystal nestled against his chest, its cool surface a tantalizing promise of escape. Yet he hesitated. The crystal was too precious a resource and finding another was unlikely.

He also sensed that the warriors had the situation under control. Their movements were coordinated and disciplined as they faced the scalemaw threat. Shon'anga watched with apprehension, hoping they would dispatch the creatures before they closed in on him.

With each passing moment, the temptation to activate the portal crystal grew stronger, its power humming like a siren's song in his mind. Yet Shon'anga remained rooted in place, torn between the desire for escape and the hope that his protectors would emerge victorious.

In a final flurry of blows, the last of the scalemaws fell, its twisted form collapsing in a heap upon the blood-stained earth. Silence descended, broken only by the ragged breaths of the warriors.

Relief flooded through Shon'anga like a cool breeze, washing away the tendrils of fear that had gripped his heart. He breathed a silent prayer of gratitude to Nergai for his deliverance from a gruesome death.

As the warriors regrouped, Shon'anga allowed himself a moment of respite, knowing the danger had passed, at least for now. But even as he caught his breath, he couldn't shake a lingering sense of unease. Was the attack an omen? A reminder of the perils that awaited them in the darkened depths of Nexus?

The warriors indicated they were ready to move on, undaunted by the loss of the fallen shaman. With a solemn nod, Shon'anga motioned for the warriors to follow as he led them deeper into the tunnels of the Scorched Mountains.

As they journeyed onward, Shon'anga's thoughts were consumed by the vision of the staff. He led the party through twisting passages and hidden crevices, each step bringing them closer to their elusive goal. And then, at long last, they stood before the entrance to the tomb.

With a sense of reverence, Shon'anga pushed open the doors, revealing the chamber within. The very air seemed burdened with history, and the walls were adorned with faded murals depicting the glory of the dragon's reign.

As they stepped into the heart of the tomb, awe washed over the warriors. Many had never set foot in the chamber before, their eyes wide with wonder at the sight before them.

Shon'anga's gaze was drawn to the center of the chamber where a huge dragon-shaped coffin lay, black and etched with countless runes. It seemed to pulse with an otherworldly energy, filling the space with an aura of power and death. The atmosphere stirred a flicker of hope in Shon'anga's spirit, a belief that, with the guidance of Nergai, he would find the powerful artefact that would change his fate.

Shon'anga ordered that the sconces be lit, providing a source of fire in the chamber. With whispered incantations he had memorized from Nergai himself, Shon'anga invoked the ancient magic of the chamber, calling upon the forces of fire to aid their quest. It took a few moments, and initially, Shon'anga worried he had failed, but then the ground grew excruciatingly hot beneath their feet as reality itself began to warp and bend. As the walls of the chamber shimmered like mirages in the desert heat, Shon'anga and his party stepped forward into the unknown, their bodies bathed in the faint glow of the shifting magic. In an instant, they were transported from the confines of the Scorched Mountains and thrust into the twisted realm of Nexus.

Darkness enveloped them like a shroud as they emerged into the desolate landscape of Nexus. Shadows danced hungrily upon the horizon, and the air was thick with the scent of decay. Strange spectre-like things lurked in every shadow, their hollow eyes fixated upon the intruders who dared to trespass upon their domain.

But Shon'anga stood resolute, his missing hand a stark reminder of the sacrifices already made in his pursuit of power. Each step into the darkness felt like an invocation of destiny, a pledge to Nergai and to himself, driving him towards the elusive prize that awaited him in the heart of Nexus.

Gunnar

Gunnar faced the entrance to the Labyrinth, his piercing blue eyes straining against the shroud of darkness veiling the depths of the trial ahead.

Havoc, perched atop Gunnar's shoulder, grew increasingly restless. The tiny Sprite had always struggled with the concept of patience, and Gunnar sent reassuring thoughts of calm and restraint pulsing through the bond between them.

Commander Aelric stood silently off to the side, as stoic and uncommunicative as ever. Gunnar briefly entertained the notion of coaxing more information about the trial from him but thought better of it. The man's stern demeanor was like an impenetrable wall, offering no glimpse of the thoughts behind that cold eye. Gunnar felt a pang of concern as Havoc's restlessness escalated, fearing he might lose control of the Stonesprite altogether. In fairness, they had been waiting in silence at the trial entrance for nearly an hour. Each minute that passed devoid of information or guidance wore Gunnar's own patience ever thinner. The oppressive silence grew heavier with each tick of the clock.

After what felt like an eternity, Gunnar's ears perked up at the distinct sound of footsteps echoing down the hallway behind him. Turning, he was greeted by the sight of Karl, his heart lifting at witnessing his fellow Dwarf's approach. A broad grin as wide as his red, hairy face split Karl's features in two.

"Took your time!" Gunnar exclaimed, his voice echoing in the cavernous space.

"Aye," Karl began, "been waiting here long then, boss?"

"Any longer and I fear Havoc would've leapt straight into the Labyrinth alone," he replied, only half-joking.

"Boss, I've made something for you…" Karl started, his voice tinged with excitement, but the sound of more footsteps approaching from behind interrupted their conversation.

As they turned, they saw Anwyn making her way towards them with Thalirion following closely behind. Gunnar's pulse quickened at the sight. Her elegance and strength were a beacon amidst the darkness, a reminder of what they were fighting for.

"Anwyn!" Karl exclaimed. "Feels like it's been an age and a half since we've all been in the same room together!"

Anwyn chuckled warmly as she embraced Karl. "It has been too long," she agreed before turning to Gunnar.

As they hugged, Gunnar felt a rush of warmth flood through him at the closeness of their bodies. He couldn't help but notice the softness of Anwyn's touch, the gentle curve of her frame fitting perfectly against his own. He felt the familiar fluttering in his chest that he always experienced when she was near.

As they stepped apart, Gunnar felt a pang of longing. He yearned for more time with Anwyn, without the constraints of duty or obligation. But for now, all he could do was offer her a weary smile and a nod of greeting.

"Anwyn," Gunnar said, his voice softening, "how do you fare? I apologize we haven't been able to spend much time together; my training has been... intense," he admitted, casting a glance towards Commander Aelric.

She chuckled and gave his hand a reassuring squeeze. "Please do not apologize, Gunnar," she said gently. "Thalirion has also been keeping me busy!"

Havoc perched on Gunnar's shoulder, telepathically inquired about Lorelei, his tiny form rum- bling with anticipation.

Gunnar glanced at Anwyn and conveyed the question that Havoc had posed. In response, Anwyn's delicate Fae companion fluttered from around her, wings shimmering like gossamer in the dim light of the chamber. With a musical tinkle, she began chattering away, and although Gunnar had no clue what she was saying, he got the impression that she was happy.

A soft smile played across Anwyn's lips as she translated. "Lorelei is well," she said fondly. "She has missed you all and longs for the camaraderie of our group once again."

Gunnar nodded, happy at the news of Lorelei's well-being and the progress they had all made despite the challenges they faced.

"Gunnar," Karl interrupted, drawing his attention. "I was just saying that I have something for you. Under Sage Thadwick's guidance, I made an axe that will serve you well in the upcoming trials." Karl slowly withdrew a large battle axe and its sheath from where it had been secured on his back and presented it to Gunnar.

Gunnar grasped the sheathed weapon with both hands, expecting the weight of the large axe to anchor him to the ground. To his surprise, the axe felt feather-light in his grip. Despite its formidable size and imposing appearance, it seemed to defy the laws of physics, its weight barely registering in his hands.

"Karl," Gunnar said, his voice filled with genuine appreciation, "this is an amazing gift. Thank you."

"Boss, take it out of its sheath and examine it. I'll explain its strengths to you," Karl responded, his own pride evident in his tone.

With a nod of agreement, Gunnar carefully unsheathed the double-headed axe, his hands trembling slightly with anticipation. As the polished frosteel blade emerged from its sheath, intricate runes etched around its curves shimmered with an unearthly green light. Gunnar sensed intuitively that each symbol bore a tale, a piece of the potent energy flowing within the weapon.

The metal of the axe was no ordinary frosteel; beautiful swirling patterns reminiscent of flowing rivers and stormy skies adorned its surface. When caught in the light, the mesmerizing patterns gleamed like liquid silver.

Gunnar ran his hand down the smooth haft, crafted from a shadowy, bone-like material. It seemed to draw in the surrounding darkness, as if channeling the very essence of the void. Gunnar could sense that Spectral Echoes lingered within its depths, reminding him of virtues like courage, strength, and honor—remnants of long-forgotten warriors.

It seemed to hum with an energy all its own, resonating with a unique bond that Gunnar couldn't quite explain—a bond that somehow felt intertwined with his friendship with Karl. With each passing moment as the weightless axe rested in his hands, Gunnar felt a profound sense of connection to the weapon, as if it had been forged specifically for him and him alone.

Glancing over at Karl, Gunnar could see the pride shining in his friend's eyes. At that moment, Gunnar knew that this gift was more than just a weapon—it was a symbol of their friendship.

Karl approached with eager anticipation, his eyes alight with excitement as he huddled around the weapon. His meaty fingers traced the intricate runes running along the curved blade.

"Each of these runes ensures a different quality," Karl explained enthusiastically. "This rune ensures the blade stays as sharp as a dragon's tooth!" He pointed to one of the many runes etched into the blade's edge.

As he continued to trace his finger along the blade, skipping some runes and pausing on others, Karl's explanations grew more animated. "This rune will enhance the blade's accuracy, ensuring that each strike finds its mark with pinpoint precision," he declared, his finger hovering over a particular rune. Then, pointing at another, he exclaimed, "And this rune enhances the blade's agility and swiftness in combat, allowing you to strike with lightning-fast speed!"

Gunnar eyed the axe with newfound respect, his admiration for Karl's craftsmanship growing with each passing moment. It was clear that Karl had poured everything he had into this weapon, and the results were nothing short of remarkable.

"You have my thanks, my friend," Gunnar said earnestly. "This axe is the finest weapon I have ever seen! It feels powerful, yet it weighs almost nothing!"

Karl chuckled softly, his eyes twinkling with amusement. "Sage Thadwick mentioned you might say something similar. When I first felt the weight of it, I was disappointed, truth be told," he confessed, his expression turning thoughtful. "It seemed too heavy to be a practical weapon. I almost threw it away and gave up. Only Sage Thadwick prevented me. You see, the haft is imbued with the virtues of powerful warriors." Karl ran his hand upon the smooth, shadowy haft fondly. "Separating virtues from the shards of Spectral Echoes is quite the challenge, might I add!" A proud grin spread across his face as he exclaimed, "But I managed it!"

He became earnest again as he described the attributes of his masterpiece. "When you pick up the axe, these virtues will manifest in you. The primary virtue imbued in the haft is strength. You'll notice that your own strength is heightened whenever you're in contact with it. That's why it feels as though it weighs nothing at all."

Leaning in conspiratorially, Karl continued, "The second virtue is courage. With the ability to face danger and overcome your fear amidst the chaos of battle, you'll be able to harness your magic to its fullest potential."

"And finally," Karl's expression lightened, his tone turning jovial, "to ensure that the power doesn't go to your head, I imbued the virtue of honor. With the haft in your hands, you'll feel a strong sense of integrity and righteousness, guiding you to always act with honor, even in the heat of battle."

Gunnar ran a spiritual scan through the weapon and could indeed sense the virtues imbued within. "It appears my debt to you is becoming harder and harder to repay, Karl!"

"I'm glad you said your debt," Havoc chuckled in Gunnar's mind. "I don't owe the oaf anything!"

Gunnar ignored the sprite as he continued to examine the weapon. "This is truly too much," he whispered.

The swirling patterns running through the frosteel of the metal blade drew his eye. "What is this pattern? It is beautiful," he asked, his curiosity piqued by its elegance.

"Ah!" Karl exclaimed proudly. "Beauty is merely a byproduct! Infused into the frosteel is the soul shard of the most powerful spectral echo we could find! It took me weeks of hammering, infusing the metal with the shard. But it was worth it. Sage Thadwick said it is one of the most powerful weapons he has ever seen! It would take the fall of the Boria expanse itself to shatter this blade!" His chest swelled with pride as he spoke, his belief in the weapon's unparalleled strength evident in every word.

Anwyn came over and eyed the weapon with awe. "This truly is amazing, Karl," she said warmly. "You should be very proud of it!"

"Indeed I am," Karl agreed, running his hand through his bushy red beard, and Gunnar almost chuckled at how many of Sage Thadwick's mannerisms Karl had adopted since spending the past few weeks with him.

"Do you mind if I scan it?" Anwyn asked hesitantly.

"Aye, Anwyn. You scan away!" Karl chuckled.

Oddly, as Anwyn's eyes went vacant, Gunnar felt the distinct tingle of a spiritual scan emanating from the weapon. As Anwyn's eyes cleared and returned to normal, she gasped. "Karl, truly you have created a magnificent weapon. You have also imbued it with your own spirit!" she gasped.

"Aye, every time the hammer struck, I poured more of my spirit into it... Although," he chuckled, "I didn't even realise I'd been doing it at first. Sage Thadwick stopped me one day, wondering what I was doing. I just said... hammering away, boss. But he decided to scan me as I was hammering, and that's when he figured it out. Apparently, it's never been done before!"

"And for good reason!" a deep voice echoed from the corridor. A few moments later, Thraxos emerged from the shadows with the human mage next to him. "Infusing one's own spirit into a weapon is dangerous for several reasons. Agreed, it will create a powerful bond between the wielder and the object. However, it is thought that this bond can become too strong, leading to the weapon exerting influence over its wielder or even attempting to possess them."

Gunnar held the axe slightly more apprehensively after Thraxos's revelation, but the large Minotaur continued. "In addition, just as the spirit can imbue the weapon with power, so too can the weapon influence the spirit. Despite Karl's insistence that the virtue of honor will prevent it from happening, if the weapon can somehow be used for dark or malevolent purposes, it is believed that it will corrupt the spirit of its wielder, leading them down a path of darkness and destruction."

Thalirion interrupted, his voice rising above Thraxos. "In- deed, Thraxos is correct. However, this is only the case when somebody infuses a weapon for themselves. In this instance, Karl is not the wielder of the weapon. The only reason that Gunnar can even hold the weapon, let alone wield it in battle, is because of the bond and loyalty between them."

Commander Aelric joined the conversation cutting Thalirion off with his gruff voice. "Are you forgetting the risk of loss, Thalirion? Or are you purposely attempting to deceive?" The Commander's voice dripped with contempt for the Elf Sage.

Thalirion scoffed. "Why would I attempt to deceive them, Aelric? It is my home realm that is under threat."

"Yet you neglected to mention that when one infuses their spirit into a weapon, they are essentially binding a part of their essence to that object. This can leave them vulnerable to harm should the weapon be destroyed." Commander Aelric spat.

Surprisingly, it was Karl who silenced the Commander. "Did you not hear what I said? It would take the fall of the Boria Stellar Expanse for this axe to be destroyed. And with all due respect, Commander, if that were to happen, who would give a flying fuck whether the axe led to my harm?"

Gunnar had to stifle a laugh at Karl's words and the Commander's angry silence.

While Aelric in silence, the group continued to examine the weapon. Even Kemp, the human mage, asked to feel its haft and look at the runed blade.

Eventually, Anwyn asked, "Gunnar, you surely have to give the weapon a name?"

Gunnar shook his head slowly. Giving the axe a name felt wrong somehow... well, that wasn't exactly true, he thought. Giving the axe a name now felt wrong. He knew that he should only name this weapon once it had tasted blood.

The axe hummed in silent acknowledgment that only Gunnar could sense.

21.
THE LABYRINTH

"The only way to find the limits of the possible is by going beyond them into the impossible."

Kemp

From high up in his control room, Kemp observed the three companions as they approached the threshold of the trials.

It was no ordinary entrance; it was a gaping maw in the ancient tower's stone façade that seemed to swallow the very light around it. Kemp couldn't help but admire their courage as he watched them disappear into the abyss, their silhouettes swallowed by the darkness.

A shiver of apprehension ran down Kemp's spine. Thraxos had explained that if they succeeded, they would emerge stronger, their spirits on the verge of Overlord. If they failed… Kemp pushed that thought aside. Only time would tell.

Kemp's role was straightforward, and it hadn't taken him long to understand how the control panel for the Labyrinth worked. Each trial required a constant flow of aura to ensure it kept running. The amount of aura needed varied depending on the challenge itself and how difficult Kemp wanted it to be.

There were three separate trials within the Labyrinth, each designed to test the challengers' strength, skill, bravery, intelligence, and how well they could operate as a team. Kemp had spent countless hours honing his skills in manipulating each of the three trials. He knew he could make them nearly insurmountable if he chose to do so. Thraxos had urged Kemp to practice using the controls until he could render the trials virtually impossible for all but the most skilled Overlords.

Just before Thraxos departed, leaving Kemp in the control room alone until who knew when, the towering Minotaur emphasized the importance of pushing the candidates to their limits if Kemp wished to continue his advancement at the Tower. His role was clear: make the trials so difficult that Gunnar, Karl, and Anwyn would give up.

The allure of becoming an Overlord dangled tantalizingly before Kemp, serving as a potent motivator to ensure that none of the challengers succeeded in passing the trials. While Kemp harbored no ill will towards the three competitors, the prospect of achieving Overlord status overshadowed any qualms he might have had about pushing them to their breaking point.

As he watched them step into the first trial, he almost felt the air crackle with anticipation. Before them lay a vast battlefield littered with obstacles and teeming with enemy soldiers. These soldiers, however, were not living beings but constructs made from spectral echo parts and fueled by the aura Kemp flooded into them.

On the competitors' side stood a unit of soldiers, also constructed from spectral echo parts. Kemp knew that the success of the challengers depended not only on their individual skills but also on their ability to work as a cohesive unit, coordinating their movements and strategies to overcome the enemy onslaught.

The trial's strengths lay in its ability to assess the challengers' teamwork, communication, and tactical prowess. It forced them to rely on each other, to trust in each other's abilities while utilizing their own strengths to support the team. The dynamic battlefield required quick thinking and adaptability, testing their ability to make split-second decisions under pressure.

However, the trial also presented significant challenges. The relentless onslaught of enemy soldiers would test the challengers' endurance and resilience, pushing them to their physical and mental limits. The presence of friendly soldiers added another layer of complexity, requiring the challengers to balance offence and defense while ensuring the safety of their allies.

Moreover, some of the constructed enemy soldiers possessed magical abilities beyond those of ordinary warriors, making them formidable adversaries. Additionally, the constant influx of aura from Kemp ensured their opponents were never tired, forcing the challengers to constantly reassess their approach and conserve their own energy wisely.

Kemp cracked his knuckles and stretched out his back, readying himself for a long night.

Gunnar

Gunnar stood at the entrance of the trial, his eyes scanning the scroll: "Just as a chain composed of individual links relies on each link's integrity to bear the weight it carries, so too does a team rely on the strength and commitment of each member to achieve success." He raised his gaze, taking in the sprawling battlefield ahead, where spectral echoes of soldiers stood in mismatched formations, bound by magic.

The scene before him stirred memories of his father's stories, tales meant to teach the value of leadership and unity. He recalled the parable of the bear and the wolves, understanding now more than ever the lesson behind it. The bear's lone strength could never match the collective power of the wolf pack. Gunnar knew he needed to embody this lesson now.

"It seems our first challenge will be a battle," he announced to his companions. "I assume we must defeat the enemy to be victorious."

Karl, examining the battlefield with a critical eye, grunted in agreement. Anwyn nodded towards the spectral soldiers. "It seems we are to work alongside these... constructs."

"Let's test the waters," Gunnar decided, stepping into the trial. The soldiers sprang to life, projectiles flying, but as he stepped back, they returned to their original positions and froze. An ominous red light bathed the field, and a shadowy clock began counting down.

"It appears we have to wait for the trial to restart," Gunnar noted.

"Aye, thank Draeg's stone balls! I could do with a nap," Havoc sighed, diving into Gunnar's cloak pocket. "Wake me when it gets interesting."

"What now, boss?" Karl asked.

Anwyn stepped into the trial, inspecting the friendly soldiers. "We have time to strategize. Perhaps this is a boon."

Gunnar doubted it but joined her. "Karl, can you sense anything from these soldiers, given your recent exposure to spectral echoes?"

Karl inspected the soldiers carefully, lifting arms, examining weapons. He even wandered to the enemy lines, muttering to himself. "Our allies are constructed from various spectral echoes, requiring an outside source of aura to function," he reported. "The enemy soldiers, however, have runes for enhanced strength, speed, and spell-casting. That one there," he pointed to a large soldier, "is heavily fortified for defense."

Gunnar nodded. "And killing them?"

"They're not alive. Animated corpses fueled by magic. Destroying them would mean outlasting the magic animating them."

Anwyn shuddered but remained focused. "There must be another way to defeat them. Let's investigate further."

The three companions explored the battlefield, studying soldiers and terrain. Even Lorelei fluttered about, searching for clues.

To Gunnar's surprise, Havoc found the answer. The Sprite emerged from Gunnar's pocket, grumbling about the lack of space. "Are you telling me you can't sense that?" Havoc asked incredulously.

"What do you mean?" Gunnar asked.

"The veins in the earth, shifting and moving. You can't feel it?" Havoc shook his head. "Come here, I'll show you." Gunnar extended his hand, and Havoc hopped on, closing his eyes and breathing deeply.

"Are you meditating?" Gunnar asked, having never witnessed the Sprite meditate before.

"Aye, now let me do this. And close your eyes for Dreyna's sake!" Havoc muttered instructions, guiding Gunnar to open his spiritual senses. Gunnar felt the aura, euphoric and vibrant, and the subtle vibrations in the ground.

"I can feel it," Gunnar gasped.

"Good," Havoc said. "Focus on the veins. They connect to that," he pointed to an obsidian sphere above the trial. "Disrupt it, and we disrupt the soldiers long enough to overpower them."

Gunnar marveled at Havoc's ability to sense so much. "Thank you, Havoc."

"Aye, now let me sleep. Wake me when the trial starts."

After Gunnar had explained the situation, they continued investigating the battlefield, following the veins of power running through the earth. Dozens of veins, each powering a different section: half for their army of constructs, half for the enemy.

Anwyn noted that although each of them could disrupt the flow of power, her connection to aura and magical abilities far surpassed the others. While Gunnar and Karl could only disrupt one section each, Anwyn could manage two, perhaps three.

Karl's experience with Sage Thadwick in Spiritsmithing meant he could create weapons from discarded spectral echo parts stored in a hut by the battlefield. It was agreed that Gunnar's skills were best used leading their army of friendly soldiers.

The following morning, just before the course reset itself, they had their plan. Anwyn would target veins powering the enemy constructs, weakening their defenses and reducing their offensive capabilities. She would also pave the way for Karl to reach the hut, where he would craft weapons for the team, providing the firepower needed to break through the enemy defenses.

Gunnar would lead the main army, ensuring soldiers deployed in sync with Anwyn's disruptions and armed with Karl's weapons, driving them to overwhelm the enemy forces.

They waited at the trial's threshold as the red light faded. Gunnar stood, his majestic battleaxe in hand, near the soldiers he would command. Havoc yawned beside him. Karl waited near the hut, ready for Gunnar's orders. Anwyn, in the battlefield's center, could disrupt magic for Karl and assist Gunnar when needed. Lorelei perched atop Anwyn's head, resolute.

"Like old times, hey boss!" Karl called out. "Aye," Gunnar replied. "Except this time there's more at stake." He nodded to his companions and stepped into the battlefield.

The constructs sprang to life, fueled by the obsidian sphere. Gunnar, unsure if the soldiers understood him, barked orders. "Soldiers, advance as a unit and overwhelm the enemy. Ready… advance!" He marched forward, the friendly soldiers following. He glanced at Karl, who dashed forward, using boulders for cover.

An enemy unit broke away towards Karl. Gunnar nodded to Anwyn. She placed her hand on the ground, sending a pulse of magic through the vein, freezing two soldiers. Another pulse, stronger, and all soldiers approaching Karl froze. Karl nodded appreciatively and sprinted towards the hut. Eight more soldiers broke away towards him. Gunnar had to focus on the advancing enemy. He placed his hand on the ground, sending a magic pulse. Several enemy soldiers froze, others pushed past.

"Form up! Shields forward, ranks tight!" he screamed. The soldiers closed ranks, shields raised. "Forward march! Steady pace!" The shield wall advanced.

As they neared the enemy, Gunnar peered over his shield. "Lock shields! Brace!" Soldiers interlocked shields. "Ready weapons! Strike on my command!" They marched two more paces. "Attack!" The soldiers charged, maintaining their shield wall, striking out with weapons. Gunnar marveled at the constructs' effectiveness.

Yet the enemy began to overpower his soldiers. They gave ground, only a few paces, but enough. He needed to turn the tide. Reaching down, he sent short pulses of magic through the veins. Some enemies jolted to a stop. His soldiers took advantage, pushing forward. Another pulse, more ground gained. One last time, and the enemy was significantly pushed back. Gunnar smiled, clenching his battleaxe.

Swinging the axe, he cleaved an enemy construct in two. His perception of time slowed, allowing him to react. No resistance; the enemy soldier split bloodlessly.

He glanced at Karl, who battled fiercely. Anwyn had cleared a path, but enemy soldiers continually peeled off, attacking Karl. He fought with an axe and short sword, his training evident. Without it, Karl would be overwhelmed.

Anwyn was locked in a magical duel with a runed soldier. One hand on the ground, the other raised, white lightning bolts streamed towards her opponent. The air crackled with her magic.

Her opponent, unaffected, stepped forward. Gunnar sought the vein powering the soldier, sending a shockwave through it. The soldier froze, arms limp, then was obliterated by lightning. Anwyn mouthed "thank you" across the battlefield.

Energized, Gunnar charged his opponents, his axe cleaving multiple soldiers. Havoc weaved between legs, causing miniature earthquakes. By the time Gunnar looked up, Karl was in the hut, crafting weapons. Anwyn, or perhaps Lorelei, had erected a magical barrier around the hut, under attack by enemy soldiers.

Suddenly, a surge of power from the obsidian sphere propelled the enemy forward. Gunnar's soldiers were pushed back. Karl retreated, blasting enemies with a cannon he had made. Anwyn strained, her spells ineffective against the enemy surge. Realizing defeat, Gunnar called for a retreat. His head hung heavy with their failure. They would rest and try again. This was not the end of their trial.

Anwyn's muscles ached with the memory of defeat, each step heavier than the last. Three weeks of relentless trials had etched lines of exhaustion on her companions' faces, their eyes shadowed with fatigue. Each day's failure had been a harsh teacher, the sting of it a catalyst that drove them to push harder, dig deeper. They had faced the trial every day, the battlefield a familiar adversary that showed no mercy. Despite Anwyn realizing that in the three weeks which had passed in Nexus, only three days had passed back in Vellhor, she still felt as though they were wasting valuable time.

The firelight flickered over Gunnar's face as he pored over the scroll, seeking any scrap of wisdom in the few sentences it contained that might help turn the tide. Anwyn admired his determination, driving himself forward despite the string of defeats. His hands were calloused from endless practice with his battleaxe, which, once merely a mighty weapon, had become an extension of his will. She sensed the aura within it getting stronger as Gunnar's efforts unlocked something deep and ancient that might finally give them the edge they needed.

Karl's hands were always busy. His nights were spent in the hut, where the air was thick with the scent of magic. Under Sage Thadwick's guidance, he had mastered the art of crafting weapons, each one a vital element in their armory. His masterpiece was an enchanted cannon designed to target the obsidian sphere. He had perfected the manufacturing process through grueling trial and error. The next time they attempted the trial, he would be able to create it in moments.

Anwyn's path had been one of deep introspection. She would sit for hours, cross-legged on the cold ground, feeling the pulse of the aura beneath her skin, sinking deeper into its flow. She could feel it now, a living current of power, more intimate than her own heartbeat. She had learned to manipulate the magical veins with precision, bending them to her will like a skilled weaver at her loom. She had grown attuned to the battlefield's energy, sensing the ebb and flow of power as naturally as she felt the wind on her face.

As they stood at the threshold of the trial once more, Anwyn felt a quiet resolve settle over her. The battlefield lay ahead, a familiar expanse of spectral soldiers and pulsing veins of magic. She could sense the power thrumming beneath the ground, a living current she was ready to harness.

She glanced at Gunnar, his eyes alight with the same determination. This was their chance to prove that the last three weeks had tempered their skills and taught them to win.

"We've got this," Gunnar said, his voice steady. The runes etched into the blade of his battleaxe gleamed an eerie green in the dim light.

Anwyn nodded, comforted by the weight of her sword in her hand. Lorelei fluttered atop her shoulder, whispering words of encouragement. Beside her, Karl adjusted his gear, his expression grim. Even the usually irreverent Havoc, was somber and serious.

As the familiar light bathed the battlefield, spectral soldiers sprang to life once more. Anwyn immediately focused on the magical veins, her aura flaring as she sent powerful pulses through the ground.

Gunnar led the friendly soldiers forward in perfect formation, their shields raised, ready to face the enemy. Anwyn began targeting multiple sections of the battlefield.

She sent disruptive waves through the veins, causing the enemy soldiers to falter and weaken. Her connection to the aura was stronger than ever, and she felt the power coursing through her.

Karl, as always, moved swiftly towards the hut using the boulders for cover as he made his way to the hut. Anwyn kept a protective eye on him, sending pulses of magic to freeze any enemies that approached. Her spells were more precise now, her control absolute.

"Anwyn, focus on the central vein!" Gunnar's voice cut through the din of battle.

Anwyn nodded, her focus narrowing to a single point. She channeled her energy into the main vein that powered a large section of the enemy forces. Immediately, she felt the resistance—a dark, pulsating force pushing back against her. The enemy's magic clawed at her, trying to repel her intrusion. She gritted her teeth, every muscle in her body tensing with the effort to maintain her hold. The magical pressure almost suffocating, but she refused to yield.

With a final effort, she collapsed the vein, causing a significant portion of the enemy soldiers to crumble. Gunnar seized the opportunity, leading a charge that pushed their advantage further.

Karl had reached the hut and began crafting the spectral parts into weapons with practiced speed. He emerged with the cannon-like device and Anwyn could feel the power emanating from it even from where she stood. Lorelei created a barrier around the Karl, shielding him from the enemy's attacks as he got into position.

Havoc, sensing the critical moment, darted through the battlefield, disrupting smaller veins with uncanny precision.

His agility and magical sensitivity proved invaluable, creating openings for Gunnar and the friendly soldiers.

Chaos engulfed the battlefield, a whirlwind of clashing weapons and arcane energies. Anwyn's breath came in ragged gasps, but she forced herself to remain focused through her exhaustion, seeking out the key nodes within the enemy's network.

She visualized the intricate web of magic and sent targeted pulses of disruptive energy through the veins. Every jolt she delivered fractured the enemy's defenses a little more, the spectral soldiers faltering as the aura supporting them failed. The strain tugged at her, but with each weakening pulse, she could see the path to victory growing clearer.

"Anwyn, now!" Gunnar's voice rang out over the fray.

Anwyn closed her eyes, drawing a deep breath as she summoned every ounce of her energy. She felt the familiar rush of the aura flowing through her, building to a fierce crescendo. With a determined exhale, she released it in a concentrated blast aimed directly at the obsidian sphere.

At that precise moment, she heard the thunderous roar of Karl's cannon. The enchanted projectile streaked across the battlefield, a brilliant arc of light. It struck the sphere with a deafening impact. Anwyn's eyes snapped open in time to see the sphere's surface spider-web with cracks, but it held firm, refusing to shatter.

Her heart sank as the enemy soldiers, momentarily stunned, began to rally. The brief glimmer of hope wavered, but she clenched her fists, feeling the residual energy of her blast still reverberating in the air. They had made a dent, but it wasn't enough. Not yet.

From her vantage point, Anwyn watched as Gunnar, his face set, refused to accept defeat. He stepped forward, his grip tightening around the hilt of his battleaxe. She could almost see the aura flowing through him, merging with the powerful weapon in his hands. Gunnar closed his eyes, centering himself, and Anwyn held her breath.

With a fierce cry, Gunnar swung the axe with all his might. The air around him seemed to ripple and bend as a shockwave erupted from the blade, tearing through the enemy. Anwyn felt the ground beneath her tremble as the sheer intensity of the attack sent vibrations through the earth. The shockwave raced forward, shattering the remaining magical veins and striking the obsidian sphere.

The sphere, unable to withstand the combined assault, splintered and exploded into fragments. The battlefield fell into stunned silence, the devastating impact of Gunnar's attack evident in the fallen enemy constructs and the quivering earth.

The remaining enemy soldiers crumbled, their magic severed and lifeless. Silence enveloped the battlefield, now bathed in a soft green light. After three weeks of enduring the ominous red glow after each attempt, the sight of the green light nearly brought tears to Anwyn's eyes.

She lowered her katana, her breath coming in heavy but triumphant gasps. Gunnar and Karl stood beside her, their faces reflecting the same sense of victory and relief.

"We did it," Gunnar said, his voice filled with pride.

Anwyn nodded, a profound sense of accomplishment swelling within her. They had adapted and grown through the countless hours of practice and moments of doubt. The lessons of teamwork and unity had finally borne fruit, their combined efforts culminating in this hard-won victory.

Havoc rumbled, his usual grin back in place. "About time," he said with a chuckle. "Now, how about a nap?"

They shared a laugh, the tension of the trial finally melting away. Anwyn's shoulders relaxed, a genuine smile spreading across her face for the first time in weeks. She glanced at her companions, noticing the sparkle in their eyes and the ease in their laughter. For the first time in a long while, hope surged within her, a warm glow reassuring her they could overcome any obstacle as long as they stood united.

22.
IN EXILE

"In the face of exile, the king's spirit remains unbroken, his eyes fixed on the horizon of his reclaimed throne."

Ruiha

The biting chill of the Frost Mountains clung to Ruiha's cloak as she trudged alongside Dakarai, Magnus, and Fellron. Their victory against the Drogo was still fresh in their minds, but exhaustion weighed heavily on them all. Fellron, led with his hood low over his face. Ruiha stole glances at him, trying to decipher the mysteries cloaking him like a second skin.

Magnus, strode confidently, eyes scanning the snow-covered landscape for danger. Ghost trotted at his side, having taken a liking to him. The Snow Wolves revered the elusive creature, their unit being named after it.

Ruiha broke the silence that had settled since their departure from the Scorched Mountains, her voice low and hoarse from captivity and battle. "Fellron, before we reach Dreynas, there's something I need to know," she began. "You mentioned our paths have intertwined for a reason. Can you explain?"

"Aye, true enough," Fellron said, his eerie black irises fixed on her intently. "You've not heard of my order before, lassie. But they have." He jerked his thumb at the Snow Wolves.

Magnus interrupted, his voice gravelly. "A Daemonseeker of the Shadowforged. My father told me of your order when I was younger. He used them to scare us, however, I do recall the respect in his stories."

Fellron raised an eyebrow. "So, ya' don't fear me then?"

Ruiha, trying to follow the story, asked, "Why would he fear you, Fellron?"

Fellron cast a meaningful glance at her before speaking. "The clans don't grasp who we are. To them, we're nought but practitioners of dark magic, beings to be feared and avoided. Yet, when desperation grips 'em, they seek our aid." He sighed, his gaze drifting to the snowy landscape.

"Because you can use dark magic?" she asked softly.

"Aye," he let out a bitter laugh. "If they knew what we give up, what they did to us, in order for us to use the dark arts, maybe they'd appreciate us more."

"Not all clans fear you. Magnus's father clearly doesn't," Ruiha stated.

"Aye, Erik the Blood. A good Dwarf, truth be told," Fellron admitted.

"You know him?" Magnus asked eagerly.

"Aye, met him once, many years ago. It was your da' who sent me after yous'."

Magnus nodded, as if he had already guessed as much. "And my brother? Any word from him?"

"No, lad. Unfortunately not. He's somehow managed to… slip through my attempts at scrying," Fellron said thoughtfully. Ruiha sensed he might be holding something back.

"What will happen when we reach Erik?" Ruiha asked. "Will he accept Drogo refugees and a human?"

"My father will likely try to make you an ally. But his allegiance will come with a price." Magnus said.

"What price?" she asked.

"Erik's thirst for vengeance runs deep," Fellron interjected. "He seeks to reclaim his place as clan chief and will stop at nothing to achieve his goal." Magnus nodded in agreement with the Daemonseeker.

Ruiha exchanged a wary glance with Dakarai. She had heard tales of Erik the Blood from the Snow Wolves, of his ruthless tactics and unmatched ferocity, but also of his loyalty to those he trusted. Surely, their common cause against the Drogo Mulik, who had imprisoned his son, would warrant his support in her pursuit of justice.

"What does he want from us?" Dakarai asked cautiously. "As Magnus said. He seeks allies," Fellron replied. "He needs warriors to help him reclaim his title."

Ruiha sucked in a breath. She was willing to fight someone else's war if it meant gaining allies for her own. But Dakarai? Would he see it as fighting and dying for another's whim, or as a chance to carve his own path to freedom. She looked over at Dakarai, searching his features for a clue to his thoughts, but the Drogo's face remained inscrutable. She sighed, knowing she would find out soon enough.

As they approached Erik the Blood's camp, Ruiha's emotions were churning with anticipation and apprehension.

Fellron's revelations colored her expectations for the impending encounter with the deposed clan chief.

The camp, nestled in a dense forest above ground, was a stark contrast to the vast, winding tunnels they had traversed in their escape. Here, the towering trees and open sky provided a semblance of freedom but also a constant reminder of Erik's exile and the betrayal that led him to this place.

As they arrived at the camp, Ruiha felt a wave of relief at Erik's joyful expression. His eyes sparkled with joy as he pulled Magnus into a warm embrace. Yet, the atmosphere shifted palpably as Erik's gaze scanned the rest of their group. His joy dimmed as he asked, "Where's Gunnar?"

Magnus's shoulders slumped, and with a heavy sigh, he began to sorrowfully recount the events that led to Gunnar's absence.

"We haven't seen Gunnar since Fort Bjerg," Magnus confessed at the end of his tale. "He was imprisoned there when the Snow Wolves departed."

Ruiha could feel the tension thickening in the air, a heavy silence settling over the camp as they awaited Erik's response.

Fellron broke the oppressive silence. With a solemnity that commanded attention, he recounted a vision that had plagued his mind since their departure from Fort Bjerg, a vivid picture of Gunnar's escape from the fortress.

He spoke of two accomplices in the escape, one an enigmatic figure shrouded in darkness. As Fellron's story unfurled Ruiha could feel the vivid imagery of his vision bringing Gunnar's perilous journey to life before her eyes.

However, as she listened, a suspicion tugged at her mind. His hesitations and the way his dark eyes flickered hinted at an incomplete truth. She noticed how his voice wavered, ever so slightly when he spoke of Gunnar's escape, and how his eyes darkened and his hands trembled when he mentioned the mysterious accomplice.

The obvious dissemblance stoked her unease. Why would Fellron hold back now, at such a crucial moment? The way he avoided eye contact when discussing certain parts of the story, the pauses as if choosing his words with care— all pointed to something unsaid, something critical. She resolved she would uncover the truth from him, no matter what it took.

At the end, Fellron reluctantly confessed that his magical senses, although honed through years of practice as a Daemonseeker, had failed him. He could no longer sense Gunnar's presence, leaving his fate frustratingly unknown.

"Is my son dead, Fellron?" Erik's asked, his voice trembling.

Fellron paused, his expression softening as he met Erik's gaze. "I cannot see him," he admitted. "But absence doesn't equate to death, lad."

Ruiha found it strange to hear Fellron, who looked far younger than Erik, call him "lad," but she noticed that none of the Dwarves batted an eye at the comment. She wondered if this was a mark of respect among them, an acknowledgment of Fellron's wisdom and experience despite his youthful appearance. She listened intently as the Daemonseeker continued.

"There are many mysteries in this world, and the absence of an explanation does not necessarily mean the worst has come to pass," he said.

Ruiha could see him grappling with his own doubts and inability to provide a satisfactory explanation for the absence of Gunnar's presence.

"As a Daemonseeker, my senses are attuned to the ebb and flow of the shadows," Fellron continued, his brow furrowing with frustration. "But there are forces at play that elude even my understanding. Whatever has befallen Gunnar remains shrouded in mystery, and until we uncover the truth, we cannot make assumptions."

"I fear he's gone," Erik said, his voice heavy with sorrow.

"I don't believe Gunnar is dead," Fellron interjected firmly.

Erik looked at him, surprise elbowing out grief. "What makes you so sure?"

"I can feel it," Fellron replied, placing a hand over his forehead and closing his eyes. "He's out there. We just have to find him."

"We've searched everywhere," Erik murmured, though his voice lacked its former certainty as grief made way for a fragile hope.

Magnus stepped forward. "If there's even a chance Gunnar is alive, we must act on it," he said. "We owe it to him to keep looking."

Erik nodded slowly, drawing strength from their conviction. "Very well," he said, the determination returning to his voice. "We will continue the search."

As the group dispersed, Ruiha watched Erik as he lingered staring out over the dense forest that now served as his refuge. The sun dipping below the horizon cast long shadows through the trees. The leaves rustled softly in the evening breeze, standing as silent witnesses to Erik's fall from grace.

Ruiha guessed that the betrayal by his brother, Wilfrid, had left scars deeper than Erik cared to admit. She watched as Magnus approached, having apparently sensed something of his father's turmoil.

"Father," he began softly, "we need to discuss reclaiming your rule. The clan is suffering under Wilfrid's tyranny. They need you."

"Aye," Erik sighed. "You're right, lad. No matter the fate of Gunnar, we have to think about the future of Dreynas."

Ruiha could see the resolve solidify in Erik's eyes, and she found herself feeling surprisingly invested in the future of Dreynas.

She glanced over at Dakarai, who was methodically organizing his people. She wondered what his plans would be once their immediate tasks were accomplished. Would he stay and help the Dwarves in their struggle against Wilfrid and the Drogo, forging a new alliance? Or would he lead his people back to Drogo Mulik, seeking seclusion and safety, hidden from the ever-looming threat of Junak? Whatever Dakarai's intentions she knew one thing for certain: she wanted her own revenge.

That evening, as the flickering flames of the campfire cast dancing shadows on their faces, Ruiha couldn't shake the gnawing questions in her mind. Did Fellron's hesitation when recounting Gunnar's fate mean he was lying? Or had she simply misunderstood him? As she replayed his tale in her mind, she felt sure he hadn't been telling the whole truth, sowing a seed of doubt she couldn't ignore.

Another question concerned Erik's fears for the future of Dreynas. She hadn't thought much about it earlier, but now, in the stillness of contemplation, she wondered why all of Dreynas was in peril. Surely, it was only the Draegoor clan that should be concerned about Wilfrid's tyranny.

"Erik," Ruiha began, "you spoke of reclaiming your rule and ending the suffering of your clan. But I don't understand why the whole of Dreynas is at risk. I thought this was only about the Draegoor clan."

Erik's expression grew more serious, and he exchanged a glance with Fellron and Magnus. He took a deep breath before answering. "It's more complicated than that, Ruiha. Wilfrid's betrayal goes beyond our clan. I have reasons to believe that he is colluding with the Drogo."

Ruiha's eyes widened. "The Drogo? Why would Wilfrid ally with them?"

Erik's gaze hardened as he continued. "I suspect Wilfrid, having used the Drogo to overthrow my rule, is now totally compromised. The Drogo have always wanted to undermine our strength. With Wilfrid as their puppet chief, they have a foothold within our clan and, the whole Frost Mountains."

Fellron nodded in agreement. "Erik is right. I've seen signs of Drogo interference and heard whispers of their presence in places they shouldn't be. This is no coincidence. If Wilfrid remains as chief, it won't just be the Draegoor clan that suffers. The Drogo will destabilize all of Dreynas, pitting clan against clan until they can sweep in and seize control."

Magnus, who had been quietly listening, finally spoke up. "The Drogo are cunning. They've always wanted our resources and our lands. With Wilfrid as their pawn, they can weaken us from within. It's a strategy that's as old as our history, and it's one we cannot afford to ignore."

Ruiha listened intently, realizing just how much she still had to learn about the intricate web of Dwarven politics. "So, this isn't just about reclaiming your rightful place, Erik. It's about protecting all of Dreynas from falling into enemy hands."

Erik nodded solemnly. "Yes. We must act not only to restore order within our clan but to safeguard the future of all Dwarves in Dreynas. The Drogo's influence must be eradicated, and Wilfrid must be removed from power. Only then can we hope to secure peace and stability."

Ruiha digested the information quietly. The stakes were higher than she had imagined. "Then we must be prepared for whatever lies ahead. The Drogo won't give up their hold easily, and by the sound of it, neither will Wilfrid."

Erik turned his gaze on Ruiha, his eyes filled with determination. "Ruiha, we need all the help we can get. By all accounts, your skills are impressive, and I can see that your spirit is strong. Will you join our cause and help us reclaim what is rightfully ours?"

Ruiha found she barely had to think. "Of course, Erik" she said. "I'll stand with you and fight for Dreynas."

As she spoke, a deeper, more personal resolve settled within her. Helping Erik wasn't just about saving Dreynas or restoring honor to the Draegoor clan—it was about confronting her own past. The Drogo had captured her, forced her into their brutal arena, and turned her life into a relentless fight for survival. She had endured their cruelty and emerged stronger, but joining Erik's cause would give her a chance for revenge against those who had tormented her.

Erik nodded gratefully, then turned to address the group of former Drogo slaves, who had been observing the exchange. "You all have suffered under Junak's yoke, and you know his cruelty better than anyone. Your strength and resilience have brought you this far. Will you stand with us in this fight to free Dreynas from his influence and ensure a future where no one else has to endure what you have?"

As Erik extended his invitation to the former Drogo slaves to join their ranks, Ruiha noticed the subtle yet clear shift in the group's demeanor—their gazes instinctively turning to Dakarai for guidance. It was as if an unspoken consensus had formed among them, their eyes conveying a silent plea for his leadership.

Ruiha could see the conflict in Dakarai's eyes, the struggle between the yearning for his own personal freedom and the call to lead his people.

"Dakarai," Ruiha whispered, stepping closer. "What will you do?" Her voice was soft but insistent, hoping to lend him the strength he needed to make this difficult choice.

He looked at her, frowning. "I... I don't know. This isn't what I envisioned for us."

"But you have the strength to lead," she urged, gesturing to the former slaves. "They need you."

Dakarai hesitated, grappling with his conflicting emotions, but then Ruiha saw the spark of decision ignite within him.. "You're right," he said, his voice steady. "I must lead."

He stepped forward, tacitly accepting the mantle of leadership. "We will join you, Erik," he declared. "Together, we will fight."

Ruiha felt a sense of pride and relief wash over her. She had lived and fought alongside him for what felt like an eternity, despite it only being weeks. Yet the bond they had been forged in the blood of the arena was unbreakable.

"Dakarai," Ruiha said, smiling at him. "You're going to make a great leader."

"We all have a part to play," he replied, a confident glint in his eye. "Let's just make sure we win this."

23.

THE CROWN

"The flames of transformation burn away the old, making way for the emergence of something new and powerful."

Gunnar

Gunnar stood tall and resolute, the weight of his battle-worn armor familiar yet strangely comforting. The leather straps dug slightly into his shoulders, a reminder of the trials he had faced and conquered. The moments of doubt and exhaustion now seemed distant, almost surreal. Beside him, Anwyn and Karl exuded a similar aura of newfound strength and camaraderie. They had completed the Labyrinth trial, a feat that would have seemed impossible a month ago. He glanced at Anwyn, noticing the quiet confidence in her stance, and then at Karl, whose eyes shone with a blend of relief and determination. The air in the grand chamber was thick with anticipation. Gunnar's senses were heightened, every sound and movement magnified as they awaited their instructors and the next steps in their journey.

Commander Aelric entered first. The burn scar glistened in the soft light of the room, whilst his neatly folded wings were barely noticeable beneath his cloak. His piercing gaze met Gunnar's, and he offered a curt nod of approval. Gunnar felt a surge of pride; earning the commander's respect was no small feat. He recalled the countless rebukes and harsh criticisms that had shaped him into the battle mage he was today.

Thalirion followed, his Elven grace matched by a stern, appraising look directed at Anwyn. Gunnar saw a flicker of recognition in Thalirion's eyes, an unspoken acknowledgment of the bond formed between mentor and pupil. Anwyn stood a little straighter under his gaze, her chin lifted with quiet pride. Gunnar knew how much this moment meant to her; Thalirion was not only her mentor, he was the Seishinmori passing down his mantle to her. His approval meant the world to her.

Sage Thadwick, with his scholarly air, completed the trio of mentors. Trinkets and charms adorned his thick beard and his eyes twinkled approvingly as his gaze landed on Karl.

As their mentors took their places, Gunnar's thoughts settled on the present. The journey ahead was uncertain, but they were no longer the same individuals who had first entered the Labyrinth. They were a team, united by their struggles and triumphs. He could feel the strength of their connection.

Kemp stood a few paces away, fidgeting with the hem of his tunic. He glanced up, his expression a mix of awe and nervousness. Thraxos, his instructor, loomed beside him, a towering figure of stoic power. Kemp had run the trial himself and knew the true extent of its difficulty. He was clearly surprised at the trio's successful completion of the challenges.

"Three weeks," Kemp murmured, shaking his head. "I can't believe you did it in just three weeks."

Commander Aelric stepped forward, his voice a deep rumble that filled the chamber. "The Labyrinth trials were designed to push your abilities to their limits, paving the way for your advancement to Overlord and preparing you for the darkest of times. You have surpassed our expectations."

Gunnar felt Anwyn's shoulder brush against his as she shifted slightly. He glanced sideways to see her eyes shining with a mixture of pride and determination. Karl, standing on his other side, looked equally resolute, his hands no longer idle, but resting purposefully at his sides.

"We must prepare you now for the final trial. The Corpselands," Commander Aelric continued solemnly. "The Corpse- lands are barren wastelands in the darkest corner of Nexus.

This desolate place is littered with powerful, natural arcane artifacts, each one capable of significantly enhancing your abilities and aiding in your advancement. However, there is a reason it's called the Corpselands. These artifacts draw in spectral echoes like bees to honey, making the spirits increasingly violent and unpredictable. It is an extremely dangerous place, where only the strongest and most prepared can hope to survive. Prepare yourselves well, for the challenges ahead will be unlike any you have faced before."

"When do we go?" Gunnar asked.

"You must first reach Overlord status," Commander Aelric replied.

Gunnar felt a wave of dejection wash over him. Becoming an Overlord seemed more distant than the faintest star in the night sky.

At the look of despair on Gunnar's face, Thalirin placed a reassuring hand on his shoulder. "Do not lose hope, Gunnar. The path to becoming an Overlord may seem long and arduous, but you are closer than you think. Every challenge you have faced, every lesson you have learned, has been preparing you for this moment. Trust in your training and in yourself. We believe in you, and soon, you will believe in yourself too."

Thalirion's words rekindled Gunnar's hope and he glanced over at Anwyn, whose evident resolve bolstered his own.

Thadwick cleared his throat, drawing their attention. "During your time in the Labyrinth, Thraxos and I took the opportunity to investigate the broken crown Kemp possessed when he arrived. Our findings are... intriguing."

Thraxos stepped forward, his deep voice resonating with authority. "The crown, as it turns out, possesses the ability to transport you back to Vellhor. However, it has bonded itself with Kemp. To access its powers, Kemp must harmonize with it."

Kemp's eyes widened, fear and excitement flashing across his face. "Harmonize? How do I do that?"

Thadwick smiled reassuringly. "It requires a deep connection, a melding of your aura with the crown's. It is a process that will take effort, but with our guidance, it is achievable."

Gunnar felt a twinge of unease. Thalirion had spoken to them of the crown before they had entered the Labyrinth, and the idea of relying on such an artifact was daunting, but he had absolute trust in his. Stepping forward he declared,

"We will support Kemp in any way we can. This is our path forward."

Commander Aelric nodded approvingly. "Indeed. Your unity and strength are your greatest assets. The trials have proven that. Now, you must prepare for the next phase of your journey."

Thalirion's voice was softer, yet no less commanding. "Re- member, the bond you share is your shield and your sword. Together, you can overcome any challenge."

As they turned to leave the chamber, Kemp fell into step beside Gunnar. "I never thought I'd be part of something like this," he admitted in an awed voice.

Gunnar clapped a reassuring hand on Kemp's shoulder. "Neither did we, Kemp. But together, we are unstoppable."

Kemp sat alone in his dimly lit dormitory that evening, the flickering candle casting elongated shadows on the walls. The events of the day weighed heavily on his mind, and he felt a strange restlessness that he couldn't quite shake. He stared at the worn book in front of him, its pages filled with spells and incantations he had read countless times before, yet tonight, the words seemed to blur together.

As he tried to focus, a faint whisper echoed in the recesses of his mind. It was barely audible, like the distant murmur of a hidden stream, but there was something unsettling about it. The whispers were dark and strange, and though he strained to understand them, they slipped elusively away just as he thought he could grasp their meaning.

Kemp shook his head, trying to dispel the uneasy feeling. He walked over to the small window and peered out into the darkness. The whispers grew louder, but he still couldn't discern any words. It felt as if shadows were dancing at the edge of his consciousness, teasing and taunting him with their presence.

A sudden knock on the door pulled him abruptly from his thoughts. He took a deep breath to steady his racing heart. "Come in," he called, his voice sounding more composed than he felt.

The door creaked open, and Thraxos stepped into the room, his imposing figure filling the doorway. "Kemp, we need to talk." His tone was serious, but not unkind. He closed the door behind him and took a seat across from Kemp, studying him with those sharp, perceptive eyes.

Kemp sat back down, the whispers fading into the background but still lingering, like a forgotten melody. "What is it, Thraxos?" he asked, trying to focus on the present.

Thraxos leaned forward, his expression intent. "Tomorrow morning, you will harmonize with the crown. This is a crucial step in your training, and it's essential that you are fully prepared. The crown has already begun bonding with you, but the harmonization process will still be challenging. You must be in the right state of mind."

Kemp nodded, though his mind was still distracted by the faint whispers. "I understand. I'll be ready."

Thraxos leant back, giant bull head cocked on one side. "And yet you seem uncertain?"

Kemp hesitated, unsure how to explain the strange whispers without sounding irrational. "It's nothing, really. Just a feeling. Maybe it's nerves about tomorrow."

Thraxos's gaze softened. "It's natural to feel apprehensive, but you must trust in your abilities. The crown will test you, but it will also reveal your true potential. Focus on your strengths and let go of any doubts."

Kemp took a deep breath. "I'll do my best."

Thraxos nodded, satisfied for now. "Good. Get some rest tonight. You'll need all your strength for the harmonization process. Remember, we believe in you, Kemp. You have come a long way, and this is just another step in your journey."

With that, Thraxos stood and gave Kemp a reassuring pat on the shoulder before leaving the room. Kemp watched him go, the whispers now a mere murmur in the back of his mind. He knew Thraxos was right; he needed to focus and trust in himself.

As he prepared for bed, Kemp wondered again about the whispers and what they might mean. Were they a sign of something deeper, a part of the process he was about to undertake? Or were they simply a manifestation of his own fears and uncertainties?

He lay down, closing his eyes and willing himself to relax. The whispers faded further, becoming a distant echo as sleep finally claimed him.

The next morning, when Kemp awoke, the whispers were nothing more than a faint memory that barely touched his consciousness. He stretched and rose from his bed, ready to prepare himself for the harmonization process.

He took a deep breath, feeling the tension in his muscles, and began his morning routine. He sat cross-legged on the floor, closing his eyes and entering a state of meditation. As he focused on inhaling deeply and exhaling slowly, the familiar rhythm helped clear his mind, and a sense of calm gradually wash over him.

Thraxos had always emphasized the importance of maintaining a strong spirit through meditation, and Kemp knew that today, especially, he would need that strength.

As he meditated, Kemp's thoughts drifted to the journey that had brought him here. The relentless challenges, the moments of doubt where he questioned if he could truly wield the amount of power he had witnessed since arriving here. He had come so far, and yet, today's trial felt like the most daunting hurdle yet. The crown awaited him, a symbol of immense power and responsibility. Harmonizing with it meant not just proving his worth but accepting the mantle that came with it.

He took another deep breath, allowing the calm to deepen. This process was about becoming one with his own spirit, understanding it on an intrinsic level. Kemp visualized the crown, imagining its energy merging with his own, a harmonious blend that would enhance his abilities and fortify his spirit.

After what felt like an eternity but was only a few minutes, Kemp opened his eyes. He felt more centered, his mind clearer and his resolve stronger. He knew the whispers might return, that doubts could creep back in, but he also knew he had the tools to push them away. Today was not just about facing a challenge; it was about affirming his growth and readiness.

After meditating, Kemp moved through a series of physical exercises designed to help control his shadow hand. Each movement was deliberate and practiced, and he marveled at how much control over it he had now. Just as he completed his final exercise, there was a knock on the door.

"Come in," Kemp called, standing up and straightening his robes.

The door opened, and Sages Thraxos, Thalirion, and Thadwick entered the room. Thraxos's imposing presence led the way, his eyes appraising Kemp. Thalirion, with his serene demeanor, nodded encouragingly, while Thadwick, adorned with his trinket-filled beard, gave Kemp a reassuring smile.

"It's time," Thraxos said, his voice steady. "Are you ready?"

Kemp nodded, feeling a flutter of anxiety in his chest but quickly pushing it aside. "I'm ready."

The Sages escorted Kemp through the winding corridors of the Tower, their footsteps echoing softly against the stone floors. They descended several flights of stairs, each step bringing Kemp closer to the moment he had been preparing for.

They finally arrived at a large chamber, its grand doors opening to reveal a laboratory filled with strange tools and arcane symbols. In the center of the room, on a pedestal, sat the crown. Its metallic surface gleamed with an ethereal light, and the air around it seemed to hum with energy.

Kemp's heart quickened as he took in the sight, the whispers faintly returning, tickling the edges of his mind. He clenched his fists, pushing the whispers to the back of his consciousness, refusing to let them distract him.

"Come forward, Kemp," Thalirion said gently, gesturing toward the pedestal.

Kemp took a deep breath and walked to the center of the room, his eyes locked on the crown. It seemed to pulse with a life of its own, the ethereal glow casting long, flickering shadows on the walls. The Sages formed a circle around him, their expressions solemn and focused, their collective presence imposing yet reassuring.

Thraxos let out a snort as he raised his hands, his fingers tracing patterns in the air that shimmered with iridescent light. Thalirion and Thadwick followed suit, their hands moving in perfect synchrony. Intricate symbols and runes appeared, weaving together to form a delicate web of magical energy. The air crackled with raw energy as their spells seemed to try and stitch the crown's aura to Kemp's own spirit.

Kemp's heart pounded in his chest, the sound almost deafening in the charged silence. He reached out and touched the crown, its surface cool and smooth beneath his fingertips. Immediately, a surge of warmth flowed through him, a rush of energy that was both invigorating and overwhelming. The whispers in his mind grew louder, insistent, but he fought to maintain his focus.

A myriad of emotions cascaded through Kemp. Excitement mingled with fear, the thrill of power blending with the terror of losing himself. He could feel the crown's essence seeping into his very being. It felt like a living force that sought to merge with his spirit. Voices in his mind, echoing a strange mix of both knowledge and dark desires, tugged at his thoughts, tempting him with visions of grandeur and dominion.

Images of his past flashed before his eyes—moments of triumph and failure, lessons learned through hardship. He remembered Ruiha, how strong she was, how she never gave up on him, despite Harald's enchantment. These memories fortified him, reminding him of who he was and why he had come to this moment. He was Kemp, not just a vessel for the crown, but a man with his own strength and will.

Kemp's resolve wavered for a moment, the weight of the crown's power pressing heavily on his spirit. He clenched his jaw, forcing himself to breathe deeply and center his mind. This was his destiny, the path he had chosen, and he would not be consumed by it. He focused on the cool touch of the crown, grounding himself with the physical sensation.

Ruiha's image lingered in his mind, a symbol of resilience and hope. Her courage inspired him, reminding him that he was not just a vessel for the crown's power, but a man capable of great things. He was Kemp, with his own strength and will, shaped by the trials he had overcome.

He concentrated on the Sages' spells, their rhythmic patterns like a lifeline in the storm of sensations. Each symbol they crafted hung in the air, glowing briefly before merging into the next. The complexity and beauty of their spell-weaving held him steady, providing an anchor as he felt the crown's energy begin to merge with his own.

Kemp closed his eyes, attempting to shut out the chaos. He could feel the essence of the crown, ancient and powerful, merging with his spirit. It was like being submerged in a river of light, every particle of his being suffused with warmth and brilliance.

The whispers became a cacophony, voices overlapping and indistinct, tugging at the edges of his mind. He gritted his teeth, using every ounce of his willpower to push them into the background. The harmonization process was both exhilarating and terrifying, a delicate balance that he struggled to maintain. Then, something shifted. Kemp's eyes snapped open, and he gasped as his vision was flooded with black shadow. His eyes flashed green for earth, and he felt a surge of vitality as tendrils of vines sprouted from the ground. They changed to red for fire, and flames erupted around him, fierce and uncontrollable. Suddenly, they were blue for water, and swirling torrents surged through the air. Then, pure white for air, and gusts of wind whipped around him, sending the runes and symbols into chaotic swirls.

Panic gripped Kemp as the elemental energies clashed violently within him, each force a wild, uncontrollable beast battling for dominance. His heart pounded in his chest, a rapid, relentless drumbeat that echoed the chaos within. Sweat dripped down his forehead, stinging his eyes, but he couldn't wipe it away. His muscles tensed, locked in a desperate struggle to maintain some semblance of control. The room around him was a maelstrom of conflicting forces, the air crackling with energy that made his skin prickle. He could feel his grip slipping, the tenuous threads of control fraying.

Cold dread settled in the pit of his stomach, a fear that he was about to be consumed, torn apart from the inside out. His mind frantically searched for a solution, but the sheer intensity of the energies made coherent thought nearly impossible.

The Sages seemed to sense the imminent danger as they intensified their own efforts. Kemp caught glimpses of their faces, masks of grim determination, their eyes sharp with focus. Their hands moved faster, injecting more power into their spells in a desperate bid to stabilize the energy coursing through him. He could feel the flickers of their magic, delicate threads trying to weave a net around the raging storm within him.

But would it be enough? Doubt gnawed at him, insidious and paralyzing. What if he lost control? What if their efforts failed? The thought of the devastation he could unleash, of the raw, unbridled power ripping free and wreaking havoc, sent a fresh wave of panic surging through him. He closed his eyes, trying to find himself, to find a calm spot within the storm. His breathing came in ragged gasps, every inhale feeling like fire, every exhale a struggle. The energies within him roared, and for a moment, he feared they would overwhelm him completely.

The pain was excruciating, a searing agony that made Kemp feel as if he were being torn apart from within. Every nerve in his body screamed, the torment pushing him to the brink of his endurance. He clenched his teeth, his vision blurring with tears as he fought to hold on, every second was felt like a lifetime of suffering. Just when he thought he could bear no more, he felt a sudden shift. The Sages' spells began to take effect, their magic weaving through the chaos within him.

There was a sharp, wrenching pull, as if his very essence were being yanked in all directions. He gasped, the sensation overwhelming, but gradually, the elemental forces began to withdraw. The chaotic energy was redirected, pulled from him with a force that left him breathless and trembling. Relief washed over him, mingling with exhaustion, as the maelstrom within him subsided.

He had been saved. The realization brought an unexpected but fleeting flood of emotion. As the chaotic energy was wrenched from him, Kemp felt an unsettling shift deep within. Something fundamental had changed. He couldn't quite grasp it, but there was an emptiness, a hollow space where the raging forces had been. It was as if a part of him had been torn away, leaving him altered in a way he couldn't yet comprehend. The relief of survival was tempered by a growing unease, a sense that he was no longer the same person he had been before the storm.

This unease deepened as the void left by the stripped elemental magic was quickly filled with a new, dark power. Black fire flickered around his shadowed hand, cold and destructive, an unsettling contrast to the warmth he had known. It felt alien, wild, and uncontrollable, yet incredibly potent. Kemp stared at his hand, a mixture of fear and fascination gripping him. This new power pulsed within him, a dark promise of strength, but its presence was a stark reminder that he was no longer who he once was, and the path ahead seemed more uncertain than ever.

Minutes stretched into what felt like hours, and then, slowly, the energy began to settle. Kemp's body trembled as the power within him stabilized, the whispers fading to a distant hum. He opened his eyes, feeling a strange mix of clarity and power. His irises, once vibrant, had turned into dark, stormy shadows swirling in his eyes. The crown had accepted him, its bond forged deeply within his spirit. Yet, he was irrevocably changed. The Sages lowered their hands, their spell-weaving complete, but their faces were etched with concern. Thraxos stepped forward, his eyes scanning Kemp for any sign of lingering instability. "You have done well, Kemp. The harmonization is complete, though not without unexpected results."

Kemp nodded. The sense of accomplishment was overshadowed by trepidation. The black fire flickered at his fingertips, a constant reminder of the power—and the danger—he now wielded. He glanced at his shadowed hand, watching the dark flames dance and flicker. This new magic was potent, almost intoxicating in its strength, but it was wild, unpredictable.

As Thraxos spoke, Kemp's thoughts whirled. He had come so far, faced so many challenges, but this was something entirely new. He would need to learn control, to master this dark fire that had replaced his elemental magic. It was a daunting prospect, but he steeled himself, drawing on the inner strength he had cultivated over the years.

24.
The Fight for Draegoor

"The calm before the storm is where warriors find their focus, their hearts steeled for the fight ahead."

Ruiha

The fire crackled, sending sparks dancing into the twilight as shadows lengthened around the campsite.

The evening air was cool, carrying the scent of pine and earth, mingling with the faint aroma of the stew simmering in a pot over the flames. Ruiha sat cross-legged on a log, sharpening her sword with deliberate, methodical strokes.

She glanced up, watching Dakarai as he stirred the pot absently, his dark eyes reflecting the firelight but clouded with doubt. Ruiha could sense his unease, but she waited, giving him the space to voice his thoughts.

"Tomorrow, we strike at Wilfrid's forces," she said at last, breaking the silence with a note of eager anticipation. "It's our best chance to weaken him before the final assault. With his defeat, Erik can finally focus on the Drogo, and Junak's days will be numbered."

Dakarai nodded slowly, his gaze falling to the flickering flames. "You seem certain of victory," he said, in a tone that betrayed his reservations.

"Because I am," Ruiha replied without hesitation. She lifted the blade to inspect its edge before turning her intense gaze on Dakarai. "This battle brings us closer to reclaiming what was stolen from us. Once Wilfrid falls, Erik will have no choice but to confront the Drogo. My revenge on Junak is within reach."

"And what of my people, Ruiha?" Dakarai said sadly. "What will happen to them in this war for vengeance?"

Ruiha's expression softened. "They fight for freedom, just as we all do. A future without Junak is worth any sacrifice."

Dakarai sighed, his shoulders slumping. "I fear the cost may be too high. The Drogo I lead... they've seen enough death, enough suffering. I wonder if I'm leading them to more of the same."

"You have given them hope, Dakarai," Ruiha said firmly. "Hope for a life beyond chains and tyranny. That is worth fighting for."

"And if we fail? Where will we go? There's nowhere else for us. We are caught between Wilfrid's tyranny and Junak's oppression."

Ruiha's expression hardened. "We won't fail. We can't afford to. And even if we end in defeat, we will face it with the knowledge that we fought for something greater than ourselves."

Her words seemed to stir something within Dakarai, a flicker of the hope she knew he had once carried so fiercely. "I wish I shared your certainty," he said quietly. "But the thought of more death... it haunts me."

Ruiha stood, her movements fluid and purposeful, and crossed to his side. She placed a hand on his shoulder, squeezing it gently. "Your fear is not a weakness, Dakarai. It shows that you care for those who follow you. But remember why we fight. For freedom. For justice. For the chance to rebuild what was broken."

He met her gaze. "For freedom," he echoed.

Ruiha watched the night deepen around them, the fire a beacon in the encroaching darkness. The vast expanse of sky above seemed to mirror the turmoil in her heart, black doubt dotted with glimmers of hope.

Ruiha's thoughts drifted to her past, to her friend Kemp, who she had lost to Junak's tyranny. Every swing of her sword, every strategic decision she made, was driven by the memories of those who had suffered. The fire's warmth on her face reminded her of the burning desire for vengeance that kept her going, even in the darkest moments.

She was glad that Dakarai now led; she had hated leading the Drogo during their escape with every life resting on her decisions. Dakarai shouldering that responsibility had lifted the burden of leadership, allowing her to focus on her personal quest for vengeance. Yet, she couldn't escape the pang of guilt that the very weight which had nearly crushed her now rested on her friend. She worried for him, knowing all too well the toll it could take.

She looked over at Dakarai. Tomorrow they would bring the fight to Wilfrid, a crucial step in their shared dream of liberation. Ruiha felt a rush of adrenaline at the thought of battle. She knew the risks, the potential for loss, but she also knew that there was no turning back from this path.

The first light of dawn crept through the flaps of Erik's tent, casting long shadows over the gathering. Ruiha could feel the palpable tension in the air. She glanced at Dakarai, taking silent comfort in his steady presence beside her, though she could sense the burden of leadership weighing heavily on him.

Magnus, as commander of the Snow Wolves, with Uleg beside him as his deputy, stood on the other side of the table. They gazed intently at the map spread across its surface, their arms folded and expressions grim as they contemplated the coming trials.

Erik, leading the council of war stood at the head of the table. Ruiha thought he looked weary but resolute. His eyes, shadowed with fatigue and haunted by the treacherous actions of his brother Wilfrid, still burned bright with a hunger to reclaim his rightful place and restore order to Draegoor. The dwarf beside him was called Arvi and Ruiha had learned it was Arvi who had helped enlist Fellron's aid. Erik had promoted Arvi from the rank of Commander that he had held under Wilfrid, to General. Ruiha wondered how he felt about his swift elevation, thrust into a position of immense responsibility at such a critical time.

The final member of the group was Fellron. The enigmatic Daemonseeker stood at the edge of the gathering. His eyes were dark and unreadable and Ruiha's instincts had warned her from their first meeting that he was holding something back. Now, she watched him closely, trying to decipher the secrets he carried.

Ruiha's mind raced with the enormity of their task. The fate of their people, the future of Draegoor, rested on the decisions made in this tent. The thought of facing Wilfrid's forces filled her with dread and excitement, knowing that each step brought her closer to her long-sought revenge against Junak.

In the midst of her allies, Ruiha felt a surge of determination. She would see this through, not just for herself, but for Dakarai, Erik, Magnus, and all those who had placed their trust in her. With the dawn light came the chance of a new beginning, an opportunity to avenge the wrongs of the past and forge a future free from tyranny.

Erik's voice drew their attention. "We need a strategy that will help neutralize the strength of Wilfrid's forces. We need to strike in the right place and at the right moment, if we are to reclaim Draegoor."

Magnus nodded. "We should use the terrain to our advantage. The mountains surrounding Draegoor can provide us cover, and the network of tunnels within the city itself can serve as a strategic asset."

Uleg added, "A frontal assault would be suicide. We need to create a diversion to draw Wilfrid's forces out into the open, away from the safety of the underground passages and fortified positions."

Erik looked thoughtful. "What if we split into two groups? One to create a diversion and the other to infiltrate the city?"

Dakarai spoke up, his deep voice resonating in the tent. "I can lead the diversion. The Drogo know how to move swiftly and strike hard."

Ruiha admired Dakarai's bravery, but her thoughts kept returning to Fellron. From the moment she had met him, she had sensed that he wasn't telling the whole truth. Now, surrounded by her comrades, she decided it was time to address her suspicions.

"Fellron," she said, her voice cutting through the discussion. "There's something you haven't told us. When we first met, I sensed you were holding back. What aren't you telling us?"

All eyes turned to Fellron, the room suddenly still. He hesitated, then sighed, a reluctant look in his eyes. "You're right, Ruiha. I haven't been entirely honest."

Magnus frowned. "Out with it, then."

Fellron took a deep breath. "I saw Hansen, the Dwarf who helped Gunnar escape Fort Bjerg, over two thousand years ago. It has been... playing on my mind, somewhat."

A shocked silence fell over the group as they digested this information. Ruiha felt her pulse quicken. Two thousand years? How could that be?

"Two thousand years?" Erik exclaimed. "How is that possible?"

Fellron nodded, his expression sombre. "I am older than I appear. My role as a Daemonseeker has granted me longevity beyond that of most. The ancient poem of the Shadowforged speaks in riddles of a time when darkness will rise, and a Daemonseeker must stand against it. This prophecy set me on my path to help save the Snow Wolves. And I cannot help but think—no, I am certain—that Hansen is intricately connected to it."

Arvi's eyes widened. "I'd heard the Shadowforged could live unnaturally long lives... it's not just a legend?"

Fellron shook his head. "No, it's real. And it is why I am still here. The shadows are rising, and Wilfrid is just a part of a much larger threat. I believe Hansen knew this. He may hold the key to our victory."

Ruiha knew that Dwarves were considered old at two-hundred and fifty years so Fellron's age and longevity were astonishing. Ruiha noted the awe and apprehension in her companions' expressions, and realized how deeply they too had been shaken by the revelation of Fellron's true nature.

Questions erupted around the tent, voices overlapping as the group wrestled with Fellron's revelation. Ruiha's suspicion of the Daemonseeker was giving way to a grudging respect. He had kept this secret for a reason, and now it was up to them to use this knowledge to their advantage.

Arvi called over the din, "Surely we need to find Hansen. He could be the key to not just defeating Wilfrid, but to facing the darkness that threatens us all."

Fellron shook his head firmly. "Finding Hansen is not worth it. I have scried for him hundreds of times since his disappearance and have never been successful. I am adamant that Hansen is no longer in this realm."

His words raised a stir of disbelief and concern. Magnus spoke up. "If what Fellron is right, then we cannot waste valuable time and resources searching for a Dwarf who may no longer be in this realm."

Erik nodded. "Agreed. We'll divide our forces as initially planned. Dakarai, you lead the diversion. Magnus, Uleg, and I will focus on infiltrating the fort. Ruiha and Arvi, you'll assist with the main assault. We need this to go right if we're to reclaim Draegoor and face this tyranny."

The camp buzzed with activity as preparations for the assault began in earnest. Ruiha watched as Dakarai gathered his group= of Drogo warriors together. His calm, commanding presence gave her a sense of reassurance, and she felt a surge of pride in seeing how much he had grown since they first fled from Junak's tyranny.

"Stay sharp," Dakarai said, meeting her eyes. "We'll draw them out. Trust in our strength."

Ruiha nodded, gripping his forearm in a gesture of solidarity, and taking comfort from the warmth of his leathery scaled skin. "And we'll be ready when you do. Good luck, Dak."

"I have faith that you will, Shadowhawk!" He grinned at her before turning to lead his team into the shadows of the surrounding mountains. Ruiha watched him go with a mix of admiration and worry. Despite his light-hearted confidence, battle was an uncertain business – its outcome never guaranteed.

Shaking off her concern, Ruiha turned to focus on her own preparations. Arvi stood nearby, adjusting his armor and checking his weapons with professional rigor. She could see the same fire in his eyes, the resolve to reclaim Draegoor and to stand against the darkness that threatened them all.

Arvi glanced across offering a small nod of encouragement which Ruiha returned. With Dakarai leading the diversion and Erik's team ready to infiltrate the fort, it was up to them to strike the decisive blow.

Magnus and Uleg's Snow Wolves formed into disciplined ranks. Erik conferred briefly with his son while Fellron watched from the edge of the group with his usual inscrutable calm. As the sun dipped below the horizon, the signal was given.

Dakarai's team moved out first, disappearing into the growing darkness. Ruiha could feel the tension in the air as they waited for the diversion to begin. Every second felt like an eternity, the silence pressing down on them like a physical weight.

Then, in the distance, the sound of battle erupted. Shouts and the clash of weapons echoed through the mountains, carried on the wind. Dakarai's team had engaged Wilfrid's forces, drawing them away from the entrance to Draegoor.

"Move out!" Erik commanded, and the main assault force surged forward.

Ruiha ran alongside Arvi, her senses heightened by the adrenaline coursing through her veins. The entrance to Draegoor loomed ahead, a gaping hole in the side of the mountain, guarded by a skeleton force of Wilfrid's soldiers. They had taken the bait.

Arvi and Ruiha led the charge, their blades flashing in the dim light as they cut through the initial line of defenders. The sound of combat surrounded them, a cacophony of clashing steel and battle cries. Ruiha's focus narrowed, each movement precise and deadly as she fought her way toward the entrance. Magnus and Uleg's Dwarven warriors surged forward, their tall shields forming an impenetrable wall as they advanced. Erik the Blood fought alongside them, his presence igniting a fierce determination in their ranks. They pushed deeper into Draegoor, the labyrinthine tunnels echoing with the sounds of their advance. Ruiha's mind raced as they navigated the twisting passages. Memories of her previous battles flashed before her eyes

Suddenly, a blinding light filled the tunnel ahead, and Ruiha skidded to a halt, shielding her eyes. A figure emerged from the light, clad in dark armor that seemed to absorb the very essence of the surrounding shadows. Wilfrid.

He stood before them, his eyes gleaming with a malevolent, almost maniacal, intent. Ruiha's breath caught in her throat as she noticed the unhinged glint in his gaze, a look that spoke of dark plans and ruthless ambition. She shivered, unable to shake the sense of dread creeping up her spine.

"Welcome, intruders," Wilfrid's voice echoed through the tunnel, cold and mocking. "You've come a long way, but this is where your journey ends."

Ruiha tightened her grip on her sword, her heart pounding in her chest. She glanced at Arvi, who met her gaze with a determined nod. They were ready to face whatever came next, but the fear of the unknown loomed large.

Wilfrid raised his hand, and the shadows around him seemed to come alive. Suddenly, from the dark corners of the tunnel, Dwarven warriors emerged, their movements almost imperceptible until they were physically upon them. Ruiha's heart skipped a beat. How had she not seen them before? The realization hit her like a punch to the gut: they had been waiting, concealed by the very shadows Wilfrid now manipulated.

As the hidden warriors surged forward, the tunnel shook with a violent tremor, causing the walls to crack and debris to fall. Ruiha's eyes widened in shock as the ground beneath her feet began to crumble. The chaos of the ambush melded with the collapsing tunnel, and she struggled to maintain her footing, her mind racing to find a way out of the trap that had so cleverly ensnared them.

25.

THE DESCENT INTO DARKNESS

"The true challenge of power is not in its acquisition, but in mastering its boundless potential."

Kemp

Kemp stood alone in the center of the training grounds, a sense of isolation amplifying the heavy presence of the crown within his core. Its weight was not a physical weight; it was a constant, dark whisper threading through his thoughts, coiling around his spirit like a serpent tightening its grip. He couldn't shake the unsettling feeling that it was slowly becoming a part of him.

Thraxos and Thalirion watched from a distance, their eyes fixed on him with a mixture of curiosity and apprehension. They had never seen anything like this strange new force that had replaced his elemental magic. When they first witnessed it, they had decided to name it Shadowfire—a name that captured the dark, eerie aura it radiated, and the way it felt to Kemp, both alien and oddly fitting.

The memory of losing his elemental powers still haunted Kemp, a void where fire, earth, water, and air had once surged through him with familiar ease. Now, in their place,

Shadowfire surged with unpredictable potency, a force far beyond anything he had ever experienced. It was as if the gods had taken from him only to bestow something far more dangerous and unique. He could feel the eyes of Thraxos and Thalirion on him, a silent testament to the significance of what he had become.

The dark flame flickered around Kemp's hand, its black and gray hues pulsating with life. He could feel its energy, a unique and potentially dangerous force that sent shivers down his spine. Shadowfire seemed almost sentient, eager to consume anything it touched.

As he stared at his shadow hand, now an extension of this dark power, a mix of fear and fascination coursed through him. It felt both foreign and familiar, as if it had always been a part of him, lurking in the shadows of his soul. Kemp flexed his fingers, mesmerized by the way the flames danced and swirled.

The eerie beauty of Shadowfire held him captive and the flames whispered secrets he couldn't quite grasp. With each flicker, he felt a deeper connection to the darkness within.

"Focus, Kemp," Thraxos commanded sternly, his face lined with concern as he watched his pupil.

Kemp nodded, taking a deep breath. He could feel the tension between Thraxos and Thalirion, their nervousness palpable. They had tried numerous tests, attempting to understand the nature of Shadowfire, but its unpredictable nature left them wary. Kemp couldn't blame them. He was wary of it himself.

As Kemp channeled the dark flames, a surge of power coursed through him, filling him with a rush that was both exhilarating and terrifying. He felt as if he was standing on the edge of a precipice, teetering between control and chaos. The Shadowfire leapt from his hand, striking the target across the field with a precision that startled him.

The wooden dummy was instantly consumed, reduced to a pile of ash. Kemp's breath caught in his throat, fascinated and horrified, at the destructive potential he now wielded. He clenched his fist, desperately commanding the flames to retract. They obeyed, but he could feel their reluctance, a lingering resistance that sent a chill through him. It was as if the Shadowfire had a will of its own, testing his resolve, probing the limits of his control. He stared at his hand, the remnants of the dark energy flickering out, and wondered how much longer he could keep this dangerous power in check.

"Good," Thalirion said, stepping forward. The Elf's eyes were sharp, calculating. "You're learning to control it, but you must be cautious. This power is unlike any other."

Kemp met his gaze, a flicker of doubt crossing his mind. "I know. It's... difficult. It feels alive, like it wants to break free."

Thraxos exchanged a glance with Thalirion. "That's what concerns us, Kemp. This Shadowfire is potent, but it has a will of its own. You need to master it completely before we can safely move forward."

Kemp nodded, his jaw set with determination. The whispers of the crown were a constant murmur, urging him to embrace the power fully, to let it devour him. He shook his head, trying to clear the thoughts. He couldn't let the crown control him, not now.

After another round of training, where Kemp managed to harness the Shadowfire with slightly more precision, Thraxos and Thalirion approached him.

"We believe you're ready for the Corpselands trials," Thraxos announced although. Kemp could se a flicker of doubt in the Minatour's eyes. "You'll be joining Gunnar, Anwyn, and Karl. It's dangerous, but we need you to be part of this."

Thalirion stood beside him, a tightness around his mouth that Kemp had come to recognize as worry, an unspoken concern that mirrored Kemp's own anxieties. They didn't want to send him——but the situation left them with no choice. He was the only one who could transport them back to Vellhor now. They needed him at his strongest, and the trial would achieve that. If it didn't kill him, that is.

Everything he had heard about the Corpselands referred to the place's brutality and the high risk of fatality. Every mage or warrior who faced them returned changed, if they returned at all.

Yet, beneath the fear, Kemp felt a flicker of determination. This would be more than a test of survival; it was a chance to prove himself, to harness the Shadowfire that had become a part of him. He knew he needed to be ready. Or at least, he needed to convince himself that he was.

"I understand," he replied, his voice steady despite the anxiety gnawing at his insides. "I'll do my best."

As they turned to prepare for the journey to the Corpselands, Kemp couldn't shake the feeling of unease. The crown's whispers were growing stronger, more insistent, like a dark melody threading through his thoughts. He could sense a darkness within him, one that the

Shadowfire seemed to amplify. Every time he closed his eyes, he saw flashes of dragons and dark, black fire. He pushed the thoughts aside, focusing on the task ahead. They all depended on him now; he was the only one who could transport them back to Vellhor. He had to control this power, for his sake and for the sake of the others.

A sudden cry broke in on his reverie as a young woman from Raaniada rushed into the grounds, panting and wide-eyed. "Masters, there's been a breach in Nexus!" she shouted, her wings twitching behind her in visible panic. "Someone uninvited has arrived."

Thalirion's eyes widened, his calm demeanor shattered by the unexpected news. Thraxos let out a huff of air from his bull-like snout. "We need to investigate immediately," he said.

As Thalirion nodded in agreement Thraxos turned to Kemp. "Stay here," he commanded, though there was a hesitation in his voice.

"No," Kemp interjected, surprising himself with the firmness in his voice. "I should come with you. My Shadowfire is the only thing that can transport us between realms. If there is an emergency, I can help you escape."

Thalirion and Thraxos exchanged another glance, before Thalirion shook his had. "No," he said, "you need to prepare for the trial. Thraxos and I will decide how to deal with this intrusion."

Thraxos nodded reluctantly, then turned to Thalirion. "Escort Kemp to Gunnar, Anwyn, and Karl while I investigate the situation."

Kemp's heart pounded in his chest but he tried to focus on the task at hand, pushing aside the nagging fears that threatened to overwhelm him.

"Stay close," Thalirion ordered as they moved swiftly through the corridors of the Tower. The air buzzed with the energy of the alarm while Sages passed them wearing expressions of concern.

Kemp's mind swirled chaotically, the whispers of the crown interweaving with his own thoughts. The Shadowfire within him stirred, its dark energy pulsing eagerly, straining against his control. He barely registered his surroundings, only the insistent pull of the energy guiding his steps.

Before he knew it, he was standing before Gunnar, Anwyn, and Karl, who were immersed in their own preparations. The journey there had been a blur, lost in the storm of his mind.

Gunnar's eyes narrowed as he looked at Kemp. "What are you doing here?"

"Kemp has merged with the crown," Thalirion explained. "He is the only one capable of transporting us back to Vellhor. These trials, though dangerous, will greatly strengthen him."

A sudden thought seemed to strike Thalirion, and he reached out to perform a spiritual scan on Kemp. Kemp felt his spirit quiver under the intensity of Thalirion's scrutiny, a sensation that was both invasive and oddly reassuring. He stood still, trying to steady his breathing as Thalirion's power coursed through him.

When Thalirion's eyes widened in surprise, Kemp's felt a sharp pang of anxiety. But the Elf announced in astonishment, "Kemp has attained the rank of Master. He now stands on equal footing with you all. These trials will pave the way for him to become an Overlord, just as they will for the rest of you."

Kemp felt a surge of pride at the realization he had truly become the equal of his three companions. However, Anwyn's gaze was fixed on Kemp's eyes, her unease palpable as she shivered involuntarily. "What happened to your eyes?" she asked, unable to keep the shock from her voice. "I've never heard of something like this happening before."

Kemp shifted uncomfortably beneath her scrutiny, embarrassment and frustration churning within him. "The harmonization process, though successful, stripped me of my elemental powers and left me with Shadowfire in their place." His voice wavered, the transformation still unsettling even to him. "It was an unexpected side effect, along with my eyes." He felt exposed and vulnerable in making the admission, worried about the judgment of his new companions.

Thalirion nodded, frowning. "It has not happened before. Both Thraxos and I are as confused as you are by this anomaly."

"Well Kemp," Gunnar greeted, his voice gruff but warm. "Eyes or no eyes, there's much to do before we embark on the trials."

Anwyn and Karl nodded in agreement, their faces serious. Kemp could see the resolve in their eyes, a mirror of his own determination.

As the group began their final preparations, Kemp tried to shake off the unease that clung to him. The crown's whispers were louder now, almost deafening, but he forced himself to concentrate.

As he glanced at his reflection in a nearby pool of water, the dark flames of his shadow hand flickered eerily, a stark reminder of the power and the curse he now carried. He clenched his fist, watching the Shadowfire flicker around his hand. The trials would be the ultimate test, not just of his strength, but of his ability to control the darkness within.

―――――✦―――――

Anwyn

Thalirion activated the Endless Bridge, a tunnel of heatless flame that would portal them from the Tower to the Corpselands. Anwyn stepped forward, feeling the familiar, comforting presence of Lorelei, whose bell-like tinkles were a constant reminder of their connection. The soft, melodic sounds reassured her, grounding her in the midst of uncertainty.

As they passed through the ethereal tunnel, Anwyn couldn't shake the sense of foreboding that settled over her like a heavy cloak. The Corpselands were notorious, a place spoken of in hushed, fearful tones. The idea of traversing such a desolate and dangerous land made her stomach churn.

Anwyn remembered the tales about the Corpselands, stories of erratic spectral echoes. Even Lorelei's lighthearted tinkles couldn't completely dispel her anxiety.

As they approached the end of the tunnel, the oppressive atmosphere intensified. Anwyn forced herself to take steady breaths. She had to be strong, not just for herself, but for the entire group. They were counting on her, just as much as she was counting on them.

When they emerged on the other side she understood immediately why it was called the Corpselands. The landscape was a barren wasteland, devoid of life, with blackened trees reaching out like skeletal hands. The aura here was even stronger and thicker than at the Tower, as if the air itself resisted their presence.

Anwyn glanced around at her companions. Gunnar stood resolute, Havoc, perched on his shoulder, no doubt communicating telepathically as always. Karl scanned the area, his expression hardening as he took in their bleak surroundings. Kemp, with his stormy eyes, seemed more at ease with the darkness, but Anwyn could sense the tension in his posture.

The spectral echoes, hundreds of them, drifted through the air, drawn to this place like moths to a flame. Anwyn could see a variety of shadow-like creatures lurking in the canopy of the blackened trees, their forms shifting and flickering in the darkness. There was no sun or light to illuminate their path, only the omnipresent darkness that was a hallmark of Nexus.

Anwyn felt Lorelei's gentle tinkle, a sound that was both reassuring and urgent. She nodded, understanding the unspoken message. They had to stay vigilant. The Corpselands were not just a barren wasteland; they were a place of danger and malevolent intent. Anwyn's senses remained on high alert, every instinct tuned to the hostile environment around them.

As the group took their first steps into the darkness of the Corpselands, Anwyn suggested, "We should start exploring.

Her voice cut through the silence. "Thalirion told me that there are valuable resources and relics here that can help us get stronger."

Gunnar nodded. "Agreed, but what exactly are we looking for?"

Anwyn began to recount the relics Thalirion had described. "There are a few specific items we should keep an eye out for. One is the Emberheart Crystal, found deep within ancient volcanic rock. It's a glowing red crystal that enhances fire magic abilities and increases resistance to heat and flames. Then there's the Stormcaller's Gem, which is infused with the power of countless storms. It grants control over lightning and storms, and enhances speed and reaction time."

Anwyn saw the shadow of disappointment crossing Kemp's features. With his powers as an elemental mage stripped away he had to work with the unknown and unpredictable Shadowfire. The mention of relics tailored to elemental mages must have been a bitter reminder of what he had lost. "I'm sorry, Kemp. I didn't mean to be insensitive."

Kemp forced a smile, though it didn't quite reach his eyes. "It's okay," he said quietly.

Gunnar, sensing the tension, shifted the focus. "What about treasures for battle mages?"

Anwyn gratefully accepted the diversion. "Yes, for battle mages, there are items like the Warrior's Aegis, an unbreakable shield that boosts physical defense and fortitude. There's also the Bloodforged Talisman, which increases physical strength and grants a berserker rage ability. And the Spectral Blade Shard allows the user to summon a spectral weapon, enhancing agility and precision in combat."

Karl, his big bushy red beard framing a face full of curiosity, spoke up next. "And for craft mages? What treasures are there for us?"

Anwyn smiled, appreciating Karl's enthusiasm. "For craft mages, there's the Artisan's Sigil, a rune-inscribed medallion that boosts crafting abilities and enhances creativity and innovation. Then there's the Weaver's Thread, a spool of shimmering, unbreakable thread that grants the ability to weave powerful magical fabrics and create protective clothing and barriers. And finally, the Rune Scribe's Ink, a vial of ever-flowing magical ink that enhances the ability to inscribe powerful runes and glyphs." Lorelei's bell-like tinkles filled Anwyn's mind, a gentle reminder of the Fae's presence and support. Anwyn felt a surge of determination. "We need to find these relics. They could make the difference between success and failure."

As they moved forward, the strange aura of the Corpselands seemed to press in on them, making every step feel heavier. The spectral echoes drifted around them, skulking in the canopy of the blackened trees, their eyes glowing with malicious intent. Anwyn kept her senses sharp. "Stay close," she advised her companions. "This place is dangerous, but if we work together, we can find what we need."

The group ventured on ever deeper into the Corpselands, led by Gunnar, with Havoc on his shoulder, alert for any sign of threat or treasure.

Gunnar

The eerie glow of the Corpselands cast long shadows across the barren terrain. The haunted land was littered with the remnants of a once-thriving civilization, now reduced to skeletal ruins and spectral echoes of the past. Gunnar didn't know what had happened to the civilization, the records lost to the annals of time, but now they were scavenging its remains, in an attempt to advance to Overlord.

Gunnar led the group, scanning the area for any signs of danger with Anwyn following closely behind, her staff held at the ready. Karl and Kemp brought up the rear, Karl's gaze fixed on the ground, searching for any relics hidden beneath the rubble, while Kemp kept glancing nervously around, his shadow arm twitching involuntarily.

Havoc perched on Gunnar's shoulder, peeking around with his mischievous purple eyes. Gunnar could sense the sprite was not enjoying this place.

Their first breakthrough came when Karl spotted a faint, glimmering light emanating from beneath a pile of debris. He knelt down and carefully unearthed a beautifully crafted Artisan's Sigil, its intricate patterns glowing with a soft, ethereal light.

"Look at this," Karl breathed, holding the sigil up for the others to see.

Before they could celebrate, a chilling wail echoed through the air, and three spectral echoes materialized, their forms shifting and flickering like smoke in the wind. They lunged towards the group, spectral weapons raised.

"Get ready!" Gunnar shouted, drawing his axe. As his fingers wrapped around the familiar grip, a rush of energy coursed through him. The runes etched into the blade began to glow a soft green, pulsing with the rhythm of his heartbeat. He felt a connection to the weapon, a sense of ancient power that always surged to life in moments of conflict. The runes' glow cast eerie shadows on the ground around them, and a hum of arcane power resonated from within the blade, as if the axe were whispering promises of strength and victory.

Anwyn moved forward with fluid grace, her katana crackling with energy, the air around her humming with magical potential.

The first echo, a bird-like creature, swept its shadowy talon at Gunnar, who blocked it with his axe. The impact sent a shockwave through his arm, reverberating up to his shoulder. The force of it was staggering, but Gunnar gritted his teeth, feeling the familiar surge of adrenaline that sharpened his focus. He pushed back with all his might. The runes on his axe flared a fierce green as he sliced through the echo's middle, watching as its form dissolved into nothingness.

Beside him, Anwyn was chanting a spell, her voice steady and commanding. Bolts of lightning shot from her staff to strike the second echo. The creature screamed in agony, twisting and writhing before it disintegrated into a cloud of spectral mist.

Gunnar found himself reminded of Thalirion, whose power had always been a source of awe and, occasionally, envy for the Dwarf. Now Anwyn seemed to be embodying the same powerful yet effortless mastery over the elements.

The third echo, a menacing figure shrouded in shadow, lunged at Karl, its spectral blade aiming for his heart. Karl, clutching the Artisan's Sigil, barely managed to dodge the initial strike. The echo's blade sliced through the air with a chilling hiss, missing Karl by mere inches.

"Hold on, Karl!" Gunnar shouted, as he charged at the echo, his axe raised high. The echo turned its attention to Gunnar, its hollow eyes glinting with malevolence. It swung its talon with deadly precision, but Gunnar parried the blow with his axe, the runes flaring a brilliant green upon impact. The force of the clash reverberated through the air, a shockwave of energy that seemed to distort the very fabric of reality around them.

Gunnar pushed back, his muscles straining with effort. He could feel the power of the axe coursing through him, guiding his movements. With a powerful twist, he disengaged from the echo's talon and brought his axe down in a mighty arc. The runes on the blade glowed even brighter, their light slicing through the darkness.

The echo let out a chilling screech as the axe cleaved through its form, the green light tearing it apart from within. Gunnar didn't relent. He swung again and again, each strike filled with the determination to protect his friends. The echo's form flickered and warped beneath the onslaught. With one final, devastating blow, Gunnar's axe cut through the echo's core, shattering it into wisps of shadow that dissipated into the air.

Breathing heavily, Gunnar turned to Karl, who still held the Artisan's Sigil. "Now, Karl! Absorb it!"

Karl, eyes wide with awe and relief, nodded. He focused on the sigil, feeling its ancient energy resonate with his spirit. As he absorbed the relic, a surge of power coursed through him, infusing his very being with newfound strength and skill. It was as if he could feel the essence of long-forgotten crafts smiths guiding his hands, their knowledge and craft becoming one with his soul.

Without hesitation, Karl picked up a fallen limb from one of the defeated echoes. He concentrated, channeling the sigil's power into the limb. A flash of energy enveloped the limb, transforming it into a gleaming hammer that radiated with power and purpose. The craftsmanship was beyond anything Karl had ever achieved before, the hammer a testament to the relic's influence.

Karl swung the hammer experimentally, feeling its weight and balance. He glanced at Gunnar and Anwyn with an exhilarated expression, reveling in his newfound power and capabilities.

Gunnar's eyes caught a glint of something metallic half-buried beneath a fallen tree trunk. He approached cautiously, pushing aside the decaying wood and debris to reveal an ancient shield. The Warrior's Aegis lay before him, its surface etched with intricate runes and symbols of protection.

As Gunnar reached for the shield, he felt a magnetic pull, an almost tangible connection between him and the relic. He lifted it, the weight reassuring in his hands, and examined the unyielding surface. The shield thrummed with a steady, rhythmic pulse, as if it had a heartbeat of its own. This wasn't just a piece of metal—it was the physical embodiment of the strength and fortitude of the warriors who had wielded it before him.

Taking a deep breath, Gunnar closed his eyes and began the process of absorption. He could feel the shield's energy merging with his own, an electric sensation that spread from his fingertips up through his arms and into his core. Memories of ancient battles and fallen heroes flashed through his mind, each one embedding itself into his consciousness.

With each passing second, Gunnar felt the shield's power integrating with his spirit, an unyielding strength settling into his very bones. He pictured the warriors who had stood their ground against insurmountable odds, their spirits now a part of him. The sensation was both humbling and empowering, a reminder of the legacy he was now a part of.

As the shield's power merged with his spirit, Gunnar kept a watchful eye on his surroundings. He saw Anwyn discover her relic, a Stormcaller's Gem hidden within the roots of a gnarled tree.

Even while focusing on his own relic, he was acutely aware of the raw energy emanating from the vibrant pulsating gem. The air around it seemed to hum with electricity, and Gunnar felt a tingle across his skin.

Anwyn knelt by the ancient tree, her fingers deftly brushing away dirt and debris. She picked up the gem with both hands, and as she did, a surge of energy rippled through the air. Gunnar felt the hairs on the back of his neck stand on end. The gem's power was almost tangible, resonating with the elemental forces of nature.

Suddenly, out of the murky gloom, spectral echoes in the form of shadow-woven tigers leaped at them, their eyes glowing with a sinister light. The air grew colder, and

Gunnar could feel the weight of their malevolent intent pressing in from all sides.

Karl, reacting swiftly, hefted his newly crafted hammer and met the first tiger mid-leap. The hammer connected with a resounding crack, the shadowy form shattering into wisps of darkness that dissolved into the air.

Before he could catch his breath, another tiger lunged at him from the side. Karl spun, the hammer a blur of motion, and struck the second tiger with a powerful swing. The creature let out a ghostly snarl before disintegrating into a cloud of shadows.

Karl glanced down with an alarmed expression. Tiny fractures were spider-webbing across the hammer's surface, the once-pristine weapon now marred by signs of deterioration. Panic flickered in Karl's eyes as he shouted across, "Gunnar, we've got a problem."

He swung the hammer again, but each strike seemed to weaken the weapon's integrity further. It was not built for prolonged use.

Havoc then sprinted out, weaving between shadowy limbs, triggering miniature earthquakes to prevent the spectral echoes from closing the distance. The ground trembled with each seismic rupture, disrupting their spectral adversaries. It helped, but it wouldn't be enough. Still absorbing his relic, Gunnar knew they needed to end this quickly, before Karl's weapon failed entirely.

"I can't fight like this forever!" Karl shouted, the hammer crumbling in his hands.

Anwyn, also locked in the process of absorbing her relic, was unable to defend herself, and Gunnar couldn't risk interrupting his own absorption. The situation was dire, and the spectral tigers were closing in. Suddenly, he sensed a protective barrier forming around them. As he glanced over, he saw Lorelei atop Anwyn's head, straining with effort to maintain the barrier and protect them while they were vulnerable.

Amidst the chaos, Gunnar caught sight of Kemp standing back, trembling. His friend's fear was palpable, but there was something else in his eyes—a flicker of determination. Gunnar's breath caught as he saw Kemp raise his shadow arm, the limb a dark contrast against the dim, ghostly light of the Corpselands. Kemp's expression shifted from fear to fierce resolve, his brow furrowing as he focused all his will into a single point. The air around him seemed to darken, and Gunnar felt a strange pull, an anticipation of power about to be unleashed.

A dark flame erupted from Kemp's shadow arm, swirling with an intense, almost malevolent energy. The flame coiled and twisted, a living entity born from Kemp's newfound power. It surged forward, seeking out the remaining spectral tigers with a predatory instinct.

The tigers, poised to strike again, hesitated as the dark flame approached. The fire engulfed them, wrapping their shadowy forms in tendrils of black flame. Gunnar watched in awe as the tigers disintegrated, their forms unraveling into the very shadows from which they had emerged. The baleful glow in their eyes faded into the consuming darkness of Kemp's flame.

Kemp stood still, his shadow arm smoking slightly, his eyes wide with a mix of shock and realization at the power he had just wielded. For a moment, the battlefield was silent, the only sound the fading crackle of Kemp's Shadowfire.

Gunnar stepped forward, placing a reassuring hand on Kemp's shoulder. "Well done, Kemp," he said, his voice steady, though his heart still pounded with the adrenaline of the fight.

Kemp nodded, still processing what he had done, as Gunnar looked around at his friends, feeling a renewed sense of hope and determination. The Corpselands were treacherous, but they had proven themselves capable.

"Looks like we've got a new weapon," Karl said, a hint of a smile on his lips.

26.
Fellron's Stand

"In the darkest moments, the light of sacrifice shines the brightest."

Ruiha

The tunnel quaked violently, the tremors splitting the walls and sending chunks of stone crashing down. Ruiha staggered, her boots slipping on the uneven ground. Panic clawed at her mind, every instinct screaming to find a way out. Her pulse pounded in her ears, melding with the cacophony of battle, as the Dwarven warriors materialized from the shadows, their ambush a brutal surprise. Axes glinted ominously in the dim light, and she tasted bitter self-reproach for not noticing them earlier.

Desperation lent speed to her strikes as Ruiha's blade danced in a blur of steel. The narrow tunnel intensified the chaos, the clash of weapons and shouts of battle echoing around them in a deafening roar. Arvi was a deadly storm at her side, but even their combined skill seemed insufficient against the relentless wave of enemies.

Sweat stung Ruiha's eyes as she blocked another blow, the impact jolting her arm. She gritted her teeth against the pain, the mounting pressure almost overwhelming. The sheer number of attackers pressed in, threatening to suffocate them. The tunnel had descended into mayhem, its tight confines making a fighting retreat nearly impossible.

Ruiha couldn't understand how they had fallen into such a perfect trap, but a cold dread of failure fueled her strikes and parries.

As another wave of attackers bore down on them, Ruiha's grip tightened on her sword. A fierce, burning refusal to be crushed by Wilfrid's subterfuge ignited within her.

Suddenly, Fellron emerged from the shadows. Grim faced and black eyed the Daemonseeker charged into the fray. As he raised his hands, faint rune scars on his skin flashed briefly, casting an eerie light before fading. The air around him darkened, shadowy tendrils snaking out and lashing at the enemy. Ghost, his loyal Snow Wolf, followed close behind, its white fur a stark contrast to the gloom. The wolf's growls mixed with the cacophony of battle, adding to the pandemonium.

Heartened at the sight of Fellron, Ruiha shouted to him, over the din, "We need to fall back!"

Fellron's unsettling eyes scanned the tunnel, quickly assessing their options. "This way!" he bellowed, pointing toward a narrow side passage. He led the charge, conjuring a wall of darkness that pushed their enemies back. Ghost snapped and lunged at their heels, driving the Dwarven warriors back with fierce determination.

As Fellron and Ghost broke through the enemy lines, Ruiha felt a surge of renewed vigor. She and Arvi followed, adrenaline pumping, knowing they had a chance to escape this trap.

The group scrambled into the passage, the walls closing in around them. The tremors continued, but the immediate threat of collapse seemed lessened. Fellron turned to face the pursuing enemies. "Go, Ruiha! I'll hold them off!"

"No!" Ruiha shouted, her voice breaking with emotion. "We can fight them together!"

Fellron shook his head, a sad smile touching his lips. "You have to lead them, Ruiha. This is your fight now."

Ruiha's heart clenched, filled with a mix of despair and admiration. She had witnessed the potency of his magic before, but now he was sacrificing himself to give them a chance at survival.

With a final, resolute nod, Fellron turned back toward the tunnel, shadows swirling around him. He raised his arms, summoning a maelstrom of darkness that enveloped the attackers. The sight of him, bathed in dark energy, was both awe-inspiring and heartbreaking. The last glimpse she had of Fellron was a blur of motion, his fierce roar echoing through the passage. A tremendous crash followed, and she knew he had made his final stand.

Ruiha swallowed hard, forcing herself to turn away. "We have to keep moving," she said, her voice choked with grief. Arvi placed a reassuring hand on her shoulder, his touch grounding her amidst the chaos and together, they led their group deeper into Draegoor.

As they pressed on, Ruiha noticed Ghost at her side. The Snow Wolf's mournful eyes met hers, and she felt his shared pain for Fellron. "Come on, Ghost," she whispered, kneeling to scratch behind his ears. "We'll honor his sacrifice."

Ghost nudged her hand, his warm presence a small comfort amidst the chaos. "Forward," she commanded, her voice steady. "For Fellron. For Draegoor."

Ruiha emerged from the narrow passage into a larger cavern, her breath catching at the sight of the vast space. Magnus and Erik stood ready with the Snow Wolves, their fierce growls echoing through the cavern.

Magnus nodded at Ruiha, his expression grim. "We need to secure the upper levels," he said. "Erik and I will take point. The Snow Wolves will flank us."

Ruiha's heart pounded, but she forced herself to focus. "I'll cover the rear," she replied, her eyes scanning the shadows for any sign of movement.

They moved swiftly, Magnus leading with a determined stride. Erik's eyes darted sharply, missing nothing. The Snow Wolves flanked them, weaving through the chaos with predatory grace.

Ruiha's thoughts drifted back to Fellron. She could still see the flash of his rune scars, feel the oppressive power of the shadows he conjured. The memory of his sacrifice burned in her mind. She couldn't let his death be in vain.

The sounds of battle grew louder. They were close to their goal, every step bringing them closer to the heart of Draegoor. The thought of facing Wilfrid sent a chill down her spine, but it also ignited a fierce resolve. They had come too far to falter now.

Suddenly, a group of Dwarven warriors charged from the shadows, their axes gleaming ominously in the dim light.

Magnus met them head-on, his shield deflecting blows while his axe struck with lethal precision. Erik moved beside him, his swings deliberate and deadly, cutting through the enemy with practiced efficiency. The sight of them fighting side by side bolstered Ruiha's resolve. Ghost lunged, teeth bared and snarls ripping through the air, his ferocity amplifying the disciplined attacks of Magnus and Erik.

Ruiha fought alongside them, her blade a blur as she parried and struck. She had found the narrow confines of the tunnel constricting, but here in the open cavern, her sword danced through the air with a renewed freedom. Sweat dripped down her brow, mingling with the grime of battle, but she hardly noticed.

As her blade connected with an enemy's weapon, the force of the clash vibrated up her arm. Around her the Snow Wolves fought with lethal efficiency, while Magnus fended off attacks with an impenetrable defense. Erik's precise strikes and Ghost's ferocity combined to push the enemy back and bring Ruiha a step closer to her revenge.

The clang of metal, the growls of Ghost, and the shouts of battle filled the cavern, creating a symphony of conflict. Ruiha's muscles burned, but she pushed through the pain. She had been through worse.

Amidst the chaos, a horn sounded from the depths of the cavern. Ruiha's heart skipped a beat as she recognized the signal. Relief surged through her as Dakarai and the Drogo warriors emerged from the shadows, their arrival well-timed and more than welcome. She could see the weariness etched on their faces, the toll of battle evident in their reduced numbers, and she felt a pang of guilt for the sacrifices made in their cause.

As the Drogo warriors joined the fray Dakarai's eyes met Ruiha's and a brief nod of solidarity passing between them. The Drogo warriors moved seamlessly, their weapons striking with fierce power. A surge of hope washed over

Ruiha. With their combined strength, they had a real chance to turn the tide.

As the final stages of the battle drew near, all eyes turned to the central dais where Wilfrid loomed, his dark armor seeming to swallow the surrounding light. Erik stepped forward, muscles tense, his gaze fixed on his treacherous brother. The space between them crackled with animosity as they began to circle each other warily and the noise of the surrounding battle seemed to fade away.

Ruiha held her breath as Erik and Wilfrid clashed. Each strike sent sparks flying, illuminating the sweat and grime on their faces. Erik fought with relentless intensity, his muscles straining with each blow. She could see the years of battles etched in his movements, the slight hesitation in his parries, the fatigue in his eyes. Wilfrid had the advantage of youth, moving with a ruthless grace as he blended strength and agility in a deadly combination.

Ruiha's heart thundered in her chest. She could feel Erik's desperation, his fierce determination to end this once and for all. But Wilfrid pressed his advantage, landing a brutal strike that nearly sent Erik sprawling. Fear clawed at her insides, but she was locked in her own battle, unable to aid the beleaguered clan chief.

She willed him to dig deep and defy the odds as she swiftly dispatched the last of her immediate adversaries, her blade finding its mark with deadly precision. She barely had time to catch her breath before more enemies surged toward her, their eyes filled with malice. She tightened her grip on her sword, feeling the familiar weight in her hand, and prepared for the next onslaught.

From the corner of her eye, Ruiha caught glimpses of Erik's battle; Wilfrid's relentless assault and Erik's determined, albeit weary, defense.

As her new adversaries closed in, Ruiha moved with a dancer's grace, her sword slicing through the air with lethal intent as she threaded her way towards Erik and Wilfrid. She parried a blow aimed at her head, countering with a swift strike to her attacker's side as she closed on the embattled brothers.

With a kick Wilfrid send Erik sprawling, but then – sensing the danger of Ruiha's approach – he turned to lunge at her, but she sidestepped, driving her blade through a gap in his armor.

The usurper staggered, his eyes widening in shock, the color draining from his face. Blood poured from the wound, darkening his armor. Erik seized the moment, his expression a mixture of sorrow and resolve, and delivered a decisive blow, driving his blade deep into Wilfrid's heart.

A stunned silence fell over the cavern, the echoes of battle fading into an eerie stillness as, with Wilfrid dead, his soldiers swiftly threw down their own weapons.

Ruiha took a deep breath, her gaze sweeping across the cavern where her comrades stood, equally stunned. Victory had come at a high cost, but it was theirs. The future of Draegoor was now in their hands.

Erik met Ruiha's gaze and she saw the exhaustion in his eyes but also the unyielding determination that had carried them through.

Magnus stepped forward, placing a hand on his father's shoulder. "Well done," he said.

Erik nodded, his expression a mix of relief and anguish. "For Gunnar," he replied quietly.

Magnus raised his weapon high, his voice booming through the cavern, "For Draegoor!"

The echo of his cry filled the space, a rallying call that reverberated off the walls and into the hearts of every warrior present. Ruiha felt a surge of pride and determination. The battle was over, but their fight for a better future had only just begun. With Ghost by her side, she followed Magnus and Erik as they led their companions deeper into the heart of the mountain, ready to rebuild and reclaim their home.

27.
UNINVITED GUEST

*"In the stillness of the shadows, an
unexpected visitor is more than a stranger;
they are a harbinger of chaos."*

Anwyn

Anwyn stepped carefully over the uneven terrain, her eyes scanning for any glimmer of the relics they sought.

The Corpselands were a harsh, desolate place, filled with spectral echoes and the remains of a civilization long lost to time.

The air felt thick with ancient sorrow and forgotten battles. Each step seemed heavier, as if the very ground resisted their intrusion. Lorelei's gentle, bell-like tinkles, provided Anwyn with a comforting presence. However, she couldn't shake the feeling of eyes watching them from the shadows. Spectral echoes waiting for a moment of weakness.

As they ventured deeper, the atmosphere seemed to press in on them even more, making each breath labored. The air of the Corpselands was thick, almost suffocating, making each step a battle against an unseen pressure.

A lucky reprieve came when Karl's sharp eyes caught a faint glimmer beneath a pile of debris. Excitement lit up his face as he knelt and carefully unearthed a beautifully crafted

Artisan's Sigil, its intricate patterns glowing softly in the dim light.

"Look at this," Karl breathed, holding the relic up for the others to see.

Anwyn's heart lifted at the sight. The delicate lines of the sigil seemed to pulse with latent energy, a promise of the power they sought. Before they could celebrate, however, a chilling wail echoed through the air. Three spectral echoes materialized, their forms shifting and flickering like smoke as they lunged towards the group, dark claws raised.

"Get ready!" Gunnar shouted, his axe already drawn. As his fingers wrapped around the grip, the runes etched into the blade began to glow a soft green, pulsing with his heartbeat.

He met the first echo head-on. The shadowy figure hurled itself at him reaching out with spectral claws, but Gunnar swung his axe in a wide arc. The blade connected with a satisfying thud, the runes flaring brighter upon impact. The echo let out a chilling wail as the axe cleaved through its form, dispelling the creature into wisps of dark mist.

Anwyn tightened her grip on her katana, its blade humming with latent energy, as she channeled her power into the weapon. She could feel the magical currents flowing through her, merging with her katana. The air seemed to crackle as she swung her blade, spitting out arcs of lightning from its edge.

The nearest echo, a shadowy figure with hollow eyes, screamed in agony as the lightning struck it. The creature's form twisted and writhed before disintegrating into shadow, its ethereal remnants swallowed by the darkness.

The stifling weight of the Corpselands seemed to lift slightly with each fallen enemy, giving a chance to glanced over at her companions. Gunnar stood like a bulwark against the shadows. Karl's eyes shone with the thrill of discovery, clutched the Artisan's Sigil as if it were a lifeline. Kemp, however, stood motionless as if afraid to unleash his newfound Shadowfire.

As another echo lunged at her, Anwyn fluidly parried its attack, her katana slicing through the air with a satisfying hum. She could feel the electricity coursing through the blade, as she reversed the motion to slice through her adversary. The creature dissolved into smoke with a final, desperate cry.

The victory lifted their spirits as they probed deeper into the Corpselands, seeking out more relics. Their determination paid off when Kemp discovered a glowing red crystal embedded in ancient volcanic rock. He pried it free, holding it up to reveal the Emberheart Crystal. The crystal pulsated with a fiery glow, and as Kemp touched it, a strange reaction occurred. The crystal's fire mingled with Kemp's Shadowfire, creating a purple tinge to the usually dark flames.

Kemp stared at the transformed fire with a mix of awe and uncertainty. "It feels… different," he murmured, the flames reflecting in his dark stormy eyes.

Anwyn watched in fascination as the transformation unfolded before her. The Emberheart Crystal, nestling in Kemp's hand, pulsed with a fiery glow that seemed to merge with his Shadowfire. She could see the flames shifting, taking on a vibrant purple hue that flickered with an intense, almost hypnotic energy.

"It's the Emberheart Crystal," Anwyn murmured, her voice almost reverent. "It enhances fire magic and increases resistance to heat and flames. It must be reacting with your Shadowfire."

Kemp stared at the swirling flames, the initial uncertainty in his expression giving way to fierce determination. He clenched his fist, the purple-tinged flames dancing around his fingers like living entities. "It's powerful, but I can control it," he said.

The purple flames cast an otherworldly glow around them, that seemed to lift the overbearing pressure of the Corpselands.

"Kemp," she said softly encouraging. "With this power, we can overcome anything."

Kemp nodded, the flickering flames casting shadows across his face. "Then let's make sure we do just that," he replied firmly.

The group uncovered several more relics as they continued their search. Karl found the Weaver's Thread, a spool of shimmering, unbreakable thread that granted the ability to weave powerful magical fabrics. Anwyn discovered the Stormcaller's Gem, a vibrant crystal that granted control over lightning and storms.

As they absorbed these treasures, a sense of hope and strength filled them. Each relic amplified their power, preparing them for their advancement to Overlord.

Suddenly, a portal tore through the fabric of reality before them. Anwyn recognized it instantly as the Endless Bridge. It emanated heatless fire, bathing their surroundings in an ethereal amber glow. The air shimmered with unnatural energy, making her skin tingle. From the depths of the

Endless Bridge, Thalirion and Thraxos emerged, their faces etched with deep concern. A chill ran down Anwyn's spine at the sight of their worried expressions. Something was wrong. Thalirion approached, his eyes locking onto Anwyn's. "We need to talk," he said heavily. "There's been a development."

Gunnar

As Thalirion and Thraxos emerged from the Endless Bridge, a knot of dread tightened in Gunnar's stomach. The expressions of concern on their faces immediately signaled that something was amiss. Gunnar desperately wanted to know more about the 'development' Thalirion had mentioned. Glancing around the group, he saw the same nervous anxiety etched into their faces.

"What happened?" he asked.

Thalirion took a deep breath. "There's been a breach in the Corpselands," Thalirion began solemnly. "As you know, someone has portalled from another realm to Nexus. However, we have recently discovered that they have deliberately entered the Corpselands."

Gunnar's mind whirled with possibilities. The Corpselands were already fraught with danger and secrets; the thought of an intruder from another realm added a new layer of complexity. Who would risk coming here? And why? His thoughts briefly flickered to the Drogo. Could this be connected?

Karl, ever the curious one, broke the silence. "Who would be stupid enough to come to this place?"

Thalirion's expression darkened, confirming Gunnar's worst suspicions. "I fear it may be related to Nergai. There are many powerful weapons hidden in the Corpselands. If this intruder is seeking to gain strength from these relics, we must stop them."

Gunnar felt a cold dread at the thought of Nergai's influence seeping into their world again. But there was no time for hesitation. "We can't let them get their hands on any more power," he said firmly. "We have to find this intruder and stop them."

Thalirion nodded, grim-faced. "Agreed. We need to move quickly and track them down before they can secure any relics or weapons."

The team set off immediately, probing deeper into the Corpselands. As they walked, the silence was occasionally broken by the distant howl of unseen echoes and Gunnar couldn't shake the feeling of being watched.

"Keep your eyes peeled," Thalirion said, his voice a low murmur. "This place is full of surprises, none of them pleasant."

Anwyn, walking beside Gunnar, glanced at him with a wry smile. "Cheerful as always, Thalirion," she whispered with a chuckle, but Gunnar could see the worry in her eyes.

As they journeyed on, the air grew colder, and the group fell into the silence of their own thoughts. Suddenly, a low growl echoed through the mist, and spectral shadowbeasts emerged from the darkness, their eyes glowing a malevolent red.

Anwyn reacted quickest, drawing her blade in a swift, fluid motion. The steel gleamed in the dim light as she lunged at the nearest shadowbeast, slashing through its ethereal form in a blur of movement. The creature howled in pain, its red eyes flaring bright before it dissipated into wisps of smoke.

Thalirion raised his staff to summon a crackling ball of energy which he hurled at another shadowbeast. The spell exploded on impact and scattering the creature into shimmering fragments.

Thraxos stood beside him, his hands weaving intricate patterns in the air. A burst of blue flame erupted from his fingertips, engulfing two shadowbeasts and reducing them to ash.

Kemp positioned himself at the rear, extending his shadow hand to conjure Shadowfire. He directed the black and purple flame precisely at the heart of each spectral echo driving them back. The creatures snarled and snapped, but Kemp's spellcraft prevented them from flanking the group.

"I see your flames have changed," Thraxos remarked between casting his own spells. "Last time I saw, they were just black and grey."

Anwyn, dodging a shadowbeast's swipe, explained, "It's the Emberheart Crystal. It altered his power."

Thraxos nodded in understanding before sending a burst of blue flame towards another enemy.

The battle raged on, the cacophony of clashing steel and crackling magic filling the air. Gunnar watched Anwyn darting between the spectral forms with a dancer's grace, her blade slicing through their ghostly bodies. Despite her skill, one of the shadowbeasts managed to slip past her defenses, its red eyes fixed on her.

Without a second thought, Gunnar summoned his battle magic. He felt the familiar rush of power as the world around him began to slow. Time crawled and the movements of the shadowbeasts became sluggish and predictable. The cool haft of his axe felt reassuring in his grip as he stepped between Anwyn and the attacking creature.

With a powerful swing, Gunnar brought his axe down. In the slowed time, he could see every detail: the shadowbeast's red eyes glistening, the ethereal tendrils of its body parting under the force of his blow. The creature dissolved into a misty vapor, its malevolent gaze extinguished. Relief washed over him, but only for a moment. He knew the fight was far from over.

Moving through the battlefield with the advantage of his time- slowing magic, Gunnar systematically targeted the spectral echoes. Between swings of his axe, he could see Thalirion's spells exploding in brilliant arcs of energy, and Thraxos's blue flames engulfing the spectral forms. Kemp's Shadowfire, tinged with purple from the Emberheart Crystal, blazed fiercely, each conjured flame striking true.

Despite their numbers and ferocity, the shadowbeasts were no match for the team's combined might and Gunnar's temporal advantage. One by one, they fell, their spectral forms disintegrating into the air.

The last echo dissolved, succumbing to the final blow from Anwyn's katana, and Gunnar released his hold on the battle magic. Time resumed its normal pace. The silence that followed was almost startling after the chaos of battle.

Gunnar's senses slowly adjusted to the absence of frenetic energy, his heart still pounding in his chest.

"Everyone alright?" Thalirion asked.

"That was too close," Kemp muttered, wiping sweat from his brow. "I thought they'd have us for sure."

"We're still here," Thraxos replied, his voice steady and reassuring. "Let's keep it that way."

With the immediate threat behind them, the team pressed on, their steps cautious and senses alert. The terrain grew more ever more treacherous until they stumbled upon an ancient, enchanted forest. The trees were black and twisted, their bark gnarled and cracked like old bones. As they passed, the branches seemed to reach out with skeletal fingers, whispering secrets in a language lost to time.

The air was thick with the forbidding aura, and Gunnar found it hard to focus. Shadows danced in the corners of his vision, giving the forest an almost sentient feel, as if it were watching their every move. The uneven ground was covered in a dense layer of fallen leaves that crunched underfoot.

"This place gives me the creeps," Karl admitted, his usual curiosity dampened by the stifling atmosphere. "What kind of power could be buried here?"

"Power best left undisturbed," Thalirion said quietly, his eyes scanning the surroundings.

As they pressed on, the landscape changed, becoming more desolate and foreboding. The ground became unstable, riddled with sinkholes and jagged rocks. They had to navigate carefully, using spells to ensure safe passage.

"Watch your step," Gunnar warned, as he reached out to help Anwyn over a particularly treacherous patch of ground.

Her hand felt warm around his, a comforting contrast to the cold, eerie forest surrounding them.

"Last thing we need is someone getting hurt," he added, holding her gaze for a moment. He steadied her, but didn't let go immediately, savoring the brief connection.

"Thanks, Gunnar," she said softly letting her hand linger in his. The warmth of her touch remained even after she'd let go.

"We need to stay focused," he said, though the danger of the forest seemed to fade for a brief second, replaced by a growing awareness of a vulnerability in her that made his heart ache.

They continued through the ominous forest until, eventually, the trees thinned and opened out into a clearing. Gunnar felt the shift in the air, a lightening of the suffocating darkness that had surrounded them.

His eyes widened as he took in the sight before him. Standing in stark contrast to the rest of the Corpselands was a large, crumbling tower. It sent a shiver down his spine, eerily reminiscent of the Tower of Absence. Time and neglect had taken their toll on the structure; the once-pristine white stone was now dirty and off-color, with green vines wrapping around the base like a constricting serpent.

Gunnar's grip tightened on his axe as he surveyed the tower. The years had taken a severe toll on the building—cracks running through the stone, windows broken and dark. He glanced across at Anwyn, who was staring up at the tower with a mix of awe and trepidation.

"This must be it," she whispered, her voice barely audible.

Gunnar nodded. "Stay close," he said, his voice steady despite the unease gnawing at him. "We don't know what we'll find inside."

The team moved cautiously towards the tower, their senses alert for any signs of danger. As they approached, the air grew colder, and a stifling silence enveloped them. The vines seemed to react to their presence, thrumming with a dark energy.

High up in one of the windows, a pulse of magic radiated outward, followed by a beaming green light. Gunnar watched as Thalirion's eyes widened. "That light... it's the same as the one from the Tower of Absence," Thalirion whispered. He turned to Thraxos. "We need to explore the tower. If that light is indeed from the Tower of Absence, we must understand its purpose here."

Thraxos nodded. "Agreed. We can't afford to ignore this."

Anwyn hesitated. "The magic here could be unpredictable and dangerous."

Gunnar took a deep breath. "We have no choice. We need answers, and the only way to get them is by venturing inside. Let's just make sure we're ready for anything."

Inside the tower, the corridors were dark and filled with debris. Every step echoed ominously, and the team stayed close together, weapons at the ready as they climbed the spiral staircase, toward the source of the green light.

"This place is a maze," Havoc grumbled into Gunnar's mind, his frustration mingling with Gunnar's own rising anxiety. Each corridor seemed designed to confuse and disorient while the flickering light of their torches only added to the eerie atmosphere.

"How are we supposed to find anyone in here?" Havoc's mental voice echoed his own doubts.

Gunnar forced himself to focus, drawing strength from the bond he shared with Havoc. "We follow the light," he communicated back, trying to infuse his thoughts with more confidence than he felt. "It will lead us to the source."

The light, a strange, almost sentient glow, seemed to beckon them onward. As they climbed the winding staircase, the air grew colder, and Gunnar's heart pounded louder in his chest. Every creak and whisper of the old stone made him tighten his grip on his axe.

Finally, they reached the top and emerged into a large, ancient chamber. Gunnar's breath caught in his throat as he took in the sight before him. The walls, lined with shelves, held dusty tomes and strange artifacts that seemed to hum with latent power. His gaze was drawn to the center of the room, where a figure cloaked in shadow stood before a glowing green crystal.

The eerie light cast grotesque, shifting shadows across the walls, creating an almost hypnotic effect.

Gunnar's heart pounded as the shadows in the chamber shifted, revealing a band of Drogo warriors and shamans emerging from the darkness, their eyes glowing with malevolent intent.

The figure at the room's center turned slowly, revealing a face twisted with dark magic. Malice and hunger gleamed in his reptilian eyes, sending a chill down Gunnar's spine. The raw, corrupted power radiating from him made Gunnar's skin crawl. In his hand he held a huge staff. The source of the green light.

Recognition struck him like a lightning bolt—this was the Drogo shaman from the battle of the Sacred Tree. He remembered severing this shaman's hand as he attacked the Sacred Tree with his magic.

"I am Shon'anga, a mere servant of Nergai," the shaman intoned, his voice a rasping whisper that seemed to echo from the depths of the earth. "I seek the power hidden in these lands, and you are unable to stop me." He let out a cackle, and Gunnar couldn't help but wonder if the power of the staff had driven him mad.

28.

Battle of the Second Tower

"Victory is hollow when the price is the heart of those we cherish."

Kemp

Kemp stood at the edge of the chamber, his heart pounding in his chest as the Drogo warriors and shamans closed in. He clenched his shadow hand, feeling the potent hum of magic pulsing through it. He had fought many battles before now, but the stakes had never felt this high.

The air crackled with energy, the tension so thick it was almost palpable. The glowing crystal in the center of Shon'anga's staff cast long, shifting shadows, adding to the eerie atmosphere. Kemp's eyes darted around, taking in the positions of his comrades—all of them poised, ready to strike.

Suddenly, a Drogo warrior lunged forward, his blade gleaming with a dark, malevolent light. Adrenaline surging through Kemp's veins. Without conscious thought, his hand shot up, and a torrent of black and purple flame erupted from his fingertips. The warrior disintegrated in an instant, leaving only ash in the air. Kemp's stomach churned with a mix of nausea and horror at how effortlessly he had taken a life.

In the stillness that followed, a faint whisper emerged from the recesses of his mind. Though the words were indistinct, a sense of reassurance washed over him, as if the whisper was trying to soothe his troubled soul.

"Now!" Thalirion's voice echoed through the chamber.

Gunnar moved like a force of nature, his axe a blur as he parried a strike from one warrior and spun, driving his enchanted blade into the next.

Thraxos stood beside him, chanting in an ancient tongue, his hands weaving intricate patterns in the air as he summoned bolts of lightning that struck down Drogo shamans attempting to cast dark spells.

Karl, having crafted a giant shield out of spectral remnant parts, held the line, bashing aside attackers with brutal efficiency. In his other hand, he held a crafted warhammer which he swung in wide arcs, crushing armor and bone with each thunderous blow.

More warriors and shamans poured into the chamber. Shon'anga stood at the back, his twisted smile never wavering as he directed the assault. Kemp could feel the dark magic radiating from him, a cold, suffocating presence that seemed to sap the very light from the room.

Kemp felt the weight of the battle pressing down on him; they had to break the enemy's momentum or be overwhelmed. He raised his hand high, delving into the deepest reserves of his power. Shadowfire erupted from his fingertips, wild and untamed, mirroring the turmoil within his soul.

As he wrestled with the volatile energy, a fleeting moment of doubt crossed his mind—was he strong enough to control this? The sight of several Drogo evaporating under the force of his attack sent a shiver down his spine, a sickening mix of horror and grim satisfaction. Panic surged as the Shadowfire resisted his attempts to rein it in, seeming to revel in the destruction it wrought.

Gritting his teeth, Kemp focused every ounce of his willpower, his mind a battlefield of concentration and fear. Slowly, reluctantly, the Shadowfire obeyed, the flames subsiding until they flickered out. He stood there, panting from the exertion, feeling the raw power still thrumming through his veins, and hearing the faint whispers at the back of his mind.

His eyes met those of his companions, who watched him with wide-eyed awe. He saw their admiration, but also a shadow of fear—fear of the power he wielded, and perhaps, fear of what he might become.

"Press the attack!" Gunnar yelled, his voice a rallying cry.

They surged forward as one, their renewed vigor driving them into the heart of the enemy formation. Thraxos hung back to weave spells of protection and support, his magic a lifeline that kept them all in the fight.

Thalirion's lightning bolts arced across the room, striking down shaman after shaman, their screams mingling with the cacophony of battle. Gunnar fought with a ferocity that seemed almost superhuman, his axe dancing through the air, green runes flashing, each strike precise and lethal. Karl and his shield were an immovable wall, every swing of his warhammer a testament to his unyielding strength.

As Kemp's gaze swept across the chamber, his eyes fell upon the obscure corner of the chamber—a faint shimmering, like a rip in the fabric of reality itself. His breath caught in his throat as he realized the truth: that was the gateway, the conduit through which the Drogo warriors poured into Nexus.

But even as that realization settled upon him, another presence drew his attention. Shon'anga, standing tall and ominous, his voice weaving through the air like a dark incantation. Kemp felt a shiver ripple through his very core at the ever-intensifying chant, as though the very stones of the chamber were responding to the dark magic.

With a sinking feeling, Kemp understood the gravity of the situation. "He's summoning something!" he called out in panic. "Something worse!"

And then, confirming his worst fears, a second portal began to materialize behind Shon'anga—a swirling maelstrom of shadow and flame, a gateway to untold horrors. The sight of the monstrous creatures emerging from the depths of that abyssal portal sent a chill deep into his bones, but he clenched his jaw, steeling himself for the inevitable confrontation. There was no turning back now—they had no choice but to stand their ground, to fight with every ounce of strength they possessed.

With a roar that echoed through the chamber, the monstrous creatures surged forward, their vicious claws outstretched, hungry for blood. Gunnar and Anwyn braced themselves, meeting the onslaught head-on, their weapons a blur of motion in the dim light.

Each clash of steel against flesh sent a jolt of adrenaline coursing through Kemp's veins. Amidst the chaos of battle,

Kemp's mind churned with the realization that couldn't afford to prolong this fight. They needed to strike at the heart of the darkness, to sever the source of Shon'anga's power before it was too late. With grim determination, he focused his energy, piecing together a plan of action. There was no room for hesitation—they had to act swiftly and decisively.

"Cover me!" Kemp's surged into the chaos of battle without even waiting for acknowledgment, his senses honed to a razor's edge, his shadow hand crackling with volatile energy.

As he closed in on Shon'anga, the shaman's gaze locked onto his with a chilling intensity, a wicked grin twisting his features into a grotesque mask of malevolence. "You cannot stop me!"

"We'll see about that," Kemp retorted.

With a surge of determination, Kemp unleashed a torrent of Shadowfire, the raw power of his magic unleashed with deadly precision. But to his shock and horror, Shon'anga countered with a dark spell of his own, a sinister energy that simply snuffed out Kemp's flames. Dread gripped Kemp's heart like a vice as he realized the true extent of the shaman's power.

Anwyn

Amidst the clash of steel and the roar of battle, Anwyn's gaze locked onto the unfolding confrontation between Kemp and Shon'anga. Her breath caught as she witnessed the shaman's dark magic repelling Kemp's Shadowfire with unnerving ease.

She threw herself back into the fray, her muscles burning with exertion as she wove through the chaotic melee. Her blade became an extension of herself, a lethal dance of steel in the dim light of the chamber, each strike finding its mark amidst the throng of Drogo warriors.

But even as she fought, unease clawed at the edges of her consciousness, like a shadow lurking just beyond the reach of the flickering torchlight. It whispered of danger, of impending doom, but Anwyn forced the intrusive thoughts aside and focused instead on the rhythmic cadence of battle, on the primal instinct that drove her ever forward into the heart of the fray.

Each clash of steel sent sparks flying, each foe defeated, bringing them one step closer to victory. But beneath the cacophony of war, Anwyn still couldn't shake the foreboding feeling that something was terribly wrong.

As the battle raged on, Anwyn felt exhaustion encumbering her limbs, each swing of her sword heavier than the last, each step forward an agonizing struggle against the weight of fatigue. The weariness seemed to seep into her bones, dragging her down into the depths of despair.

Just when she thought she could fight no longer, a surge of power came so potent, so overwhelming, that it left her gasping for breath. It was unlike anything she had ever experienced, a raw, primal force that coursed through her veins like wildfire, setting every nerve ablaze with its searing intensity.

Anwyn cried out in agony as the magic seemed to consume her spirit, its tendrils wrapping around her very soul. It was as if she had been thrust into the heart of a raging inferno, every fiber of her being consumed by the infernal blaze.

In that moment of unbearable anguish, Anwyn felt as though she were teetering on the edge of oblivion, her spirit torn asunder by a sensation beyond comprehension, beyond anything she had ever imagined possible.

And yet, even as the darkness threatened to consume her, she fought on, her willpower the only thing standing between her and annihilation. For in battle, there was no room for weakness, no time for surrender. There was only the relentless pursuit of victory, no matter the cost.

Anwyn felt her form engulfed in a blinding aura of light, her own screams of pain echoing through the chamber. She was dimly aware of Thalirion's presence nearby, his heartache palpable as he witnessed her plight. But in the throes of agony, she knew that this battle was hers alone to fight.

And then, with a final, heart-wrenching scream, Anwyn collapsed to the ground, her body wracked with pain and exhaustion. The world around her blurred into darkness as consciousness slipped away, leaving her at the mercy of the encroaching shadows.

The last thing she saw before succumbing to unconsciousness was Gunnar rushing to her side, face, his expression creased with worry, his outstretched hand reaching for her a beacon of hope in the encroaching darkness. And as darkness claimed her, Anwyn prayed that somehow, someway, they would find a way to emerge victorious against the forces that sought to destroy them.

Gunnar

Panic surged through Gunnar when he saw Anwyn collapse. Although he had known her for only a few weeks, he had fallen for her, her strength and resilience, and the fierce spirit that burned within her. Dread filled him as she crumpled to the floor, as if the ground had given way beneath him, pitching him into an abyss of fear and helplessness.

Gunnar charged through the melee, his focus solely on reaching Anwyn. Around him, the clash of steel and the roars of monstrous foes filled the air, but all he could see was her prone form. His mind raced with thoughts of what might have happened, the worst-case scenarios playing out in vivid detail. What if she was already beyond saving? What if he was too late?

He dropped to his knees beside her, his calloused hands shaking as he gently lifted her head. The warmth of her skin against his fingers was a small comfort, a sign that she was still alive. But her pallor and the limpness of her body were terrifying. "Anwyn," he called, his voice breaking with fear. "Stay with us."

Karl, standing nearby, deflected a Drogo warrior's blow with his shield. He glanced over at Gunnar and Anwyn, his face grim. "We need to hold the line!" he shouted, raising his shield to block another attack.

The words barely registered in Gunnar's mind. All he could think about was Anwyn, lying motionless in his arms.

Kemp, his Shadowfire searing through the ranks of Drogo and monsters alike, spared a glance towards them.

"We can't let them break through!" he called, his voice strained with effort.

An awareness of his surroundings gradually returned to Gunnar. He realized they were still in the midst of a battle, and Anwyn's life depended not just on his care, but on the outcome of this fight.

Havoc caused the ground to tremble as he ran in between the Drogo legs, creating earthquakes and tremors that disoriented their enemies. Gunnar took heart from Havoc's relentless efforts. They still had powerful allies, and together they might just stand a chance.

Thalirion appeared beside Gunnar, his face etched with worry. "She has advanced to Overlord," he said, his voice tight. "It's not a good thing. Her spirit... it's more than likely damaged. If we can't bring her back soon, she may die."

The Elf's words hit Gunnar like a hammer. He had thought reaching the Overlord status was a mark of power, an advantage in this dire battle. But now he realized the cost might be Anwyn's life. Gunnar's confusion gave way to fury. The idea that this incredible Elf might die because of her power was unacceptable. Anger surged through him, white-hot and all-consuming. He felt a primal need to protect her, to save her at any cost.

Roaring in defiance, Gunnar rose to his feet, gripping his battle axe with renewed determination. The weapon, enchanted and extraordinarily powerful, felt like an extension of his rage. His mind was a storm of emotions— fear for Anwyn, fury at their enemies, and a fierce determination to see them all through this alive.

With a bellow, he flung himself at Shon'anga, his strikes fueled by the desperate need to protect Anwyn. Every swing of his axe was a declaration of his resolve, each blow a promise that he would not let her down.

Shon'anga, sensing the imminent danger, raised his staff, dark magic crackling around him like a storm waiting to be unleashed. The malevolent energy pulsed in the air, but Gunnar's fury was a force of nature, an unstoppable tidal wave fueled by desperation and a single, powerful drive to protect Anwyn.

With a primal roar, Gunnar swung his battle ax. The weapon felt like an extension of his own wrath, slicing through Shon'anga's dark defenses. The blow was a release of his pent-up rage, a physical manifestation of his refusal to lose Anwyn. His axe cleaved through the shaman's protective magic, cutting deeply into flesh and bone.

Shon'anga staggered, bloodied and beaten, but his eyes still gleamed with a dark resolve. Gunnar watched, breathless and trembling with adrenaline, as the shaman, in a final, desperate act, lifted his staff towards the tower's ceiling. Gunnar's heart skipped a beat as he realized what was about to happen.

The ancient stones around them began to tremble, a deep, foreboding rumble that echoed through the chamber. Cracks snaked through the walls, spreading like a web of doom. Shon'anga's dark magic sought to bring the entire tower down upon them, to bury them all beneath its ruin. The realization hit Gunnar like a physical blow—this wasn't just about defeating a foe; it was about surviving an impending cataclysm.

In that moment, Gunnar's fear for Anwyn's life intensified. He couldn't let her die here, not like this, not after everything they had fought for.

"Take cover!" Thalirion's voice cut through the din of battle. Karl raised his shield, ready to protect those he could, but Gunnar knew it wouldn't be enough.

With a final, devastating swing, Gunnar's battle axe cleaved through Shon'anga's chest. The shaman let out a guttural cry, his eyes wide with shock and pain, before crumpling to the ground. His staff slipped from his grasp, clattering uselessly on the stone floor. Yet even in death, the magic Shon'anga had unleashed was unstoppable. The tower groaned and trembled, the cracks in the walls widening ominously.

Gunnar barely had a moment to catch his breath. His gaze snapped back to Anwyn, lying motionless on the ground. Fear gripped his heart, but he pushed it aside, sprinting towards her, and scooping her into his arms. Her body felt fragile and alarmingly light, her breathing shallow. "We need to get out of here, now!" he yelled.

Thraxos, his normally calm demeanor shattered by the impending disaster, looked up sharply. "Kemp! Use the crown! Portal us to Vellhor – it is our only chance!"

Kemp's face was a mask of fear and panic, his eyes wide as he looked at the collapsing tower. He raised both hands, his shadow hand twitching uncontrollably. Gunnar could see the strain in his posture, the sweat beginning to bead across his forehead. Kemp's brow furrowed in intense concentration, the pressure of their survival weighing heavily on his shoulders.

For a moment, the chaos of the collapsing tower seemed to freeze. Then, with a blinding flash, they were enveloped in a tunnel of brilliant light. The world around them dissolved, replaced by a rush of colors and sensations that defied description.

Gunnar clutched Anwyn tightly, his heart pounding. The light was overwhelming, yet he forced himself to focus on her, feeling the faint rise and fall of her chest. They were moving, escaping, but the uncertainty of their destination gnawed at him. He could only hope Thraxos's plan would work, that they would emerge from this tunnel of light into safety, and not into another perilous situation.

As the light began to fade, Gunnar's mind raced. He thought of Anwyn, of the promise he had made to himself to protect her, and of the battle that had brought them to this moment. No matter what awaited them on the other side, he would fight for her, for all of them, until his last breath.

29.
REUNITED

"The longest journeys lead to the most heartfelt reunions."

Kemp

Kemp's entire body ached with exhaustion, the toll of transporting them through the portal sapping the last of his strength. He stumbled as they emerged from the tunnel of brilliant light, praying silently that they had reached Vellhor. His vision was blurred, and he fought to stay conscious, leaning heavily against a nearby rock for support.

As the light receded, Kemp blinked, trying to make sense of their surroundings. Instead of the familiar architecture of Vellhor, they found themselves in the damp, dimly lit bowels of a mountain. The air was thick and musty, the walls rough-hewn from ancient stone.

"Where are we?" Kemp muttered, his voice hoarse. His heart sank as he realized this was not the safe haven he had hoped for. He glanced around at his companions, noting Karl's puzzled expression as he surveyed their new environment.

Karl's eyes widened in recognition. "We're in Draegoor," he said, a note of excitement creeping into his voice.

Gunnar and Thalirion were preoccupied with Anwyn, desperately trying to revive her. Thalirion's hands moved with practiced urgency, his face a mask of concentration, while Gunnar hovered anxiously, his face lined with worry.

Thraxos turned to Kemp, his expression a mix of confusion and urgency. "How did you transport us here, Kemp?"

Kemp shook his head, trying to gather his thoughts. His mind was a fog of fatigue and confusion. "I… I tried to portal us to Vellhor," he explained, struggling to make sense of what had gone wrong. "When I concentrated, I thought of Ruiha—the last person I saw in Vellhor. I was certain that would take us there."

"But this is Draegoor," Thraxos replied, his voice tinged with frustration. "Why here?"

Kemp's brow furrowed as he tried to piece it together. "I don't know. Ruiha shouldn't be here. Why would she be in Draegoor?"

Before they could ponder further, a group of Dwarven warriors emerged from the shadows, encircling them. The Dwarves' armor was battered, their faces grim and determined, each holding weapons at the ready.

"Who goes there?" demanded the lead dwarf, his voice a deep rumble that echoed off the stone walls. His eyes were sharp and suspicious, clearly not in the mood for any nonsense.

Thalirion looked up from Anwyn, meeting the dwarf's gaze. "We mean no harm. We were trying to escape a dire situation and ended up here by mistake."

The dwarves exchanged glances, their expressions hard to read. Finally, the leader stepped forward, his eyes locking onto Gunnar. A broad grin spread across his face, delight and disbelief mingling in his expression. "Gunnar! By the gods, it's really you!"

Gunnar glanced up at his name. "Magnus? Magnus!" Even as astonishment washed over him at his brother's presence, he was turning back to Anwyn. "We need help." His voice was strained. "It's Anwyn—she's hurt."

Magnus nodded quickly grasping the urgency of the situation. "You're fortunate it's us who found you and not something worse. Draegoor is dangerous right now. We'll take you to the city. Father will be overjoyed to see you."

As they walked, Thalirion explained to Magnus what had happened, recounting their desperate escape and the unexpected arrival in Draegoor. Magnus listened, his eyes never leaving Anwyn's pale face.

As the dwarves led them deeper into the mountain, Kemp suddenly spotted Ruiha entering the cavern. A wave of emotion swept away his exhaustion. He ran to her, legs moving almost involuntarily, driven by pure instinct and longing. As he embraced her tightly, the familiar comfort of her presence washed over him, soothing his frayed nerves. He could feel her warmth, smell the faint scent of her hair, and the reality of her in his arms was almost surreal. Tears of joy welled up in his eyes.

"Kemp," Ruiha whispered. "I thought I'd never see you again."

"I missed you so much," Kemp replied, his voice cracking. "Every day felt like an eternity. I can't believe you're here."

As she pulled back slightly, her eyes widened with concern. "What happened to your hand?"

Kemp glanced down at the magical prosthetic, a faint glow emanating from the intricate runes etched into its surface. "I lost it in an attack. Thraxos replaced it with magic," he explained, flexing the fingers to show her.

Ruiha's gaze moved to his eyes, now bearing an ethereal, almost otherworldly gleam. "And your eyes...?"

Kemp sighed, the memory still fresh and painful. "During another magical spell, things went wrong. I thought I was going to die. The magic changed me, but I survived."

She reached up to touch his face gently, her fingers tracing the lines of worry and fatigue. "I've been forced to fight as a gladiator for the Drogo Mulik," she said quietly, her voice tinged with bitterness and sorrow. "It's been a constant battle, every day a fight for survival."

Kemp's heart ached at her words, and he pulled her close again, holding her as if he could shield her from all the pain she had endured. "We'll find a way out of this," he promised. "Together, we'll fight for our freedom."

Ruiha nodded. "Together," she echoed. The cavern around them seemed to fade into the background as they held onto each other until, with a final squeeze, Kemp stepped back, a fire in his eyes. "Let's find a way to end this," he said, taking her hand in his.

They turned to follow the dwarves deeper into the mountain, ready to face whatever challenges lay ahead.

Gunnar

As the group descended the narrow, winding tunnel leading to the underground city of Draegoor, Gunnar's heart tightened with every step. The once bustling entrance, a grand stone archway carved with intricate runes, was now marred by the signs of recent conflict. Scorch marks and debris littered the passage, and the air was thick with the acrid scent of smoke.

Each step echoed through the tunnel, mingling with Gunnar's racing thoughts. He couldn't shake the image of Anwyn, pale and unconscious, from his mind. Her usually vibrant eyes were closed, her body limp. He had seen Thalirion work miracles before, but this time felt different. The stakes were higher, and the urgency gnawed at him.

"Stay close," Magnus commanded, his voice a low growl that echoed off the stone walls. Gunnar glanced at his brother, noticing the tension in his posture, the rigid set of his shoulders. Gunnar had always been the strong one, the leader, but now, as Magnus took charge, Gunnar felt a swell of pride. Even though Magnus seemed strained under the weight of recent events, he stood firm, embodying the strength their family needed.

Gunnar's gaze shifted back to Anwyn. His heart clenched at the sight of her, so fragile and still. Thalirion and Thraxos were already murmuring incantations, their hands glowing with faint magical auras. Desperation clawed at Gunnar's chest, making it hard to breathe.

"Keep her alive," Gunnar implored, his voice cracking with anguish. "Do everything in your power…" The words felt like a prayer, a plea to the gods, but it was all he could do. He felt utterly helpless.

Thalirion looked up, meeting Gunnar's eyes with a firm nod. "We will, Gunnar. She is strong."

Reluctantly, Gunnar turned to follow Magnus deeper into Draegoor. The city unfolded before them, its grandeur now tinged with the scars of battle. The usually vibrant market stalls lay in ruins, and the echo of their footsteps was accompanied by the distant cries of the wounded. Gunnar's heart ached for his home, now a place of pain and suffering.

Amid the destruction, Gunnar caught sight of Karl reuniting with the Snow Wolves. Their relieved laughter and firm embraces brought a brief smile to his face. Despite the chaos, their camaraderie was a reminder of what they were fighting for.

The Great Hall loomed ahead, its imposing stone doors splintered but still standing. Gunnar felt a knot in his stomach tighten as they approached. Inside, the hall's grandeur remained, the tall pillars and vaulted ceiling untouched by the conflict outside. Torches flickered, casting long shadows that danced along the stone walls.

At the far end, his father stood surrounded by loyal warriors, his presence commanding despite the clear toll the conflict had taken. Gunnar's heart swelled with emotion as his father's eyes widened in disbelief and joy.

"Gunnar, my son!" Erik's voice boomed, and he enveloped Gunnar in a familiar bear-like embrace.

He clung to his father, feeling like a child again, seeking comfort in the midst of chaos. "Father, there's much I need to tell you," Gunnar began urgently as they pulled apart. "I met Draeg."

Erik's expression shifted to one of concern and curiosity. "Draeg? The god of chaos?"

"Yes," Gunnar confirmed. "He revealed to me a dire threat. The Drogo are attempting to resurrect their god Nergai. If they succeed, Nergai will bring utter destruction upon us all. Draeg said that I must unite the clans of Dreynas and lead the fight against Nergai."

A heavy silence settled over the hall, as Gunnar's words sunk in. Erik's face hardened. "We will not let Nergai's darkness consume our world," he declared. "We will gather the clans, and we will fight."

Magnus stepped forward, his eyes blazing with determination. "Wilfrid's betrayal nearly broke us, but we are stronger now. We will reclaim what is ours and forge new alliances."

One of Erik's retinue raised his voice. "Gunnar, you speak of uniting the clans, but you know our ways. The dwarven clans of Dreynas have always been led by a democratic council. We are fiercely protective of our power and autonomy."

Another grizzled warrior standing behind Erik nodded in agreement. "Our council prides itself on these principles. The idea of uniting under a single leader is unthinkable. How can we ask the clans to forsake their votes and their voices?"

Gunnar took a deep breath, feeling the weight of their concerns. "I understand, I do. But this is not just about our traditions. This is about our survival. Draeg was clear: if I do not lead the clans against Nergai, we will all fall."

Erik nodded thoughtfully. "We would not be asking the clans to abandon their voices, so much as trust in a unified command for the sake of our survival. This is a matter of life and death, and we must come together."

Magnus added, "The threat we face requires us to adapt. We must rise above our old ways and embrace a new path."

The warrior nodded slowly. "It will be difficult. Many will resist. But if this is our only hope, we must make it work."

Erik placed a firm hand on Gunnar's shoulder. "You have brought us a great challenge, my son." He paused, a softer expression crossing his face. "Despite this, I am glad you are alive and well. It brings me great relief to see you here with us."

Gunnar nodded, feeling a spark of hope ignite within him. The path ahead was fraught with danger, but he was ready.

They all were.

As the fires of determination blazed in the eyes of those around him, Gunnar knew this was not the end but the beginning of a new chapter. A battle for survival, unity, and the future of not only Dreynas but the whole of Vellhor.

The subterranean winds carried the promise of change as the first echoes of preparation resounded through the caverns. The fight against Nergai would be their greatest challenge yet, but together, they would forge a legacy of courage and hope.

As the warriors celebrated their hard-won victory over Wilfrid, the hall buzzed with festive energy. Tankards clinked in jubilant toasts, and the air was filled with the murmur of animated conversations and tales of valor, each story of bravery adding to the collective pride and relief of the gathered dwarves.

Gunnar's attention was drawn to Kemp, sitting in the corner deep in conversation with a striking human woman. She exuded an air of quiet strength, her dark skin a stark contrast to the giant white snow wolf standing loyally by her side. The wolf's intelligent eyes surveyed the room with a watchful gaze. Gunnar's curiosity was piqued, and he couldn't help but wonder about the connection between Kemp and this formidable woman, and what tales of adventure and survival lay behind their acquaintance.

Magnus, noticing Gunnar's interest, approached with a chuckle. "That's Ruiha, also known as the Shadowhawk," he explained, his voice tinged with a hint of admiration. "She helped lead the Snow Wolves' escape from captivity in the Drogo Mulik lands, where they had been forced to fight as gladiators. She's quite the legend."

Intrigued, Gunnar followed Magnus over to meet her. As they approached, the white wolf's ears perked up, and Ruiha turned to greet them, her eyes sharp and assessing. Magnus introduced them, "Ruiha, this is my brother, Gunnar."

Ruiha extended her hand with a firm grip, her gaze steady. "It's an honor to meet you, Gunnar. Your reputation precedes you."

"The honor is mine," he replied, offering a genuine smile. He felt an immediate respect for her, recognizing a kindred spirit of resilience and leadership.

Their exchange was brief, but Gunnar sensed the depth of her character in that short moment. Before he could delve further into conversation, he heard his father's voice calling for him. With a respectful nod to Ruiha and a glance at Magnus, they excused themselves.

As Gunnar and Magnus made their way back to their father, the weight of his responsibilities pressed heavily on Gunnar's shoulders. The recent victories had been sweet, but the path ahead remained fraught with challenges. His thoughts drifted to Anwyn; the memory of her lying still and vulnerable gnawed at him, a stark reminder of what was at stake. Yet, meeting allies like Ruiha gave him hope. With such formidable companions by his side, they stood a fighting chance against the darkness that threatened their world. Protecting Anwyn, his family, and his people was paramount, and for that, he would draw strength from every ally and every ounce of his resolve.

Erik led them through the throng of dwarves until they reached the center of the hall and a hush fell over the crowd. Erik turned to face Gunnar. With deliberate movements that blended formality and deep emotion, he knelt before his son.

"Gunnar," Erik began, his voice steady but filled with warmth, "today we honor you as the Dwarven Prince. Your courage and vision have brought us together, and for that, I am not only grateful but proud."

Gunnar felt a rush of emotions at his father's words. Although he had never truly wanted to lead, he had always striven to be worthy of his father's legacy. Yet, the mantle of leadership felt heavy, an immense responsibility now resting on his shoulders. The eyes of the gathered dwarves bore into him, their hopes and expectations palpable. Gunnar took a deep breath, drawing strength from his father's unwavering gaze and the supportive presence of Magnus beside him. He vowed silently to live up to their trust and to lead with the same courage and vision he had shown.

Magnus followed suit, kneeling beside Erik. "Brother," he said, his tone reverent yet familiar, "we pledge ourselves to your leadership. Your strength has always guided us, and now, more than ever, we need you."

Gunnar stood before them both, feeling a mix of pride and awkwardness. He was unaccustomed to such reverence. He looked around the silent hall, seeing the faces of his people—filled with hope, determination, and trust.

Taking a deep breath, Gunnar nodded solemnly. "I accept this mantle with a humble heart. Together, we will face whatever comes, united in our purpose and unbroken in spirit."

As he spoke, a renewed sense of purpose filled the hall. The dwarves, once fragmented, now stood united under a common cause. The subterranean winds seemed to carry the promise of change, echoing through the caverns as the first preparations for battle began.

Gunnar knew this was not the end but the beginning of a new chapter. A battle for survival, unity, and the future of Dreynas lay ahead. As they prepared to face the looming threat, he vowed silently to save Anwyn, protect his family, and lead his people at all costs.

Thank You for Embarking on *The Vellhor Saga*!

I hope you enjoyed *Battle Mage*! To show my appreciation, I'm offering you another **exclusive, free short story** that delves even deeper into the world of Vellhor. Each book in *The Vellhor Saga* comes with its own unique short story, available **only** to my mailing list subscribers.

Follow the Link to get your first story and continue your adventure with the characters you've grown to love.

https://dl.bookfunnel.com/c8wdy2g4ll

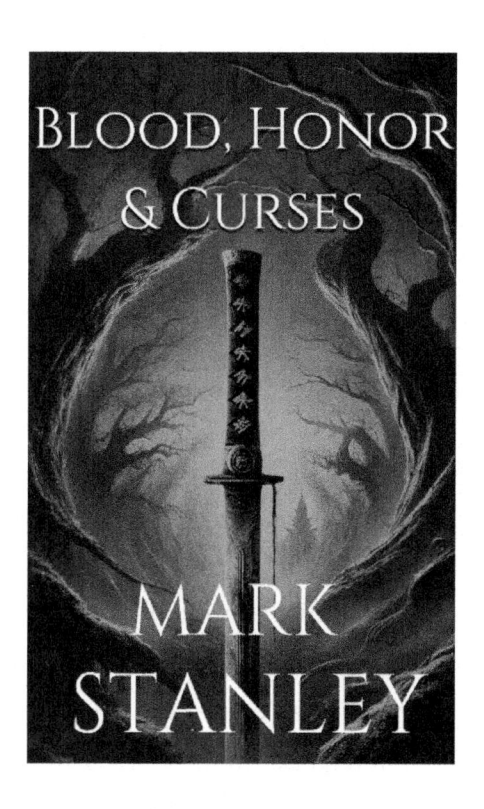

What You'll Get When You Sign Up:

- **Exclusive Short Stories:** Unlock new tales from Vellhor, not available anywhere else.
- **Insider Updates:** Be the first to know about upcoming books, special events, and more.
- **Early Previews:** Get sneak peeks at new releases before anyone else.
- **Special Offers:** Access discounts and offers available only to my mailing list subscribers.

Don't miss out on these exclusive extras
Join now and keep the adventure going!

Love the Series? Want More? Support the Saga on Patreon!

If you'd like to see more of the Vellhor world—faster, deeper, and bolder—consider joining me on **Patreon**.

Your support helps me write full-time and unlocks:

🔥 **Early access to chapters**
🛠 **Behind-the-scenes development logs**
📖 **Worldbuilding extras, character sheets, and maps**
📃 **Monthly short stories voted on by patrons**
✏ **Live Q&As, polls, and manuscript previews**

☞ **Become a patron here:**
patreon.com/MarkStanleywrites

And help shape the future of Vellhor.

Stay Connected!

I'd love to stay in touch with you! Follow me on Facebook and Instagram for the latest news, behind-the-scenes content, and to connect with other fans of *The Vellhor Saga*. Plus, be on the lookout for special giveaways and exclusive content just for my social media followers!

Facebook - https://www.facebook.com/profile.php?id=61561728111921

Instagram - https://www.instagram.com/markstanleywrites/

Mark Stanley

AFTERWORD

A Sneak Peek at Book 3 – Dwarven Prince

Gunnar stepped into the chamber, and the sheer grandeur of it all struck him like a hammer blow. The air was thick with the heady fragrance of burning incense, mingling with the faint, musty aroma of ancient parchment and burning torches. The walls, a testament to centuries of unparalleled dwarven craftsmanship, gleamed with intricate carvings that seemed to come alive in the flickering torchlight. Each stone whispered of ancient battles and hard-won victories, echoing the legacy that now rested on his shoulders. Gold and gemstones sparkled from the very rock, a silent, glittering reminder of his new status as Dwarven Prince. Yet, amid all this wealth and history, a seed of doubt gnawed at him. Could he ever measure up to the legacy of those who had come before? As his gaze drifted to Anwyn's bedside, the weight of his responsibilities pressed harder, his chest tightening with the enormity of it all. Ready or not, his time had come. The question was, would he rise to the occasion, or crumble beneath the weight of his destiny?

He moved to Anwyn's bedside, his steps slow and deliberate. She lay motionless on the plush silk bed, her honey-colored hair spilling like liquid sunlight across the pillow. The sight of her, so still and fragile, pierced his heart like a dagger. The warm glow of the lanterns cast an ethereal light on her delicate, serene features. Despite the pallor of her magically induced coma, her beauty remained undiminished. Gunnar's heart ached with worry for her, a pain that gnawed at him constantly. He longed to brush his fingers against her porcelain skin, to feel the warmth of her breath against his hand. But the fear of disturbing her fragile state held him back. For now, all he could do was sit vigil and pray for her recovery.

Lorelei's delicate, shimmering form darted closer, her tiny face etched with worry. She whispered tinkling words in the tongue of the Fae, hoping to reach Anwyn's spirit. The sound was like a gentle breeze, soothing yet filled with urgency. Gunnar, lost in his own turmoil, barely registered her presence. His world had narrowed to the rhythmic rise and fall of Anwyn's chest, each breath a fragile promise that she was still with him.

Gunnar's rough hand gently held hers, the contrast between his calloused skin and her delicate fingers stark. He had spent endless hours here since her coma began, his mind consumed with finding a way to heal her. The room bore silent witness to his despair, the walls absorbing his whispered vows and muffled sobs. The fiery spirit that had drawn him to her lay dormant, and he desperately missed the spark that had once danced in her eyes. Their bond, forged in battle and bloodshed, had never had the chance to blossom in peace. Now, in his home, with the illusion of peace finally present, he longed for them to have the chance to explore their relationship further.

His shoulders slumped, a deep sigh escaping his lips. His gaze remained fixed on Anwyn's face, the one constant in his chaotic world. "Anwyn," he whispered, his voice a mix of pleading and desperation. "I will find a way to save you, no matter what it takes."

The echo of his words lingered in the air, a promise to the sleeping figure who had come to mean so much to him. Just as he was about to lose himself in his thoughts, the sound of approaching footsteps pulled him back to the present. He blinked, focusing on the here and now, pushing away the swirling storm of emotions. He squared his shoulders, drawing strength from the resolve that had seen him through countless battles. Gunnar looked up to see his brother Magnus entering the chamber, his presence a steadying force amidst the turmoil.

Magnus filled the doorway, his strong posture tinged with concern. The soft light caught the worry lines etched into his face, highlighting the shared burden they both carried. His eyes, mirrors of Gunnar's own, reflected the silent pact between them—duty above all.

"Gunnar," Magnus called gently, his voice echoing off the stone walls. "Father needs us in council."

Gunnar tightened his grip on Anwyn's hand momentarily before he reluctantly let go. He stood, his stature imposing despite the weariness in his eyes. "What does he want?"

Magnus's gaze softened as he glanced at Anwyn. "It's about the council. There are murmurings of dissent. Some do not believe uniting under one leader is the right path."

Gunnar nodded, though doubt gnawed at him. "They fear change, even when it is necessary for our survival."

Magnus moved further into the chamber, placing a reassuring hand on Gunnar's shoulder. "We need a strategy to get them on board. You have the strength to convince them, but we must plan carefully. You are our prince now, and soon, you will be more."

With one last look at Anwyn, Gunnar followed Magnus out of the chamber. Each step felt like a march toward an uncertain destiny. His heart felt heavy, a fire of determination burning within him, but doubt shadowed his resolve. He wondered if he could truly unite the clans, especially once they learned about his ability to practice magic—a fact he had yet to disclose to his father. Would they see him as a leader or as a threat?

As the doors closed behind them, the torchlight flickered, casting long shadows that danced across the room. And in the quiet of the chamber, Anwyn's chest rose and fell in a steady rhythm, as if even in her deep slumber, she waited for him to fulfill his destiny. The silent room held its breath, bearing witness to the unfolding saga of love, duty, and the quest for unity.

About the Author

Firstly I'd like to say a big thank you to all you wonderful readers who have stumbled upon my writing and have stuck around to actually give it a read!

So, born in the amazing 80s (1984 to be precise), I'm Mark Stanley, and my life's been quite a journey, fueled by a mix of optimism and the occasional misadventure.

Following in my old man's footsteps, I did a stint in the British army where I saw some of the best and the worst the world has to offer, but, no matter where I was in the world, there would always be a book in my pack.

Then, I ventured into the world of international intrigue with NATO for a solid three years. Let me tell you, writing international policy is nowhere near as exciting as conjuring up fantasy realms!

Alongside my partner-in-crime (and life), Katie, we run a recruitment agency that's ticking along nicely, all while I'm secretly plotting my next epic fantasy masterpiece.

Family is my anchor in life. Three crazy kids—Luis, Ava, and Owen keep me on my toes, along with our crazy spaniel, Stanley, and the majestic feline queen, Tia.

Fun fact: my love for the fantasy genre? You can blame my mum's creative disciplinary tactic of making me read as a punishment!

When I'm not crafting stories, you'll find me experimenting in the kitchen or sweating it out at the gym, trying (and often failing) to keep pace with Katie.

Now for some insight into my academic credentials: I've got a CIPS Level 3 Certificate in Procurement and Supply and an LLB Hons Law Degree from the University of Hertfordshire. But let's be realistic, formalised education and my ADHD? Let's just say they didn't always see eye to eye.

I am an avid reader and writer inspired by the captivating works of *Michael R. Miller, Philip C. Quaintrell, John Gwynne, Will Wight, David Estes* and *Jefferey Kohanek*. Drawing from the rich worlds and compelling characters created by these authors, I craft stories that blend fantasy and adventure, aiming to transport readers to realms filled with wonder and excitement. With a passion for storytelling and a dedication to the craft, I continually try and explore new narratives and share them with my growing audience.

So, that's me in a nutshell—full-time writer, full-time dreamer, family man, and eternal seeker of the next great adventure. Thanks for joining me on this wild ride called life!

Printed in Dunstable, United Kingdom